TH

Khardan charged through the crowd, his torch held high, his eyes rushing from one black-robed figure to another; he impatiently lashed out at anyone who got in his way. At last he found the one for whom he had been searching. Slimmer than the rest, moving with an unmistakable grace, this figure—dagger in hand—was grimly facing an opponent whose saber must within seconds slice her in two.

"Mine!" shouted the Calif, urging his horse forward at a gallop. Neatly cutting between the attacker and his black-robed victim, Khardan struck the man's arm down with the flat of his own blade. Leaning over, he caught hold of Zohra around the waist and hoisted her—headfirst, kicking and screaming—up and over his saddle.

"Death will not rob me of my chance to see you humbled, wife!" Khardan cried, grinning.

"Oh, won't he?" Zohra muttered viciously. Dangling head down, fighting to free herself, she raised her dagger.

THE ROSE OF THE PROPHET
Volume One

THE WILL
OF THE
WANDERER

MARGARET WEIS AND TRACY HICKMAN

BANTAM BOOKS
TORONTO • NEW YORK • LONDON • SYDNEY • AUCKLAND

THE WILL OF THE WANDERER

A Bantam Spectra Book / January 1989

ISBN 0-553-27638-7

Published simultaneously in the United States and Canada

Bantam Books are published by Bantam Books, a division of Bantam Doubleday
Dell Publishing Group, Inc. Its trademark, consisting of the words "Bantam
Books" and the portrayal of a rooster, is Registered in U.S. Patent and Trademark
Office and in other countries. Marca Registrada. Bantam Books, 666 Fifth Avenue,
New York, New York 10103.

PRINTED IN THE UNITED STATES OF AMERICA

O   0 9 8 7 6 5 4 3 2 1

Foreword

Look where you will, bold adventurer, for as far as the eye can see, there is nothing.

You stand near the Well of Akhran, a large oasis located in the center of the great Pagrah desert. This is the last water you will find between here and the Kurdin Sea, which lies to the east. The rest of the party, delighting in the first signs of life they have seen after two days of travel through rolling, empty dunes, revels in the shady greenness, lounging beneath the date palms, dabbling their feet and hands in the cool water that bubbles up from somewhere underground. You, however—by nature restless and wandering—are already tired of this place and pace about, eager to leave and continue your journey. The sun is dipping down in the west and your guide has decreed that you must spend the night riding, for no one crosses the stretch of desert to the east, known as the Sun's Anvil, during the hours of daylight.

You look to the south. The landscape unfolds before you, an endless expanse of windswept granite whose broad, brownish, reddish monotony is occasionally relieved by touches of green: the feathery-limbed tamarisk, the tall acacia, man-shaped cacti, scrub pine, thorn trees, and clumps of a silvery-green grass (which your camels love to eat) that springs up in odd and unexpected places. Continue traveling to the southwest and you will enter the land of Bas—a land of contrast, a land of huge cities of vast wealth and primitive tribes, skulking on the plains.

Glancing to the north, you see more of the same monotonous windswept land. But well-traveled as you are, you know that if you journey several hundred miles north, you will eventually leave the desert behind. Entering into the foothills of the Idrith mountains, you follow a pass between the Idrith and the Kich ranges and arrive at a well-traveled highway built of wood over which rolls innumerable wagons and carts, all heading still farther north for the magnificent Kasbah of Khandar, the once-great capital city of the land known as Tara-kan.

Irritably slapping your camel stick against your leg, you glance about to see that your guides are loading the *girba,* the waterskins, onto the camels. It is nearly time to leave. Turning to the east, you look in the direction you are to travel. The patches of green grow less and less, for that way lies the eerily singing, shifting white sands, known appropriately as the Sun's Anvil. Beyond those dunes to the east, so it is told, is a vast and locked ocean—the Kurdin Sea.

Your guide has informed you that it has another name. Among the desert nomads it was once known scornfully as the Water of the Kafir—the unbeliever—since they had never seen it and therefore assumed that it existed only in the minds of the city-dwellers. Any statement made within the hearing of a nomad that he believes to be a lie is received with the caustic remark, "No doubt you drink the Water of the Kafir as well!"

You are sorry not to have seen any of these fierce *spahi*— the nomadic desert horse riders—for you have heard many tales of their daring and courage. When you mention this to your guide, he coolly replies that though you do not see them, they see you, for this is their oasis and they know who comes to its banks and who goes.

"You have paid well for the privilege of using their water, *Effendi.*" Your guide gestures to where the servants are spreading out a fine blanket upon the sand near the banks of the lake, heaping it with gold and semiprecious gems, baskets of dates and melons brought from the cool lands to the north. "There," he says in a low voice, pointing. "You see?"

You turn swiftly. A tall sand dune to the east marks the beginning of the Sun's Anvil. Standing upon that dune, silhouetted against the emptiness of the sky behind them, are four figures. They ride horses—even from this distance you can appreciate the magnificence of their animals. Their *haiks*—or head cloths—are black, their faces are shrouded in black masks. You wave to them, but they neither move nor respond.

"What would have happened had we not paid their tribute?"
you ask.

"Ah, *Effendi,* instead of *you* drinking the blood of the
desert, it is the desert who would be drinking your blood."

Nodding, you look back, only to see the dune is once more
barren and empty. The nomads have vanished.

Your guide hurries off, shouting at the servants, the sight
obviously having disquieted him. Your eyes—aching from
the glare of the sun off the sand—turn westward to find rest.

Here a line of red rock hills thrusts abruptly out of the
desert, looking as if some gigantic hand had reached down
and dragged them up out of the ground. This is country you
left two days ago and you think back on it fondly. Icy-cold
streams meander through the hills, to finally lose their way in
the hot sand. Grass grows in abundance on the hillsides, as
do juniper trees, tall pines, cedar, willows, and bushes and
shrubs of all description. Entering the hills was, at first, a
welcome relief after traversing the desert land that lies between
these foothills and the mountains of Kich. But you soon found
that the hills are—in their way—every bit as eerie and
forbidding as the desert.

Jagged cliffs of red rock, whose very redness is enhanced
by the contrasting green of the trees, soar into the overcast
skies. Gray-white clouds hang over them, trailing long wisps
of rain that drag across the hilltops. The wind howls among
the crags and crevices, the chill streams rush wildly over
smooth rocks as though they know their destination is the
desert and are trying in vain to escape their destiny. Occasionally, upon a hillside, you can see a patch of white that
moves across the green grass in an odd, undulating, flowing
motion—a flock of sheep being driven to new pasture by the
sheepherding nomads who dwell in this region; nomads who—
you understand—are distantly related to those you have just
seen.

Your guide hastens back with word that all is ready. You
cast a final look about your surroundings and notice—not for
the first time—the most unusual phenomenon in this strange
landscape. Immediately behind you stands a small hill. It has
no business being in the desert; it is sadly out of place and
appears to have been left behind when the bigger hills ran off
to play in the west. As if to further emphasize the hill's

incongruity, your guide has told you that a plant growing on this hill grows nowhere else in the desert, or in the world for that matter.

Before you leave, you walk over to examine the plant. It is an ugly, lethal-looking species of cactus. Squat, with fat, bulbous, pointed-tip leaves, it sprouts slender needles that must leap out at their victim, for you swear that you do not go near the plant, yet you find—when you look down—the wicked-looking thorns sticking in the tops of your boots.

"What is the name of this abhorrent cactus?" you ask, plucking out thorns.

"It is called the Rose of the Prophet, *Effendi*."

"What a beautiful name for something so hideous!" you remark, astonished.

Your guide shrugs and says nothing. He is a city-dweller, uncomfortable in this place and impatient to leave. You look again at the strange hill in the middle of the desert and at the even stranger plant growing on the hill—the ugly plant with the beautiful, romantic name.

The Rose of the Prophet.

There must be a story here, you think as you rejoin the waiting caravan.

There is, fellow wanderer, and I—the *meddah*—will tell it to you.

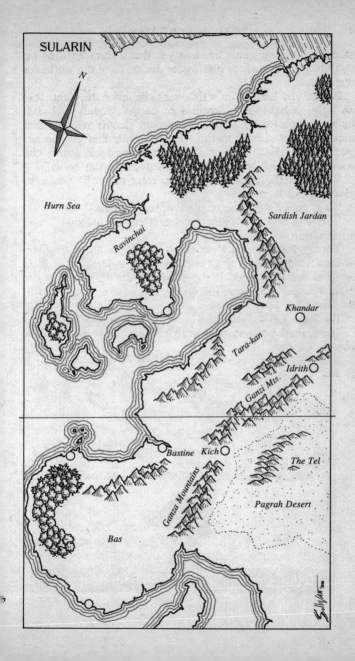

THE BOOK
OF THE GODS

The universe, as everyone knows, is a huge twenty-faceted jewel that revolves around Sul, Truth, the center. The Jewel rotates on an axis that has Good at the top and Evil at the bottom. The twenty facets of the Jewel are made up of connecting triangles, each triangle sharing sides with four other triangles. The nexus of their sides—the points on the Jewel—number twelve and represent the twelve philosophies of Sul. The positive philosophies—Good (at the top), Mercy, Faith, Charity, Patience and Law—are balanced by the negative—Evil (at the bottom), Intolerance, Reality, Greed, Impatience, and Chaos. Each of the twenty Gods combines three of these philosophies to make up one facet of Sul. Thus each God reflects a different facet of the Center's Truth.

Five Gods at the top touch the axis of Good. These are the Gods of Light. Five Gods at the bottom touch the axis of Evil. These are the Gods of Darkness. Ten Gods exist in the middle, touching both Light and Darkness. These are the Neutral Gods.

When the world of Sularin was first created, it glowed brightly in the universe because each God remained joined to his fellows and Truth's Jewel shone as a single, brilliant planet in the heavens. Man worshiped all the Gods equally, speaking to them directly, and there was peace in the world and in the universe.

But as time went by, each God began to focus only on his or her facet of the Truth, coming to see that particular facet as *The* Truth and pulling away from the others. The light of the Jewel became fragmented, starting to shift and vary among the Gods as they fought with each other.

In order to increase his power, each God sought to outdo the others by showering blessings down upon his mortal worshipers. As mortals will, the more blessings they received, the more they sought. Men began to call upon the Gods day and night, demanding favors, boons, gifts, long life, wealth, fair daughters, strong sons, fast horses, more rain, less rain, and so forth and so on.

The Gods became deeply involved in the petty, day-to-day affairs of mortal men on Sularin, and the universe began to suffer, for it is written in Sul that the Gods must look not upon the light of one sun as it rises and the darkness of one night as it falls but must see the rise of an eternity of suns and the fall of an eternity of nights. Because the Gods looked increasingly at the world and less at the heavens, the Jewel of Truth began to totter and wobble.

The Gods were at a loss. They dared not offend their followers, or it would mean losing their own existence. Yet they had to get back to the business of keeping the universe in motion. To help with this problem, the Gods summoned forth the immortals. A gift from Sul to the Gods, the immortals were beings created in the image of the Gods and given eternal life, but not unlimited power. Divided up equally among the Gods, these immortal beings had originally been performing the task of greeting the deceased after their departure from Sularin and escorting them to the Realms of the Dead.

"From now on, however," said the Gods to the immortals, "*you* will be the ones who must listen to the bleating and whining and incessant 'I want's of mortal man. You will deal with those wants that are within your power to provide— gold, jewels, horses, assassinations, and so forth. Other matters more difficult to arrange, such as marriages, babies, and rainfall, you will continue to bring to us."

The immortals were delighted with this new service; the Realm of the Dead being, as one might imagine, an extremely dull and boring place. The Gods, in vast relief, began to distribute their share of immortals as each God thought best.

As the nature of the Gods differed, so did the nature of the immortals and their workings among men. Some of the Gods feared that the immortals might become as great a nuisance as man himself, while others desired to protect their immortals from the follies and vagaries of man. These Gods established a hierarchy of immortals, assigning the lower echelon to act as emissaries to ones above.

For example, the immortals of Promenthas—God of

Goodness, Charity, and Faith—instructed his immortals, whom he called angels, to speak to only the most holy and pious of mankind. These men became—in time—priests of Promenthas.

The worshipers of Promenthas brought their wants and needs to the priests, who brought them to the angels, who brought them to the archangels, who brought them to the cherubim, who brought them to the seraphim, who brought them finally—if the wants and needs were truly important—to the attention of the God. This arrangement proved a satisfactory one, providing a well-ordered and structured society of humans who dwelt primarily in large cities on the continent of Tirish Aranth. Promenthas's priests grew in power, religion became the center of the lives of the people, and Promenthas himself became one of the most powerful of the Gods.

Other Gods differed in their ways of utilizing the immortals, however, just as they differed in their ways of looking at Truth. Akhran—the God of Faith, Chaos, and Impatience—was also known as the Wandering God, for he could never stay in any one place for any length of time but was constantly roaming the universe, seeking out new ideas, new scenes, new lands. His followers, being like their God, were nomads who roamed the desert lands of Pagrah on the continent of Sardish Jardan. Not wanting to be bothered with his faithful—who returned the favor by not wanting to be much bothered with their God—Akhran turned over almost all his power to his immortals, then handed out the immortals freely as gifts to his followers. Known as djinn, these immortals lived among men and worked with them on a day-to-day basis.

Quar, God of Reality, Greed, and Law, took his time and studied the various methods of deploying immortals—from Promenthas's hierarchy of angels to Akhran's jumble of djinn. While Quar admired the firm grip Promenthas's priests kept on the people with their highly structured system of rules and regulations, Quar found the bureaucratic stratification of the angels cumbersome and unwieldy. Messages were often garbled in translation, it took endless amounts of time to get anything done, and—as Quar watched closely—he saw that in small matters mankind was starting to depend upon himself instead of bringing matters to the attention of Promenthas.

Promenthas was, so Quar thought, unreasonably proud of this freedom of thought among his followers. The God of Light enjoyed the philosophical and theological discussions carried on among his people. A studious lot, the people of Tirish Aranth never tired of probing into the mysteries of life, death, and the hereafter. They relied on themselves to find gold and jewels and marry off their sons and daughters. Quar did not like to see man assuming such responsibilities; it gave him grandiose ideas.

But neither did Quar ascribe to Akhran's heedless casting away of all responsibility into the increasingly fat laps of the djinn, who were meddling in the mortal world with lively enthusiasm.

Quar chose a middle ground. He established priests or *Imams* who ruled over the people of his realm, Tara-kan, on the continent of Sardish Jardan. The Imams were each given djinn of a lower nature who, in turn, reported to higher djinn known as 'efreets. Quar also distributed djinn to certain people in power: Emperors, Empresses, Sultans, Sultanas, their viceroys—the Wazirs—and the generals of the armies—the Amirs. Thus the Imams did not become too powerful . . . and neither did the Emperors, the Sultans, the Wazirs, or the Amirs.

Mankind fared well, all things considered, as each God—acting through his immortals—sought to outdo the others in terms of blessings.

Thus began the Cycle of Faith that is set forth in the Book of the Gods:

"As a man waters a bed of flowers, so the Gods pour down streams of blessings from the heavens. The immortals catch the streams in their hands. Walking upon the world, the immortals let fall the blessings from their fingers like drops of gentle rain. Man drinks the blessing of the Gods and gives the Gods his faithful following in return. As the numbers of the faithful increase, their faith in one God becomes vast and wide as an ocean. The God drinks from the water of the ocean and in turn grows stronger and stronger. Thus is the Cycle of Faith."

The Gods were well-pleased with the Cycle, and once each God had his affairs in order, he was able to return to performing Godlike works—that is, bickering and fighting with the other Gods about the nature of Truth. Because of the Cycle of Faith, the Jewel of One and Twenty became more or less stabilized and continued revolving through the centuries.

Until now the time had come for a meeting of the Gods of

Sularin. The Cycle of Faith had been broken. Two of their number were dying.

It was Quar who summoned the Twenty. During past centuries Quar had worked untiringly to try to mend the rift between Evren, Goddess of Goodness, Charity, and Faith, and Zhakrin, God of Evil, Intolerance, and Reality. It was the constant strife between these two that had disrupted the Cycle of Faith.

Due to their strife, the blessings of the two Gods were falling on mortal man not as a steady stream but as an intermittent drizzle. Their immortals, all vying for the meager drops of blessings, were forced to resort to trickery and scheming—each immortal determined to grab a cupful of blessing for his particular master.

Such blessings, doled out in miserly portions like coppers to a beggar, did not satisfy the wants and needs of mortal man, who turned from the immortals in anger. Those among mortal men who remained loyal to their Gods withdrew into secret societies—living, working, and meeting in secret places throughout the world; writing volumes of secret texts; fighting bitter, secret, and deadly battles with their enemies. The oceans of faith of the two Gods dwindled to a trickle, leaving Evren and Zhakrin nothing to drink. And so these two Gods grew weaker, their blessings grew less, and now it was feared that their oceans of faith might dry up completely.

All of the Gods and Goddesses were upset and naturally took steps to protect themselves. The turmoil and strife spread quickly to the plane of the immortals. The djinn snubbed the angels, whom the djinn considered a snobbish, prudish band of elitists. The angels, on the other hand, looked upon the djinn as boorish, hedonistic barbarians and refused to have anything to do with them. Two entire civilizations of humans—those on the continent of Sardish Jardan and those on the continent of Tirish Aranth—eventually refused even to acknowledge the other's existence.

To make matters worse, the rumor began to spread that the immortals of certain Gods were disappearing.

At the urgent behest of Quar, therefore, the Twenty came together. Or perhaps we should say nineteen came together.

Akhran the Wanderer—to the surprise of no one—did not make an appearance.

In order to facilitate matters during the meeting, each God assumed a mortal form and took mortal voice for ease of communication—speaking mind-to-mind becoming a bit confused when twenty minds are all endeavoring to talk at once as was usually the case when the Gods came together.

The Gods met in the fabled Jewel Pavilion located on top of the highest mountain peak on the very bottom of the world in a barren, snow-covered land that has no name. A mortal who climbs that mountain would see nothing but snow and rock, for the Jewel Pavilion exists only in the minds of the Gods. Its look varies, therefore, according to the mind of each God, just as everything else varies according to the minds of the Gods on Sularin.

Quar viewed the Pavilion as a lush pleasure garden in one of his turreted palaces in one of his walled cities. Promenthas saw it as a cathedral made of marble with spires and flying buttresses, stained-glass windows, and gargoyles. Akhran, if he had been there, would have ridden his white steed into a desert oasis, pitching his tent among the cedars and junipers. Hurishta saw it as a grotto of coral beneath the sea where she dwelt. To Benario, God of Faith, Chaos, and Greed (Thieves), it was a dark cavern filled with the possessions of all the other Gods. Benario's opposite, Kharmani, God of Faith, Mercy and Greed (Wealth) viewed it as an opulent palace filled with every material possession coveted by man.

Each God sees the other nineteen entering *his* particular surroundings. Thus, the dark-eyed Quar, attired in a *burnoose* and silk turban, looked barbaric and exotic to Promenthas in his cathedral. The white-bearded Promenthas, dressed in his surplice and cassock, appeared equally ridiculous, lounging beneath the eucalyptus in Quar's pleasure garden. Hammah, a fierce warrior God who dressed in animal skins and wore a horned metal helm, stomped about the cherry trees of a tea garden belonging to Shistar, the monk Chu-lin sat in a cross-legged meditative pose on the freezing steppes of Hammah's home in Tara-kan. Naturally this gave each God—comfortable in his own surroundings—good reason to feel superior to the other nineteen.

At any other time a meeting of the Twenty would have

been a forum of discussion and argument that might have gone on for generations of mortal man had not the situation been of such severity that—for once—petty differences were put aside. Each God, glancing about the sea or the cavern or the garden or wherever he happened to be, noticed uneasily that in addition to Akhran (whom no one counted) two other Gods were missing. These were two of the major Gods— Evren, Goddess of Goodness, Charity, and Faith, and Zhakrin, God of Evil, Intolerance, and Reality.

Promenthas was just about to question their whereabouts when he saw a decrepit and wasted man enter the Pavilion. The steps of this man were feeble. His ragged clothes were falling off, exposing his limbs, which were covered with sores and scabs; he seemed afflicted by every disease known to mortal man. The Gods stared in shock as this wretched being crept down the red-carpeted aisle of the cathedral or among the splashing fountains of the pleasure garden, or through the waters of the sea, for the Gods recognized him as one of their own—Zhakrin. And it was obvious, from his cadaverous face and emaciated body, that the God was dying of starvation.

His eyes dull and glazed, Zhakrin looked around the assembled multitude, most of whom could not hide the signs of appalled horror on their human faces. Zhakrin's feverish gaze skipped over his fellows, however, obviously searching intently for one he did not, at first, see.

Then she entered—the Goddess, Evren.

The Gods of Light cried out in anger and pity, many averting their gaze from the ghastly sight. The once beautiful face of the Goddess was wasted and skull-like. Her hair was white and hung from her shriveled head in ragged wisps. Her teeth were gone, her limbs twisted, her form bent. It seemed she could barely walk, and Quar hastened forward to catch hold of the poor woman and aid her faltering steps.

At sight of her, Zhakrin sneered and spit out a curse.

Evren, with a strength unimaginable in her thin and wasted body, shoved Quar away from her and threw herself at Zhakrin. Her clawlike hands closed around his neck. He grappled with her, the two falling to the red carpet of the cathedral or to the mosaic tile of the garden or the bottom of the ocean floor. Shrieking and howling in hatred, the battling Gods rolled and writhed in what seemed a hideous parody of lovemaking—a bitter struggle to the death.

So frightful was this that the other Gods could do nothing but watch helplessly. Even Quar appeared so sickened and stunned by the sight of these two dying Gods—each attempting with his or her last strength to murder the other—that he stood staring at the twisting bodies and did nothing.

And then, slowly, Zhakrin began to fade away.

Evren, screaming in triumph, scratched at his vanishing face with her nails. But she was too weak to do him further injury. Falling backward, she lay gasping for breath. Quar, moved by pity, knelt down beside her and took the Goddess in his arms. All could see that she, too, was beginning to disappear.

"Evren!" Quar called to her. "Do not let this happen! You are strong! You have defeated your enemy! Remain with us!"

But it was useless. As she shook her head feebly, the Goddess's image grew fainter and fainter. Zhakrin could no longer be seen at all, and within moments Quar found himself kneeling on the tile of his perfumed garden, holding nothing in his arms but the wind.

The other Gods cried out in anger and fear, wondering what would happen now that the order of the universe was thrown completely out of balance. They began taking sides, the Gods of Darkness blaming Evren; the Gods of Light blaming Zhakrin. Quar—one of the Neutral Gods—ignored them all. He remained on his knees, his head bowed in profound sorrow. Several of the other Neutral Gods moved to his side, offering condolences and adding their praise for his unrelenting attempts to mediate between the two.

At that moment the air whispering through the eucalyptus, the silence of the cathedral, the murmuring of ocean water was broken by a harsh sound, a shocking sound, a sound that caused all argument and conversation to suddenly cease. It was the sound of hands clapping, the sound of applause.

"Well done, Quar!" boomed a loud baritone voice. "Well done! By Sul, I have been standing here weeping until it is a wonder my eyes didn't run from my head."

"What irreverence is this?" Promenthas said severely. His long white beard falling in shining waves over his gold-embroidered surplice, the hem of his cassock rustling around his ankles, the God strode down the cathedral aisle to confront the figure who had entered. "Be off with you, Akhran the Wanderer! This is a serious matter. You are not needed here."

Folding his arms across his chest, Akhran gazed around him loftily, not at all disconcerted by this distinct lack of welcome. He was not attired in robes of honor as were the other Gods. Akhran the Wanderer wore the traditional dress of the *spahi*, a desert rider—a tunic of white over white woolen trousers, cut full for comfort and tucked into the tops of shiny black leather riding boots. Over the tunic and trousers he wore long black robes that brushed the floor, their flowing sleeves covering his arms to the elbow. A white woolen sash girdled his waist. When he gracefully tossed the folds of his robes over his arm, the blade of the scimitar and the jeweled hilt of a dagger could be seen, flashing in the light of Sul.

As he stared coldly at Promenthas, Akhran's bearded upper lip—barely visible above his black face mask worn with the black turbanlike *haik*—curled in a sneer, his teeth showing gleaming white against his brown, weather-lined skin.

"What is the meaning of this outburst?" Promenthas demanded sternly. "Did you not witness the tragedy that has occurred here this terrible day?"

"I witnessed it," Akhran said grimly. His smoldering black eyes went from Promenthas to Quar, who—with the help of his fellows—was rising slowly to his feet, his pious face drawn with grief and sorrow. Lifting a brown, weathered hand, Akhran pointed at the pallid, slender, and elegant Quar. "I have seen it and I see the cause of it!"

"Fie! What are you saying?" Indignation rustled among all the Gods, many of whom gathered about Quar, reaching out to touch him in respect and regard (Benario managing at the same time to acquire a fine ruby pendant).

At Akhran's speech, Promenthas's beard quivered with suppressed anger, his stern face grew sterner still. "For many, many decades," he began, his low voice sounding magnificently through the cathedral, less magnificently in the pleasure garden, where it was competing with the shrill screams of peacocks and the splashing of the fountains. In the oasis, where Akhran stood, regarding the Gods with cynical amusement, the white-bearded Promenthas's sonorous tones could barely be heard at all above the clicking of the palm fronds, the bleating of sheep, the neighing of horses, and the grumbling of camels.

"For many decades, we have watched the untiring efforts of Quar the Lawful"—Promenthas nodded respectfully to the God, who received the accolade with a humble bow—"to end this bitter fight between two of our number. He has failed"—Promenthas shook his head—"and now we are left in a state of turmoil and chaos—"

"—That is of his making," Akhran said succinctly. "Oh, I know all about Quar's 'peace efforts.' How many times have you seen Evren and Zhakrin on the verge of burying their differences when our friend Quar here brought the skeletons of their past grievances dancing out of the tombs again. How many times have you heard Quar the Lawful say, 'Let us forget the time when Evren did such and such to Zhakrin, who in turn did so and so to Evren.' Fresh wood tossed on dying coals. The fire always flamed up again while friend Quar stood looking on, biding his time.

"Quar the Lawful!" Akhran spit upon the floor. Then, amid outraged silence, the Wandering God pointed at the place where Evren and Zhakrin had breathed their last. "Mark my words, for I speak them over the bodies of the dead. Trust this Quar the Lawful and the rest of you will suffer the same fate as Evren and Zhakrin. You have heard the rumors. You have heard of the disappearance of the immortals of Evren and Zhakrin. Some of you others have lost immortals as well." The accusatory finger rose again, pointing at Quar. "Ask this God! Ask him where your immortals are!"

"Alas, Akhran the Wanderer," Quar said in his soft, gentle voice, spreading his delicate hands. "I am grieved beyond telling at this misunderstanding between us. It is through no fault of my own. It takes two to make a quarrel, and I, for my part, have never been angered with you, my Brother of the Desert. As for the disappearance of the immortals, I wish with all my heart I could solve this mystery, especially"—Quar added sadly—"as mine are among those who have vanished!"

This was shocking news. The Gods sucked in a collective breath, exchanging glances that were now fearful and wary. The news appeared to take Akhran by surprise; his tanned face flushed, his bushy black brows came together beneath his *haik,* and he fingered the hilt of his favorite dagger.

Promenthas, perhaps slightly unnerved by the sight of Akhran running his broad thumb over the jeweled hilt of the weapon, took advantage of the sudden silence to inform the Wandering God once again that his presence was not wanted. It was obvious he was doing nothing but breeding discord and discontent among the Gods.

At this, Akhran cast a dark glance at Quar. Stroking his black beard, he gazed around at the other Gods, who were glaring at him disapprovingly. "Very well," he said abruptly. "I will leave. But I will be back, and when I return, it will be to prove to those of you who still survive"—his voice was tinged with irony—"that this Quar the Lawful intends to become Quar the Law. Farewell, my brothers and sisters."

Turning on his heel, his scimitar clashing against the wooden pews with a ringing sound, Akhran stalked out of the doors of the cathedral of Promenthas, trampled the flowers of the pleasure garden of Quar. The other Gods watched him go, muttering among themselves and shaking their heads.

Fuming, Akhran paced the silvery-green grass of his own oasis. After many hours of walking back and forth, staring at the bright light of Sul that burned above him hotter than the desert sun, Akhran finally knew what to do. His plan formed, he summoned two of his immortals.

It took some time for these immortals to answer the summons of their God. Neither had been contacted by Akhran in eons, and both were more than a little startled to hear the words of their Eternal Master booming in their ears.

The djinn Sond, hunting gazelle with his mortal master, Sheykh Majiid al Fakhar, blinked in astonishment at the sound and glanced around, wondering why there was thunder in a perfectly sunny sky. The djinn Fedj, tending sheep with his mortal master, Sheykh Jaafar al Widjar, was so thoroughly unnerved that he leaped out of his bottle with a shrill yell, causing the herdsmen to start up in panic.

Both djinn repaired immediately to the plane of their God, finding him pacing back and forth beneath a towering fan palm, muttering imprecations on the heads of each of the other nineteen—now unfortunately seventeen—Gods. The two djinn, prostrating themselves humbly before their Master, kissed the ground between their hands. Had Akhran been more observant and less absorbed in his own anger, he would have noted that each djinn—while appearing to have eyes only for his Eternal Master—was in reality keeping one eye upon his Deity and one eye—a wary, unfriendly eye—upon his fellow djinn.

Akhran the Omnipercipient did not notice, however.

"Stop that nonsense!" he commanded, irritably kicking at the djinn groveling on their bellies before him. "Get up and face me."

Hurriedly the djinn scrambled to their feet. Taking the forms of mortal men, they were both tall, handsome, and well-built. Muscles rippled across their bare chests; gold bracelets encircled their strong arms; silken *pantalons* covered their powerful, shapely legs; silk turbans set with jewels adorned their heads.

"It is my pleasure to serve you, O *Hazrat* Akhran the Omnipotent," said Sond, bowing three times from the waist.

"It is an honor to stand before you once again, O *Hazrat* Akhran the Omnibenevolent," said Fedj, bowing four times from the waist.

"I am highly displeased with you both!" Akhran stated, his black brows coming together over his hawklike nose. "Why didn't you inform me that Quar's djinn were disappearing?"

Sond and Fedj—enemies suddenly drawn together to face a common foe—exchanged startled glances.

"Well?" growled Akhran impatiently.

"Are you testing us in some way, *Effendi*? Surely you who are All-Knowing know this," said Sond, thinking quickly.

"If this is a test to see if we are remaining alert, O Wise Wanderer," added Fedj, taking up the reins of his companion's horse, as the adage goes, "I can answer any question concerning this tragedy which you care to put to me."

"Not as many questions as I can answer, *Effendi*," interposed Sond. "I would obviously know more about this important matter than one who spends his time with sheep."

"I am the more knowledgeable, *Effendi*," countered Fedj angrily. "I do not waste my time in mindless gallopings and *thieving*!"

"*Thieving!*" Sond turned upon Fedj.

"You cannot deny it!" Fedj turned upon Sond.

"If your grass-killing beasts stray upon our land, consuming the sustenance which is meant for our noble steeds, then it is the will of Akhran that we in turn consume your beasts!"

"*Your* land! All the world is Your Land, according to your four-legged master, who was born thus because his father visited his horse in the night instead of the tent of his wife!"

Daggers flashed in the hands of the djinn.

"*Andak!*" thundered Akhran. "Stop this! Attend to me."

Breathing heavily, glaring at each other, both djinn reluctantly thrust their weapons into the sashes around their slim waists and turned once again to face their God. A final exchange of looks, however, promised that the quarrel would be continued at a more convenient time in more private surroundings.

Akhran—who was all-knowing when he cared to be—saw and understood this exchange. He smiled grimly.

"Very well," he said, "I will 'test' you both. Are the disappearances of Quar's djinn similar in nature to the disappearance of the immortals of Evren and Zhakrin?"

"No, O Ominiprevelant One," said Sond sullenly, still rankling at the insult to his master. "The immortals of the Two Dead—Evren and Zhakrin—dwindled away even as the faith in their Gods dwindled away."

"Quar's power is not lessening, O Omniparent," added Fedj, fingering the hilt of his dagger with a vicious, sidelong glance at his companion. "Rather, it grows, which makes the disappearance of his djinn all the more mysterious."

"Is he dealing with mortals directly?" Akhran asked in astonishment and some disgust.

"Oh, no, *Effendi*!" Both djinn—seeing once again the dull and boring Realms of the Dead loom in their vision—hastened to reassure their God. "In place of the many djinn who once dwelt with Quar's people, the God is consolidating more and more power in the hands of one Kaug—an 'efreet."

Sond's lip curled in anger as he spoke this name. Fedj's hand closed tightly about the hilt of his dagger.

Akhran noted this reaction, and obviously disturbed at this news, which shouldn't have been news had he been paying attention to what was transpiring in the world and in heaven, he stroked his beard thoughtfully. "An ingenious move," Akhran muttered. "I wonder . . ." He bowed his head in deep thought, the folds of the *haik* falling forward to hide his face in shadow.

Fedj and Sond stood before their Master in silence, their tension growing with each passing moment. Though each djinn had been somewhat disturbed at the strange disappearances and the increasing turmoil among the immortals, these djinn—like their God—had considered themselves above the fray. They were lucky, in fact, that they knew anything about it at all. Though neither admitted it, both had received their information from Pukah—an inquisitive, meddling young djinn belonging to the Calif, Khardan, son of Sheykh Majiid al Fakhar.

Sensitive to the feelings and desires of their mortal masters, the djinn were also sensitive to the moods of their Eternal Master. Danger clung to him like a heady perfume. Catching a whiff of it now, the djinn felt their skin prickle and twitch like dogs who scent an enemy. They knew suddenly that they were no longer going to be above the fray, but in it.

Finally Akhran stirred. Lifting his head, he fixed each djinn with a piercing, black-eyed gaze. "You will take a message to my people."

"Your wish is my command, *Effendi*," said Sond, bowing.

"To hear is to obey, *Effendi*," said Fedj, bowing lower than Sond.

Akhran gave them the message.

As they listened to it, Sond's mouth fell open so wide that a swarm of bats might have taken up residence within the cavernous opening. Fedj's eyes bulged from his head. When the God had completed relaying his instructions, each djinn glanced at the other, as if to ascertain from the face of his companion that he had heard the words of his Master correctly.

There was no doubt. Fedj had gone three shades paler. Sond was slightly green around the nose and lips. Both djinn, swallowing, attempted to speak. Sond, the quicker-thinking, as usual put a voice to his opinion first. But his throat thickened and he was forced to cough several times before he could get the words out.

"O *Almost* Ominiscient Akhran, this plan of yours is a good . . . I may truthfully say a *great* plan . . . to discomfit our enemies. There is just one small detail you *may*, in your vast genius, have overlooked. It is, I hasten to add, a very *small* matter . . ."

"*Very* small," interjected Fedj.

"And that is?" Akhran glared impatiently at the djinn.

Nearby, the God's noble white steed was pawing the ground, wanting to be off and riding with the winds of heaven once more. It was obvious that Akhran, who had been in one place longer than he liked, shared his horse's desire.

The two djinn stared at their bare feet, shuffling in the sand, one thinking with longing of retreating to his golden bottle, the other to his golden ring. The great horse neighed and shook his white mane. Akhran made a rumbling sound, deep in his chest.

"Master," began Sond, the words bursting from him, "for the last five hundred years our two families have killed each other on sight!"

"*Arghhh!*" Akhran's hand clenched around the hilt of his scimitar. Drawing it forth from its metal scabbard with a ringing sound, he brandished it threateningly. Both djinn dropped to their knees, cowering before his rage. "Petty human frailties! This childish quarreling among my people must end or Quar will take advantage of it and devour us one by one as so many seeds in a pomegranate!"

"Yes, *Hazrat* Akhran!" cried the quivering djinn.

"You will undertake what I have told you," continued Akhran in a towering fury, slashing recklessly about him with the scimitar, "or I swear by Sul that I will cut off your ears, your hands, and your feet, seal you up in your vessels, and hurl you into the deepest part of the Kurdin Sea! Is that understood?"

"Yes, O Most Gentle and Merciful Master," wailed the djinn, their heads nearly buried in the sand.

With a final "*Humphf!*" Akhran put his leather-booted foot on the posterior of each djinn and with a kick, sent each sprawling on his belly in the sand. Stalking off without another word, the God mounted his horse. The animal leaped into the starlit sky and the two were gone.

Picking themselves up, spitting sand from their mouths, the djinn looked at each other suspiciously, warily.

"*Akhran* be praised," said one.

"All praise to His name," said the other quickly, not to be outdone.

And may He find a *qarakurt* in his boot this night, added both silently as they reluctantly returned to the world of mortals to bring their people a startling message from their Wandering God.

THE BOOK
OF AKHRAN

Chapter 1

"It is the will of Akhran, *sidi,*" said Fedj.

Sheykh Jaafar a! Widjar groaned. "What have I done that *Hazrat* Akhran brings this curse upon me?" he wailed, flinging his arms wide, questioning the heavens through the hole in the roof. "Explain this to me, Fedj!"

The two, djinn and master, sat in the Sheykh's spacious yurt, set up in the Hrana tribe's winter camp. The sheepherding Hrana lived among the red rock hills that thrust up out of the western edge of the Pagrah desert. In the summer the sheep were pastured up in the higher elevations. Winter forced the nomads down into the desert, where their flocks lived off the sparse vegetation found there until the snow receded and they could move back to the hills in the spring.

It was a difficult life, every day proving a constant struggle to survive. The sheep were the tribe's lifeblood—their wool providing clothing and shelter, their milk and their flesh providing sustenance. If *Hazrat* Akhran was good to the Hrana and the herds grew large, sheep and lambs could be taken to the city of Kich and sold in the *souks*—the bazaars—providing money for such luxuries as silk, perfume, tea, and tobacco. If *Hazrat* Akhran forgot his people, their herds dwindled and no one thought of perfume, only of surviving the winter in the desert.

Fortunately the last few years had been prosperous—no thanks to Akhran, Fedj thought angrily, though he did not dare say such a sacrilege aloud. How could the djinn answer his Sheykh's plea for understanding? Fedj could not very well reveal the turmoil among the Gods to the mortals who looked up to them. And he didn't see how this crazed scheme of his Eternal Master was going to help matters in that direction anyhow. Crouched on his knees before his mortal master, the djinn glanced about the yurt helplessly, seeking inspiration from the designs in the many-colored carpets that covered the felt walls.

Fedj had known Jaafar would take this badly. His master took everything so personally! Let a lamb be born dead, a tarantula bite a child—the Sheykh was certain to blame the catastrophes on himself and wander about in a state of gloom for days. Now this blow. Fedj heaved a sigh. Jaafar might well never recover.

"Cursed! Cursed!"

The Sheykh rocked back and forth on the bench among his cushions. Certainly it seemed the fates were conspiring against the Sheykh, beginning with his appearance. Although only in his late forties, Jaafar appeared older. His hair was almost completely gray. His skin was deeply tanned and lined from years spent in the hills. He was short and thin, with scrawny, sinewy limbs that resembled the legs of a bustard. The long, flowing robes of the shepherds enhanced his short stature. Two streaks of gray in his beard trailed from the corners of his mouth in a perpetual frown that was not fierce— only sad. His black eyes, almost hidden in the shadows of his *haik*—long folds of white cloth bound around the head with an *agal,* a golden cord—were large and liquid and always slightly red around the rims, giving the impression that he was about to burst into tears at any moment. The only time these eyes were seen to lose their sorrow was at the mention of the name of his mortal enemy—Majiid al Fakhar, Sheykh of the Akar.

The sad eyes had flashed fire only moments before, and Fedj had some hope that hatred and rage might take the place of Jaafar's missing backbone. Unfortunately the flames had been quenched by the Sheykh's customary whining over his ill luck.

Fedj sighed again. The yurt offered no help to the djinn. He looked up through the hole in the top of the tent, seeking advice from the heavens. That was a joke, he realized, watching the smoke from the charcoal brazier spiral up and out of the tent. Night in the desert can get very cold, and the warmth of the burning charcoal was welcome to the djinn, who had lived among mortals so long he had fallen into the habit of experiencing physical sensations.

The round yurt, about six feet in height, was twenty-six feet in diameter. The skeleton of the semipermanent tent was made of strong wooden poles lashed together with thin leather thongs to form the side walls. On top of these, bent poles were lashed to a circular hoop about the size of a cart wheel. This central ring was left open to provide ventilation and to carry off the smoke of the burning charcoal, which—in a tightly closed area—could suffocate a man. The skeleton of the yurt was covered with felt—made of matted camel hair— both inside and out; the felt held fast with cords tied firmly around it. The inner walls were sometimes stamped with colorful designs, or in richer dwellings such as the Sheykh's, the walls were covered with colorful carpets, woven by his wives.

The floor of the yurt was made of thick felt, a layer of dried grass, then another layer of felt, leaving a clear space in the center for the brazier. The wooden-frame door was left open in the summer, covered in the winter with curtains of felt rugs. Fedj was thankful it was covered. Only the servants crouched near the back of the tent were witness to their master's display of weakness.

Fedj had made certain that he and Jaafar would be alone before breaking the news of the God's command to the Sheykh. At this time of night—after *eucha* or suppertime— there would normally have been many of the Sheykh's friends seated with him in the yurt, drawing smoke through the water of the hubble-bubble pipes, drinking bitter coffee and sweet tea, and regaling each other with stories that Fedj had heard a thousand times, told by their grandfathers and great-grand-fathers. After a few hours they would disperse, the men going to the tents of their wives or heading for the flocks if it was their turn to take over the night watch.

Sheykh Jaafar al Widjar himself would select the tent of the wife he currently preferred, taking elaborate precautions to visit her tent in secrecy. This was an old custom, handed down from more violent days when assassins lurked in the shadows, waiting to murder the Sheykh when he was at his most vulnerable—alone with his wife.

Having been around in the old days and having seen relative peace settle at last over the various desert tribes, Fedj had always considered these precautions ludicrous and had hinted to Jaafar on occasion that they should be abandoned. Now, however, the djinn was moved to thank Akhran that his master had—out of nothing more than a childish love for pretending there were ghuls lurking beneath the bed—kept up the old customs. In the land to the west—land of their ancient enemy the Akar—these precautions against knife thrusts in the dark would undoubtedly be useful.

The Sheykh let out another wail, clasping his bony hands together. Fedj cringed, wondering what new calamity had struck Jaafar—as if this one wasn't bad enough.

"Who will tell her?" the Sheykh demanded, peering around the tent with his sorrow-filled eyes that were, at the moment, glittering with fear. "Who will tell her?"

The servants huddled as far back into the shadows of the tent as was possible, each striving to avoid catching his master's eye. One—a large, muscular man—seeing the Sheykh's gaze linger on him, threw himself flat on the floor, scattering cushions and knocking over a brass water pot.

"O master! What crime have I committed that you should torture me thus? Even though I earned my freedom a year ago, haven't I remained to serve you faithfully out of nothing but my love for you?"

And your love of the bribes paid by those seeking the Sheykh's favor and the leftovers from the Sheykh's table, thought Fedj. The djinn did not waste time considering the plight of the servants, however. It was time now for him to retire. He had delivered his message, listened to his master's wailings and commiseratings, done all that could be expected of him. His eyes went to the golden ring on his master's left hand. . . .

"No, you don't!" snapped Jaafar, clapping his right hand over the ring with an unusual amount of spirit.

"Master," said Fedj, squirming uncomfortably, his gaze fixed upon the hand covering the ring whose somewhat cramped interior had never seemed more welcome, "I have performed my duty as given to me by *Hazrat* Akhran in delivering his message. There will be much work to do tomorrow, what with packing and preparing for the long march to the Tel, in which duties you can be assured of my help, *sidi*. I therefore beg leave to retire and rest. . . .''

"*You* will tell her," pronounced Jaafar al Widjar.

The slave in the corner gasped in relief and crept back into the shadows, throwing a rug over his head in case the Sheykh should change his mind.

If Fedj had possessed a heart, it would have sunk at that moment.

"Master," the djinn began desperately, "why waste my valuable services by using me for duties fit for slaves? Give me a command worthy of my talents. Say the word, I will fly to the far ends of the world—"

"I'll bet you would! So would I, if I could," said Jaafar gloomily. "I cannot even begin to imagine what she will do when she hears this!" The Sheykh shook his head, shuddering from scrawny neck to slippered feet. "No, you tell her, Fedj. Someone has to, and after all, you're immortal."

"That only means I will suffer longer!" snapped the djinn viciously, cursing *Hazrat* Akhran from the bottom of his imagined heart.

Fedj kept his eyes fixed hopefully on his master's hand, praying for a glimpse of the ring, but the Sheykh, with unusual stubbornness born of sheer terror, kept his fingers closed over it tightly. Rising from the bench, Jaafar gazed down upon the prostrate djinn.

"Fedj, I command you to carry the news to Zohra, my daughter, that one month from this day, by command of *Hazrat* Akhran, she is to marry Khardan al Fakhar, Calif of the Akar, son of my hated enemy, Majiid al Fakhar—may *Hazrat* Akhran infest his trousers with scorpions. Tell her that if she does not do this thing and remain married to the Calif until the Rose of the Prophet blooms upon the Tel, that it is the will of *Hazrat* Akhran that her people will all perish. Tell her this," said the Sheykh morosely, "then bind her hand and foot and surround her tent with guards. You"—he gestured to a servant—"come with me."

"Where are you going, *sidi*?" demanded Fedj.

"To—to inspect the flocks," said Jaafar, throwing on a cloak to ward off the night's chill. He started for the door of the yurt, nearly falling over the servants, who were—contrary to normal—racing to do their master's bidding.

"Inspect the flocks?" Fedj's mouth gaped open. "Since when have you decided to do this, *sidi*?"

"Since . . . uh . . . receiving reports that those thieving Akar—the sons of horses—have been raiding again," Jaafar said, sidling past the djinn on his way to the door, his hand covering the ring.

"They are always raiding us!" Fedj pointed out sourly.

The Sheykh ignored him. "Come to me later . . . and—er— tell my daughter's reaction to the . . . uh . . . joyous news of her betrothal."

"Where will you be, *sidi*?" the djinn demanded, rising to his full height, his turbaned head poking out of the hole in the ceiling of the yurt.

"Akhran willing—far, far away!" said the father fervently.

Chapter 2

"Sond!" Majiid al Fakhar cried joyously as the djinn materialized inside the Sheykh's tent. "Where have you been? We missed you last night, on the raid."

Raid! Sond winced. "Who did you strike last night, *sidi*?"

"The Hrana! The sheepherders, of course."

Sond groaned inwardly. Sheykh al Fakhar made a gesture of his brown, weathered hand. "Stole ten fat ones, right out from under their noses." He snapped his fingers. "I even caught a glimpse of that piece of camel dung—Jaafar al Widjar—sitting among his shepherds." Majiid's booming laughter shook the poles of the striped tent. " '*Salaam aleikum*, greetings to you, Jaafar!' Khardan called out to him as we galloped past, the carcasses of Hrana sheep bouncing on our saddles." The Sheykh laughed again, this time with pride. "My son Khardan, what a prankster!"

"I wish you had not done that, *sidi*," said Sond in a low, subdued voice.

"Bah! What's the matter with you this morning, Sond? Some little djinniyeh say no last night, did she?" Majiid smote the djinn a blow upon his bare shoulders that nearly sent the immortal sprawling to the felt-covered tent floor. "Come along. Cheer up! We are having a game of *baigha* to celebrate."

The Sheykh turned to walk out the tent entrance—propped up by strong poles, the front of the spacious tent was open to catch the breeze—but he stopped in some astonish-

33

ment as Sond laid his hand firmly upon Majiid's strong arm. "I beg that you will take a moment to listen to my news, *sidi*," said the djinn.

"Make it quick," Majiid demanded irritably, glaring at Sond. Outside, the Sheykh could see his men and their horses assembling, eager for the game.

"Please lower the flaps, that we may have privacy."

"Very well," Majiid growled, instructing the servants with a wave of his hand to lower the tent flaps—an indication to all who passed that the Sheykh was not to be disturbed.

"Out with it. By Sul, man, you look as though you've swallowed a bad fig!" Majiid frowned, his thick, grizzled mustaches bristling. "The Aran, those camel-riding swine, have been using the southern well again, haven't they?" Majiid's big fist clenched. "This time, I'll rip out Zeid's lungs—"

"No, *sidi*!" Sond interrupted desperately. "It is not your cousin, Sheykh Zeid." His voice lowered. "I was summoned last night into the presence of *Hazrat* Akhran. The God has sent me with a message to you and your people."

Sheykh Majiid al Fakhar literally swelled with pride—in itself an imposing sight. The djinn, Sond, stood seven feet tall; Majiid came to his shoulder. A gigantic man, everything about the Sheykh was equally large and impressive. He had a thunderous voice that could be heard above the most furious battle. Fifty years old, he could lift a full-grown sheep with one arm, consume more *qumiz* than any man in camp, and outride all but the eldest of his many sons.

This eldest son, Khardan—Calif of his tribe—was the light of the sun in his father's eyes. Twenty-five years of age, Khardan—although not as tall as his father—resembled Majiid in nearly every other aspect. The Calif was so handsome that the eligible daughters of the Akar, peeping at him from the slits in the tent as he rode by, sighed over his blue-black hair and his fiery black eyes that—so it was said—could melt the heart of a woman or scorch that of an enemy. Strong and muscular, Khardan held his own in the tribe's friendly wrestling matches, once even throwing the djinn, Sond, to the ground.

The Calif had ridden on his first raid at the age of six. Seated behind his father on Majiid's tall horse, screaming in excitement, Khardan never forgot the thrill of that wild ride—

the tense, exciting moments sneaking in among the stupid sheep; the howls of triumph when the *spahis* galloped off, bearing their booty; the howls of rage from the shepherds and their dogs. Since that night Khardan lived for raiding and for war.

The Akar were among the most hated and feared tribes in the Pagrah desert. Blood feuds existed between them and every other nomadic band of people. Hardly a week went past that Khardan didn't lead his men on a sheep-stealing raid, a skirmish with some other tribe over disputed lands, or strike at another tribe in revenge for a wrong committed by one great-great-great-grandfather against another great-great-great-grandfather a century ago.

Arrogant, a skilled rider, fearless in battle, Khardan was adored by the Akar. The men would have followed him into Sul's Hell, while there wasn't an unmarried woman in camp from the age of sixteen and over who wouldn't have gladly carried her bed, her clothes, and all her worldly possessions to his tent and humbly laid them at his feet (the first act a woman performs following her wedding night).

But Khardan was not yet married—an unusual state for a man of twenty-five. It had been spoken at his birth, by the djinn Sond, that the God Akhran himself would choose the Calif's wife. This had been considered quite an honor at the time, but as the years went by and Khardan watched the *harems* of men he considered beneath him grow, waiting for the God to make a decision was getting a bit tiresome.

Without a *harem* a man lacks an important power—magic. A gift from Sul to women alone, the art of magic resided in the *seraglio,* where the head wife—generally chosen for her skill in this art—oversaw the usage of it. Khardan was forced to wait until he had a wife to obtain the blessings of magic, as well as the other blessings that come from the marriage bed.

"*Hazrat* Akhran speaks to me!" Majiid said proudly. "What is the will of the Holy One?" His mustaches twitched eagerly. "Has it to do at last with the marriage of my son?"

"Yes—" began Sond.

"Akhran be praised!" Majiid shouted, raising his hands to heaven. "We have waited five and twenty years to hear the will of the God in this matter. At last my son will have a wife!"

"*Sidi!*" Sond attempted to continue, but it was useless. Hurling aside the tent flaps with such force that he nearly upset the entire structure, Majiid burst outside.

The *spahis*—the horsemen of the desert—do not live in the yurts, the semipermanent dwellings of their cousins, the sheepherders of the hills. Constantly on the move to find grazing grounds for their herds of horses, the Akar travel from oasis to oasis, their animals feeding off the grasses in one area, then drifting on when the grass is gone to return again when it has grown back. The Akar lived in tents made of strips of wool that has been stitched together by the fingers and held together by the magical arts of the women of the *harem*. Khardan's mother—a sorceress of considerable skill—boasted that no storm wind that blew could upset one of her tents.

The Sheykh's tent was large and roomy, for here Majiid held council nearly every day, hearing petitions, settling disputes, passing judgement among his people. Though plain-appearing on the outside, Majiid's tent was adorned inside with the luxuries of the nomad. Fine woolen rugs of shimmering color and intricate design hung from the tent walls and ceilings. Silken cushions lined the floors (the Akar scorned to sit or sleep on wooden benches, as did their cousins the Hrana.) Several hubble-bubble pipes, an ornate silver-trimmed saddle used to lean against while seated as well as for riding, a few brass water pots, coffee and tea pots and Sond's golden bottle stood in an orderly row near an outer tent wall. A finely carved wooden chest that had come from the city of Khandar held Majiid's weapons—scimitars, sabers, knives, and daggers.

As with their cousins the Hrana, the past few years had been prosperous ones for the Akar. This news would mark the rising of Khardan's star in the heavens. Truly now the Akar would become the most powerful tribe in all of Pagrah.

"Men and women of the Akar. Now we truly have something to celebrate!" Majiid's voice boomed through the camp. "*Hazrat* Akhran, all praise to His name, has made His will known concerning the marriage of Khardan!"

Sond heard resounding cheers from the assembled people. Eligible daughters gasped, giggled, and clasped each other's hands in hope. Mothers of the eligible daughters began planning the wedding in their minds, while their fathers hastily began to think of the *dot*—or dowry—each girl takes with her.

Sighing, the djinn looked longingly at his golden bottle that stood in a corner of Majiid's tent, near the Sheykh's favorite hubble-bubble pipe.

"I will double the prize money! Let the game begin!" Majiid called out.

Peering from the tent flaps, Sond saw the Sheykh, clothed in his black robes and the full-cut white trousers of the horsemen, leap onto the back of his tall steed—a pure white horse with a long, flowing mane and a tail that swept the sands.

"Sond! Come here! We need you!" Majiid shouted, twisting in his saddle to look back at his tent. "Sond, you son of a— Oh, there you are," the Sheykh said, somewhat discomfited to see the djinn spring up out of the desert and stand by his stirrup. Majiid waved a hand. "Take the carcass out." He gestured some two hundred yards away. "When all is ready, give the signal."

Sond made one last attempt. "*Sidi*, don't you want to know who *Hazrat* Akhran—"

"Who? What does it matter who? A woman is a woman. Beneath the neck, they are all the same! Don't you see, my men are eager for their sport!"

"First things first, Sond," said Khardan, galloping up and wheeling his horse around and around the djinn. "My father is right. Women are as plentiful as grains of sand. The ten silver *tumans* my father is offering as prize are not so easily come by."

Heaving a profound sigh and shaking his silk-turbaned head, Sond lifted the freshly slaughtered sheep's carcass from where it lay on the ground. Flying up into the air, the djinn skimmed over the windswept rock floor of the desert. When he found a suitable site, he first cleared the area of brush and cacti, then dropped the bloody carcass on the ground. Standing beside the carcass, his *pantalons* flapping in the desert wind, Sond gave the signal. A ball of blue fire burst in the air over his head. At the sight, with wild, shrill yells, the *spahis* kicked their horses' flanks and began their mad dash for the prize. Sond, head bowed and feet dragging, slowly began to drift back to the side of his master.

"I gather by the length of your face that the will of *Hazrat* Akhran is going to be difficult for my master to swallow," said a voice in Sond's ear. "Tell me the girl's name!"

Startled, Sond glanced about to find Pukah, the djinn belonging to Khardan, hovering at his elbow.

"You will hear with everyone else," Sond snapped testily. "Certainly I will not tell you when I have not told my master."

"Have it your way," Pukah said easily, watching the horsemen gallop toward the sheep's carcass. "Besides, I already know the name."

"You don't."

"I do."

"Impossible."

"Not so. I talked to Fedj last night. Or what was left of him after Zohra was finished."

Sond drew a seething breath. "You consort with our enemy!"

"Nay, no enemy! Have you forgotten? I consort with our *brother*!"

"Why would Fedj, that son of a goat, tell you?" Sond demanded, nettled.

"He owed me," Pukah replied, shrugging his shapely shoulders.

"Have you told—"

"My master?" Pukah glanced at Sond in mocking amusement. "And find myself sealed up in my basket for the next twenty years for being the bearer of such tidings? No, thank you!" He chuckled, folding his arms across his chest.

Pukah's words brought back an unpleasant reminder. Thinking of Akhran's threat, Sond turned moodily away from the grinning young djinn and pretended to be concentrating on watching the game.

The object of *baigha* is to see which rider can bring the largest portion of the sheep's carcass to Sheykh Majiid. Sixty horses and their riders were now galloping wildly across the desert, each one determined to be the one to carry the prize back to his Sheykh. Khardan's fast horse and skill in riding giving him the advantage; the Calif was almost always the first to reach the carcass. He did so now, but that didn't mean he had won. Leaping off his horse, Khardan grabbed the bleeding carcass and was struggling to lift it up to his saddle when he was overtaken by at least ten other men.

Nine jumped from their saddles. Falling bodily on Khardan, they attempted to wrestle the carcass away from him, almost immediately dismembering the sheep. One rider—Khardan's younger brother Achmed—remained on his plunging horse, leaning down from the saddle at a perilous angle in an attempt to grab a share of the prize and race off with it before the others could remount. By this time the rest of the riders had arrived to join in the fray. From the sidelines the spectators cheered madly, though nothing could be seen except clouds of sand and occasionally, a glimpse of a rearing horse or a toppling rider.

Each man struggled ferociously to yank a portion of the carcass from his comrade's hold. Blood-soaked riders were down, then up, then down again. Hooves flailed; horses whinnied in excitement, sometimes slipping and falling themselves, only to clamber back to their feet in well-trained haste. Finally Achmed—having possessed himself of a hind leg—galloped off, dashing back to the cheering Sheykh.

Leaping onto their horses, several men left the group still fighting over the remainder of the carcass to pursue the victor, Khardan in the lead. Catching up with his brother, the Calif jumped from his saddle, dragging Achmed, sheep, and horse down into the sand. The three other riders—unable to stop their maddened horses—hurtled over the bodies rolling on the ground. Wheeling their steeds, the *spahis* rode back and the fight began all over again.

Several times the Sheykh himself had to gallop out of the way in order to escape the melee that surged around him, his thundering shouts and cheers and laughter adding to the confusion. At the end of an hour everyone—man and horse—was exhausted. Majiid ordered Sond to signal a halt. A ball of fire—this one red—burst in the air with an explosive bang right above the heads of the contestants. At least twenty of them—laughing, bruised, battered, and covered with blood (some of which belonged to the sheep)—staggered up to their Sheykh, gory trophies grasped in their hands.

At a gesture from Majiid one of the *aksakal*—a tribal elder—rode forward, carrying in his hand a crude balance. Sitting on his horse, he carefully weighed each bloody, sand-covered hunk of meat in turn, finally pronouncing Achmed the winner of the ten *tumans*.

Clasping his strong arms around his seventeen-year-old half brother, Khardan hugged the panting boy close in congratulation, advising him to save the money for their annual horse-selling trip to the city of Kich.

Achmed turned to his father to receive a similar reward—a reward that would have been more precious to him than silver. But Majiid was far too excited over the forthcoming revelations from the God concerning his eldest son to pay any attention to the younger one. Elbowing Achmed aside, Majiid gestured for Khardan to approach.

Achmed fell back a pace, giving way—as usual—to his older brother. If the young man sighed over this, no one heard him. In the heart of another there might have been bitter jealousy over such favoritism. In Achmed's heart there was only admiration and love for the older brother, who had been more father to him than sibling.

His arms and chest smeared with sheep's blood, his mouth split in a grin—white teeth shining against his black beard— Khardan accosted the somber djinn.

"Very well, Sond," the Calif said laughingly. "I have lost at *baigha*. Certainly I will prove more lucky at love. Tell me the name of my betrothed, chosen by the Holy Akhran Himself."

Sond swallowed. From the corner of his eye he saw Pukah leering at him wickedly, making a gesture as of a man stopping a bottle with a cork then tossing it away. Flushing angrily, the djinn faced Sheykh Majiid and his son.

"It is the will of *Hazrat* Akhran," said Sond in a low voice, his eyes on the feet of his master, "that Khardan, Calif of his people, wed Zohra, daughter of Sheykh Jaafar al Widjar. The wedding is to take place on the Tel of the Rose of the Prophet before the next full moon." The djinn spread his hands deprecatingly. "One month from today. Thus speaks *Hazrat* Akhran to his people."

Sond kept his gaze on the ground, not daring to raise it. He could guess the reaction of his master, the Sheykh, from the terrible, thundering silence that was crashing about the djinn in waves. No one spoke or made a noise. If a horse so much as grunted, it was stifled by its master's clasping a swift hand over the beast's nose.

The silence lasted so long that Sond at last risked a glimpse, fearful that perhaps his master had fallen into a fit. This seemed not unlikely. The Sheykh's face was purple, his eyes bulged in rage, his mustaches stood nearly straight out in bristling fury. Sond had never seen his master so angry, and for an instant the bottom of the Kurdin Sea was a haven of peace and calm by comparison.

But it was Khardan who spoke, breaking the silence.

"The will of *Hazrat* Akhran," he repeated, drawing a deep, shivering breath. "The will of *Hazrat* Akhran that I mingle the tainted blood of Hrana"—he exhibited his crimson-stained hands, glaring at them in disgust—"with the noble blood of the Akar!" The young man's face was pale beneath his black beard, the dark eyes glinted more brightly than the sun off polished steel. "Here is what I think of the will of *Hazrat* Akhran!"

Catching up the sheep's head from the pile of legs and guts and ribs and haunches, Khardan hurled it at the feet of the djinn. Then—drawing his scimitar—he plunged the blade through the animal's skull.

"There is my answer, Sond. Take that to your Wandering God—if you can find Him!"

Khardan spit on the sheep's head. Reaching out, he laid a bloody hand on the shoulder of a man standing near him, who cringed at the touch. "Abdullah? You have a daughter?"

"Several, Calif," said the man with a profound sigh.

"I will marry the oldest. Father, make the arrangements." Turning on his heel, without a glance at the djinn, Khardan stalked off toward his tent, wiping the blood of the sheep from his hands as he went.

That night the desert of Pagrah was hit by the worst storm in the memory of the oldest *aksakal*.

Chapter 3

The day had grown increasingly hot, unusual for late winter in the desert. The sun beat down unmercifully; it was difficult to breathe the scorched air. The horses were nervous and uneasy, nipping at each other and their herders, or standing, huddled together, in what shade could be found from a tall sand dune that cut across the northern side of the oasis where the Akar were currently camped.

Late afternoon, one of the herders sent a boy running with a message for the Sheykh. Emerging from his tent, Majiid cast one look at the ominous sight on the western horizon and immediately cried out the alarm. A yellow cloud, standing out vividly against a dark-blue mass of clouds behind it, was rolling down out of the foothills. Seemingly as tall as the hills themselves, the yellow cloud was moving against the wind at an incredible rate of speed.

"Sandstorm!" Majiid shouted above the rising wind that, in sharp contrast to the searing heat, was damp and bitterly cold.

Men, women, and children of the encampment ran to their tasks, the men securing the tents while their wives cast magical spells of protection over them, the children driving the goats and other small animals inside or running to the pools of water in the oasis to fill waterskins. Some of the women of the *harems* ran to the horse herds where the herdsmen were hobbling the animals in the shelter of the dune. Around the necks of the beasts the women hung *feisha*—

amulets—magically endowed with soothing calm to settle the frightened horses, allowing the men to wrap the animals' heads in soft cloths to protect them from the stinging, blinding sand.

Favorite horses were taken inside the tents; Khardan himself led his black stallion, allowing no one else to touch the animal, whispering words of courage into the horse's ears as he took the animal into his own dwelling place. Majiid's wives returned, leading his horse. Watching the progress of the storm, the Sheykh gestured for them to lead the animal into his tent.

"Sond!" he bellowed, peering into the stinging sand that was billowing around them even though the main storm was some distance away. "Sond!"

"Yes, *sidi*," the djinn responded, springing up out of the sands.

"Look . . . there!" Majiid pointed. "What do you see?"

Sond stared into the approaching storm. His eyes narrowed, he looked back at his master with a grim expression. " 'Efreet!"

The yellow cloud rolled down on them. Leading it, as generals lead an advancing army, were two great beings tall as the clouds of sand, surging over the desert before it. Lightning flared from their eyes, thunder roared from their mouths. In their hands they held uprooted trees, their giant feet kicked up huge clouds of dust as they sped down upon the camp. Nearer and nearer the 'efreet came, whirling and dancing over the sands like dervishes.

"Have they been sent by *Hazrat* Akhran?" Majiid roared.

A gust of wind hit him, nearly blowing the big man off his feet. Seeing that everyone in the camp had taken shelter within their tents, he made his way back to his.

"Undoubtedly, *sidi*," Sond shouted back.

Majiid shook his fist at the 'efreets defiantly, then ducked inside the tent, his djinn hastily seeking shelter in his bottle. The Sheykh's servants were endeavoring to calm Majiid's horse, who was plunging back and forth nervously, threatening to tear down the tent.

"Get away!" Majiid shouted at the servants. "He smells your fear!"

Stroking the horse's nose and patting him reassuringly on the neck, the Sheykh calmed the frightened animal. Under no circumstances had Majiid ever allowed women's magic to touch his horse. Seeing the animal tremble, its eyes rolling in its head, the Sheykh began to think that this time he might make an exception.

He was just about to go to his head wife's tent, seeking her, when he heard a rustling sound and smelled the scent of roses that, no matter where he was, brought the image of Khardan's mother to his mind.

"You read my thoughts, Badia," he said gruffly as she approached, and realized then that she must have been sitting quietly in his tent the entire time.

In her late forties, the mother of seven children, Badia was a handsome woman still, and Majiid regarded her with pride. Though he rarely slept in her bed—he preferred his younger wives for his pleasure—Majiid often visited Badia's tent at night anyway, to talk and receive her counsel, for he had come, over the years, to depend upon her wisdom.

Smiling at her husband, Badia hung the *feisha* around the horse's neck and whispered arcane words. Heaving a deep sigh, the animal sank down, resting its head in its master's lap. Its eyes closed in peaceful sleep. Stroking his horse's mane, Majiid reached out his hand, gripping his wife's arm as she was about to leave.

"Don't go out there, my treasure," he said. "Stay with me."

The tent walls heaved and billowed like a live thing, the chill wind sang a strange and threatening song in the ropes that held the tent fast. The light was a sickly ocher color, so murky it was as hard to see as if it had been night. Outside could be heard a low, grinding sound—the cloud of sand, accompanied by the 'efreets, drawing nearer.

Sitting on cushions beside her husband, Badia laid her head on his arm. Her face was veiled against the storm. She was dressed in her winter cloak made of fine brocade, embroidered with golden thread and lined with fur. Rings adorned the fingers that held fast to her husband's strong arm, gold glinted from her earlobes, the bangles on her wrists jingled softly. Kohl lined her eyes, her black hair—streaked with gray—was thick and long and fell in a single braid down her shoulder.

"It will be a bad storm, husband," she said. "You saw the 'efreets that travel with it?"

At that moment a blast of sand-laden wind struck the tent. Although protected by magic and the skill of the nomads in securing their dwellings against the storms of the desert, Majiid and his wife were nearly suffocated by the sand that swirled in every opening, seeming to penetrate the sturdy fabric of the tent itself.

Casting a cloth over his head, cradling his wife protectively in his arms as she buried her face in his breast for protection, Majiid wished briefly he could ask her to cast a spell of calm over him. He could hear the 'efreets stomping through the camp, battering against the tents with their giant fists, their voices howling in rage. The Sheykh's nose, mouth, and ears filled with sand; drawing breath was a painful sensation. Out in the camp he heard shrill screams and hoarse cries and realized that someone's tent had not been properly secured; probably a young man who had not established his *harem* yet and who perhaps had no mother to cast the spell of protection for him.

There was nothing anyone could do for him but hope he found shelter in the tent of a friend or relative.

An hour passed, and the storm did not diminish in fury. Rather, it appeared to grow worse. The yellow light deepened to an ugly brown. The wind pounced on them from every conceivable direction. Above the howling of the 'efreets, Majiid could hear the wailings of his people, children crying, women sobbing, and even his brave men raising their voices in terror.

"Sond!" shouted Majiid, coughing and spitting sand from his mouth.

"*Sidi?*" came a tinny-sounding voice from inside the golden bottle.

"Come out here!" Majiid demanded, half-choked.

"I would prefer not to, *sidi*," returned the djinn.

"How long will this cursed storm last?"

"Until your noble son, Khardan, agrees to do the will of the most holy Akhran, *sidi*," replied the djinn.

Majiid swore bitterly. "My son will not marry a sheepherder!"

The giant hand of an 'efreet tore at the Sheykh's tent, ripping loose the strong ropes and lifting one of the tent walls. Badia cried out in terror and prostrated herself on the floor, calling to *Hazrat* Akhran for mercy. The servants fled, lunging out beneath the flaps of the shaking tent, howling at the top of their lungs. Majiid, his face twisted in anger that vied with his fear, raised his face cloth to protect his skin from the stinging, biting blasts of sand as he staggered out of the tent to try to secure the ropes once more.

Instantly the 'efreets caught hold of him. Whirling him around until he didn't know his front from his back, they sent the Sheykh on a tumbling, staggering dance through the camp—tossing him back and forth from one to the other, hurling him up against tents, throwing him down into ravines, nearly burying him in sand. Disoriented, almost completely blind from the sand in his eyes, near suffocation from the dust in his mouth and nose, Majiid was finally blown completely off his feet. Catching hold of him, the 'efreets rolled his body over and over, sending him spinning across the rocky, windswept ground until he came to a sudden and painful stop, brought up by a palm tree bent double by the gale, its fronds kissing the earth in obeisance to the God of the desert.

Rubbing the grit from his eyes, Majiid peered upward, groaning in pain. The 'efreets towered above him, spinning so swiftly it made the Sheykh dizzy to watch. In their huge hands they held fragments of tents. Lightning flared from eyes that stared down at the Sheykh without visible emotion as their bodies surged around him.

For the briefest instant the storm abated, as though the 'efreets were holding their breaths, waiting. Majiid groaned again; he had broken ribs in his wild dance through the camp, he thought he might have sprained an ankle tumbling down that last ditch. The Sheykh was a fighter from a long line of fighters. Like any veteran warrior, he knew overwhelming odds when he saw them.

One could not—it seemed—fight a God.

Sheykh Majiid al Fakhar cursed. Clenching his fist in impotent anger, he beat it into the sand. Then, lifting his head, he stared up grimly at the grinning 'efreets.

"Sond!" he roared, a shout that carried clear across the camp. "Bring me my son!"

Chapter 4

Although the mapmakers of the Emperor of Tara-kan had undoubtedly given it some fanciful name, the outcropping of rock that jutted up unexpectedly and inexplicably in the center of the Pagrah desert was called by the dwellers of the desert the Tel, a word meaning hill. A forthright, laconic people, whose harsh surroundings had taught them to be sparing of everything including breath, they saw no need to call things other than what they were or to add any frivolous embellishments. It was a hill, so name it a hill.

The highest point of land for hundreds of miles in any direction, located in the heart of the desert, the Tel naturally became a prominent landmark. Distance was measured by it—such and such a well was three days' ride from the Tel, the Sun's Anvil was two days' ride east from the Tel, the city of Kich was a week's ride west from the Tel, and so forth. Situated in the center of nothing, the Tel and its surrounding oasis was, in fact, at least two days' ride from anywhere— which is what made it so remarkable to find two tribes of nomads camped on either side, one to the east and one to the west.

South of the Tel, standing in a spot that was equidistant from each tribe's encampment, stood a huge ceremonial tent. Measuring seven poles long and three across, it was made of wide woolen bands sewn together—bands that appeared to have come from two different sources, for the colors of the tent clashed wildly, one side being a dark, sober-minded crimson and the other a flamboyant, dashing orange. A *bairaq,* tribal flag, fluttered in the desert breeze at either end of the tent—one flag was crimson, the other flag orange.

The ceremonial tent—sturdy and stable at the far ends—appeared to be unstable in the center, as if the workmen of the two tribes erecting it had become distracted by something. Several splotches of blood on the ground near the middle of the tent may have accounted for the wobbling centerpoles.

Perhaps it was these splotches of blood that also accounted for the unusually large numbers of carrion-eating birds that circled above the huge tent. Or perhaps it was simply the unusually large number of people camped around the oasis. Whatever the reason, vultures wheeled in the skies above the Tel, their wings, black against the golden twilight, casting shadows that flowed over the huge tent—an ill-omen for a wedding day.

Neither bride nor groom noticed the bad luck sign, however. The groom had spent the day being plied with *qumiz*—fermented mare's milk—and was, by evening, so drunk that he could scarcely distinguish sky from ground, much less notice the scrawny birds flapping in eager anticipation above his head. The bride, dressed for the occasion in a *paranja* of finest white silk embroidered with golden thread, was heavily veiled; one might say extremely heavily veiled, since it was *not* generally the custom among her people to blindfold the bride before the wedding ceremony.

Nor was it the custom to bind the bride's wrists tightly together with strips of sheepskin, or to have the bride escorted to the tent by her father and his strongest men rather than her mother, sisters, and other wives of the *seraglio.* The bride's mother was dead, she had no sisters, and the other wives of her father were shut up in their tent, ringed round by guards, as they were when a raid was expected.

No music accompanied the bride's procession through her camp to the wedding tent. There was no strumming of the *dutar,* no clashing of tamborine, no wailing of the *surnai.* The journey was completed in silence, for the most part; silence broken only by the oaths and cursings of the men responsible for bearing the blushing bride to the ceremonial tent, the bride taking every occasion possible to kick the shins of her escorts.

At last the bride, still struggling, was dragged into the garish, unsteady wedding tent. Here her escorts relinquished her thankfully to her father, whose only comment on receiving his daughter on her wedding day was, "Make certain she doesn't get her hands on a knife!"

The groom's procession through his camp was considerably less painful for his escorts than the bride's, this being due to the fact that most of the escorts were in the same state of drunken euphoria as the groom. His djinn, Pukah, had passed out cold. Several of the *aksakal,* tribal elders, had remained sober—on orders of Sheykh Majiid—or the groom might never have arrived at his wedding at all; that small matter having slipped the besotted minds of the Calif and his *spahis,* who were reliving glorious raids.

At *aseur,* when the desert sun was sinking down behind the far-off foothills, the groom was lifted to his feet and hauled bodily into the ceremonial tent, accompanied by those of his companions who could still walk.

Inside the tent the groom's father met his son. At the sight of Majiid, Khardan's handsome face split into a grin. Spreading his arms wide, he lurched forward, wrapped his strong arms around his father's shoulders, and belched.

"Get him up to the center of the tent," commanded the Sheykh, casting a nervous sidelong glance at the unusually stern-faced and formidable-appearing Sond, who was standing near the centerpole.

The *aksakal* went into action. Without further ceremony Khardan al Fakhar, Calif of his tribe, was pushed and pulled over to stand unsteadily next to the centerpole. His drunken friends, shoving their way in behind their Prince, took their places on the right-hand side of the tent. They did not sit down as was customary, but remained standing, glaring balefully at the escorts of the bride, who were on the left-hand side.

The sight of the shepherds effectively sobered most of the *spahis.* Laughter and the crude jokes and boasts about the groom's prowess in the marriage bed died upon the warriors' bearded lips, some still frothy white from the *qumiz.* Armed to the teeth, the Akar and Hrana fingered the daggers thrust into their sashes or fondly caressed the hilts of scimitars and sabers, a low muttering rising from their throats as the bride and groom were being shoved and jostled into position.

"Let's get this travesty over with!" gasped Sheykh Jaafar al Widjar. Sweat poured from beneath his headcloth, both arms encircled his struggling daughter. "I can't hold her much longer, and if that gag comes loose from her mouth . . ." His voice trailed off ominously.

"Gag! How is she going to say her vows if she's gagged?" demanded Majiid al Fakhar.

"I will say them," grunted Jaafar al Widjar.

Traces of blood decorated the sleeves of his daughter's wedding gown, her hands twisted together as she fought to free herself of the bindings around her wrists.

Noting that Majiid al Fakhar looked dubious, Jaafar added harshly, "If she is allowed to speak, she might use her magic, and she is the most powerful sorceress in my wife's *seraglio*!"

"Bah! Women's magic!" snorted Majiid scornfully, but he glanced somewhat uneasily at the heavily veiled bride nonetheless. Reaching out, the Sheykh caught hold of his drunken son, who was slowly listing to one side, and yanked him upright. "Sond! If Jaafar speaks his daughters vows, will she and my son be married in the eyes of *Hazrat* Akhran?"

"If Zohra's father's camel said her vows, his daughter would be married in the sight of *Hazrat* Akhran!" growled Sond, exchanging glances with Fedj.

The other djinn nodded in agreement, making a gesture with his hand. "Get on with it!" The light of the hanging oil lamps flashed off golden bracelets ringing muscular arms.

"Very well," Majiid agreed with an ill-grace. Taking his place between the couple, flanked on either side by the grim-faced djinn, the Sheykh raised his eyes defiantly to heaven. "We, the chosen of the Most Holy and Beneficent God Akhran the Wanderer, have been brought together by a message from our great Lord"—a note of bitterness here—"to the effect that our tribes be joined by the marriage of my son, Khardan al Fakhar, Calif of his people, to this daughter of a sheep—"

A shrill scream from the bound and gagged Zohra and a sudden lunging of the bride in the direction of Majiid al Fakhar caused a momentary interruption in the ceremony.

"What insult is this 'daughter of a sheep'? Zohra is the

daughter of myself, Jaafar al Widjar, princess of her people!''
yelled Jaafar, catching hold of his daughter around the waist
and wrestling her backward.

"Zohra, princess of sheep,'' resumed Majiid coolly.

"Better than a four-legged son of a horse!''

Hanging onto his kicking, screaming daughter with one
hand, Jaafar reached out and shoved the reeling, grinning
groom with the other. His face flushed in drunken anger,
Khardan staggered back into his parent, nearly knocking them
both over, then lurched forward to take a wild swing at his
future father-in-law.

The low mutterings on both sides of the ceremonial tent
broke into open, shouted insults. Loud cries and the clashing
of blades being drawn on the bride's side of the tent precipitated
a clashing of steel on the groom's side. Sayal, one of the
bride's brothers, hurled himself at Achmed, one of the groom's
brothers, cousins of both gleefully joining the fight. A glorious
brawl was in the offing when a blinding flash of light and
deafening explosion knocked the combatants to the ground
and caused the center post of the tent to sway in an alarming
manner.

Stunned, the brothers and cousins rubbed their dazzled
eyes and their ringing ears, wondering what had hit them.

Sond's turbaned head brushed the topmost part of the
seven-foot-high tent. He stood in the middle of the melee, his
muscled arms folded across his bronze, glistening chest, his
black eyes flashing in anger.

"Attend to me—djinn of Sheykh Majiid al Fakhar, djinn to
his father before him, djinn to *his* father before him, djinn to
his father before *him*, and so on for the past five hundred
generations of the Akar! Hear the will of the most Holy
Akhran the Wanderer, who has deigned to speak to you
foolish mortals after over two hundred years of silence!''

"May His name be praised,'' muttered Majiid caustically,
holding up Khardan, whose knees were giving way beneath
him.

Sond heard Majiid's sarcastic remark but chose to ignore it.
"It is the will of Akhran the Wanderer that you two ancient
enemies—the Akar and Hrana—be brought together in peace
through the marriage of the eldest son and the eldest daughter
of the tribal rulers. It is the will of Akhran that neither tribe shall

shed the blood of a member of the other. It is further the will of Akhran that both tribes shall make their camps at the foot of the Tel until such time as the flower sacred to the great and mighty Akhran the Wanderer, the flower of the desert known as the Rose of the Prophet, blooms. This is the will of *Hazrat* Akhran.

"In return for their obedience"—Sond saw the groom's eyes start to glaze over and spoke more rapidly—"the Holy Akhran promises his people his blessing and assistance in the times of strife that are forthcoming."

"Strife! Hah!" muttered Jaafar to his daughter. "The only people we ever fight are each other, and we are forbidden to do that!"

Zohra shrugged. She had suddenly ceased to struggle and slumped against her father's chest in what he assumed was exhaustion. He did not notice, in the confusion and turmoil, that his dagger was missing from its customary place in his sash.

"Skip the rest," ordered Fedj, holding out the ceremonial cord that officially bound the two people together as husband and wife. "Get on with the vows."

"In the name of Akhran the Wanderer, do you, Princess Zohra, daughter of Sheykh Jaafar al Widjar, come here of your own free will to marry Calif Khardan al Fakhar?"

A bitter curse from the bride was cut off by her father, who wrapped his hand around her throat. "She does," he said, breathing heavily.

"In the name of Akhran the Wanderer, do you, Calif Khardan al Fakhar, son of Sheykh Majiid al Fakhar, come here of your own free will to marry Princess Zohra, daughter of Sheykh Jaafar al Widjar?"

A vicious poke in the back from his father brought Khardan standing bolt upright, staring around with blinking eyes.

"Say *bali*! *Bali!*" ordered Majiid. "Yes! Yes!"

"*B-bali!*" cried Khardan with a triumphant gesture of his hand. His mouth gaped open, his eyes rolled back in his head, he swayed where he stood.

"Quickly!" shouted Fedj, holding out the binding to the two fathers.

Generally made of finest silk, the cord symbolizes the love and loyalty that bind husband and wife together. For this hasty wedding there had not been time to journey to the walled city of Kich to purchase silken cord, so a substitute was made of strong desert hemp. And as Pukah stated, it seemed more suitable to the occasion anyhow.

"Take it!" Fedj ordered.

Both fathers hesitated, glaring at each other. The mutterings in the tent swelled to a loud rumbling. Sond growled ominously, Fedj flexed his strong arms. A sudden gust of wind brought a small sand devil swirling into the tent through the open flap.

Memories of the 'efreets in his mind, Majiid grabbed the cord. With an ill-will, he and Jaafar bound the hemp around their offspring and tied it in a love knot, a bit more tightly than was absolutely necessary.

"In the name of Akhran the Wanderer, you two are married!" gasped Sond, wiping the sweat from his brow as he gloomily surveyed the bound couple—the groom leaning heavily against the bride, his head lolling on her shoulder.

There was the flash of a knife, the hemp cord parted as did the bindings on the bride's hands. The blade flashed again and might have ended the wedding day as well as any other future days for the groom had not Khardan pitched face-first onto the floor. Seeing that she had missed, Zohra jumped over the comatose body of her new husband and ran for the tent opening.

"Stop her!" Majiid yelled. "She tried to kill my son!"

"You stop her!" Jaafar roared. "You could probably beat a woman in a fair fight!"

"Dog!"

"Swine!"

The fathers drew their scimitars. Cousins and brothers leaped for each other's throats.

Hearing the clash of steel, Khardan staggered to his feet. He felt blindly for his scimitar—only to realize dimly that he was not wearing it on his wedding day. Cursing, he surged forward weaponless to join the brawl.

Steel clashed on steel. The tent poles swayed dangerously as bodies crashed into them. A shriek, a curse, and a groan coming from one of the guards standing near the tent entrance indicated that the knife-wielding bride had made her way that far, at least.

The two djinn stared around in exasperation. "You go after her!" Sond shouted. "I'll put an end to this!"

"Akhran's blessing be with you!" cried Fedj, vanishing in a swirl of smoke.

"That's just all I need!" muttered Sond.

Grabbing hold of the central tentpole with his strong hands, the djinn glared at the sword-slashing, dagger-wielding, heaving and plunging bodies. Then, his lips coming together in a grim smile, Sond jerked the tentpole up out of the ground and neatly snapping it in two, let it fall.

The tent collapsed like a deflated goatskin, narrowly missing the bride, smothering the groom, effectively ending the fighting of fathers, brothers and cousins. Dagger in hand, Zohra fled into the desert. The *qumiz* going to his head, Khardan lay snoring blissfully beneath the folds of the ceremonial tent as the air whistled out of it with a whoosh, effectively extinguishing—for the time being—the flames of hatred that had burned hot within the hearts of these people for centuries past remembering.

Chapter 5

Deep night had fallen over the desert. Around the Tel, however, the flames of a hundred small suns lit the night almost as bright as day, the night air resounded with drunken laughter. These celebratory measures were not so much in honor of the wedding but in commemoration of the glorious fight that had taken place following the wedding, and in expectation of more glorious fights to come. The largest bonfire burned outside Khardan's tent. Surrounded by weaving, dancing black shapes, the flames licked hungrily at the wood as dogs lick up blood.

A silver slit appeared in the black sky; Achmed's youthful voice, more sober than the rest, shouted out that the moon was rising. This was followed by a cheer, for it was the signal to escort the groom to his bridal tent where, presumably, the bride waited in perfumed, bejeweled splendor. Everyone (more or less) surged forward—the groom in the lead. Many of his companions clung to each other for support, either too drunk or too injured to walk without help.

No one had died in the skirmish in the wedding tent—for which the fall of the pole could undoubtedly be thanked—but there were several on both sides who'd been carried to their tents feet-first and were being tended by their wives. One of these was Zohra's father, Jaafar. A lucky swipe of Majiid's saber just as the tent collapsed on top of them caught Jaafar across his skinny chest. The wound opened a bloody gash in his flesh, ruined his best robes, and neatly sliced off the bottom half of his long, white beard, but it did little other damage, not even penetrating as far as the bone.

Nonetheless, this injury done to their Sheykh would have precipitated a bloodbath among the tribes had not Sond threatened to transport the first man who raised his dagger into the Sun's Anvil, stuff his mouth with salt, and leave him tied to a stake with a waterskin hanging just beyond his reach. Grumbling and muttering threats into their beards, Jaafar's men limped out of the tent, bearing their fallen Sheykh, stretched out on a blanket, between them.

Jaafar himself had only one command to make: "Find my daughter."

The men of Hrana glanced uneasily at each other. Zohra was still armed, not only with her knife but with her magic, which, though it could do nothing deadly to them, could still make their lives more miserable than Sul's Hell. The men therefore hastened to assure their Sheykh that Zohra had been located. She was in the bridal tent.

This wasn't a lie—no honorable man would have told an untruth to a member of his own tribe. Someone had actually seen Zohra heading in the direction of the bridal tent following her escape from her wedding. What for, no one knew, but bets were being placed among the Hrana on how long Khardan would remain alive once he entered that tent. Nothing over five minutes was getting any odds at all.

Jaafar appeared dubious upon receiving the news that his daughter had—apparently—decided to meekly submit to this marriage. But before he could say anything further, he lost consciousness. Leaving their wounded Sheykh among his wives, the men of Hrana stealthily followed the groom's procession to the bridal tent, hoping to find a way to disrupt it without being caught by the djinn.

As it turned out, all of these proceedings in the camps were being observed by two black, scornful eyes. Supposedly in her bridal tent, lounging in a silken gown among silken cushions with kohl on her eyelids, henna on her fingertips, attar of rose, jasmine, and orange blossom perfuming the air, Zohra instead was standing on the very top of the Tel, dressed in an old caftan and trousers that she had stolen from her father. Her hand on her horse's bridle, she looked down into the camp one last time before leaving it forever.

The horse was a magnificent stallion—a wedding gift from Majiid to Jaafar. (Actually it was a gift from Sond to Jaafar. The djinn knew that Majiid would reluctantly hand over his son in marriage, but the Sheykh of the Akar would never— no matter how many storms *Hazrat* Akhran visited on him— give one of his horses to a Hrana. Therefore Sond had taken it upon himself to present the suitable gift. Majiid had no idea that the horse was missing. Sond had created a passable substitute that fooled everyone until the first time Majiid attempted to ride it. An unfortunate leap into the nonexistent saddle revealed that the horse was an illusion. It took a month for the Sheykh's bruises to heal, and it was weeks before he could speak to Sond without exploding in rage.)

Jaafar had been pleased with the horse, but he never rode it, preferring to ride the ancient, mangy camel he had purchased long ago from the tribe of Sheykh Zeid. His daughter Zohra, however, had fallen in love with the animal and determined to learn to ride if she died in the attempt. She practiced several times in secret during the month before the wedding, galloping among the hills, and being naturally athletic, she had become quite skilled. She had another motive in learning to ride: this gave her the means to escape her dire fate.

Stealing from a member of one's own tribe was an unforgivable act, but—since the horse was a wedding gift— Zohra considered that she had more right to the animal than did her father. After all, she was the one who had been insulted by that mockery of a wedding ceremony. She deserved this wonderful beast. And she had left all her jewels behind to pay for it. Surely they were worth more than one horse.

At the thought of her jewelry Zohra sighed softly and rubbed the horse's nose. The animal nuzzled its head against her neck impatiently, longing for a gallop, urging her to get on with her journey. Zohra patted it soothingly.

"We'll go soon," she promised, but she didn't move.

If there was one weakness in this strong woman, it was a love of jewelry. To hear the jingle of golden earrings, to see the flash of sapphire and ruby bracelets on her slender arms, to admire the sparkle of turquoise and silver on her fingers, this was almost worth being born a female. Almost . . . Not quite. That was the real reason she had gone to the bridal tent—to look for the last time on the jewelry that had been given her. Jewelry meant to adorn her body for—for what? To make her worthy in the eyes of some horseman?

Zohra's lip curled in a sneer. In her mind she envisioned the man's heavy, clumsy hands snatching the rings from her fingers, tugging the bracelets from her arms, and hurling them carelessly into a corner of the tent as he . . . as he . . .

The horse neighed suddenly, tossing its head. Gripping the knife, Zohra whirled around, stabbing with a quick, skillful thrust, not caring whom or what she hit.

A strong hand closed painfully over Zohra's wrist. Holding on to the woman, the djinn Fedj stared down at the blade sticking from his chest. Grimly plucking out the dagger, the djinn returned it to the fuming bride.

"I command you! Leave me! Return to your ring!" ordered Zohra in a quivering voice.

"I am your father's djinn and therefore subject to no one's commands but his, Princess," answered Fedj coolly.

"Did he send you after me? Not that it matters. I'm not going back," Zohra stated defiantly, a defiance whose strength was severely diluted by the knowledge that the powerful djinn could return her to her father's tent in the blink of an eye.

Fedj was just about to respond when a shout of drunken laughter coming up from the desert floor drew the attention of both. Looking down, they saw the groom's procession wend its way slowly through the camp. Khardan had apparently sobered up following the fight in the wedding tent, for he was walking upright without help, laughing and joking with several less steady companions, who staggered along at his side. Snatches of his conversation, carried clearly on the crisp, chill desert air, came to Zohra.

"I've heard stories about this she-devil of a sheepherder." Khardan's voice was rich and mellow, a deep baritone, his laughter infectious and arrogant. "I heard that she has vowed to the God that no man will possess her. An unholy vow! To be honest, my friends"—Khardan turned to face his companions, who were regarding their Calif with profound admiration—"I have come to believe that this sacrilegious vow is the reason *Hazrat* Akhran brought the Akar together with the tribe of our enemies. These shepherds have been living too long among their sheep. Akhran needed a man to take this woman and teach her the duties of her sex—''

Zohra gasped. Her dark eyes flashed, her hand curled tightly over the hilt of the dagger. ''I have changed my mind,'' she said, breathing rapidly. ''Send me back to the bridal tent, Fedj. That filthy *spahi* will learn what are the 'duties' of a woman!''

The djinn's own face was pale with fury as he glared down upon the swaggering prince, who was boasting of his prowess with women. ''Believe me, Princess! Nothing would give me greater pleasure than to run a hundred cactus thorns through the portion of his anatomy that this young man values most, but—''

Raucous laughter drifted up from the Calif's companions. Turning unsteadily, Khardan once more proceeded slowly and leisurely to the tent of his bride. With a sigh Fedj laid his hand over the dagger-wielding hand of the Princess.

''But what?'' she cried angrily.

''But I dare not. *Hazrat* Akhran has ordered that this union shall be so and so it shall be. You two must remain married and no blood must be shed between the two tribes until the Rose of the Prophet blooms.''

''Why?'' Zohra asked bitterly. ''What is the God's reason? Look at the ugly plant!'' She kicked irritably at one of the many Rose cactis growing at her feet. Sprawled against the hillside, it looked, in the bright moonlight, like a dead spider. ''The leaves are withered and turning brown, curling in upon themselves . . .''

''It is winter, Princess,'' said Fedj, glancing at the cactus with equal disgust. ''Perhaps this is its habit in the winter. I am not familiar with the customs of this flower, except I know that it grows here and nowhere else in the world—one reason why you have been commanded to reside in this place. As for the 'why' of *Hazrat* Akhran in forcing you to make this hateful marriage, I know something of the mind of the God, and—if it will comfort you—I can tell you that the boastings of that puffed-up prince are arrows shot wide of the mark. I can also tell you, Zohra,'' said Fedj, his tone growing more serious, ''that if you do not go back to your people, they and perhaps all the people of the desert are doomed.''

Zohra glanced at the djinn from the corner of her black eyes. Though shadowed by thick, long lashes, the fire in their depths burned more hotly than any blazing log.

"Besides, Princess," continued Fedj persuasively, moving nearer Zohra, "Akhran said only that the two of you had to be married. He did *not* say that the marriage had to be consummated . . ."

Zohra's black eyes narrowed thoughtfully, and there was, Fedj was relieved to see, a glimmer of amusement in them— malevolent amusement, but amusement nonetheless.

"You would be Khardan's head wife, Princess," Fedj suggested softly, feeding the fire. "He would not be allowed to take another into his *harem* without your permission."

The glimmer of amusement became a flaring spark.

"And it is only a few weeks until spring. When the Rose of the Prophet blooms, the command of the God is fulfilled. You may do what you like to your husband then, after having made his life miserable in the interim."

"Mmmmm," Zohra murmured. Near her, the horse shifted restlessly, either wanting to take flight through the desert or return to his mares.

"If I agree to go back," Zohra said slowly, her fingers tracing the intricate designs carved into the bone handle of the dagger, "I want one more thing."

"If it is in my power to provide it, I will, my lady," answered Fedj cautiously. There was no knowing what this wildcat might ask him for—anything from a *sirocco* to blow her enemies off the sands of the desert to a carpet to fly her to the other side of the world.

"I want my own immortal to serve me."

Fedj checked a deep sigh of relief. Fortunately a djinn was easy to provide. Fedj had one in mind, in fact—a low-ranking immortal who owed him a favor from three or four centuries back. Not only did this djinn—one Usti—owe Fedj a favor, but Fedj owed Usti a nasty trick. Fedj had been biding his time, savoring revenge for several hundred years. Here was his chance.

"Your wish is my command, Princess," said Fedj, bowing humbly. "In the morning you will find upon the floor of your tent what appears to be a small, brass charcoal brazier. Take up the brazier in your hand, tap it gently three times with your fingernail, and call the name 'Usti.' Your djinn will appear."

"I would prefer a female."

"Alas, Princess. The djinniyeh are the highest ranking of our kind and rarely deign to have dealings with mortals. And now, will you return to the bridal tent?'' Fedj asked, holding his breath in anxiety.

"I will," said Zohra magnanimously.

Smiling broadly, Fedj patted the Princess's hand. The djinn could not see Zohra's face, hidden as it was by the folds of the headcloth she wore, or he might have been less pleased with himself.

"Shall I transport you, Princess?"

"No, you take care of the horse." Zohra stroked the animal's nose with regret, "We will have our ride another day," she promised the stallion.

"What about the guards?" Fedj gestured to several stalwart men of her father's tribe who were standing around the tent. At that moment he noted that one of the guards was leaning at an odd angle against a straggly-looking palm tree. "Ah, I see you've taken care of them. He's not dead?"

"No!" Zohra said scornfully. "It is a magic spell used to soothe teething babies to sleep. He may wake screaming for his mother"—the princess shrugged—"but he *will* wake, Farewell, Fedj."

Zohra began to make her way down the side of the Tel, slipping in the loose sand and gravel. Suddenly she stopped and looked back up at the djinn. "By the way, how is my father? I heard he was wounded in the fight."

"He is well, Princess," Fedj answered, noting that Zohra had not asked this question earlier. "The sword thrust penetrated no vital areas."

"It would have served him right if it had," Zohra remarked coolly. Turning, she made her way down the side of the hill, heedlessly trampling the Rose of the Prophet beneath her booted feet.

Zohra's mother, dead these ten years, had been an intelligent, strong-willed, and beautiful woman. A powerful sorceress, she was not only Jaafar's head wife but his favorite wife as well, bearing him many fine sons and a single daughter.

This one daughter, Jaafar used to say sadly, gave him far more trouble than any of his sons. Intelligent and strong-willed, and even more skilled in magic, Zohra, at the age of twelve, had the misfortune to lose the influence of her mother. Fatima could have shown her daughter how to use that intelligence for the good of her people, how to use the magic in order to help them survive their harsh way of life. Instead, without her mother's guidance, Zohra used her gifts to run wild.

The men of her tribe were responsible for the sheep, herding them from pasture to pasture, driving off predators. The women were responsible for the camp, using their magic in domestic matters from the building of the yurts to the cooking of food and the healing of the sick. Zohra found women's work boring, the confinement of the *seraglio* stifling. Dressing in her older brother's cast-off clothes, she constantly escaped the *harem*, preferring to play at the boys' rough sports. Jaafar's wives dared not correct the girl, for Zohra's doting father—grieving over his favorite wife's death—could not bear to see the daughter who resembled her made unhappy.

"She will outgrow it," he used to say fondly when his wives came to him with tales of Zohra seen running among the hills with the sheepdogs, the skin of her face and arms brown as that of a boy's.

Time passed, Zohra outgrew her brother's cast-off clothes, but she did not outgrow her wild and rebellious nature. Her brothers—grown men with wives of their own—were now scandalized by their sister's unwomanly behavior and tried to persuade Jaafar to control his daughter. Jaafar himself began to think uneasily that somewhere along the road he had made a mistake, but he could not figure out how to correct it. (His sons had suggested a sound beating. The one time Jaafar had attempted to beat Zohra, she had grabbed the stick from his hands and threatened to beat him!)

When Zohra was sixteen, the Sheykh let it be known among the Hrana that he was interested in contracting his daughter's marriage. This announcement precipitated a sudden outbreak of weddings in the tribe, the eligible men all hurrying to marry someone else—anyone else! Those ending up without brides disappeared into the hills, preferring to live among the sheep. They returned only when it was known that Zohra had publicly vowed to *Hazrat* Akhran that no man would ever possess her.

Moaning the usual—that he was cursed—Jaafar gave up all hope of changing his daughter and retired to his tent. Zohra, triumphant, continued to roam the hills dressed as a young man—her long black hair tangled and windblown, her skin deeply tanned from the sun, her body growing lithe and strong. She was twenty-two years old and could proudly boast that no man had laid a hand on her.

Then her world collapsed. The Wandering God abandoned her, casting her into the arms of her enemy as if she had been nothing more than a slave. She had refused to marry Khardan, of course, and would have run away from her home the moment she heard the news had not Fedj set himself to guard her day and night.

Then came the storm, terrifying her father and the rest of the weak-hearted cowards of her tribe. Jaafar decreed that she would marry Khardan and in this he stood firm, the 'efreets scaring him more than his daughter. Leaving the sheep with a few guards in the hills, the rest of the Hrana tribe made the long journey into the middle of the desert to the Tel, dragging their princess every degrading inch of the way.

These thoughts and memories a jumble in her mind, Zohra stopped again, halfway to the bridal tent. She had very nearly made good her escape this time. Why not try again? Surely Fedj would be occupied with watching the men. . . .

Biting her lip, looking at the bridal tent, Zohra sighed. Fedj's words returned to her. *If you do not go back to your people, they and perhaps all the people of the desert are doomed.* Although at times the princess thought her people as stupid as the sheep they tended, she loved her tribe fiercely. She didn't understand it. It seemed ludicrous. How could they be in such danger? But if they were, it would not be *she* who brought the wrath of the God down upon her people!

Zohra felt pleased with herself; she was making a noble sacrifice, and—by Sul—the Hrana would never be allowed to forget it!

Creeping past the slumbering guard, the princess crawled beneath the opening left between the tent wall and the felt floor. The tent flaps were lowered. Outside she could hear the groom's drunken procession wending its way through the camp, coming closer and closer. Stripping off the caftan and trousers and hurriedly stuffing them beneath a cushion, Zohra dressed herself in the silken bridal gown. Adorning herself with her jewelry, the princess sat before her mirror and began brushing out her waist-long black hair.

To be head wife . . . wife of the Calif . . .

Zohra smiled at her reflection.

She would make this Khardan wish he had never been born!

Chapter 6

The desert slept in the moonlight, languishing like a woman in her lover's arms. Khardan breathed deeply, joyfully inhaling the air scented with the smoke of burning juniper, roasting meats, and the elusive, mysterious fragrance of the desert itself.

He called to mind a story about a nomad who had become so exceedingly wealthy that he moved to the city. The nomad built a splendid palace, causing each room to have the perfume of thousands of crushed flowers blended with the clay of its walls. A visitor entering room after room was overwhelmed with the scents of roses, orchid, orange blossoms. Finally, however, the visitor came to the last room, which had no windows or doors but was open to the air.

"This," said the nomad proudly, "is *my* room!" He drew a deep, satisfied breath.

The visitor sniffed curiously. "But I smell nothing," he said, puzzled.

"The scent of the desert," replied the nomad with wistful longing.

And the desert had a fragrance—a clean, sharp perfume that was the smell of the wind and the sun and the sand and the sky. Khardan breathed again and again. He was young and alive. It was his wedding night. He was being awaited by a virgin of twenty-two who, though reputedly spirited, was also reputedly extremely beautiful. The thought was more intoxicating to him than the *qumiz*.

The Calif had not seen Zohra, nor had any of the men of his tribe. But he knew what she looked like. Or at least he supposed he did. Once Majiid had made his will known that his son would marry the Hrana's princess—Khardan had secretly sent Pukah, his djinn, to investigate.

Hovering about the shepherd's camp, completely invisible, the djinn followed a veiled Zohra for days, and at last his patience was rewarded when the woman—out on one of her solitary rambles—decided to strip off her clothes and bathe in a rushing stream. The djinn spent an afternoon observing her, then went—not to his master—but to Fedj, Jaafar's djinn.

Pukah found the older immortal lounging inside his ring. Although somewhat smaller and more cramped than most dwellings of the djinn, the ring suited Fedj to perfection. He was an orderly djinn, liking things neatly arranged, each in its proper place. The ring was sumptuously decorated, but it was not cluttered with furniture—as were some immortal dwellings. A carved wooden chair or two, a bench with silken cushions for his bed, a fine hubble-bubble pipe in the corner, and several very rare tapestries embellishing the ring's golden walls made up the djinn's establishment.

"*Salaam aleikum,* O Great One." Pukah performed the obeisance due to this older and higher-ranking immortal. "May I enter?"

A djinn may not cross the threshold of the dwelling place of another unless he has been invited.

"What do you want?" Fedj, drawing smoke up through the water of the hubble-bubble pipe, glanced at Pukah with distaste. He neither liked nor trusted the young djinn and liked and trusted him still less when Pukah was respectful and polite.

"I have been sent on an errand from my master, the Calif," replied Pukah humbly. "And knowing your wisdom, I am seeking advice about how to discharge my errand, O Intelligent One."

Fedj scowled. "You may enter, I suppose. But don't get the idea that just because our tribes are uniting means anything else but enmity exists between us. Your master could marry a thousand daughters of my master and I would just as soon see the eyes in his head eaten by ants as not. And that goes for your eyes, too.''

"A blessing upon your eyes as well, O Fedj the Magnificent," said Pukah, seating himself cross-legged on a cushion.

"Well, what do you want?" said Fedj, glaring at the young djinn, not certain but having the feeling he'd been insulted. "Be quick. There's a redolent odor of horse in here I find nauseating."

"My master requested that I view his bride and ascertain her beauty," said Pukah glibly, his face smooth as goat's milk.

Fedj tensed. Slowly he lowered the stem of the hubble-bubble from his mouth, his enjoyment of his quiet smoke ruined. "Well, have you seen her?"

"Yes, O Exalted One," Pukah replied.

"Then return to your master and tell her he is marrying the most beautiful of women and leave me in peace," Fedj said, lounging back among his cushions.

"I would that I could, O Peerless One," Pukah said sadly. "As I have said, I have *seen* the princess. . . ."

"And are not her eyes the soft and gentle eyes of the gazelle?" demanded Fedj.

Pukah shook his head. "The eyes of a prowling leopard."

Fedj flushed in anger. "Her lips, red as the rose!"

"Red as the persimmon," said Pukah, his mouth puckering.

"Her hair, black as the feathers of the ostrich—"

"The feathers of the vulture."

"Her breasts, white as the snows of the mountain tops."

"That much I'll concede. But," Pukah added sadly, "after viewing her from the neck up, my master may never get that far down."

"So what?" Fedj retorted. "He's been ordered to marry her and marry her he will, be she as ugly as the bustard. Or does he want to contend with another of *Hazrat* Akhran's 'warnings'?"

"My master has the courage of ten thousand men," returned Pukah loftily. "He offered to challenge the God, Himself, in single combat, but his father forbade and my master is a most dutiful son."

"*Humpf!*" snorted Fedj.

"But if I return with a report like this . . . well"—Pukah sighed—"I cannot be held responsible for the consequences."

"Let the hotheaded Calif fight *Hazrat* Akhran," Fedj sneered. "I will enjoy watching the 'efreets rip his arms from his body and wipe his face with the bloody stumps."

"Alas, I fear you would miss the spectacle, O Salty One," said Pukah. "I doubt if much would be visible from the bottom of the Kurdin Sea."

Fedj glowered at the young djinn, who gazed at him with limpid, innocent eyes. "What do you want?"

"Flying on the wings of love, I will return to my master and tell him that his bride-to-be is truly the loveliest of women with eyes of the gazelle, lips of roses, breasts of whitest snow, thighs—"

"What do you know of her thighs?" Fedj roared.

Pukah bowed his turbaned head to the ground. "Forgive me. I was carried away by my enchantment over the beauty of your mistress."

"Well," continued Fedj, eyeing the djinn warily, "you will tell your master this—in exchange for what?"

"Your thanks are all I desire—"

"And I'm Sul. What do you want."

"If you insist on giving me some reward, I ask only that you promise to do me a like favor some day, O Magnanimous One," Pukah said, his nose pressed into the carpet.

"I would sooner cut out my tongue than make such a promise to the likes of you!"

"*Hazrat* Akhran might be able to assist you in that," Pukah said gravely.

Remembering the God's threat if the djinn failed in his assigned task, Fedj choked.

"Very well," the djinn snarled, fighting a momentary longing to grab up Pukah and stuff him bodily into the hubble-bubble pipe. "Now leave."

"You agree to do me a like favor someday?" Pukah persisted, knowing that a "very well" would not be acceptable as evidence before a higher tribunal of djinn in case Fedj ever tried to worm out of his agreement.

"I agree . . . to do you . . . a . . . favor . . ." muttered Fedj sourly.

Pukah smiled sweetly. Rising to his feet, the young djinn

exhibited every sign of respect, backing out of the ring, his hands pressed together over his forehead. *"Bilhana!* Wishing you joy! *Bilshifa!* Wishing you health!"

"Wishing you devoured by demons!" muttered Fedj, but he waited to say this until Pukah had vanished. Moodily the elder djinn sought solace in his pipe once more, only to discover that the charcoal had gone out.

Now, on this moonlit night, his wedding night, Khardan approached the bridal tent, images of his bride—as described by an effusive Pukah—filling his mind and causing his blood to burn.

So what if she was the daughter of a shepherd? She was a beautiful daughter by his djinn's account, and anyway, this marriage only had to last until some wretched cactus flower bloomed. That would be, when? A matter of a few weeks until spring?

I will amuse myself with her until then, Khardan reflected, and if she grows wearisome, I will take a wife of my own choosing and relegate this shepherd's daughter to her proper place. If she proves too difficult, I will simply return her to her father.

But that was in the future. For now, there was the wedding night.

Turning to face his companions, who were weaving unsteadily on their feet, hanging on to each other's shoulders, Khardan bid them farewell. Sending him forth with several final, ribald suggestions, the men of the Akar turned and staggered off, never noticing that several cold-sober Hrana left the shadows to follow them.

Khardan reached the bridal tent just as the moon attained its zenith. The guards—members of the bride's tribe—stared stonily straight ahead, refusing to look at him as he approached. Khardan, grinning, wished them an impertinent, *"Emshi besselema*—good night," pushed past them, shoved aside the flap of the bridal tent, and entered.

A soft light glowed within the tent. The fragrance of jasmine met his nostrils, blended—oddly—with the faint smell of horse. His bride lay reclining upon the cushions of the marriage bed. In the dim light she was a shadowy figure against the pure white of the bridal sheets. Struck by a sudden thought, Khardan turned and poked his head out the tent flap.

"In the morning," he said to the Hrana, "enter and see by the blood upon this sheet that I have done what you sheep followers could not do; see what it is to be a man!"

One of the guards, with a bitter curse, made a lunge for his scimitar. The sudden appearance of Fedj, springing up out of the sand, his arms folded across his massive chest, caused the Hrana to contain himself.

"Leave," the djinn commanded, "I will stand guard this night."

Fedj did not do this out of love for Khardan. At this moment he would have enjoyed nothing more than seeing the Hrana's blade rip the braggart Calif from crotch to throat.

"Akhran commands," he reminded the guards.

Muttering, the Hrana left. The djinn, full seven feet tall, took his place before the tent.

Khardan, laughing, ducked back inside and shut the tent flaps. Turning, he approached the bed of his bride.

She was dressed in her white wedding gown. The light sparkled off the golden threads of the elaborate embroidery that lined the hem of gown and veil. Jewels sparkled on her hands and arms, a band of gold held her veil upon her head. Drawing nearer, Khardan could see the swelling curves of her breasts rising and falling beneath the folds of the filmy material that swathed her body, the full curve of her hips as she lay upon the bed.

Sinking down upon the cushions beside Zohra, Khardan reached out his hand and gently removed the white veil from her face. He could feel her trembling, and his excitement mounted.

Khardan breathed a soft sigh.

From Pukah's description the Calif had expected a lovely woman, an ordinary woman—a woman like his mother and his sisters. "Eyes like the gazelle, lips like roses, breasts like snow. . . ." So Pukah had glibly reported.

"Djinn, where are your eyes?" Khardan said to himself, letting the silk of Zohra's face-veil slip between his fingers and fall to the bed.

He had seen the pet gazelles in the palaces of Kich, he had seen the animal's adoring gaze cast down when a man stroked the creature's neck or fondled the soft ears.

The large, liquid black eyes that fixed him with an

unwavering stare were nothing like that. There was flame in them, they gleamed with an inner light that the intoxicated Calif mistook for love. The petal softness of Zohra's cheeks were a dusky rose, not pasty white as other women's. Her black hair shone sleek and smooth like the mane of the Calif's own horse. Falling over her shoulders, her hair brushed against the wrist of his hand that rested lightly upon the white sheets of the bridal bed, sending a fire crackling through his body as though he'd been touched by a flail.

"Holy Akhran, my sincerest apologies for ever doubting your wisdom," Khardan breathed, moving nearer his bride, his eyes upon the red lips. "I thank you, Wandering God, for this gift. She truly pleases me. I—"

Khardan stopped speaking, his voice arrested by the blade of a dagger pressed against his throat. His hand, which had been about to part the silken fabric of the *paranja,* halted in midair.

"Touch me and you die," said the bride.

The Calif's face flushed in anger. He made a movement toward Zohra's knife-hand, only to feel the metal of the blade—warm from having been hidden against the bride's breast—prick his skin.

"Your thanks to your God are premature, *batir*—thief!" Zohra said, her lip curling. "Don't move. If you think that I—weak female that I am—do not know how to use this weapon, you are wrong. The women in my tribe butcher the sheep. There is a vein right here"—she traced a line down his neck with the tip of her dagger—"that will spill your cowardly blood and drain you of life in seconds."

Khardan, sobering rapidly, knew suddenly that he was seeing his bride truly for the first time. The black, fiery eyes were the eyes of the hawk swooping in for the kill, the trembling he had mistaken for passion he realized now was suppressed fury. The Calif had faced many enemies in his life, he had seen the eyes of men intent on killing him, and he knew the expression. Slowly, breathing heavily, he withdrew his hand.

"What is the meaning of this? You are now my wife! It is your duty to lie with me, to bear my children. It is the will of *Hazrat* Akhran!"

"It is the will of *Hazrat* Akhran that we marry. The God (

said nothing about bearing children!'' Zohra held the knife firmly. Her black eyes, staring into Khardan's, did not waver.

''And what will happen tomorrow morning when the bridal sheet is exhibited to our fathers and there is no blood to give proof of your virginity?'' Khardan asked coolly, lounging back and folding his arms across his chest. His enemy had made a mistake, opening up an area vulnerable to attack. He waited to see how she countered.

Zohra shrugged her shoulders.

''That is *your* disgrace,'' she said, lowering the dagger slightly.

''Oh, no, it isn't, madam!'' Lunging forward, Khardan skillfully pinned Zohra's knife-wielding hand to the bed cushions. ''Quit struggling. You'll hurt yourself. Now listen to me, she-devil!'' He shoved his bride down upon the bed and held her fast, his arm over her chest. ''When that sheet is exhibited tomorrow morning, Princess, and it is white and spotless, I will go to your father and tell him that I took you this night and that you were *not* a virgin!''

Zohra's face went livid. The hawk eyes glared at him with such fury that Khardan tightened his grip on the woman's wrist.

''They will never believe you!''

''They will. I am a man, Calif of my tribe, known for my honor. Your father will be forced to take you back in disgrace. Perhaps he will even cut off your nose—''

Zohra twisted in Khardan's grasp. ''My magic—'' she gasped.

''Cannot be used against me! Would you have yourself proclaimed a black sorceress as well? You would be stoned to death!''

''You—'' Struggling to free herself, Zohra mouthed a filthy name.

Khardan, his eyes widening in pretended shock, grinned. The Calif's gaze went to the high, firm breasts he could feel rising and falling rapidly beneath the silk. The fragrance of night-blooming jasmine wafted through the air. His bride's black eyes were fierce as any hunting bird's, but her lips were red and warm and glistened warmly.

''Come, Zohra,'' he murmured, leaning to kiss her. ''I like

your spirit. I had not expected such a thing from the daughter of a sheepherder. You will bear me many fine sons—*hhhhiii!*''

"You wanted blood on the sheet!" Zohra cried in triumph. "There, you have it!"

Gritting his teeth against the pain, Khardan stared in amazement at a deep gash in his upper arm.

Dagger pointed at her husband, Zohra slid back away from him as far as she could on the cushions of the bridal bed whose white silken sheets were now stained crimson red.

"And what will you tell your father? That his stallion was a gelding?" Zohra laughed mirthlessly, pointing at the wound on his arm. "That *you* were the virgin? That it was the bride who conquered?"

Her earrings jingling in triumph, Zohra flung back her head proudly and started to rise up out of the bed. A strong hand caught hold of her wrist, yanking her back down onto the cushions. Screaming a curse, she tried to lash out with the dagger, only to find her knife-hand caught in a grip of iron. There was a cracking sound, and gagging with pain, Zohra dropped the weapon.

Smiling grimly, Khardan flung his bride back onto the bed. "Do not fear, *wife*"—he spoke with mocking irony—"I will not touch you. But you are not going anywhere. We must spend this night as man and wife and be found together in the morning or *Hazrat* Akhran will vent his wrath upon our people."

He gazed down upon her as she lay among the cushions, nursing her bruised wrist. Her hate-filled eyes burned through a tangle of sleek black hair. Her gown had been torn in their struggles; it fell down over one shoulder, revealing smooth, white skin. The slightest touch would displace it completely. Khardan's gaze lowered, his hand moved slowly. . . .

Snarling like a wildcat, Zohra grasped hold of the flimsy fabric and drew it closer around her.

"Spend the night with you. I would sooner sleep with a goat! Pah!" She spit at him.

"And I likewise!" Khardan said coldly, wiping spittle from his face.

The groom was stone-sober now. There was no passion in his eyes as he gazed upon is bride—only disgust.

Zohra clutched her clothes around her. Wriggling as far

from her husband as she could get, she huddled among the cushions at the head of the bed.

Khardan climbed out of bed and stripped off his torn and bloodstained wedding shirt. Rolling it into a ball, he threw it into a corner of the tent, then tossed a cushion over it. "In the morning, burn it," he ordered without turning around or looking at his bride.

The tan skin of his strong shoulders glistened in the flickering light. Removing the headcloth, he shook out his curly, black hair. *Shir,* he was called among his people—the lion. Fearless and ferocious in battle, he moved with a catlike grace. The scars of his victories were traced over his lithe body. Going to a water bowl in the tent, he bathed the wound on his arm and clumsily bandaged it as best he could with one hand.

Glancing at his bride's reflection in one of many small mirrors that had been woven into a tapestry hanging upon the wall before him, Khardan saw to his astonishment that the fire of anger had died in the dark eyes. There was even, he thought, a smoldering glimmer of admiration.

It was gone in an instant, as soon as Zohra realized the Calif was watching her. The soft red lips that had been slightly parted over the even white teeth curled in a sneer. Flipping her long black hair over her shoulders, Zohra coldly averted her face, but he could see the slits of black eyes watching him.

Khardan's hand moved to the waist of his trousers, and he heard a snarl of warning from the bed behind him. His lips twisting in a grim smile, the Calif—with an emphatic gesture—cinched his trousers more tightly. Walking to the front of the tent, he searched the felt floor. Finding what he sought, he returned at last to the bridal bed. In his hand was the dagger.

Without a glance at Zohra, he tossed the weapon down upon the cushions. Blood glistened on the dagger's blade, its handle facing the bride. Lying down upon the right-hand side of the bed, the dagger separating him from his wife, Khardan turned his bare back to Zohra. He rested his head upon his arm, made himself comfortable, and closed his eyes.

Zohra remained where she was, crouched at the head of the bed, watching her husband warily for long moments. She could see blood beginning to seep through the crude bandage he had wound around his arm. The gash was open, bleeding freely. Hesitantly, moving slowly and quietly, Zohra removed a bracelet, ornamental with blood stone, she wore upon her arm and held it out toward Khardan.

The Calif, sighing, shifted his weight. Zohra snatched her hand back. Dropping the bracelet, her fingers hovered over the handle of the dagger. But Khardan only burrowed further down into the soft cushions. Zohra sat, waiting, unmoving, until the man's breathing became even and regular. Then, picking up the bracelet again, she lightly passed the jewels over the injured flesh.

"By the power granted to woman by Sul, I conjure the spirits of healing to close this wound."

The bracelet slipped from her hand. Her fingers lingered on the man's muscular arm, their light touch sliding up the smooth skin.

Khardan stirred. Hastily, fearfully, Zohra snatched her hand away. There was no change in his breathing pattern, however, and she relaxed. *Qumiz* often sent men to sleep's realm quickly, buried them deeply. She stared closely at the wound, wondering if her spell had been successful. It seemed that the bleeding had stopped, but because of the bandage she could not be certain, and she dared not untie the cloth to examine it, for fear of waking the man.

Zohra had no reason to doubt her power, however. Nodding to herself in satisfaction, she blew out the light of the lamp then gingerly laid herself down upon the bed, keeping her body as far as possible from Khardan's, nearly rolling off the edge of the cushions in the process. For some reason she could still feel the touch of his skin, warm beneath her fingers. Glowering into the darkness, the princess reached behind her with her hand for the dagger and found the hilt, cold and reassuring, lying on the silken sheets between them.

The wound was healed, vanished as if it had never been. The scar would be just one more taken in battle. But what an ignominious defeat for the warrior!

Zohra smiled. Exhausted from the day's events, she sighed, relaxed, and soon fell fast asleep.

Lying next to her, Khardan stared into the darkness, still feeling the touch of fingers upon his skin, fingers as soft and delicate as the wings of the butterfly.

*   *   *

The next morning the two fathers approached the bridal tent. Jaafar walked stiffly. Though his wives had used their magic to seal his wound, the cut had been deep enough to require a bandage and a healing potion spread over it to prevent the tainting of the blood. The Sheykh of the Hrana was surrounded by armed guards who glared at the Sheykh of the Akar as Majiid swaggered into view, surrounded by his own armed *spahis*.

The procession of the two fathers was not, therefore, the joyous walk with arms around each other customary to the morning after the wedding night. They did not speak but growled at each other like fighting dogs, their followers keeping their hands closed over the hilts of dagger and sword.

The men of the Hrana and the Akar gathered around the bridal tent, waiting in silence. Fedj, his face grim, turned and faced the tent, calling out a cold morning greeting to bride and groom. The djinn, having heard the commotion in the bridal tent during the night, had no idea what they would find upon entering. Two lifeless corpses, hands on each other's throats, wouldn't have much surprised him.

After several moments, however, the groom emerged, carrying the white silken sheet in his hand. Slowly he unfurled it to flutter like a banner in the desert wind. The splotch of red was plainly visible.

A cheer went up from the Akar. Jaafar regarded Khardan with amazed, if grudging, respect. Majiid clapped his son upon his back. Pukah, sidling over, nudged Fedj in the ribs. "Five rubies you owe me," he said, holding out his hand.

Scowling, the djinn paid up.

The fathers reached for the bridal sheet, but Khardan kept it away from them.

"*Hazrat* Akhran, this belongs to you," the Calif cried to the heavens.

He held the sheet out. The desert wind filled the bridal sheet. Khardan loosed it and a sudden strong gust sent it skipping along the sands. The silken sheet fluttered through camp, dancing like a ghost, the wind driving it toward the Tel. Long, sharp needles of a shriveled and brown cactus—the ugly plant known as the Rose of the Prophet—caught the sheet and held it fast.

Within seconds the whipping, angry wind had ripped the bridal sheet to shreds.

THE BOOK OF
PROMENTHAS

Chapter 1

Leaning upon the ship's rail, the young wizard breathed deeply, his lips parted as though he could drink in the fresh wind that billowed the sails and sent the galleon scudding over the waves. Sunlight danced on the smooth blue water of the Hurn Ocean, clouds white as angel's wings floated in the sky.

"A day like this is a gift of Promenthas," said the wizard to his companion, a monk, who stood beside him on the foredeck.

"Amen," replied the monk, taking the opportunity to rest his hand lightly upon the hand of the wizard. The two young men smiled at each other, oblivious to the coarse remarks and nudgings among the galleon's rough crew.

The wizard and the monk were just entering young manhood—the magus only eighteen, the monk in his early twenties. The two had met aboard ship. It was the first time either had been away from the rigorous, cloistered schooling both Orders required of their members, and now they were on an adventure, voyaging to a world rumored to be fantastic and bizarre beyond reckoning. As they were the youngest of each of their Orders present, an immediate friendship had developed between them.

That friendship had deepened during the long voyage, becoming—on both sides—something more serious, more profound. Unaccustomed to relationships of any kind, having been raised in strictly ordered and highly disciplined schools, neither young man sought to rush this one. Both were content to wait and enjoy the long, sunlit days and the warm, moonlit evenings in each other's company; nothing more.

A step behind them caused the hands to separate quickly. Turning, each bowed reverently to the Abbot.

"I heard the name of Promenthas," said the Abbot gravely. "I trust it was not being taken in vain?" His gaze went to the young wizard.

"Indeed not, Holiness," replied the wizard, flushing. "I was thanking our God for the beauty of the day."

The Abbot nodded. His gravity easing as he looked upon the two young men, he smiled at them benignly before continuing his morning stroll around the deck. Glancing back over his shoulder, he saw them grinning at each other and shaking their heads, undoubtedly laughing at the foibles of their elders.

Ah, well . . . the Abbot recalled what it was to be young. He had seen the growing affection between the two; one would have had to have been blind to miss it. He was not overly concerned. Once they arrived in Bastine, the two would be kept busy with the duties of their Orders, and though the party of wizards and monks traveled as a group for safety's sake, the young men would find little time to be alone together. If their relationship was a solid one, the hardships of the journey would strengthen it. If not, as well to find out before either was hurt.

The Abbot, his constitutional taking him around to the starboard side of the ship, found his gaze following his thoughts, returning once again to the two young men standing opposite him. A school of dolphins was swimming alongside the ship, their graceful bodies leaping through the waves. Brother John, the young monk, was leaning over the rail in an effort to gain a better view; a feat that obviously disturbed his companion.

Odd, thought the Abbot. One generally sees solemnity in those of *my* Order. In this instance, however, it was the wizard Mathew who was the more solemn and serious of the two. Such a remarkable-looking young man, too, the Abbot noted, not for the first time.

Mathew was a Wesman, a race celebrated—men and women alike—for their beauty and their high-pitched, fluting voices. His hair was a coppery auburn, his face so white as to be almost translucent, his eyes green beneath feathery chestnut eyebrows. The men of Mathew's race did not grow beards—

his face was smooth, and though the bone structure was delicate, it was strong, marked by a serious, thoughtful expression that was rarely broken. When the young wizard smiled, which was rarely, it was a smile of such infectious warmth that one was instantly moved to smile back.

He was as intelligent as he was attractive. His Master had informed the Abbot that Mathew had been at the head of his class since he was a boy. This journey was, in fact, a reward granted upon his recent graduation to the rank of apprentice wizard.

Mathew was also devoutly religious, another reason he had been chosen to accompany the priests upon their missionary travels. Forbidden by Promenthas, their God, to fight, the priests often employed wizards to act as bodyguards when traveling to the lands of infidels, preferring the more gentle, refined defenses of magic to the swords and knives of men-at-arms.

So dangerous and uncertain was this trip, however, that the Abbot almost regretted not bringing knights with him, as had been urged by the Duke. The Abbot had pooh-poohed the idea most heartily, reminding His Grace that they traveled with the blessing and guidance of Promenthas. Stories he had since heard from the ship's captain, however, had given the Abbot pause.

Of course he believed the captain to be exaggerating; obviously the man enjoyed scaring the naive representatives of God. Stories of djinn who lived in bottles and brought their masters gold and jewels, carpets that flew through the air—the Abbot smiled at the captain indulgently over the dinner table, wondering how the man thought adults could take such outlandish tales seriously.

The Abbot had studied the lands and languages of the continent of Sardish Jardan. Such study was requisite for both priests and magi, for they must all speak the language of the infidel fluently in order to bring them to the knowledge of the true Gods, and they had to know something of the land through which they were going to travel. The Abbot had read, therefore, many of these stories but took them about as seriously as he took the tales of guardian angels related to him as a child. The idea that mankind could communicate directly with immortal beings! It was . . . sacrilegious!

The Abbot believed in angels, certainly. He would not have been a faithful representative of Promenthas if he had not. But it was only the most exalted, the most holy of men and women who were granted the rare privilege of talking with these radiant beings. And for an immortal to live in a bottle! The thought brought a chuckle to the Abbot that he immediately suppressed as bordering on blasphemy.

One had to make allowances for sailors, he reminded himself. The ship's captain had, after all, not been pleased at carrying the priests to Sardish Jardan. Only through the Duke's intervention and a payment of almost three times the amount of money paid by other passengers was the captain finally prevailed upon to take the missionaries on board. The Abbot suspected the man was getting his own back by telling every gruesome tale he had ever heard.

Unfortunately, several stories of the captain's did, on more than one occasion, keep the Abbot awake long hours into the night: stories of slave traders, of strange Gods who decreed that those not of their faith should be put to death, of flesh-eating cannibals, of savage nomads who lived in uninhabitable deserts. The Abbot had read something of these in the books written by adventurers who had visited the land of Sardish Jardan, and he felt his qualms about this journey growing as each passing day brought them nearer.

It was all very well to remind himself that he should have faith in Promenthas, that they were traveling on the God's work, and that they were going to bring the light of the God's countenance to shine upon these infidels. The Abbot, after listening night after night to the captain, had begun to think that maybe the light shining off a few sword blades might not be such a bad thing.

A cry brought the Abbot's thoughts back to the ship. At sight of the dolphins, the sailors lined up at the rail began casting golden rings into the sea and crying out to the dolphins to grant them a safe voyage. Apparently the young monk, excited by the sight, had nearly fallen overboard in an effort to see the dolphins catch the rings on their long snouts. Only the quick-thinking action of this friend had saved him from tumbling into the ocean.

His feet once more firmly on deck, Brother John was wiping salt spray from his blond beard and laughing at the wizard, Mathew, whose face was so white that the Abbot feared for a moment the young magus might faint. Mathew managed a wan smile, however, when his friend clapped him on the back, and he managed to suggest—in a low, trembling voice—that they go below and play a game of chess.

Brother John agreed readily, and the two left the deck, the long, black, gold-embroidered robe of the wizard and the plain gray robe of the monk whipping around their ankles in the freshening wind. The Abbot, watching them, frowned slightly. The young wizard had truly been unnerved by the trivial incident. He had acted swiftly and responsibly in catching hold of the monk's rope belt and dragging him back over the railing. But Brother John had not been in any real danger; the seas were so calm that even if he had fallen into them, the dousing would have done him no harm.

The Abbot had suspected that Mathew was overly sensitive, and this sign of weakness did not bode well, coming as it did upon the heels of the Abbot's dark thoughts about the possible dangers they might face.

Resolving to say a word about this matter to the Archmagus, the Abbot made his way below deck. Passing the cabin where the lower members of both Orders had their berths, the Abbot saw the two young men bent over a chessboard, the carved pieces having been fitted with pegs so that the listing of the ship did not cause them to slide around. The young wizard's long red hair fell over his shoulders, almost touching his elbows. Absorbed in his game, Mathew had apparently forgotten his fright. The long, delicate fingers moved a piece. Brother John, not knowing the Abbot was observing them, muttered a mild oath, tugging at his beard in irritation.

Folding his hands in his long sleeves, the Abbot made his way to the cabin of his longtime friend, the Archmagus, where he was greeted warmly and invited to sit down for a cup of tea.

"What is the matter, Holiness?" the Archmagus asked, lifting the teapot that bubbled over a magical fire he had conjured up in a small iron brazier. "You have been unusually solemn these past few days."

"It is these tales the captain has been telling," the Abbot admitted, settling himself down on a bench bolted to the deck. "You have studied this land, more than I. Am I leading my flock into the jaws of the wolf?"

"Sailors are a superstitious lot," the Archmagus said comfortingly. Pouring the tea carefully into a cup, he took care not to allow the swaying of the ship to cause him to dump hot water upon the lap of his companion. "You saw the goings on up there just now?" He nodded above deck.

"Yes, what was that?"

"They are sacrificing to Hurishta, Goddess of the Sundering Seas. Thus the golden rings. They believe the dolphins are her daughters. By giving them these rings, they insure a smooth passage."

The Abbot stared at him, incredulous.

The Archmagus, pleased at the monk's reaction, continued, "They even claim, if you will believe me, that these daughters of Hurishta bear a great love for sailors, and that if any man falls overboard, they will carry him safely to shore."

The Abbot shook his head.

"And tonight," continued the Archmagus, who was a traveled man, "you will see something even stranger. They will cast iron rings into the sea."

"Certainly more economical than gold," remarked the Abbot, who had been thinking regretfully of that money falling into the ocean instead of into his church's poor box.

"That is not the reason. The iron rings are for the Inthaban."

"Another Goddess?"

"A God. He, too, supposedly rules the sea, but on the other side of the world. He and this Hurishta, however, are presumably jealous of each other and constantly invade each other's territory. Wars break out frequently, and when they do, terrible storms erupt. Therefore the sailors always play it safe, sacrificing to both during an ocean crossing so as not to offend either."

"Has no one ever attempted to bring these benighted souls to the knowledge that the seas are ruled by Promenthas in His grace and mercy?"

"I would strongly advise against such a thing, my friend," the Archmagus counseled, seeing an expression of eager, holy zeal start to light the Abbot's face. "The sailors already fear that your presence angers both God and Goddess. They have sacrificed more than normal during a voyage, and it is only the lasting fair weather we've experienced that has kept them in such good humor. I shudder to think what might happen if we were to run into a storm."

"But this isn't the time of year for storms!" the Abbot said impatiently. "If they only took the time to study the oceans and the tides and prevailing winds instead of believing in such childish nonsense—"

"Study?" The Archmagus looked amused. "Most of them can't read or write so much as their names. No, Holiness, I suggest that you do your proselytizing among the more educated people of Sardish Jardan. The Emperor, so I have heard, not only is conversant in several languages but can read them as well. His court is a haven for astronomers, philosophers, and other learned men. It is this very intelligence, in fact, that makes him so dangerous."

The Abbot cast the Archmagus a sharp glance. "You and I have not spoken of this—," he began in a low voice.

"Nor should we," the Archmagus said firmly, glancing out the door to see that no one was near.

"I am not quite so much in the dark as you think," the Abbot responded crisply. "The Duke sent for me the night before we sailed."

Now it was the Archmagus who cast a penetrating glance at his friend. "He told you?"

"Some. Enough to understand that he and His Royal Highness view this Emperor as a threat—unlikely as that appears to me, with an entire ocean between us."

"Oceans may be crossed and by more than ships. If you believe the captain—"

"Bah!" The Abbot dismissed the idea with a sniff.

Setting down his empty teacup, the Archmagus gazed out the porthole into the rolling seas; his face, with its long gray beard, troubled. "I will not hide from you, my friend, that we are entering a strange land, populated by a cruel and savage people who believe in alien Gods. The fact that you enter as priests threatening their Gods, and that we enter as spies threatening their government, places us all in gravest danger that no ship's captain can exaggerate. We must be wary, watchful, every moment."

"Why, if this is so, did you bring Mathew?" the Abbot asked after a moment's pause. "He is so innocent, so naive

. . . so . . . so''— the Abbot fumbled for a word—"young,"
he said finally, lamely.

"Precisely why I brought him. It is his youth and his very
lack of guile that will protect us from suspicion. He has a gift
for languages and can speak the tongue of this land better
than any of us. It is the Duke's suggestion, in fact," continued
the Archmagus, sipping his tea, "that if the Emperor takes a
fancy to him—and the Emperor is known to be attracted to all
things beautiful and charming—we leave him behind in the
court."

"Is he aware—"

"Of the true nature of our mission? No, of course not.
Nor, I think, could he ever be told. Mathew's is a transparent,
trusting nature. He could not, I believe, keep a secret to save
his life."

"Then how could you possibly think of leaving him?"

"We will tell him that he is being placed here to study
these people, to report to us on their culture, their ways, their
language. He will innocently transmit all he learns through
our magical means. We will be able to read between the lines
and thus discover the Emperor's true plans and motives."

Uncomfortable at such duplicity, the Abbot sighed and
shifted about uneasily on his hard bench. Fortunately the
Church did not involve itself in politics. He had only to save
souls. Their talk turned to other, less dark subjects, and after
an hour the Abbot prepared to take his leave.

"I suppose I shouldn't worry," he said on departing,
intending to snatch a nap before dinnertime and more of the
captain's night-disturbing tales. "After all, Promenthas is
with us."

The Archmagus smiled and nodded. But after his friend
had left, the wizard gazed out at the sparkling water where
the dolphins played alongside, sporting with the golden rings
cast to them by the sailors. His face grew troubled. "Promenthas
with us? I wonder. . . ."

Chapter 2

The voyage eastward across the Hurn sea from Tirish Aranth to Sardish Jardan was, as the Archmagus said, a swift and a calm one. The galleon had been favored with a steadily blowing wind, warm weather, and clear skies during the whole of the two-month trip. Whether credit for this was due to Hurishta and Inthaban or to the fact that it was late winter and the storms that swept the ocean early in the year had abated depended entirely upon one's point of view.

So calm had been the voyage that the sailors—ever superstitious—were relieved when a minor leak was discovered belowdecks, forcing all hands to take a turn manning the pumps. This, the sailors said, cut the luck that had been running too good. Although their work nearly doubled, the sailors' spirits improved immeasurably after finding the leak. They sang as they cheerfully pumped the seawater out of the ship, and there were only mild grumbles when the dolphins suddenly left them the morning before they were due to arrive in Bastine. The reason for this premature leave-taking of the daughters of Hurishta was undoubtedly the sight of a whale, known to be a son of Inthaban, spouting off the starboard bow. The sailors tossed iron rings in the whale's direction and gleefully pointed out the route the daughters of Hurishta had taken for the whale's benefit.

Although not yet within visual contact of land, the sailors and their passengers knew they were close, and this caused a rise of spirits of everyone aboard ship. Palm fronds could be seen floating past, along with trash and other marks of civilization. There was a noticeable change in the smell of the air as well, which the sailors claimed was the "land" smell but which the Abbot thought was probably the increasingly strong stench of the bilge. There were sharks in these waters, too. The captain took grim pleasure in pointing them out, saying that they were the sons of Hurishta keeping watch for Inthaban. Be that as it may, there were no more games for wizards or monks at the ship's rail.

About midafternoon of the day before they were due to sail into the port city of Bastine on the western coast of Sardish Jardan, the sailors' songs ceased. Casting grim glances at the priests, the sailors went about their duties in silence or gathered together in knots, talking among themselves. The captain walked the deck, a preoccupied, worried expression on his face.

Catching sight of one of the monks, he motioned. "Call up your masters," he said.

Within moments the Archmagus and the Abbot were on deck. Looking to the east, they saw the sky turning a most peculiar color—a dreadful greenish black. Banks of heavy gray clouds floated over the water, lightning flickering along the fringes. Thunder could be heard booming sullenly across a sea.

"What is it?" questioned the Abbot.

"Hurricane, most likely," said the captain.

"But that's impossible at this time of year!" the Archmagus scoffed.

"You must be mistaken, Captain," added the Abbot. "Look, the sea is completely calm!" He pointed to the waters, which were smooth and flat.

"Lubbers!" muttered the captain, and proceeded to tell them that the seas were flat because the strong wind was cutting off the tops of the waves.

A sharp command from the captain sent the sailors scrambling aloft to set the storm sails. Catching sight of the other monks and wizards hurrying up on deck to view the ominous-looking clouds, the captain was just about to order everyone below when a tremendous blast of wind hit the ship, laying it over on its side.

Sailors lost their footing and fell from the masts into the sea. The helmsman fought the wheel, the captain shouted orders and cursed the landlubbers, who had scattered all across the deck, getting in the sailors' way. The Abbot, having tumbled into a pile of ropes, was struggling to regain his feet when he saw the monster.

"Promenthas, have mercy!" the Abbot cried, staring in shock.

A gigantic man rose up from the ocean, rearing up out of the water as though he had been crouched there, waiting for them. When he reached his full height, he was three times taller than the ship, the deep seawater coming to his waist. His skin was the same greenish color as the sky, gray cloud banks formed his hair, seawater streamed from his bare chest in cascades. Lightning flared in his eyes, his thundering voice boomed over the water.

"I am Kaug," the creature roared. "Who are you who trespass upon my seas without offering the proper sacrifice?"

"Now just a minute!" the captain roared back, glaring at the creature with—to the Abbot—unbelievable courage. "We've made the sacrifices! We've given gold to Hurishta and iron to Inthaban—"

"What have you given to Quar?" bellowed the creature.

The captain turned pale.

"Quar? Who is this Quar?" muttered the Abbot, hurrying to the side of the Archmagus. "Some king?"

"Quar is the God of the infidels of this land," said the Archmagus.

"What is that . . . that thing?" The Abbot endeavored to control the tremor in his voice.

"Possibly an immortal known among them as an 'efreet," returned the Archmagus, regarding the huge creature with an air more scholarly than fearful. "I have read reports of them, but I must say, I never believed that they truly existed. This is indeed a most remarkable occurrence!"

"Nonsense! It is an archfiend of the Demon Prince Astafas!" said the Abbot angrily. "Sent to test our faith!"

"Whatever he is, he seems capable of doing that," returned the Archmagus coolly.

"We are a trading vessel on a peaceful mission," the captain was shouting. "Your God knows us. We carry the required sacrifices with us. Quar may rest assured that we will visit his shrine when we first set foot upon land!"

"Liar!" snarled Kaug, his blasting breath hitting the ship

and sending it rolling in the water. "You carry on board priests of Promenthas, who come here to try to turn the people from the worship of their true God."

"By doing this, do we offend Quar?" the captain inquired meekly, possibly for future reference.

In answer a lightning bolt splintered the mast.

The captain, nodding gravely, turned around. "Throw the priests overboard!" he commanded his crew.

"Touch these holy men at your peril!" snarled the Archmagus, leaping forward to halt the attacking sailors.

At a word from their leader, the four other wizards ranged themselves alongside the Archmagus, including the young wizard Mathew. Although his face was deathly white and he was trembling visibly, he took his place beside his leader on the heaving deck. Hastily gathering his flock around him, the Abbot stood behind the protecting wizards.

"Promenthas, come to our aid! Save us from this archfiend!" prayed the Abbot, and his prayer was fervently repeated by the twelve members of his Order.

"Don't let that bunch of old women stop you!" howled the captain, raging at his men. "Twenty gold pieces to the first man that sends a priest to the sharks!"

The Archmagus cried out arcane words and lifted in his hand a black obsidian wand that burst into black flame. The other wizards did the same, raising wands of clear quartz or red ruby or green emerald, each flaring with different color of fire. The sailors, who had surged forward again, hesitated.

Laughter thundered over the ocean. Kaug lifted both his arms high over his head. Blue fire leaped from his hands, green fire shot from his eyes. His hair was red flame, whipped about wildly by the storm winds that swirled around him.

Grimly the Archmagus held his ground, although his puny magic appeared like a tiny candle clutched in the hands of a child compared to the blazing flames in the fingers of Kaug. The priests' prayers grew more fervent, several of the monks falling to their knees to beseech Promenthas's protection. The other magi flanked their leader, waiting for his signal to hurl their spells, the red-haired young wizard keeping a bit nearer the monks than his fellows, particularly one monk who had not fallen to his knees but remained standing, tense and alert, near his friend.

For an instant it seemed time itself stopped. No one moved. The sailors, caught between the fire of the magi before them and the fire of the 'efreet behind them, stared at each other uncertainly. The priests continued their prayers, the magi stolidly guarding them.

Then, tiring of the game, Kaug shrugged his massive shoulders and began to wade toward the ship. The waves stirred up by the approach of his gigantic body sent the galleon rolling, hurling sailors and landsmen alike off their feet. Reaching out with his huge hands, Kaug caught hold of the vessel at the prow and the stern and lifted it from the water.

Howling in panic, the captain fell prostrate on his face, promising the God everything from his firstborn child to a share in next year's profits if Quar would only spare his ship. The priests slid about the deck; they had no breath left for prayers. The Archmagus, eyes closed as he clung to the rigging, appeared to be conjuring some powerful spell to deal with this dread apparition that had sprung from the seas.

Carrying the boat effortlessly, Kaug waded through the ocean. Storm winds blew before him, flattening the waves at his approach. Rain lashed the decks, lightning twined about the masts, thunder boomed incessantly. The men aboard the ship held on to anything they could find, clinging to the deck, the ropes, the wheel, for dear life as the ship rocked and heaved in the 'efreet's hands.

"So, Priests, you have come to teach Quar's people of other Gods!" shouted Kaug as he neared the land. "Quar gives you your chance."

So saying, the 'efreet set the ship back into the water. Sucking in a breath so deep that he inhaled clouds and rainwater, Kaug leaned down behind the vessel and blew upon it.

The gusting blast of the 'efreet's breath carried the ship skimming over the waves at an incredible rate of speed. Salt spray lashed the decks, the wheel spun out of control, the wind whistled in the rigging. Then came a shattering crash and a sudden jarring jolt. The ship's forward motion halted abruptly, sending everyone slithering along the wet decks.

"We've run aground!" screamed the captain.

Laughter boomed behind them. A giant wave lifted the ship, slamming it into the rocks.

"She's breaking up!" the sailors wailed in terror.

"We'll have to abandon ship," gasped the Archmagus, helping the Abbot struggle to his feet.

Wood splintered, masts fell, men cried out in agony as they were buried in the debris.

"Keep together, brethren," ordered the Abbot. "Promenthas, we commend our souls into your care! Jump, my brothers, jump!"

With that, the priests and wizards of Promenthas leaped over the side of the sinking ship and disappeared into the frothing, swirling waters of the Hurn.

Chapter 3

The young monk staggered ashore, his arm around his friend, half-carrying, half-dragging the young wizard out of the waves. The wizard sank down weakly upon the beach, the monk collapsing beside him. Coughing and gagging, gasping for breath, they lay on the beach, shivering with the cold and fear.

Gradually, however, the sand—baked by the bright sun—warmed their water-soaked robes. Mathew closed his eyes in thankful rest. The horror of the leap into the swirling water, the panic of being sucked under the waves, began to fade, replaced by the remembrance of a strong arm's catching hold of him and dragging him to the surface, the relief of drawing that first deep breath and knowing that he wasn't going to drown.

The sand's warmth seeped into his body. He was alive, saved from death. Reaching out, he touched the hand of his friend. Mathew smiled. He could lie upon this beach with this feeling in his soul forever.

"Why did you lie to me, Mathew?" asked the monk, coughing. His throat was raw from vomiting salt water. "You can't swim a stroke!"

Mathew shook his head. "I had to tell you something. You wouldn't have left me behind."

"Jumping in the water like that! You could have drowned! Should have! Would have served you right!"

Mathew, opening his eyes, glanced over to see John grinning—somewhat shakily—at him.

"Promenthas was with us!" Mathew said softly.

"Amen!" John said, looking back out at the raging seas with a shudder.

Above them the sky was clear. Angry waves still crashed upon the shoreline, though the storm was far out to sea. What had happened to the ship neither could tell, for both had immediately been swept under the swirling water and had lost sight of the vessel. Bits and pieces of splintered wood, floating up onto the beach, appeared to tell the grim story.

"What will we do now?" John asked after a pause. "No food. No water. At least you can speak the language."

"Yes, but I've lost all my scrolls and my crystal wand," Mathew said, looking down ruefully at the place on his belt where his scroll case used to hang. "You know, I had the strangest feeling that they were taken from me deliberately! Look!" He exhibited the metal chain to which they had been attached. "It's broken, as though it had been ripped apart!"

"Bah! Are there pickpockets in the ocean? You just lost them," John replied, shrugging. "As violent as those waves were, it's a miracle we've still got our clothes!"

They both stared out to sea, each wondering—now that they were safe—what would become of them, lost and alone in a strange land, when movement farther down shore caught John's attention. "Mathew, look!" he cried excitedly, sitting up in the sand and pointing along the barren shoreline. Several gray- and black-robed figures could be seen staggering out of the water. "Our brethren! Do you have the strength to reach them?"

Speechless with relief, Mathew nodded and held his hand out to his friend. John helped him stand, and limping wearily, the two made their way along the windswept beach until they reached the main body of the priests and wizards who had managed to make it ashore.

The Abbot, his wet bald head shining in the fading sunlight, was clucking over them like a distracted hen. "Who is missing? Please stay together so that I can count—Brother Mark, Brother Peter . . . Where's Brother John? Ah, there you are, my boy! And Mathew here, too! Archmagus! Mathew is safe! We have all been spared! Let us thank Promenthas." The Abbot lifted his eyes to heaven.

"Time for that later," the Archmagus said crisply. More interested in what was transpiring below than above, the wizard had been exploring the beach, investigating their surroundings. "Look there."

"Where?"

"Up there, on the crest of that hill."

"People! A caravan! They must have seen the wreck and have come to help us! Truly Promenthas is great! Blessed be His Holy name!"

"I don't think you need make spectacles of yourselves," the Archmagus counseled his followers, several of whom were shouting and waving their arms to attract attention. "They have seen us. Let us behave with some dignity."

The Archmagus wrung water from his beard. The Abbot twitched his sodden robes into place, and each leader glanced about at the others of their Orders, motioning them to do what they could to make a more presentable appearance.

Still, they did not look at all prepossessing, Mathew thought. Huddled together, half-drowned and exhausted, they were nothing more than flotsam cast up on a foreign shore.

The beach upon which the shipwrecked survivors stood gradually rose to form a sandy hill. Covered with long grass that waved sinuously in the wind, it was dotted here and there with scrub bushes. Large rocks, wet with salt spray, jutted out of the sand. Mathew saw, lined up on the top of the hill on what was apparently a road of some sort, a group of men mounted on horseback staring down at them.

Following along after the horsemen was a palanquin—a large, covered sedan chair. Hung with white curtains, the the chair rested on two large poles that were being carried by six turbaned *mamelukes*. An impossing sight, these slaves were dressed in matching black silk pantalons, their muscular chests and arms bare and glistening with oil rubbed into their skin. Behind the palanquin, the curtains of which were tightly drawn, strode several tall animals—the likes of which the men of Tirish Aranth had seen only in their books. Brown and ungainly, with long, curved necks, a ridiculously small head for such a large body, and thin, scrawny legs with huge, splayed feet, the animals carried striped, hoop-shaped tents upon their humped backs.

"Promenthas be praised!" the Abbot breathed. "Such wondrous beasts *do* exist! What is it they are called?"

"Camels," replied the Archmagus matter-of-factly, endeavoring to look unimpressed.

But what caught Mathew's attention was the group that came up behind the camels—a long line of men straggling over the road, marching with heads bowed. Each man had an iron ring around his neck. A long length of chain running through the rings, binding the men together. Mathew sucked in his breath in horror. A slave caravan! The Abbot, seeing them, scowled darkly, and the Archmagus, shaking his head, frowned in anger and sorrow.

Riding behind the chained men—obviously their guards—came another group of mounted men. The uniformed horsemen were a bizarre sight to the men of Tirish Aranth, who were accustomed to seeing the hose and doublets, feathered hats, and flowing capes of His Majesty's Royal Guard.

Each of these soldiers wore a short, dark-blue coat that came to his waist. Decorated with golden embroidery that flashed in the sunlight, the coat covered a white shirt that was open at the neck. Bright red trousers, as full as a lady's skirts, billowed about their legs and were tucked into tall black riding boots. Small cone-shaped red hats, adorned with jaunty black tassels, perched atop their heads. The hats looked extremely comical. Mathew, grinning, giggled and nudged John, only to receive a swift, rebuking glance from the Archmagus.

Acting on some unheard order, the entire caravan came to a halt. The chained slaves, glad for any excuse to rest, slumped to the ground. Mathew saw a white hand emerge from the folds of the curtains of the palanquin and make a single, graceful gesture toward the beach. At this, the leader of the horsemen turned his horse's head and skillfully guided his animal down the sandy hill, his troop following in orderly fashion behind him.

"Slave trader," muttered the Abbot, watching, scowling. "I want nothing to do with this evil person."

"I am afraid we cannot afford the luxury of picking and choosing our companions," the Archmagus said softly. "We have lost all our magical paraphernalia and without it, as you know, we are unable to cast spells. We have lost our maps, we have no idea where we are. Besides," he added smoothly, knowing how to handle the Abbot, "this may be your opportunity to bring a soul walking in darkness to the light."

"You are right. Promenthas, forgive me," the Abbot said instantly, his face clearing.

"Whoever that person is, he must be wealthy to keep his own *goums*." The Archmagus used the word of this land with the aplomb of the seasoned traveler.

"Wealth obtained from trading in human flesh," the Abbot began bitterly, but he hushed upon receiving a glance from the Archmagus, warning him that the soldiers were within earshot.

The *goums* in their colorful uniforms were truly an awesome sight. Reaching the shoreline, they rode their magnificent steeds with skill and precision along the wet, packed sand, their horses' manes and tails streaming behind them like banners in the remnants of the storm wind. The setting sun, breaking occasionally through the ragged clouds, glinted on the hilts of the sabers they wore at their sides. Instinctively the small group on the shore huddled closer together as the Abbot and the Archmagus stepped forward wearily to greet their saviors.

The leader rode his horse at a gallop straight for the Abbot, turning the beast aside with a flourish at the last possible moment, the horse's hooves flashing within inches of the priest. Reining in his mount, the *goum* raised his hand, bringing the riders behind him to a halt. Another gesture sent them cantering out in a straight line on either side of him, the horses dancing sideways in remarkable precision. The priest and the wizard watched, apparently unmoved by this spectacle, although their followers could not forbear to whisper among themselves in amazement and wonder.

The *goum* slid down from the saddle, approaching them on foot, his shining black boots crunching across the wet sand.

"*Salaam aleikum!*" said the Abbot, bowing, his greetings being echoed by the Archmagus. "*Bilshifa! Bilhana!* May you have health and joy."

Mathew cringed, wishing the Archmagus would let him do the talking. The Abbot may have been able to speak the language, but his clumsy pronunciation was that of a child saying his first words.

"Aleikum salaam," returned the leader, eyeing the wet, bedraggled band of men with cool curiosity. He was a short man with brown skin, dark eyes, and a small black mustache over his lip. "You speak our language well, but your tongue gives the words strange emphasis. Where are you from?"

"We come from across the sea, *sidi,*" said the Abbot, waving his hand westward. "A land called Tirish Aranth."

"Across the sea?" The man's eyes narrowed suspiciously as he gazed out into the crashing waves. "Are you birdmen? Have you wings beneath those robes?"

"No, *sidi.*" The Abbot smiled over such naïveté. "We came by *dh-dj*—" He struggled for the word in the foreign tongue.

Mathew, forgetting himself, impatiently supplied it. *"Dhows."*

"Thank you," said the Abbot, glancing at the young wizard gratefully. *"Dhows.* A galleon. It was attacked by an archfi—"

" 'Efreet," the Archmagus hastily interposed.

"Er, yes." The Abbot flushed. "What you call an 'efreet. I fear you will not believe us, *sidi,* but I swear by my God, Promenthas, that this creature rose up out of the water and—"

"Promenthas?" The leader repeated the name, mouthing it as if it tasted bad. "I do not know this God." Glaring at the Abbot, he frowned. "You come from a land I have never heard of, speaking our language with strange accents, talking of a God that is not ours. What is more, you have, by your own admission, brought down the wrath of an 'efreet upon us, whose anger has wreaked havoc among several small towns along the coast. Their destruction has delayed my lord's journey and caused him great inconvenience."

The Abbot blanched, glancing at the Archmagus, who looked grave.

"We—we assure you, *sidi,* that the coming of this horrible creature was not our fault," stammered the Abbot. "It attacked us, too! It sank our ship!"

The *goum* appeared unconvinced, and the Archmagus thought it best to intervene, steering the subject into safer waters. "We are cold and exhausted by our ordeal. We do not want to add to the inconvenience of your master by further delaying his journey. If you could but direct us to the town of Bastine, we have important friends there who can help us. . . ."

This last was an outright lie, but the Archmagus did not like the look of this *goum* and did not want him or his master to think them completely friendless in this alien land.

"Wait here."

Remounting, the *goum* wheeled his horse, dashing up the shoreline at a gallop. Coming to a halt before the palanquin, he leaned down to speak to the person inside.

The priests and wizards remained standing on the shore, casting sidelong glances at the riders, who, for their part, gazed out across the ocean at the slowly sinking sun with magnificent unconcern. After a brief conversation with the unseen person in the palanquin, the leader returned, cantering along the sand.

"My master has decreed that you find food and rest this night."

The Abbot sighed, clasping his hands together. "Promenthas be praised," he murmured. Aloud he said, "Please express our grateful thanks to your master—"

The Archmagus cried out a warning. The priest stopped talking, his tongue cleaving to the roof of his mouth. The leader of the riders had drawn his saber. The sunlight, breaking through the clouds, glinted on the wickedly curved blade. Behind their leader, each *goum* did the same.

"What . . . what is the meaning of this?" the Archmagus demanded, staring at the swords with narrowed eyes. "You said we were to have food and rest. . . ."

"Indeed you will, *kafir*. This night, you will dine in Hell!"

Digging his heels into his horse's flanks, the leader rode straight for the priest and before the astonished man could even cry out, drove his saber through the Abbot's stomach. Jerking the blade free, he watched the priest's body sag to the ground, then swung the bloodstained saber around, cleaving open the head of the Archmagus.

Shouting wildly, the *goums* attacked. The wizards met their deaths without a fight. Bereft of magical wands and scrolls and all else needed to cast their spells, they were helpless. The *goums* cut them down within seconds, stabbing them with their sabers, trampling their bodies beneath the flashing hooves of their steeds. The monks, true to their calling, fell to their knees, crying out to Promenthas. Sharp steel brought their prayers to an agonized end.

Mathew stared numbly at the writhing body of the Abbot, lying on the sand. He watched the *goum* slay the Archmagus, he saw their leader riding his horse directly at him, and suddenly, with no clear idea what he was doing, he caught hold of John's hand and turning, began running down the beach as fast as he could.

Seeing two of his prey escaping, a shout came from the leader. Behind him, Mathew could hear the pounding of hooves, the shrill cries of the *goums* giving chase, the dying screams of his companions.

Hearts nearly bursting from their chests, their lungs burning with fear, the two young men fled in blind panic, running without direction, without hope.

Mathew stumbled in the wet sand and fell. John stopped, reached out his hand to his friend, and pulled him back up. Though each knew that their flight must inevitably end in death, the two ran desperately, driven by the thudding of hoofbeats coming closer and closer, the whistling sound of sabers slashing through the air, the laughter of the *goums,* who were clearly enjoying this wild chase.

Then Mathew experienced the strangest sensation. It seemed a hand touched his forehead, his black hood flew back, his red hair streamed out behind him. He glanced about to see who was near him, fearful it was the *goum*. But the man was still some distance behind him, riding his horse at a canter, obviously playing with his helpless victims.

Blood pounding in his ears, Mathew turned his head and continued running. Even in his terror he moved with the grace inborn in his people, one hand holding on to John, the other clutching his robes so that he could run without tripping. He did not see the swift change of expression on the leader's face, he did not hear the new, shouted command to the rider pursuing him.

Mathew's strength was flagging. He heard cries directly behind him now and knew any moment he would feel burning pain, feel the blades pierce his body. Horses' hooves drummed next to him, he could hear the animal's harsh breathing. John's hand clung to his with a deathlike grip. . . .

A heavy weight struck Mathew from behind, knocking him

off his feet and sending him tumbling to the ground. A man was on top of him. Mathew struggled, but the *goum* struck him a blow across the face that stunned him, and the young wizard froze in the sand, sobbing in terror, waiting for death. But the *goum,* seeing his quarry subdued, rose to his feet. Sick and dizzy, Mathew turned his aching head, looking for John. He saw his friend, kneeling in the sand beside him, his head bowed. He was praying.

The leader of the *goums* dismounted and came up behind John. Raising his blade, the goum held it poised above the monk's neck.

Screaming, Mathew hurled himself forward. His guard struck him again, dashing him to the ground.

The sword fell, the blade flashing red in the light of the dying sun.

John's headless body slumped sideways into the sand. Warm blood, spurting from the neck, splashed on Mathew's outstretched arms. Something landed with a horrible, sickening thump in the sand right beside him.

Mathew saw a gaping mouth, its last prayer on its lips. He stared into wide-open, empty eyes. . . .

 **Chapter 4**

Water splashed in his face. Sputtering, shaking his head, Mathew regained consciousness. At first he could remember nothing. He knew only that there was a hollow, burning emptiness inside him, and he wondered, too, that he was not dead.

Dead. The word brought back the memories, and he moaned. He saw the sword flash red in the sunlight. . . .

"Remarkable hair, unusual color," came a harsh, deep voice quite near him. "Soft white skin. Now you must find out—"

The voice sank too low to hear; another responded. Mathew paid little attention to the words. At the time he wasn't even aware that he understood them. Shock and horror had temporarily driven the skill of speaking and understanding the language from his head. Later he would remember the words he'd heard and realize their portent. Now he only wondered what they were going to do to him.

He was lying on the ground, somewhere near the ocean, he presumed, for he could hear the waves crashing against the shore. There was a feel of grass beneath his cheek instead of sand, however, so he assumed they must have moved him from the beach. He couldn't remember. He couldn't remember anything except John's eyes, staring at him reproachfully.

I am dead. You are not.

Mathew moaned again.

Why has my life been spared? Some foul torture perhaps.

His stomach wrenched. He turned his own reproach upon Promenthas. Why didn't You let me die with John?

Hands caught hold of Mathew, dragging him to his feet. A sharp command and a slap across the face caused him to open his eyes.

It was twilight. The sun had set, the afterglow lit the sky. He was on the road above the beach, standing in front of the palanquin. The litter's curtains remained drawn. Two of the *goums* had hold of him by the upper arms, but once assuring themselves that he could stand on his own, they shoved Mathew forward. Their leader caught the young wizard as he stumbled and yanked him nearer the palanquin.

The leader grabbed hold of Mathew's chin, forcing his head up. Rough fingers, clamped beneath his jaw, turned the young wizard's head to the left and then the right, as though exhibiting him to the unseen person behind the curtains. At length a voice spoke from inside the palanquin. It was a man's voice—harsh and deep, the voice that had spoken earlier. Mathew caught a glimpse of a bejeweled, slender hand, holding the curtain aside the tiniest crack.

The leader of the *goums* let Mathew go. At the same time he asked him a question—or at least Mathew assumed he was being questioned, for the *goum* looked at him expectantly, obviously awaiting a response. The young wizard shook his head dully, not comprehending, waiting only for them to kill him and end the burning ache within his breast. The *goum* repeated the question, more loudly this time as if he thought Mathew might be deaf.

The voice from within the palanquin spoke sharply, and the leader, turning to face Mathew, made a crude gesture with his hand, a gesture whose sexual connotation transcends all languages, is known the world over. The leader made the gesture, then pointed at Mathew's private parts, then made the gesture again.

The young wizard regarded the man with disgust. He understood, he thought, what the man was trying to say. But what did it have to do with him?

Bleakly, angrily, he shook his head. The *goum*, after studying his face intently, laughed and said something to the man in the palanquin.

The man, with a nod barely discernible from behind the curtains, spoke again. Somewhere in another part of his brain

Mathew understood the man's words. He stared at the white curtains in a daze.

"Yes, I agree with you, Kiber. She is a virgin. See to it that she remains one until we reach Kich. Put her in one of the *bassourab*, so that the sun may not blemish such a delicate flower."

The jeweled hand reached out from the curtains, the man gestured. The litter bearers lifted up their poles and carried the palanquin down the road.

She! Her! Mathew understood that much in the confusion of his mind and suddenly everything became clear.

They had mistaken him for a woman!

Kiber, the leader of the *goums,* took hold of his arm and led him away. Walking almost blindly, Mathew stumbled at the side of his captor, the realization of his plight striking home with the sharp bite of a steel blade.

This was why he had not been slaughtered with the others. In his mind he saw the Abbot, the Archmagus, John—bearded, all of them. All except Mathew, the Wesman, whose race did not grow facial hair.

They have mistaken me for a woman! Now what will they do with me? Not that it matters, he thought numbly. Sooner or later they must discover their mistake. And then it will all be over. Certainly it would be better to undeceive them, to lift his robes, reveal his maleness. Undoubtedly he would die swiftly at the hands of this savage. John had died swiftly . . . very swiftly indeed. . . .

Mathew shuddered, his stomach turning, bile flooding his mouth. He saw his comrades butchered before his eyes, he saw himself dying the same way. The shining blade plunging though flesh and bone, the terrible, bursting pain, the final, dreadful scream torn from his lungs.

Mathew's legs gave way and he fell. Crouched on the road, he retched. I don't want to die! I don't!

Kiber, with a look of irritation, waited until Mathew had emptied his stomach, then hauled him to his feet, hurrying him along.

Shivering all over, Mathew trembled so that he could barely walk. He was growing light-headed and knew he would not be able to go much farther. He was going to faint. . . . Fear hit him like cold water in the face. He dare not lose consciousness; his secret might be discovered.

Fortunately they did not have too far to go. With a grunted command the *goum* jerked Mathew to a halt in front of one of the long-legged, grotesque-looking camels. Resting on its knees on the ground, the beast gazed at Mathew with an incredibly vicious, stupid expression. Taking hold of the young wizard's wrists, Kiber bound them together swiftly and skillfully with a strip of leather. The *goum* pulled aside the flap of the dome-shaped tent atop the camel saddle and gestured for Mathew to enter.

Mathew stared at the strange-looking saddle and the precarious tent covering it without the vaguest idea what to do. He had never ridden a horse, let alone any creature this big. The camel snaked its head around to look at him, chewing its cud like a cow. Its teeth were enormous. Kiber, anxious to get the caravan on its way, reached out his arms, obviously intending to pick Mathew up bodily.

Fear jolted the young wizard to action. Not wanting the man to touch him, he clumsily scrambled up into the odd-looking saddle. With gestures the *goum* indicated Mathew was to curl one leg around the horn of the saddle, locking it in place by placing the other over it. Then, either to prevent his prisoner from escaping or because he had noted Mathew's deathly pale face and the greenish shadows beneath his eyes, Kiber tied the young wizard to the saddle and to the sides of the camel tent with long lengths of cloth.

Pulling the curtains of the *bassourab* shut, the *goum* shouted, "*Adar-ya-yan!*"

Grumbling, the camel rose to its feet, moving with a rolling motion that brought back memories of the storm-tossed ship.

Mathew blessed the tent surrounding him, for it prevented him from seeing how high he was off the ground. Kiber shouted again and the beast started walking. Mathew's queasy stomach lurched with every step. Slumping over the saddle and thankful that no one could see him, the young wizard gave himself up to dark despair.

Everything had happened so swiftly, so suddenly, one moment he was standing on a sun-drenched beach with John. The next moment, John was dead and he was captured. And every moment from now on, Mathew would live with the edge of a knife constantly at his throat. And he knew, sooner or later, the blade would jab home. Sooner or later he must be discovered. He was spinning out the thread of his life for a few minutes, an hour, perhaps a day, two at most. He was alive, but what kind of life was he facing? A life of constant torment, a life without hope, a life of looking forward to death.

Tell them the truth. Do you want to live with this fear, waiting in terror for the moment that will come—yes, it *will* come—when you are found out? End it quickly! Die now! Die with your brothers. Die bravely. . . .

"I can't!" Mathew's teeth clenched together, cold sweat slid down his body. He saw John's headless trunk slumping to the sand, he felt the warm blood splashing on his hands. "I can't!" *Hiding behind a woman's skirts*—an old and shameful saying in his country. What about hiding *in* a woman's skirts! What greater shame was that? He moaned, rocking back and forth. "I am a coward! A coward!"

Mathew was sick again—the stench of the camel, the jolting motion, his fear, and his memories of the terrible sights he had witnessed all combining to twist his bowels and wrench his stomach. Clinging to the saddle, he shook with pain and terror, providing further proof for himself that he was a craven coward.

He never stopped to consider that he was young, lost, alone in a strange and terrible land, that he had seen those he loved murdered before his eyes, that he had been beaten, was sick and in shock.

No, in Mathew's eyes he was a coward, unworthy of having lived when those so much braver and better than he had given up their lives for their faith.

Their faith. His faith. Mathew tried to whisper a prayer, then stopped. Undoubtedly Promenthas had abandoned him as well. All knew the God took the soul of the martyred to dwell with him in eternal bliss forever. What about the soul of the coward? How would Mathew face Promenthas, John, the Archmagus? Even after death, there would be no comfort for him.

The journey was a nightmare that seemed to last for endless days, although in reality it was only an hour. With the advent of night the caravan came to a halt. In a stupor from his agony of mind and body, Mathew had only the vaguest comprehension of the camel he was riding lurching awkwardly to the ground. He remained where he was, lost in misery, until a hand thrust aside the curtain. Two *goums* untied Mathew, grabbed hold of him, and dragged him from the saddle.

At first he was afraid he could not walk. The moment his feet touched the ground, his knees buckled. Falling, he saw his captors bending down to lift him up and carry him. Terror revived him. Shaking off the hands of the *goums*, Mathew staggered to his feet.

The moon was full and bright. Glancing around, Mathew saw that they had traveled inland and were now far from the sea. He heard the sound of water, but it was a river. The camp was being established on its banks in the middle of a vast expanse of grassy plain. The smell and sound and sight of the river water made him realize how thirsty he was. His throat was parched and hurting from the seawater and his sickness. But he dared not call attention to himself by asking for something to drink.

To distract himself he continued looking around. The palanquin had been carried to the front of a large tent, surrounded by a bevy of slaves. The *goums* were working efficiently to set up tents, groom and water the horses, spread out fodder for the camels. Several women, their heads and bodies swathed in black silk, were being assisted out of other *bassourabs* and taken to small tents. Most of the women, Mathew saw, had their hands bound like his.

The men with the iron collars slumped to the ground where they stood. Sitting with heads bowed between their legs, their hands dangling in front of them, they took no interest in anything going on around them.

Once again Mathew wondered, What are they going to do to me? His gaze returned to the palanquin in time to see a man dressed in white robes, his head and body covered by the folds of white *burnoose*, leave the litter. A canopy had been erected by the slaves in front of the tent, cushions were carefully arranged on the ground. The man ducked beneath the canopy and settled himself among the cushions. Lounging on one arm, he made several gestures that sent slaves flying to do his bidding. Mathew was watching in weary, numb fascination when Kiber, jabbing him, pointed at a tent.

Nodding, Mathew started to walk toward it, hoping he had the energy to travel the short distance. The tent was a small one. Made of strips of wool sewn together, it was barely large enough for one person. It didn't matter. Ducking inside, Mathew fell thankfully to the firm, solid ground.

He was just realizing that he would have to go in search of water soon or perish when a head thrust itself into the tent. It was Kiber. Hastily Mathew sat up, his hands reaching instinctively to gather his robes close around his body.

The *goum* tossed a waterskin onto the floor of the tent. Snatching it up, Mathew drank greedily, gulping the water down, never minding that it tasted of camel. Watching him, Kiber gave a grunt of satisfaction, then threw down a bundle at Mathew's feet. Taking a sharp dagger from his belt, the *goum* crouched down in front of Mathew, and the young wizard's raw throat constricted in terror.

Kiber was not going to kill him, however. With a quick slice the *goum* neatly severed Mathew's wrist bonds, then gestured from the bundle to Mathew and back to the bundle again.

Mathew stared at the bundle, puzzled.

Picking it up, Kiber thrust it into his hands. Mathew examined it, and slowly it occurred to his stupefied brain what he was holding.

Clothing. Women's clothing.

He looked up at the *goum,* who gestured again peremptorily, adding something in a sharp tone and pointing with a grimace of disgust to Mathew's own filthy robes.

It was obvious what the man meant. Mathew clutched the bundle tightly. This was the moment. This was the time to make his stand. Firmly, courageously, he would rise to his feet. He would reveal the truth and accept his fate, dying bravely, dying with dignity.

Dying. . . .

Fear clenched his stomach. He tried to stand, but he had no strength in his legs. Tears blurred his vision. Finally, gulping, he bowed his head. Kiber, with another grunt, left the tent.

Spreading out the women's clothes upon the ground, Mathew slowly began to strip off his bloodstained robes.

Chapter 5

The women's clothing fit easily over Mathew's slight, slender frame, the sheer bulk and graceful folds of the fabric concealing his flat chest and narrow hips, aiding in his disguise. It was certainly different from the low-cut, full-skirted dresses worn by women in his own land—dresses that revealed a broad expanse of snowy-white bosom, of powdered shoulders, dresses whose silken fabric swept the floor and could be raised to show the turn of an ankle.

Fingers trembling, fearing to hear footsteps outside, he hastily drew on the silken, full-cut cotton trousers. Similar to those the men wore, they fit tightly about his ankles. A gauze smock covered his upper body, its sleeves reaching to the elbow. Over this fit a buttoned waistcoat with long sleeves to the wrist, then—over everything—an ankle-length black caftan, and finally a black veil that covered face and head, soft leather slippers for his feet.

Viewing these clothes in the dim moonlight that filtered through his tent, Mathew saw a mental image of himself, running along the beach, his black robes fluttering about him. The *goums'* mistake was understandable, perhaps inevitable.

He must look, he thought, like a walking black cocoon—a cocoon concealing a worm doomed to die.

What would happen to him now?

Dressed in the women's clothing, Mathew huddled inside his tent, not daring to sleep. The young wizard had lived a cloistered life, having spent his childhood and youth in the closed and secret school of the magi, but Mathew knew enough of the ways of men and women to understand that his greatest danger lay in the hours of darkness. He recalled the touch of the man in the palanquin—the jeweled hand stroking his cheek—and his heart sank.

Bitterly he regretted the loss of his magical devices—amulets and charms that could send a man into sweet slumber, spells that would disorient a man, making him think he was somewhere he wasn't. Mathew could produce them, but that would take time and material: the quill of a raven to write the arcane words, parchment made of sheepskin, blood. . . .

Blood. . . . He saw John, falling. . . .

No! Mathew shut his eyes, driving the gruesome vision from his mind. If he dwelt on that, he would go mad. And it was no use dreaming about magic defenses he didn't have and couldn't acquire. To keep himself occupied and hopefully discover some clue about what they planned to do to him, Mathew began going over the words he'd heard people speaking, trying to remember exactly what had been said, trying to translate the phrases.

At first it seemed impossible; the language that he had studied so painstakingly for so many months had vanished from his head. Stubbornly Mathew forced himself to concentrate. He'd understood a few words, enough to know that they thought he was female. "She." "Her." And another word. "Virgin." Yes, Mathew remembered that word clearly, mainly because Kiber had repeated it often, coupling it with that crude gesture. He knew now what the *goum* had been asking: Have you lain with a man? Mathew couldn't recall what he had responded, but he guessed that the look of disgust upon his face had been sufficient answer.

A light step sounding outside caused the young wizard to catch his breath in fear. But it was a woman. Parting the tent, peering inside, only her eyes visible above her veil, she thrust a bowl of food into Mathew's hands, then withdrew.

The wizard's stomach wrenched at the smell of the stuff—a glob of rice mixed with meat and vegetables. He started to shove the bowl back out, then stopped. This again would call attention to himself. It was impossible to eat. Even if he knew what the meat was, he could never keep it down. Furtively slipping the bowl out of the back of his tent, he dumped the food out into the grass, hoping some animal would come by and eat it before it was discovered in the morning.

This accomplished, he set his mind back to its problem. There had been those words spoken when he was half-conscious. "Red hair." Yes, they had been talking about his hair, which he knew from his studies would be considered an unusual color among the mostly dark-haired, dark-eyed people of this land. There had been something else. Something to do with his skin. . . .

Again, footsteps. These were heavy, booted, and definitely coming this direction. Holding his breath, Mathew waited grimly, almost eagerly. He had decided what to do. The man would almost certainly be wearing a dagger—he had noticed that they all did, carrying one or more tucked into their belts. Mathew would grab the dagger and use it. The wizard had never attacked a man before, and he doubted if he would be able to do much damage to his enemy before the man killed him. At least it would lend his death some semblance of dignity.

The steps came nearer and nearer, then stopped right outside the tent. He heard voices. There were two of them! Mathew swallowed the terrible taste in his mouth and tried to force himself to stop trembling. Soon it would be over—the fear, the pain. Then peace, eternal peace with Promenthas.

The two men, talking to each other, laughing, crouched down. Mathew tensed, ready to spring. But neither man entered the tent. Listening, longing to look outside but not daring to stir, Mathew thought he heard them settling themselves on the ground before his tent. His fear easing, he tried to concentrate on what they were discussing, hoping to discover his fate.

They spoke the language much faster than he was able to understand, however, and at first he caught only about one word in five. Listening closely, sorting out the strange accent, he began to comprehend more and more. The men were reliving the exciting event of the day—the slaughter of the *kafir*. Hearing them argue over how many of the unbelievers each had slain, and whose victims had died slowest and screamed loudest, Mathew gritted his teeth, fighting a longing to lash out in a rage and anger that surprised him, treading as it did on the heels of his fear.

"The one man, he squealed like a hog when I stuck him. Did you hear? And the two who ran. A fine chase we had, along the shore. The captain himself beheaded the man—a

swift, clean stroke. Robbed us of fun, but *he*—the master—
was in a hurry."

Beheaded! They were talking about John! Mathew wanted
to stuff something in his ears, shut out the voices and the
memories. But he couldn't afford the luxury. Grimly he
forced himself to keep listening, hoping to discover his fate.

After the murders of the *kafir* had been discussed, disputed,
and enjoyed to the fullest, the *goums'* conversation turned to
their journey. They were bound for Kich, Mathew managed
to make out, catching the name and recognizing it as being
one of the major cities in Sardish Jardan. The caravan had
made good time today, despite stopping to sport with the
kafir, and the *goums* hoped, if the weather held, to be in Kich
within a week. Once there, they would sell their wares,
collect their wages, and spend some time indulging in the sins
to be found in the rich city.

Sell their wares.

Remarkable hair, unusual color. Soft white skin.

Mathew bit his tongue to keep from crying out. What a
fool he'd been, not to have thought of this. The women with
their hands bound. . . .

*A virgin. See to it that she remains one until we reach
Kich.*

That explained the reason the men were outside. They were
guards, responsible for keeping the "wares" undamaged! So
that was his fate. He was to be sold as a slave!

Mathew sank back upon the few cushions that had been
tossed carelessly into the tent for his use. At least I am in no
immediate danger, he thought. If I manage to maintain my
disguise, which—considering how segregated the women are
being kept from the men—shouldn't be too difficult, I might
well live a while longer, until we reach the slave markets.

He felt no relief at this, only empty and disappointed, and
he smiled bitterly. Of course he had secretly been hoping it
would all end quickly, this night.

Now he looked forward to nothing but torturous days of
constant fear; torturous nights spent lying awake, starting at
every footstep. And at the end of it all? What then? He would
be placed upon the slave block and sold as a woman, then
meet his death—probably a horrible one—at the hands of
some defrauded buyer.

Terror, shame, and guilt burst from Mathew's throat in an anguished cry. Hastily he tried to choke back his tears, wondering if the guards had heard him, afraid that they might come in to find out what was wrong. But he could not help himself, grief and fear overwhelmed him. Stuffing the veil in his mouth to muffle his despairing sobs, the young man rolled over on his stomach, buried his face in the cushions, and wept.

Night, black and empty, came upon the plains. The guards outside Mathew's tent dozed fitfully. They had heard his choked cries but only glanced at each other with sly grins, each urging the other to creep into the tent and "comfort" the captive. Neither moved to do so, however. Kiber was a good captain, discipline was maintained. The last man who had gained a little private pleasure from the slaves had been dealt with swiftly and severely. One stroke of his captain's sword and the wretched *goum* was now a eunuch in the *seraglios* of Kich.

As for the faint sobs coming from the tent, more than one captive was likely wailing over her fate that night. It was none of their concern. So the guards slept, not overly worried that anyone might slip past them.

Someone did slip by them, however. It was not anyone either *goum* could have stopped had they been awake. It was not one either could have seen, asleep or awake. The angel, her white, feathery wingtips brushing the ground, stole into the tent with less sound than the soft breeze whispering across the sand. Bending over the weeping Mathew, the angel touched him gently upon the cheek, brushing away his tears even as her own fell fast.

At her soft touch, the young man's wrenching sobs ceased. He drifted into a deep, dreamless sleep. The angel gazed at him with deep pity and compassion. Slipping back out of the tent, she glanced furtively around her, then swiftly and silently spread her wings and soared into the heavens.

Chapter 6

Promenthas paced solemnly the long length of the red-carpeted aisle that ran straight and narrow between the hard, wooden pews in his cathedral. The God's face was grave, he stroked his white beard thoughtfully, his white brows bristling. An angel waited at the far end of the aisle, her silver hair shining in the soft light of hundreds of flickering votive candles. A sound behind her caused her to glance around. Seeing who it was that entered the great wooden doors, the angel slipped silently away to wait within the dark shadows of the nave.

"Promenthas, I understand that you wished to speak to me."

"I do and over a matter of extreme gravity." Promenthas's gentle voice shook with grief and anger. "How dare you murder my priests?"

Dressed in a fantastically embroidered silk caftan with long, flowing sleeves, Quar looked particularly exotic and outlandish in the austere setting of Promenthas's cathedral. But Quar did not see himself in the gray marble edifice. He was strolling about the grounds of his palace. To him it was Promenthas who was out of place, the God's plain, gray robes appearing poor and shabby amid the sumptuous setting of orange trees, fountains, and peacocks.

Coolly regarding his angry fellow, Quar raised his eyebrows. "If we are accusing one another of misdeeds, how dare you send your missionaries to subvert the faith of *my* people?"

"I cannot be accountable for the zeal of my followers!"

Quar bowed. "My answer as well."

"There was no need to slaughter them! You could have

114

attempted to gain them for yourself.'' Promenthas's face flushed in anger.

"According to the new belief spreading among my followers, a *kafir*—an unbeliever—leads a misguided life that is doomed to end only in sorrow and tragedy. By cutting short such a wretched existence, my followers consider that they are doing the *kafir* a favor.''

Promenthas stared in astonishment. "Never before have any of us propounded a doctrine such as this! It is murder in the name of religion!''

His hand absently stroking the neck of a fawn that he kept as a pet in his garden, Quar appeared to muse upon the matter. "Perhaps you are right,'' he admitted after several moments of profound thought. "I had not looked at the incident in that light.'' He shrugged delicately. "To be truthful, I had not really given the encounter much thought. These are mortals we are discussing. What can one expect of them except to behave foolishly and irrationally? But now that you have brought this to my attention, I will discuss the matter with my Imam and attempt to discover who is teaching such a potentially dangerous doctrine.''

Promenthas appeared somewhat mollified. "Yes, you had better look into it. And put an end to it.''

"Rest assured, I will do what I can.''

Promenthas did not much like this answer, nor did he like Quar's easy dismissal of the shocking murders. But Promenthas was not entirely satisfied in his own conscience that his people had been completely in the right, so he let the matter drop.

Changing the topic of conversation to less volatile subjects, he escorted Quar to the massive carved wooden doors of the cathedral. In Quar's view the two walked together to the wrought-iron gates of the palace garden. Bowing to each other coolly, the Gods parted.

But left alone, Promenthas returned his thoughts to the murdered priests and magi. His head bent, his hands clasped behind his back, the God was walking down the aisle when—to his astonishment—he glanced up to see someone standing before the altar.

"Akhran,'' said Promenthas, not overly pleased. The

followers of the Wandering God had been known to commit their share of murder, although—he had to admit—not in the name of religion. More often it was in the name of theft, blood feud, war. "What business brings you here?"

The Wandering God, dressed in flowing black robes worn over a white tunic and trousers, his head and face swathed in black cloth, looked as if he were standing in the midst of a raging sandstorm instead of the quiet of the cathedral. Two piercing black eyes beneath straight-edged brows stared intently into Promenthas's mild eyes—eyes that were now shadowed with worry.

"I warned you," came the deep voice, muffled behind the *haik*. "You would not listen to me."

Promenthas frowned. "I don't know what you mean."

"Yes, you do. *Jihad*."

"I'm sorry, I do not understand—"

"*Jihad*. The word of my people for 'holy war.' It has already begun. Evren and Zhakrin are dead, their immortals vanished. Now your followers, butchered in the lands of Quar."

Promenthas regarded the other God in silence. Akhran—as always—seemed too big, too wild, too savage, to be contained within the stone walls of the cathedral. The Wandering God himself was obviously ill at ease. Removing the face cloth from his mouth, sucking in a deep breath of air, he looked longingly to the wide wooden doors that led outside. But Akhran remained where he was—standing tall, straight— keeping himself under rigid constraint.

By Sul, Promenthas realized in astonishment. Akhran really *is* in the cathedral! The Wandering God has left his beloved desert, has deliberately entered my dwelling place! Such a thing had not happened since the beginning of time.

Promenthas knew he should be pleased, flattered. He felt neither, only chilled. Quickening his steps, he approached the altar.

"If what you told us that terrible day is true," he said slowly, coming to stand before Akhran, "why then are Quar's own immortals disappearing?"

"I have an idea, but I have no proof. If what I fear is correct, then our danger is very great."

"And what do you fear?"

Akhran shook his head, the black brows beneath the twisted black folds of the headcloth drawing together like the wings of a falcon above the smoldering eyes.

Promenthas moved to smooth his beard as was his habit when disturbed and noticed that his hand trembled visibly. He clasped his fingers together in an unconscious, prayerful attitude. "Perhaps you are right, Akhran. Perhaps we have let Quar make fools of us all. But what does he want?"

"Surely that is obvious. To become the Supreme God, the Only God. Little by little, his Emperor is extending his rule, his Imams are gaining strength. Those people they conquer are either killed instantly, as were your followers, or given the choice of the *jihad*—convert or die. Little by little we will lose our worshipers. We will dwindle and . . . eventually . . . vanish."

"That is impossible!"

"Is it? You saw it happen before your own eyes. Where now are Evren and Zhakrin?"

Promenthas was silent long moments, mulling over in his mind the account the angel had given him of the slaughter of his followers. *Jihad.* Holy war. Convert or die. Frowning, he glanced back at the Wandering God.

"This affects you most closely, Akhran. The lands of your people border on those of Quar's faithful. What are you doing?"

The Wandering God cast Promenthas a scornful look and lifted his head proudly. "My people are not like yours. They do not go meekly to their deaths with prayers upon their lips. They fight."

Promenthas smiled slightly. "Quar or each other?"

Akhran's eyes blazed fiercely, then his shoulders sagged, his mouth twisted. "One should never be angry to hear the truth. That, in fact, is the reason I have come. I seek your help. Your people are much different from mine, they are noted for their wisdom, their compassion, their patience. . . ."

Promenthas regarded the Wandering God in astonishment. "That may be true, but how can my people help you, Akhran? They are an ocean away—"

"Not all of them."

Promenthas, taken aback, appeared startled. "No," he murmured, glancing at the angel who was waiting patiently in the nave and who appeared extremely alarmed by the turn of the conversation. "No," the God repeated. Troubled, Promenthas rested his hand upon the altar rail, absently caressing the oiled wood with his gnarled, wrinkled fingers. "That is true."

Akhran laid his suntanned, weather-hardened hand upon Promenthas's. "Do not deceive yourself, my friend. An ocean will not stop Quar."

Promenthas's gaze went to the angel. "The poor lad to whom you refer has undergone a frightful experience. His suffering has been immense. I had thought to give him a swift and easy death."

"And will you do the same for the tens of thousands who will not be so fortunate?" Akhran asked sternly.

Promenthas stared thoughtfully at the angel. The silver-haired woman regarded her God with beseeching blue eyes, mutely pleading with him not to change his mind.

At length Promenthas, turning abruptly, looked back at Akhran. "So be it," he said gruffly. "I will do what I can. I promise nothing, however. After all, one can only accomplish so much with mortals."

Akhran smiled, a brief smile that vanished in an instant, his face returning to its accustomed gravity and severity. Wrapping the black cloth over his mouth and nose, he nodded to Promenthas—the closest the Wandering God ever came to a bow—and took his leave, walking hastily back down the red-carpeted aisle, his strides growing increasingly longer as he neared the bright sunlight he could see shining outside the massive wooden door.

"Come, One Who is Swifter Than the Starlight!" he called out commandingly.

In answer, Promenthas heard the sound of hooves clattering up the marble stairs of his cathedral, followed by the shocked voices of his angels raised in protest. The white head of a stallion appeared in the doorway, shaking its mane in impatience, its shrill whinny splitting the sanctuary's holy silence. With a parting wave of his hand Akhran vaulted easily into the saddle. The horse reared, hooves flashing in the light, then it leaped into the air. Indignant seraphim and cherubim gazed after it in dismay, loudly exclaiming over horse manure on the marble steps.

Shaking his head, sighing, Promenthas turned and beckoned to the droop-winged, disconsolate guardian angel.

THE BOOK
OF THE
IMMORTALS

Chapter 1

The scent of roses hung heavy in the air. A nightingale trilled unseen in the fragrant shadows. Cool water fell from the marble hands of a delicate maiden, spilling into a large conch shell at her feet. The multicolored tiles, laid out in fantastic mosaics, sparkled like jewels in the twilight. But Quar took pleasure in none of this beauty. The God sat upon the tiled rim of a fountain's basin, absently tearing apart a gardenia, moodily tossing the waxy, white petals into the rippling water.

The luck of Sul, that's what it was. The luck of Sul, which was no luck at all. The luck of Sul had taken those damned and blasted priests of Promenthas's into the way of a few dozen of Quar's faithful. At least he assumed they had been his faithful. The God had not realized his followers had grown quite that fanatical. Now Promenthas was angry and not only angry, suspicious as well. Quar was not prepared for this. He had intended to deal with Promenthas, of course, but further—much further—down the long and twisting road of his scheming.

And there was Akhran to consider. He would act swiftly to take advantage of the incident. The Wandering God was undoubtedly persuading Promenthas to some sort of action. Not that Promenthas could do much. His followers had all died on the swords of the righteous. Hadn't they? Quar made a mental note to check. But now that Promenthas was alerted, he would be watchful, wary. Quar would have to move faster than he'd anticipated.

Akhran the Meddler. He was the scorpion in Quar's bed sheets, the *qarakurt* in Quar's boot. Just days ago Quar had received a report that two tribes of Akhran's followers had banded together in the Pagrah desert. Relatively few in number compared to Quar's mighty armies, these nomads were more of a nuisance than a direct threat. But Quar had no time for nuisances right now.

The one factor on which Quar had counted in his design to overthrow Akhran was the constant feuding and strife among the Wandering God's followers. The old axiom: divide and conquer. Who would have imagined that this Wandering God, who seemingly cared for nothing except his horse, would have been observant enough to detect Quar's plotting and move swiftly to forestall it?

"It was my fault. I concentrated on the other Gods of Sardish Jardan. I saw them as the threat. Now Mimrim of the Ravenchai, feeling herself weakening, hides on her cloud-covered mountain. Uevin of the Bas takes refuge behind his politics and siege machines, never realizing that his foundation is being undermined and soon he will fall through the cracks. But you, Horse God. I underestimated you. In looking west and south, I turned my back upon the east. It will not happen again."

The vase, once broken, cannot be mended with tears, Quar reminded himself severely. You have realized your mistake, now you must act to remedy it. There is only one way Akhran could have united his feuding tribes—through the intervention of his immortals. There were reports of Akhran's 'efreets whipping up fearsome desert storms. Apparently the unleashing of the mighty power of the djinn was enough to frighten those thick-headed nomads—

Quar paused, absently crushing the last blossoms of the ravaged gardenia in his hand.

The djinn. Why, that was his answer.

Tossing the dead flower into the pool, Quar rubbed his hands together, sniffing the essence of the perfume that clung to the shell of human flesh with which the God frequently chose to surround his ethereal being. Rising to his feet, he left the pleasure garden and entered his palace, proceeding to his own private salon. The room was sumptuously furnished, the walls hung with bright-colored silks, the floors carpeted with thick tapestries made of the finest wool. In the center of the room stood a black lacquer table on which rested a small copper-and-tin gong.

Lifting the mallet, Quar struck the gong three times, waited for the count of seven, then struck the gong three times again. The resultant quavering tone was vaguely disturbing. Setting the teeth on edge, it caused the very air to shiver. As the last note died in the still, perfumed air, a cloud of smoke began to take human shape and form around the gong, coalescing into a ten-foot-tall 'efreet.

"Salaam aleikum, Effendi," said the 'efreet, folding its hands together before its turbaned forehead. Clad in red silken pantalons girded with a red sash around its massive stomach, the 'efreet bowed with a grace remarkable in such a hulking body. "What is your wish, my Master?"

"I grow weary of Akhran's meddling, Kaug," said Quar languidly, seating himself upon a silken couch. "I have received reports that two of his tribes have united. How is this possible?"

"They have united through the efforts of two of Akhran's djinn—one Fedj and one Sond, O Most Holy Being," replied Kaug.

"I thought as much. I find it most annoying."

"I can see the solution in your mind, my Master. Your plan is an excellent one. Be at peace, *Effendi*. The matter is easily handled. And now, allow me to bring you some refreshment to ease the worries this has brought upon you."

Kaug clapped his hands, the thunderous sound calling into being a pot of thick, sweet coffee and a plate of candied rose petals, sweet figs, and pomegranates. Nibbling a rose petal, Quar watched appreciatively as Kaug poured the sweet, syrupy coffee into a fragile porcelain cup.

"It is a trifling thing, an irritation," said Quar. "But such is the delicacy of my nature that these small upsets disturb me unduly. I can rest assured, then, that this matter is in your capable hands, my loyal servant?"

"Consider the scorpion relieved of his sting, the spider crushed, Magnificence," replied the 'efreet, falling to his knees and bowing so low that the front of his turban brushed the carpet.

"Mmmm." Quar picked at the pomegranate with a golden

knife, poking out the ruby seeds and crunching them, one by
one, between his teeth. Scorpions and spiders. Exactly what
he'd been thinking. He did not like Kaug's penetrating his
mind, and the God wondered, not for the first time, how
much of his inner thoughts the 'efreet was coming to know as
Kaug grew in strength and power.

"Is there anything else my Master desires?"

"Information. The murder of these wretched priests of
Promenthas—"

"Ah!" Kaug frowned.

"What is it?"

"I knew such violent a deed would upset you, Master, and
so I have endeavored to discover what I could. Unfortunately
a dark cloud hangs over those who committed the act, obscuring
my sight."

Quar's eyes narrowed. "A dark cloud. What does that
mean?"

"I do not know, *Effendi*."

"Perhaps it is some trick of Promenthas's. All the followers
are dead, are they not?"

"As far as I can tell—"

"Promenthas's followers are dead. Yes or no, Kaug?"
Quar repeated softly.

The chastised 'efreet, unable to reply, crouched on the
floor before his Master, shoulders hunched, his huge body
quivering.

Sincere abjection? Or a very fine act.

"Very well, if you do not know, you do not know. You
are dismissed," Quar said, making a negligent gesture with a
jeweled hand.

"My Master is not angry?"

"No, no," Quar said, barely concealing a yawn behind
sugar-covered fingers. "My time is too valuable to waste on
such trivial circumstances. I assume that, in your hands, all
will be acted upon and settled satisfactorily."

"I am honored by your confidence, my Master, and blessed
by your patience with my shortcomings." The 'efreet bowed
again, humbly, thankfully.

Quar did not reply. Reclining upon the couch, he closed
his eyes as though asleep. In reality he had stepped out of the
human body and was watching Kaug with invisible eyes,

scrutinizing the 'efreet carefully, searching for traces of smugness, self-satisfaction, or an inner conviction that this matter with Akhran and the priests was a greater threat than his Master was letting on. Quar saw only serious, conscientious devotion on Kaug's massive face.

Returning to his body, Quar blinked, yawned, and rubbed his eyes sleepily.

"Is there anything else I can do for you, Exalted One?"

"No. Proceed with your tasks."

Bowing again, the 'efreet's hulking form dissolved to a cloud of billowing smoke that spiraled around the gong, then vanished suddenly, sucked up by the copper metal.

Left alone, Quar rose from the couch. Perfume filled the air around him, his heavy brocade robes brushed against the thick carpet. Hands behind his back, his head bowed, he began to pace in the small amount of space in the room that was cluttered with carved wooden chairs, tables, couches, huge standing vases of porcelain, flambeaux with thick beeswax candles, golden pipes and pots, and flowering trees.

Back and forth he walked; not the restless, nervous pacing of one who is indecisive or uneasy in his mind. This was the pacing of one who walks the miles his thoughts travel, the footsteps of one mentally traversing desert and city, making new plans, refining old ones.

At the end of an hour's pacing, Quar—lingering near the black lacquer table in the center of the room—reached out to gently stroke the gong with his fingers, a slight smile upon his lips. His plans were coalescing in his mind, much as the 'efreet coalesced around the gong.

Quar's faithful follower, the Emperor, would be instructed to act at once to secure the God's position in southern Sardish Jardan. Once conquered, the southern lands of Bas would provide wealth and slave labor to complete the building of the Emperor's grand fleet. In the name of Quar, the Emperor would sail west, across the ocean, aiming to strike at the gold-laden, heavily populated continent of Tirish Aranth—the stronghold of Promenthas.

The war in heaven would move to the world.

Jihad.

Chapter 2

When the Gods decided that the immortals were to be freed from their boring task of guarding the Realms of the Dead and assigned to the more interesting—if occasionally more stressful—task of interacting with mortals, each God was initially granted an equal number of immortal beings to serve him. This number either grew or diminished as the God's power in the world increased or waned. Ranking among the immortals was, therefore, usually based on age. The older, wiser immortals took over the leadership roles. Young immortals were assigned the low-ranking, menial tasks— generally that of working directly with the humans.

Unfortunately the young immortals, because they lived half on the mortal plane and were deeply involved with mortals, tended over the centuries to take on mortal characteristics— particularly mortal weaknesses.

Promenthas's angels were arranged in a strict hierarchy, as has been discussed; guardian angels being the youngest and lowest in rank, up through archangels, seraphim, and cherubim. Each angel had his or her assigned task, his or her appointed superior. Only in times of dire emergency or disaster—such as the murder of his followers—would Promenthas invite a guardian angel to report to him directly. Others of the Gods were more relaxed in their dealings with immortals, structuring them loosely as suited their needs. Then, of course, there were those such as Akhran, the Wandering God, who had no discipline or structure at all.

This lack of organization at first led to much confusion

among Akhran's immortals. Each was constantly getting in the other's way. Some tribes had a surfeit of djinn, while others had none at all. The 'efreets fought among themselves, unleashing violent storms that occasionally came near to wiping Akhran's followers from the face of the planet.

All this was brought to Akhran's attention—when he could be found. Beyond scowling in irritation at being bothered and lopping off a few heads to serve as a warning, the Wandering God did little that was useful. Seeing that their God took no interest in them, and becoming more than a little fearful for their heads, Akhran's immortals attempted to form some sort of organization.

This worked out as well as might have been expected. The powerful 'efreets demanded control of the wild and reckless forces of storm, volcano, and shaking ground. They were granted these without question. The elder djinn refused to have anything to do with humans since that onerous duty required one to live upon the mortal plane, subject always to the whims of humans and bound to a material object. This—to the elder djinn—was a humiliating way in which to live out eternity. They chose, therefore, to remain on the immortal plane and send the young djinn down to do the dirty work.

The young djinn did not mind this so much, most enjoyed the exciting, ever-chaotic world of humans. But the elder djinn did something else that drove the younger to distraction. In order to liven up eternity's nights, the elder djinn chose to keep the djinniyeh—the female djinn—on the immortal plane with them. As might be imagined, this angered the younger djinn and nearly precipitated outright war. The rebellion came to nothing, however. Each rebel djinn felt the blade of Akhran's sharp sword at his throat and meekly, if reluctantly, backed down.

Attended by the beautiful djinniyeh, the elder djinn lived in heavenly splendor, performing such tasks as distributing their less worthy brethren among the mortals, hearing disputes between djinn, and judging complaints from mortals about their djinn. The young djinn (or an older djinn who'd had the misfortune to cross a powerful peer) were sent to the world below, each immortal's essence entrapped inside a material object made by mortal hands—such as a lamp, a ring, a bottle. This bound the djinn to the mortal plane and made it impossible for him to survive long outside of it.

Of course there was always the possibility for advancement from the mortal realm to the immortal, and the younger djinn were ever on the watch for the opportunity to perform some miracle that would attract Akhran's attention. As a reward the God would elevate the djinn from his humble lamp in a sheepherder's yurt to a dwelling among the clouds, with the djinniyeh to supply one's every need, wish, and desire.

To live in luxury, entwined in the arms of the djinniyeh, was every djinn's dream, for if there was one human frailty above all others to which the djinn were subject, it was love. Intrigues and assignations between the djinn below and the djinniyeh above were common; particularly among the young and lovely djinniyeh of an elderly djinn, whose afterdinner delights consisted of a pat on a well-rounded bottom and falling asleep with his head on a perfumed bosom.

One djinn, in particular, was notorious for his affairs of the heart. Strong and handsome, as brave and daring as his sheykh, Sond could often be found scaling the walls of the cloud palaces, slipping among night's shadows into perfume-scented gardens, whispering words of love to some beautiful djinniyeh who trembled in his strong arms and begged him not to wake the Master.

Sond had long avoided falling victim to love, however. He had a roving eye and varied tastes. His conquests among the djinniyeh were many and he always escaped unscathed. But like every gallant warrior, he was finally vanquished on the field. The weapon that brought him down was neither sword nor arrow, but something infinitely more painful and piercing —a pair of violet eyes. Red, pouting lips inflicted wounds in Sond too deep to ever heal. Soft, white breasts, pressed against his flesh, forced him to plead for terms of unconditional surrender.

Now the eucalyptus trees of other cloud gardens saw Sond no more. Other djinniyeh waited and sighed for their lover in vain.

Her name was Nedjma, which means "the star," and she was the light of his heart, his soul, his life.

On this particular night Nedjma's master—an elderly djinn who remembered (or insisted that he did) the creation of the world—had been in his silk-cushioned bed well over an hour. His current favorite was with him, destined for a boring evening of listening to the old djinn's snores. The rest of the djinniyeh remained in the *seraglio,* chattering and gossiping, playing at games of chance, or—if they were fortunate—slipping away for more thrilling games of love.

Nedjma went out for a breath of fresh air, or at least that is what she told the guards. Some might have thought it strange that no fresh air could be found near the palace but was only obtainable in the darkest part of the garden that stood farthest from her master's dwelling. Here, in this secluded place, a pool as deep and dark as Nedjma's eyes reflected the light of stars and a full moon. The eucalyptus scented the soft night wind, its fragrance mingling with the smells of roses and orange blossoms.

Nedjma looked carefully around, not really expecting to see anyone, of course, since no one ever came here. Feeling certain (and perhaps a little disappointed) that she was alone, she posed herself gracefully upon the marble lip of the pool. Leaning over, she idly trailed her hand in the water, sending the goldfish darting about in a frenzy.

She was a sight as beautiful as the night itself. Pantalons made of silken gauze spun as fine as cobweb softly draped the curves of her shapely legs. The diaphanous fabric was clasped about her waist with a jeweled girdle, leaving bare her shell-white midriff. Her small feet were adorned with jewels and rouged with henna. Her thick honey-colored hair was worn in a long coil, and her enchanting face could be seen through the soft folds of a gold-embroidered veil.

Entirely absorbed in contemplating the water, the fish, or perhaps her own bejeweled hand, Nedjma was perfectly unconscious of the fact that, when she bent over the pool, her breasts in their tight-fitting bodice were an enticement, her soft lips a temptation, her voice, as she sang sweetly to herself (or perhaps to the fish), an invitation.

Believing herself to be alone, Nedjma was considerably startled to hear a rustling in the gardenia near the wall surrounding the garden. Lifting her head, she glanced about in pretty confusion, a blush on her cheeks, her body trembling.

"Who is there?" Nedjma called.

"The one for whom you've been waiting," answered a deep voice from the wall.

"Sond!" Nedjma exclaimed indignantly, drawing her veil close about her face and glancing in the direction of the voice with eyes that sparkled like the star for which she was named. "How dare you be so bold? As if I would wait for you or any man," she continued loftily, rising to her feet with the grace of the willow swaying in the wind. "I came out here to taste the beauties of the night. . . ."

"Ah, that is my desire as well," Sond replied, slipping through the shadows of the foliage.

Her eyes cast down in charming embarrassment, Nedjma turned—not very quickly—as if to leave, accidentally allowing one small hand to flutter behind her. Sond caught hold of that hand and pulled her easily into his strong arms. Clasped close against the djinn's muscular chest, Nedjma could have struggled and screamed for help—she had done that before, just to keep her admirers eager and alert. But there was something different about Sond tonight—a fierce passion gleamed in his eyes; a passion that would not be denied.

A weakness swept over Nedjma. She had long considered surrendering herself to the handsome djinn. Besides, struggling took so much energy, screaming gave her a sore throat. Melting in the djinn's warm embrace, Nedjma closed her eyes, tilted back her head, and parted her glistening red lips.

Sond tasted the beauties of the night; not once, but several times. When it seemed he was nearly intoxicated from the wine of love, he reluctantly loosened his grasp on the beautiful djinniyeh.

"What is it, my own? What is wrong?" Nedjma asked, snuggling near him once again, her breath coming in quick pants. "My master sleeps soundly this night!"

"My bird, my blossom," Sond whispered, running his hand through the honey-colored hair, "I would give my life to be with you this night, but it may not be. My own master requires me soon."

"You came only to toy with me." Nedjma let her pretty head droop, her lips forming a charming pout.

"Cruel one! You have toyed with me for months! But no. I came to bring you a gift."

"A gift? For me?" Nedjma looked up, her eyes pools of

moonlight so lovely that Sond was forced to kiss her again. One arm around her, holding her close, he drew forth from a pouch he wore on his sash an object and placed it Nedjma's delicate hands.

The djinniyeh squealed softly in delight. It was an egg, made of pure gold, decorated with jewels. No djinn or djinniyeh can resist material objects from the mortal world; particularly those made of costly metals and jewels. It is one of their failings, and thus the elder djinn and occasionally some powerful mortal are able to entrap the souls of the unwary in such devices.

"Oh, Sond! It is beautiful!" Nedjma sighed. "But I cannot accept it." Holding the precious egg in her hand, she did not return it but gazed at it with longing.

"Certainly you can, my dove," Sond said, brushing his lips against the hair that had escaped from the veil. He closed his fingers over the hand holding the jeweled egg. "Do you fear me? Your Sond?"

Nedjma peeped up at him from beneath long, thick eyelashes. "Well," she murmured, lowering her head to hide her blushes, "perhaps just a little. You are so strong. . . ."

"Not as strong as your master," Sond answered with some bitterness, releasing her hand. "You belong to him. No poor device of mine could ever contain you."

"I don't know," Nedjma faltered, uncurling her fingers to look at the fabulous egg once more. Its gold gleamed in the moonlight, its jewels winked and sparkled like the eyes of a teasing maiden. "It is so very lovely!"

"And look," Sond said, exhibiting it with the proud eagerness of a small boy. "Look what it does."

Flicking a hidden catch, the djinn caused the egg to split open. A tiny bird in a gilt cage rose up from the bottom half of the eggshell. The bird's tiny beak parted, the cage began to whirl around and around, and sweet, tinkling music trilled in the air.

"Ohhhh!" Nedjma breathed. Her gentle hands, cupped around the egg and the singing bird within, trembled with delight. "I've never seen or dreamed of anything so exquisite!" She clasped the egg to her bosom. "I accept it, Sond!" Looking into the djinn's eyes, Nedjma moistened her red lips with the tip of her tongue. "And now," she whispered, closing her eyes and pressing near him, "take your reward. . . ."

"I will," came a cruel voice.

Nedjma's eyes opened wide, the breath caught in her throat. Her scream was cut off by a rough hand that closed over her mouth and nose. Now the djinniyeh struggled, but it was useless. The 'efreet's huge arms held her easily; his hand smothered her cries.

"I will satisfy your desires," Kaug laughed harshly, "with my own body, not that of your puny lover." Ripping open the silken bodice, the 'efreet ran his coarse hands over the djinniyeh's soft breasts. Choking in disgust and terror, Nedjma writhed in his grasp. "Come now, quit fighting. Is this the thanks I get in return for my little present?"

His arms loosened their grip somewhat as he bent his head to kiss her. With a twist of her lithe frame Nedjma managed to free herself. In her struggles she had dropped the golden egg. It lay on the tiles of the garden between them, gleaming in the moonlight, apparently forgotten. Clutching her torn clothing about her as best she could, Nedjma's form began to shimmer, changing to a column of gracefully twining smoke. Her eyes flashed scorn and hatred.

"You have violated the sanctity of the *seraglio* and laid violent hands upon my person!" she cried, her voice quavering with fear and anger. "I go to wake the guards of my Master! For having dared touch that which is not yours, your hands will be stricken from your wrists—"

"No, my lady," said Kaug. Reaching down, he picked up the golden egg and held it up before her. "You accepted my gift."

Nedjma's eyes, the only part of her body visible through the billowing smoke, stared with horror at the golden, jeweled object—an object made in the mortal world by mortal hands. Moaning, she attempted to flee. The smoke that was her body wafted through the garden's perfumed air. The 'efreet watched, unconcerned. Flicking the catch, Kaug caused the egg to open, the singing bird in the cage to rise up out of the bottom.

The 'efreet spoke a word of command. The smoke wavered in the air, fighting the invisible force that was pulling her inexorably toward the egg. Nedjma's struggles were feeble.

Kaug was too powerful, the djinniyeh's magic could not hope to prevail against that of an 'efreet.

Slowly Nedjma's being was sucked into the egg. Her ragged wail of despair, drifting unheard through the garden, was blown away by the night wind.

Chapter 3

Sond climbed over the garden wall, his heart beating to the rhythm of the words of the message he had received. "Come to me, come to me. . . ."

Nedjma had never sent for him before, preferring to tease and torment him until finally allowing him a single kiss, won after considerable playful struggle. But last time there had been a look in her eyes following that kiss—a look the experienced Sond knew. She wanted more. Her sending for him could mean only one thing: he had conquered.

Tonight Nedjma would be his.

Hiding in the gardenias near the pool—their meeting place— Sond looked about for his beloved. She was not there. He sighed, smiling. The cunning *houri*—she would tease him to the very last, it seemed. Stepping softly onto the multicolored tiles around the still pool of water, he called her name.

"Nedjma!"

"Come here, beloved. Keep hidden, out of the moonlight," came a sweet voice in return.

Sond's heart pounded, the blood beat in his head. He pictured her awaiting him in some dark, fragrant bower, her white body, modestly cloaked in the shadows of the night, trembling, eager to yield to him. Hastening toward the sound of the voice, Sond crashed through shrubs and bushes, heedless of the noise he was making, thinking only to end the ache of his desires in sweet bliss.

In a sheltered corner of the garden, far from the main dwelling and ringed round by pine trees, Sond caught a glimpse of bare skin gleaming white in the moonlight. Leaping through a tangled thicket of roses, he reached out, caught the figure to him—

—and found his face pressed against a hairy chest.

Deep laughter boomed above him. Angry and humiliated, Sond stumbled backward. Looking up, he saw the cruel, heavy features of an 'efreet.

"Kaug!" Sond glared at the 'efreet in a fury that he was forced to conceal, knowing as he did that the powerful Kaug could roll him into a ball and toss him from the heavens if he chose. "Do you know where you are, my friend?" Sond tried to look as if he cared. "You have mistakenly wandered into the realm of *Hazrat* Akhran! I advise you to leave before the guards of the mighty djinn who dwells here discover you. Quick, hurry!" He gestured toward the wall. "I will cover your retreat, my friend!"

"Friend!" Kaug said effusively, placing his huge hand upon Sond's shoulder and squeezing it painfully. "My good friend, Sond. Almost more than friends for a moment there, weren't we, though? Ha! Ha!"

"Ha, ha." Sond laughed feebly, gritting his teeth.

The 'efreet's grip on him tightened. Cartilage twisted, bone cracked. The body had existed in the mind of the djinn so long that the pain was very real. Though he gasped with the agony, Sond grimly stood his ground. Kaug might twist his shoulder off. He refused to let the 'efreet see him suffer.

A knife's blade of fear had pierced Sond, more painful than the 'efreet's torture. Kaug had obviously not come here by accident. What then was the reason for his appearance in this garden at night? What did it have to do with Sond? More frightening, what did it have to do with Nedjma!

Laughing again, Kaug released his hold. "You are brave! I like that, my friend. I like that so much, my friend, that I am going to give you a gift!"

Clapping his hand on Sond's back, Kaug knocked the breath from the djinn's body and sent him staggering headlong into an ornamental pool.

Sond teetered precariously on the edge of the water. Recovering his balance, he paused before turning around, attempting to catch his breath and master his overpowering rage. It was not easy. His hand, of its own volition, crept to the hilt of his saber. It took a strong, physical effort to wrench it back. He had to find out what Kaug was doing here. What did he mean by a gift? And where was Nedjma? By Sul, if he had harmed her . . . !

Sond's fist clenched. Slowly, forcing himself to relax, he drew several deep breaths and turned back to face the 'efreet.

"Really, a gift is not necessary, my friend!" Sond made a deprecating gesture with his swordhand, a gesture that kept it hovering near the scimitar's hilt. "To have earned the praise of one as powerful as yourself is a treasure priceless beyond all measure—"

"Ah!" Kaug shook his head. "Do not make such rash statements, my friend. For I have here in my palm a treasure that is *truly* priceless beyond measure."

Unrolling the fingers of his huge hand, the 'efreet exhibited an object that glittered in the moonlight. Growing more and more perplexed, Sond stared at it closely, suspiciously. It was an egg, made of gold, encrusted with costly jewels.

"Truly, that is a rare thing," he said cautiously, "and therefore a gift far beyond my humble aspirations, my friend. I am not worthy of such a precious object."

"Ah, my friend!" Kaug sighed gustily, the 'efreet's breath fluttering the leaves of the trees and causing ripples to mar the smooth surface of the pool. "You have not yet seen what a wondrous device this is. Watch carefully." Flicking a latch, Kaug opened the egg. A gilt cage rose up from the bottom. "Sing, my pretty bird!" Kaug said, tapping at the cage with a large fingernail. "Sing!"

"Sond! Help me! Sond!"

The voice was faint but familiar; so familiar that Sond's heart nearly burst from his chest. He stared into the gilt cage in horror. Trapped in the cage was not a bird, but a woman!

"Nedjma!"

"My love! Help me—"

Sond grabbed for the egg, but Kaug—with a deft motion— closed his hand over it, snapping shut the device and smothering the djinniyeh's despairing plea.

"Release her!" Sond demanded. His chest heaving in fury be no longer bothered to conceal, the djinn drew his scimitar and leaped threateningly at the 'efreet. "Release her or, by Sul, I'll slit you from throat to navel!"

Kaug laughed heartily and tossed the golden egg playfully into the air.

Sond attacked him, slashing wildly with his blade. Kaug spoke a word, and the djinn found himself tickling the 'efreet with the plume of an ostrich. Undaunted, Sond hurled the feather to the ground. Speaking a word of his own, he summoned up a gigantic two-handed saber. Wielding the blade, twirling it over his head until it made the air whistle, Sond made a dive for the 'efreet.

Kaug, grinning, held the golden egg in the path of Sond's savage swing. The djinn halted his deadly stroke just inches from the glittering golden surface. Kaug spoke again and the saber blade flew from Sond's hands. The 'efreet's fingers closed over the hilt—the great two-handed saber looked like a small dagger in Kaug's huge fist. Holding the egg in his palm, Kaug brought the sharp edge of the blade level with it.

"It would be a shame to crack the shell. I think the pretty bird inside would die," Kaug said coolly.

"What do you mean 'die'?" Sond demanded, struggling to breath over the tightness in his chest. "That's impossible!"

"Where now are the djinn of Evren and Zhakrin? Where now are the djinn of Quar?"

"Well, where?" Sond asked, his anguished eyes upon the golden egg.

Kaug slowly lowered the saber. "An interesting question, is it not, my friend? And one for which our pretty bird might discover a most unpleasant answer." The weapon disappeared from Kaug's hand. Reaching out one long finger, he began to stroke the egg.

"Or perhaps I will command the pretty bird to sing for me," he said, a lascivious leer on his face. "I will accompany her on my instrument, of course. Who knows, she may like my playing better than yours, friend Sond."

"What do you want in exchange for her?" Quivering in barely suppressed anger, Sond wiped sweat from his face. "It cannot be wealth. For that you would go to her master."

"I have more wealth than you can possibly imagine. Quar is generous—"

"Ah, Quar!" Sond ground his teeth. "Now we come to it!"

"Indeed, you are swift of thought, my friend—like the

falcon swooping down to peck out the eyes of the gazelle. My Most Holy Master is disturbed, you see, by rumors that have reached his ears concerning a uniting of the tribes of Akhran.''

"Well, what of it?" Sond sneered. "Is your great and powerful Master frightened?"

Kaug's laughter boomed over the garden, causing Sond to glance around nervously. He had no doubt that if they were discovered by the elderly djinn's guards, Kaug would vanish, leaving Sond to his fate.

"Is my Master frightened of the fly that buzzes around his head? No, of course not. But that fly is an annoyance. It irritates him. He could smack it and end its puny life, but Quar is merciful. He would much prefer that the fly go away. You, as I understand it, Sond, were instrumental in bringing the fly into my Master's presence, so to speak. It would be much appreciated if you would drive it off."

"And if I don't?"

"Then my Holy Master will be forced to kill the fly—"

"Hah!" Sond burst out.

"—and crush this most fragile golden egg," Kaug finished imperturbably. "Or, since that would be a grievous waste, Quar might decide to keep the egg for himself, enjoying it until he tired of toying with it, then pass it on to a devoted servant like myself—"

"Stop!" Clutching his chest, feeling that his heart must crack from the pain, Sond swallowed the bile rising in his throat. "What . . . what must I do?"

"Hatred smolders like hot coals at the feet of the two tribes. See to it that this flame is fanned until it is a roaring fire that engulfs the fly. When this is done, when the fly is either dead or departed, Quar will return this most enchanting bird's egg to one who could find it a nest."

"And what if I fail?"

Kaug popped the golden egg into his mouth and began to suck on it with lewd smacking sounds.

Sond's stomach wrenched and he doubled over in agony. Crouching on his hands and knees at Kaug's feet, he was violently sick. Kaug watched, grinning. Then, leaning down, he patted Sond solicitously on the back.

''I have faith in you, Sond, my friend. I don't think you will fail me.''

The 'efreet's laughter rumbled in Sond's ears, eventually dying away in the distance like a departing storm.

Chapter 4

Spring came to the desert at last, arriving in a week of drenching rain that turned the sea of sand into a sea of mud and the placid, underground river that fed the Tel oasis changed to a raging torrent. The rushing water found the tiniest crevice and carved it into a ravine. The desert floor collapsed in several places as the river ate away at the rock and sand. The rain slashed down like knives. Firewood was soaked and would not light. A cold wind blew constantly, chilling the blood, whipping through clothes that were never dry.

Nevertheless, spirits in the camp were high. All knew the rain would end soon, and when it did, the desert would blossom. And surely then the Rose of the Prophet would bloom. The Hrana could go back to their sheep and their hills. The Akar could move their horses to summer pastures farther to the north.

Khardan, lying in his tent in enforced idleness, listened to the rain drumming on the sand outside and thought about the rain's bringing life to the desert and wondered what it would bring to him.

When the Akar left the Tel, would Zohra come with him?

There was some astonishment among the Akar that Khardan had not taken another wife, since he had now fulfilled the god's wish and married Akhran's chosen. Several fathers had hinted openly that they had daughters available, and though modesty and tribal custom forbade the girls from making known their interest in the handsome Calif openly, they never failed in any opportunity to cross his path, peeping at him from above their veils.

Khardan ignored the hints and the sidelong glances. Akar gossip finally agreed that he did not want to grant his Hrana woman any increase in power by providing her with a *harem*— traditionally a stronghold of magic—over which she, as head wife, would rule.

Khardan let them think what they liked, perhaps even accepting this reason himself for his lack of interest in other women. There were times, however, when he admitted to himself that the eyes of the sparrow were dull and lackluster after one has looked into the fiery black eyes of the hawk.

Could one live with the hawk? Yes, if she were tamed. . . .

Closing his eyes, listening to the rain, Khardan smelled again the scent of jasmine and felt the touch of her fingers, soft and light, against his skin.

Zohra, hearing the monotonous dripping of the rain spilling from the folds of the tent's strong fabric, imagined it nourishing the Rose of the Prophet, tried to imagine the ugly cactus bearing a beautiful flower.

She herself wondered at Khardan's refusal to take another wife. Deep within, some wayward part of her was glad—the same part that persisted, during the long nights, in remembering the warmth of his smooth skin beneath her fingertips, the play of strong muscles across his back and shoulders as he had lain beside her in their bed on their wedding night.

She had won her victory, she had inflicted on this proud warrior his one and only defeat. That would be a memory to treasure all her life, something between the two of them that neither could ever forget. He had accepted his defeat with grace, she had to admit. Perhaps it was now up to her to accept her victory in the same way?

Her hand closed over the hilt of the dagger she kept beneath her pillow. Drawing it out, she gently pressed her lips against it, closed her eyes, and smiled.

The next day, just as suddenly as it started, the rain ended. The sun appeared. The desert burst into life.

The fronds of the date palm stirred in a mild breeze that bore with it the scents of the wild desert blossoms, lacy tamarisk, and sweet-smelling sage. The horses nibbled tender sweet grasses that sprang up around the oasis. Newborn foals staggered about awkwardly on unsteady legs as mothers looked on with pride, while some of the younger stallions forgot their newly acquired dignity and gamboled like colts.

That morning the Hrana and the Akar, led by their Sheykhs, eagerly gathered around the Tel. Pointing and shouting, the people began to sing hymns of praise to Akhran. Although the Rose of the Prophet had not bloomed with the rains, the cacti had turned green, their fleshy leaves and stems swelling with life. Many among both tribes swore they could actually seen the budding of blossoms. Khardan glanced at Zohra. Zohra, catching his gaze, lowered her eyes, a flush staining her face a dusky rose, more beautiful than any desert flower.

The djinn Sond watched the two of them intently, cast a grim glance at the Rose of the Prophet, and disappeared.

As Jaafar was returning to his tent, rubbing his hands with glee and already preparing for his tribe's imminent departure, he noticed someone falling into step beside him on his right-hand side.

"Congratulations, my Sheykh, on so fortunate an occurrence," the man said.

"Thank you," Jaafar responded, wondering who this fellow tribesman was. He could not see his face, hidden by the *haik,* though he thought the voice sounded vaguely familiar. "Give praise to our Wandering God."

"Praise be to Akhran," the man said obediently, bowing his head. "I presume we will be leaving soon, returning to our flocks in the hills?"

"Yes," said Jaafar, still attempting to place this person, unwilling to risk insulting him by asking his name. Trying to get a closer look at the man's face without seeming to do so, the Sheykh increased his pace to gain a step or two on the man, peering back at him. This didn't work, however. The man eagerly quickened his steps and popped around to come up unexpectedly on his Sheykh's left.

"Eh?" said Jaafar, astonished, turning to talk to the man on his right, only to find him gone.

"Here, my Sheykh."

"Oh, there you are. What was it you were saying? Something about leaving—"

"Yes, my Sheykh. And after having lived with these horse

people for so long, an idea has struck me. Wouldn't it be an excellent thing to have horses of our own? How much simpler guarding the sheep would be if we did it on horseback! How much better to have horses to drive off the wolf in the night. And other enemies besides the wolf," the man added in a low voice, with a sidelong glance at the Akar's side of the camp.

"What an interesting idea," began Jaafar, turning to his left only to find the man on his right again. "Where? Oh! I—I didn't you see move around." The Sheykh was becoming increasingly rattled.

"Then, too"—the man's voice dropped even further—"it would be some payment for what they have stolen from us over the years."

"Yes," muttered Jaafar, his brows drawing together, the old bitter hatred that had been forgotten in the celebrations of the morning burning with a new flame. "I like this suggestion. I shall myself broach it with Sheykh al Fakhar—"

"Ah, do not trouble yourself, *sidi*!" the man said smoothly, drawing his face mask even more closely around his nose and mouth. "After all, you have a daughter who is married to the Calif. Tell her to make of her husband this one small request. Surely he can refuse her nothing, least of all this. Go to her now. Press upon her the importance. It is a matter of pride, after all. You deserve nothing less, Sheykh of Hrana, who have given these Akar so much."

"You're right!" Jaafar said, his usually weak eyes gleaming. "I will go to my daughter and ask her to see the Calif without delay!"

"But she is not to go as a beggar!" the man warned, laying his hand upon the Sheykh's arm. "She is not to demean herself before that man!"

"My daughter would never do such a thing!" Jaafar shouted fiercely.

"Forgive me my eagerness to see all go well for you, my Sheykh," the man said humbly, placing his hand over his heart and bowing his head low.

"Humpf!" Jaafar, with a snort, headed off for his daughter's tent. He had completely forgotten his curiosity over who this strange tribesman might be. His eyes were on the herds of horses pastured around the oasis. Already he felt himself their proud owner.

"So much," said Sond softly, causing the robes of the Hrana he wore to melt away into the sweet spring air, "for the blossoming of the Rose or any other flower."

Chapter 5

"Couscous! Ah, what a treat!"

The djinn sniffed at the dish with the critical air of one who is accustomed to dining well and often, his large belly and several chins shaking appreciatively as he dipped the fingers of his right hand into the steaming delicacy.

"The secret is in the proper roasting of the meat," the djinn remarked, his mouth full of almonds, raisins, and lamb. "Too long and it becomes tough and dry. Too little and . . . well, there is nothing worse than underdone lamb. You, my dear Sond"—the djinn kissed his fingers to the other djinn opposite him—"have acquired the proper technique to perfection."

Following this compliment, the two djinn ate rapidly and without talking, for to speak during eating is to insult the meat. Finally, with a deep sigh and a belch of satisfaction, the fat djinn leaned back upon his cushions and swore that he could not consume another bite.

"Delicious!" he said, bathing his hands in the lemon water his host poured out in a basin before him.

"I am honored by the praise of one so knowledgeable as yourself, my dear Usti. But you really must try these almond cakes. They come all the way from Khandar."

Sond offered a plate of the sticky sweets to his guest, who could not offend his host by refusing. In truth, it appeared from his rotund stature that this djinn had not offended a host in the past six centuries.

"And a pipe to finish off a good meal," said Usti.

147

The djinn watched with appreciation as Sond placed the hubble-bubble pipe between them. Taking up one of the mouthpieces, he inhaled the tobacco smoke; the water in the pipe gurgling a soothing accompaniment. Sond puffed on the other mouthpiece, both djinn smoking in companionable silence for long moments, allowing their immortal bodies to attend to the important, if illusionary, human function of digestion.

As the two smoked, however, it became apparent to the rotund djinn that Sond was studying him with sidelong glances, and that Sond's face, as he did this, was becoming increasingly grave and solemn. Whenever Usti looked directly at Sond, however, the tall, handsome djinn instantly glanced away. Finally Usti could stand this no longer.

"My dear friend," he wheezed, his breath being constricted both by the tobacco smoke and his large belly, "you look at me, then when I look at you, you're not looking at me, then when I look away, you're looking at me again. By Sul, tell me what is wrong before I go mad."

"You will forgive me, friend Usti," said Sond, "if I speak plainly? We have known each other such a short time. I fear I am being presumptuous."

Usti waved this away with a graceful gesture of a sugar-coated hand.

"It's just that I note you are not quite well, my friend," Sond continued solicitously.

Usti heaved a mournful sigh, wisps of smoke trailing from the corners of his mouth.

"If you knew the life I led!" The djinn laid his hand upon his breast.

In contrast to Sond's bare chest and shoulders, Usti's large body was swathed in the folds of a silken blouse, a pair of voluminous trousers, and a long silken robe. A white turban adorned his head. The temperature inside Sond's lamp, where the two were dining, was warm, and Usti mopped sweat from his face as he expounded upon his woes.

"May *Hazrat* Akhran forgive me for speaking ill of my mistress, but the woman is a menace, a menace! Zohra—the flower." The djinn snorted, blowing smoke out his nose. "Zohra—the nettle. Zohra—the cactus. This"—he waved his hand over the dishes—"is the first good meal I've had in days, if you will believe me!"

"Ah, truly?" said Sond, gazing at the djinn with pity.

"It never fails. I am in the midst of a quiet little dinner when 'tap, tap, tap' "—Usti bit the words—"comes on the outside of my brazier. If I don't respond immediately, if, for example, I decide to drink my coffee while it is hot and *then* attend to my mistress's demands, she flies into a rage, which generally ends"—Usti paused for effect and breath—"in hurling my dwelling place into a corner of the tent."

"No!" Sond was appropriately horrified.

"The mess it makes." Usti shook his turbaned head mournfully. "My furniture is all topsy-turvy these days. I don't know whether it is right side up or wrong side down! To say nothing of the broken crockery! My pipe has sprung a leak. It is impossible for me to entertain!" The djinn put his head in his hand, his shoulders heaving.

"My dear friend, this is intolera—"

"And that isn't the half of it!" Usti's many chins quivered in outrage. "The demands she makes of me! And against her husband, who only tries to persuade her to behave properly. She refuses to milk goats, churn the butter, do her weaving, cook her husband's food. If you will believe me"—Usti, reaching out, tapped Sond upon his knee—"my mistress spends all the day riding horses! Dressed as a youth!" Leaning back into the cushions, Usti regarded his host with the air of one who has said it all, amen, nothing more.

Sond's eyes opened wide. The matter being too shocking for words, the djinn squeezed Usti's flabby arm in brotherly sympathy.

"But Zohra is a beautiful woman and spirited," Sond began suggestively. "Surely the Calif, Khardan, son of my master, his certain compensations—"

"If he does, he derives them from his imagination!" Usti grunted. "Which is not to disparage the Calif, may *Hazrat* Akhran look upon him with favor. He proved his manhood on his wedding night with the lioness. Why sleep with claws at his throat? It is just as well Sul, in his infinite wisdom, did not give this woman the power of black magic. I dread to think what she might do to her husband if she could. Speaking of which, are you familiar with the story of Sul and the Too-Learned Wizards?''

''No, I don't believe so,'' replied Sond, who had first heard the story four centuries earlier but who knew the duties of a host.

''When the world was young, each of the Gods, may their names be praised, had his own gifts and graces which he bestowed upon his faithful. But Sul—as center of all—alone possessed the magic. He shared this gift with humans of learned and serious mien who came to him in · humility, pledging to serve him by spending their lives in study and hard work; not only of magic but of all things in this world.

''The wizards did as they promised, studying magic, languages, mathematics, philosophy, until they became the most learned and wise men in the world. And so, too, did they become the most powerful. Since they had all learned each other's languages and customs, they came together and exchanged information, further increasing their knowledge. Then, instead of each looking to his own God, they all began to look increasingly to Sul, the Center. All gradually became of one mind, and this mind told them to use their powerful magic to supplant the Gods.

''As you can imagine, the Gods were furious and reproached Sul, demanding that magic be taken away from the humans. This Sul could not do, magic having become too pervasive within the world. But Sul himself was angered at the wizards, who had become arrogant and demanding. And so he dealt with them harshly, in order to teach them a lesson.

''Bringing the wizards together on a pretense of celebrating their newfound power, Sul took each man and cut out his tongue so that he no longer had the power to speak any language at all.

'' 'For,' spoke Sul, 'it is meant that men should speak to each other through the heart and this you have forgotten.'

''Next Sul decreed that, since magic was still in the world, it should be given into the hands of women, who are, most of them''—Usti heaved a sigh—''gentle and loving. Thus magic would be used for purposes of good, not evil. Sul stated, further, that magic must be based in material objects—charms, and amulets, potions, scrolls, and wands—so that those who practice it are constrained by the physical properties of the objects in which the magic resides as well as by their own human limitations.

"Thus spoke and did Sul, and the Too-Learned Wizards went home to discover that their wives had the magic and that they—as punishment for their arrogance—were forced to eat soup and gruel the rest of their tongueless days."

"All praise to the wisdom of Sul," said Sond, knowing what was required at the end of this story.

"All praise," repeated Usti, mopping his brow. "But Sul did not have my mistress in mind when he did such a thing. My mistress's words are sharper than the cactus and sting worse than the scorpion. Just between you and me, my friend"—leaning forward, Usti placed a fat finger on Sond's chest, poking at him to emphasize his words—"I do not think the Calif regrets overmuch that his wife does not cook for him, if you take my meaning."

"No!" remonstrated Sond, aghast. "Surely he doesn't think she would . . . she would—"

"Poison him?" Usti rolled his eyes. "The woman is a menace, a menace!"

"Zohra would not dare go against the decree of Akhran!"

Usti said nothing, but raised his hands to heaven.

Sond appeared appropriately alarmed. Lowering his voice, he glanced around the confines of the lamp and then he, in his turn, drew near Usti.

"I do not want to pry into private matters between djinn and master, but has your mistress ever asked you to . . . well, you know . . ."

Usti's eyes rolled back into his head so far that only the whites showed. "Not death," he said softly. "Even my mistress would not dare bring down the wrath of *Hazrat* Akhran by ordering me to assassinate her husband, when she knows that first I must have the God's sanction to take a mortal life. But . . . other . . . ." He whispered in Sond's ear, making explanatory gestures with his hands.

Sond's face registered horror. "And what did you do?"

"Nothing," puffed Usti, fanning himself with a palm frond. "I pleaded the excuse that several hundred years previously Khardan's great-great-great-grandfather freed me from the spell of an evil 'efreet and that I am bound to do the family no harm of *any kind*"—he emphasized the words—"for a thousand years. Which is true," he added, "to a certain extent, although the nature of the oath is not quite so binding as I have led my mistress to believe. Since then, however"— the djinn groaned—"my life has been one of torment. If I appear, my mistress throws pots at me. If I hide in my dwelling, she throws *me* at the pots!"

"What precipitated all of this? It seemed they were getting along so well. . . ."

"Sheep! I like sheep in their way," Usti said with a fond glance at the carcass of the lamb, "but I cannot fathom why such fuss is being made over them. It all has to do with this decree of *Hazrat* Akhran that the tribes remain camped around the Tel until the Rose blooms, which I may add, it seems to me further from doing than ever. I think, in fact, if I may speak candidly, my friend?"

"You may."

"I think the wretched plant is dying. But that is neither here nor there. From what I can gather, it seems that Zohra's people are being forced to trek between this Tel out in the middle of the desert and the foothills to the west where they pasture the sheep. Consequently their tribe is split. Those who are living here worry about those who are living there. They fear raiders from the south. They fear wolves. They fear wolves from the south. I don't know!"

Usti wiped his sweating forehead.

"My mistress's father—may *Hazrat* Akhran bury him to his eyebrows in a hill of fire ants—gave her the idea that if the Hrana had horses it would solve all their problems. Zohra went to Khardan and demanded that he give her people horses to herd sheep."

Sond gasped.

"Precisely the Calif's response," Usti said gloomily. He lowered his voice, imitating Khardan's deep baritone. " 'Our horses are the children of *Hazrat* Akhran,' he told my mistress. 'They are ridden for His glory—to make war, to participate in the games that celebrate His name. Never have they borne a burden! Never have they worked for their food!' " Usti began to shout. " 'Never will our noble animals be used to herd sheep! Never!' "

"*Shhh!* Hush!" Sond remonstrated, though he carefully suppressed a smile of delight.

Usti's conversation, like the sheep they were discussing, was being led along Sond's path. Taking advantage of a lull in the talk occasioned by Usti's recent passionate outburst's having temporarily caused a severe constriction of his breathing passages, Sond poured sweet, thick coffee and produced a plate of candied locusts, dates, and other delicacies. Usti's eyes actually grew moist with pleasure at the sight.

"Truly our horses *are* sacred to us, as the Calif says," Sond stated, sipping his coffee and nibbling on a fig. "Even when we move from camp to camp, our beloved animals are never ridden, but walk proudly with the people. However," the djinn continued solemnly, "it is required of us that we look at the world from the back of another's camel. I can understand your mistress's point of view. It is not good in these unsettled times for the tribe to be divided. Speaking of which, camels would, of course, be the ideal solution, but where are they to come from? The prices which that bandit Zeid demands for his *mehari* are outrageous. My master has long considered beating some humility into him."

"Ah, I agree. But as the proverb relates, it is difficult to beat the man who owns a large stick."

"True." Sond sighed. "The Aran outnumber my people two to one and their *mehari* are swifter than the wind. Those racing camels of Zeid's are famous even in Khandar."

"Why dream of camels? We may as well dream of flying carpets, which, by the way, was one of my mistress's demands, if you can believe it. I told her that sending carpets into the heavens was perfectly well for legends and lore but absolutely impractical when it came to the real thing.

" 'What would you do if you met a storm 'efreet?' I asked her. 'One puff and you're among the heathens on the opposite end of the world. And there's no way to control the silly things. They have a decided propensity to flip over. And did you know that if you fly too high, your nose starts to bleed? *That's* something they never mention in those fool stories. To say nothing of the sheer energy involved in getting one off the ground and keeping it aloft.' No, I told her it was impossible."

"What did she do?"

"She brought the tent down on top of me. And see this mark?" Usti exhibited a bruise on his forehead.

"Yes."

"An iron skillet. My ears still ring. And now, just because I refused to carpet the sky, my mistress has commanded *me* to come up with a better solution or she threatens next time to throw my brazier in quicksand. I didn't sleep a wink, all night! Oh, why was I forced into all this?" Usti gazed beseechingly at the heavens. "Of all djinn, I am the most unfortunate! If that *nesnas* had not captured my poor master and killed him and made me prisoner, I would not now be beholden to Fedj for having rescued me, and I would not now be in the clutches of this wild woman to whom—all things considered—I think I prefer the *nesnas*!"

Letting his turbaned head sink into his hands, Usti moaned in misery.

"And yet," said Sond cautiously, "if there *was* a way to make your mistress happy . . ."

Usti ceased wailing and opening one eye, peered out between his fingers. "Yes? You said a way to make my mistress happy? Go on."

"I'm not certain that I should," Sond said, upon deep reflection. "You are, after all, the enemy of my master."

"Enemy!" Usti spread his hands. "Is this the body of an enemy? No! It is the body of one who wants only to get a good night's sleep! To eat a meal while it is hot! To find his furniture on the floor and not the ceiling!"

"Ah, you tear out my heart!" said Sond, placing his hand on his bosom. "I am truly sorry for your plight and you do look unwell."

"Unwell," cried Usti, tears flooding his eyes. "If you only knew the half of it! This is the first solid food I've been able to keep down in days! I shall soon be skin and bones!" He put his hands together pleadingly. "If you have an idea that will put an end to my mistress's tantrums, I would be eternally in your debt! Rest assured, I will give you all the credit!"

"No, no!" said Sond hastily. "This is to be *your* idea. The credit will all belong to you." Reaching out, he squeezed Usti's fat hand. "My reward will be to see a brother djinn grow happy and well once more."

"You are kind, my friend! Kind!" murmured Usti, his

tears losing themselves in the creases of his chins. "Now, what is this idea?"

"Suggest to Zohra that her people steal the horses."

Usti's eyes opened wide. The tears stopped. "Steal?"

"It is fitting, after all. My people have stolen from them for years. Now the Hrana have a chance to get back at us. Zohra's father, Sheykh Jaafar, will be happy. Zohra will be happy. What's more, she will be grateful to you for suggesting something so brilliant! She will make your life a paradise! Nothing will be too good for you."

"Forgive my ignorance, my friend," Usti said cautiously, "I do not know much about your people, not having lived among them long, but it seems to me—and I intend no disrespect—that the Akar are . . . one might say . . . volatile. Isn't this proposed thievery likely to . . . uh . . . upset them?"

"My master will be angry for a day or two, but—in the end—he will respect the Hrana for showing some spirit. And the sun will freeze to a ball of ice," Sond added beneath his breath.

"What did you say?" Usti cupped his hand over his ear. "It's this ringing in my head—the skillet, you know."

"I said my master will think it all very nice. In fact," Sond continued, carried away by his enthusiasm, "this event may well solidify the friendship between our two tribes. It will provide the Hrana with the horses they need. They will be content. It will show the Akar that the Hrana are courageous and daring. My people will be content. And all because of you, Usti! *Hazrat* Akhran will undoubtedly reward you handsomely."

"My own little dwelling among the clouds," said Usti, gazing upward at the ceiling of the lamp wistfully. "Just a small one. No more than eighty rooms, ninety at the outside. A lovely garden. Djinniyeh to scratch my back where I cannot reach, rub my temples with rose water when I have the headache, sing to me sweetly. . . ."

Absorbed in his dream, Usti did not notice that at this remark about the djinniyeh, his host became exceedingly pale.

"It will be no more than you deserve, my friend," Sond

said, rather more harshly than he intended. He cleared his throat. "Well, will you do it?"

"I will!" Usti said with sudden resolve. "Are you certain, my friend," he added warily, "that you will not demand—I mean accept—any of the credit?"

"No, no!" Sond said, shaking his head emphatically. "I beg that you leave me out of this. Surely one so wise as yourself would have thought of this idea eventually."

"Ah, that is true," said Usti gravely. "In fact, it was on the tip of my tongue even when you spoke."

"There, you see!" Sond said, slapping his friend on his large back.

"I would have spoken it first," pursued Usti, "except that I was drinking this delicious coffee and I feared to insult you by putting the cup down."

"And seeing you thus pleasantly engaged, Akhran caused your thought to fly to my mouth, your words to come from my throat. I am honored"—the djinn bowed from the waist—"to have served as your vessel."

Smiling warmly, Sond propped himself up among his cushions on one elbow and passed the plate of candied fruit to his guest.

"Another fig?"

Chapter 6

"Another fig?" mimicked a disgusted voice outside the lamp, a voice so soft that neither of the two enjoying their repast inside heard it.

A djinn may not enter the dwelling of another djinn unless he receives an invitation, but it is possible for one djinn to listen in on conversations held inside the dwelling unless the master of the dwelling takes precautions to protect himself. Sond, upset and desperate, was so intent on the seduction of Usti that he carelessly forgot to place the magical seal around his lamp.

Pukah stood in Majiid's tent, his ear over the lamp spout. He had been standing there, invisible, listening to every word spoken by the two for the past hour, and now the young djinn was in a state of turmoil and confusion not to be believed.

Having been ordered by his master to keep a watch on the comings and goings of Zohra, Pukah had instantly noted the sudden disappearance of Usti—a highly unusual occurrence. Usti had not been known to voluntarily leave his dwelling since coming into Zohra's possession. Fearing mischief of some sort directed against Khardan, Pukah immediately searched the camp, eventually discovering the fat djinn's whereabouts in the last place he had expected—being entertained in the lamp of his enemy!

Just what was Sond up to? Pukah hadn't any idea. He knew Sond didn't care a horse's droppings for the fat djinn.

"If I hear one more honey-coated 'Usti, my friend' come from your lips, I'll gag," Pukah told the lamp.

He listened in amazement to Sond's casual suggestion of
the horse-thieving raid. Pukah knew—if the thickheaded Usti
didn't—that the theft of the horses would *not* bring about
everlasting friendship between the two tribes.

"Everlasting bloodshed is more like it," Pukah said grimly.
Why was Sond risking the wrath of *Hazrat* Akhran by
suggesting such a thing?

"Even if Akhran does think it's Blubber-belly's idea, he'll
be so mad he'll throw us all into the Kurdin Sea! And Sond
knows it."

Pukah pondered the matter as he returned to his own
dwelling—a woven basket that had once been used by a
snake charmer to house his reptile. It was an unusual dwelling
place for a djinn. Pukah had been only a very young djinn
when he'd come across the snake charmer squatted in the
road near Bastine. Fascinated by the snake, who swayed its
deadly head hypnotically to the music of its master, Pukah
slipped inside the basket to get a better view. He was promptly
captured by the snake's owner and spent the next twenty
years traveling the lands of Sardish Jardan, doing all sorts of
interesting jobs for the snake charmer, who also happened to
be a worshiper of Benario, God of Thieves, on the side.

Other than having to share his dwelling with the snake,
who—as it turned out—was an incredibly boring individual,
Pukah enjoyed his life on the road. He came to know all
manner of people, visit all manner of cities and villages, and
was taught a number of ways to enter houses where one
hadn't been invited. He also became acquainted with nearly
every immortal being between Bas and Tara-Kan.

Then one day his master was caught worshiping Benario
not wisely but too well. The wealthy merchant he was
attempting to rob chopped the charmer into pieces small
enough to have fit inside his own basket. This left Pukah and
the snake to their own devices. The snake, in return for its
freedom, gave Pukah the basket.

Hoping to escape the notice of Akhran's elder djinn, who
would have assigned him to a mortal, Pukah transported
himself and his basket to the *souks* of Kich, hoping to pick
out his own human. Liking the looks of Badia, Khardan's
mother, he planted his basket on the back of her donkey,
hiding among the other baskets until she arrived at her tent—an

old trick taught him by his master, who often used this to gain access to rich houses.

When Badia opened the basket, Pukah leaped out, threw his arms around her, and swore her eternal service in return for having freed him from his captivity. The young djinn was presented to Khardan on his twelfth birthday, and although Pukah was far older in years than his master, the two might have been said to have grown up together, for djinn must mature just like their mortal counterparts.

Therefore, though one was two hundred and the other but twenty-five, the same lust for action and excitement burned in the heart of the djinn that burned in the heart of his master. Pukah was equally ambitious, determined to rise high in the estimation of his God. He looked down upon Sond and Fedj with scorn. Content with their lives, the two older djinn had—or so he had always supposed—no desire to better their lot.

"I will not wait until I am old and toothless before I have a palace," Pukah resolved. "And when I get one, it will be located here in *this* world, not up there. Besides, mortals are incredible fun."

All Pukah's bright dreams were dashed when Akhran spoke—actually spoke—to Fedj and Sond, giving them the command that would eventually bring the two warring tribes together at the Tel. Pukah had nearly turned inside out with envy. What he would have given if only the Wandering God had spoken to him! And then he was forced to watch as the great fools Sond and Fedj—("They must have sand in their heads in place of brains!")—went about grumbling and complaining instead of taking full advantage of the situation.

But now, here was Sond doing what Pukah would have done all along—he was almost certainly taking this opportunity to become a hero in the eyes of *Hazrat* Akhran.

"But how oddly he's going about it!" Pukah said to himself, pacing back and forth in his basket. "I don't understand! Usti! Horse stealing! What would I do if I were in Sond's lamp? Aha!"

The young djinn snapped his fingers. Coming to a halt before a mirror that hung in a prominent location on the wall of his basket, he expounded the matter to himself as was his custom, having had, for long years, no one to talk to other than the snake.

"Well, what is it you would do, Pukah, if you were not Pukah but Sond?"

"Well, Pukah, since you asked, if I were Sond and not Pukah, I would get that triple-chinned ass, Usti, to go to his mistress with this wild scheme of stealing horses. Then I—Sond—would go to *Hazrat* Akhran and tell the God that I had learned that this disaster was about to take place. I would beg Akhran to intervene. He would do so, peace would be restored, and I—Sond—would be a hero in the eyes of Akhran!"

Pukah, proud of his plan, gazed gleefully in the mirror at Pukah, who gazed gleefully back until it occurred to both of them that they were Pukah, not Sond.

"That," said Pukah gloomily to Pukah, "is exactly what I would do if I were Sond. The swine!"

The two Pukahs put their heads together, literally, both leaning against the mirror.

"Pukah, my man, aren't you every bit as smart as Sond?"

"Smarter," replied Pukah stoutly.

"And aren't you as clever as Sond?"

"Cleverer!"

"And aren't you, Pukah"—Pukah raised his head to look himself straight in the eye—"destined to be a hero? Don't you deserve it more than that great hulking oaf who thinks only of his handsome face and his broad shoulders and whose ambition in life is to find a garden wall he hasn't scaled, a pair of legs he hasn't straddled?"

(It must be noted here that Pukah was slight and slender of build, with a face rather too long and narrow to be considered in any way handsome, and whose attempts to endear himself to certain comely djinniyeh had thus far resulted in having his pointed jaw soundly slapped.)

"You deserve it! You do!" returned Pukah warmly.

"Then, Pukah, it is up to you to ruin Sond's plans to become a hero, or if that is not possible, to come up with a plan of your own to outhero him. Now, how can this be accomplished?"

The Pukah standing in front of the mirror began pacing back and forth in the basket. The Pukah in the mirror did the same, the two coming together occasionally to inquire, with raised eyebrows, if either had an idea. Neither did, and the Pukah in the mirror—for one—was beginning to grow increasingly glum.

"There's no use in trying to talk Usti out of presenting this crazy scheme to the wild Zohra. The fat djinn is too enamored of it. He's even decided it was all his idea. I'd never be able to convince him to drop it. So, let him go ahead and let Zohra plot to steal the horses. I could go to her and tell her it was a trap. . . ."

Pukah considered this a second, but the Pukah in the mirror shook his head. "No, you're right. Zohra hates me almost as much as she hates my master. She would never believe me."

"*You* could be the one to tell Akhran you have uncovered the plot," suggested the Pukah in the mirror.

Pukah reflected upon this suggestion, and at length he announced that if they couldn't come up with anything better, it would have to do. "But," he added desperately, "there must be something I can do that will blow Sond off his camel—"

"Camel. . . ."

Pukah stared at his image, who stared at him right back, both faces taking on a look of foxish cunning.

"That's it!" they cried together. "Camels! Zeid!"

"Sond and Fedj bring two tribes together in peace. Pooh! What is that? It is nothing! A child could do the same if he put his mind to it. But if *three* tribes come together in peace! Now that would be something! Such a miracle has never occurred in all the history of the Pagrah desert!"

"Quar would not dare to even think of bothering us!"

"Kaug would leap into the ocean and drown himself in sheer frustration!"

"Akhran will be victorious above. The Akar will be victorious below, and it will all be due to me!"

Dancing in delight, Pukah began to caper about his basket, the Pukah in the mirror prancing about just as merrily.

"Me! Me! Me! *I* am the one who will be the hero. Sond and Fedj are dogs compared to Pukah! Akhran himself will bow before Pukah. 'Without you, my hero,' our God will say as he takes me in his arms and kisses both my cheeks, 'I would be lost! I would be licking Quar's boots! Here's a palace, here's two palaces, here's a dozen palaces and ten dozen djinniyeh!' ''

"Let Sond play his games! Let him plot his plots and scheme his schemes! Let him think he has won! I will snatch the fruit from his mouth and it will be so much the sweeter for having the marks of his teeth on it! Now, to make my plans. What is the name of Sheykh's Zeid's djinn?"

"Raja," supplied the Pukah in the mirror.

"Raja," murmured Pukah.

Once again he resumed his pacing, this time with such concentrated thought that he completely forgot the Pukah in the mirror, who—nevertheless—did not forget him but kept up with him step for step until night fell and both were swallowed by darkness.

Chapter 7

Peering out from a hole in the charcoal brazier that sat within the entrance to his mistress's tent, Usti watched a young man—at least it appeared to be a young man—stride through the camp of Sheykh Majiid al Fakhar early in the morning, almost three weeks following the arrival of spring to the Tel. The young man's boots were dusty, his robes coated with a fine film of sand, the *haik* covered nose and mouth. It was obvious that he had been out riding in the cool of the day. There was nothing unusual in this. It should not have attracted any particular attention to him. It did, however, and the attention was not of a flattering kind.

Women carrying firewood to cook the noonday meal stopped and stared at the young man with cold, unfriendly eyes or whispered to each other before hurrying on their way. Their husbands, standing about discussing the relative merits of one horse over another, glanced at each other as the young man walked by them, their eyebrows rising significantly. Conversations fell silent, the eyes of the men and the women turned to the tent of their Calif, who was just emerging, his falcon on his wrist, preparatory to a day's hunting.

The djinn saw that the young man was aware of the glances and undoubtedly heard the whispered words, for his head tilted higher, the lips pressed firmly together. Ignoring the stares and the mutterings, looking neither to the right nor the left but straight ahead, the young man continued walking through the camp.

His way led him directly past the Calif, who was watching

his coming with a face devoid of all expression. Usti held his breath. Nearing Khardan, the young man—for the first time—shifted his eyes from the tent that was his destination. The gazes of the two met and crossed like saber blades; the djinn swore that he could hear the clash and see the sparks.

Neither the Calif nor the young man spoke. The young man, with a contemptuous toss of the head, walked past his Calif. Khardan went his own way, crossing the compound to his father's tent. The women continued their chores, the men picked up their conversations, many looking after their prince with sympathy and respect, praising his patience, speaking of him as they might speak of a martyr who was being tortured for his faith.

Seeing the young man approach, Usti groaned and immediately thrust several fragile items beneath a mound of clothes. He himself took refuge in his brazier in the sunken tiled bath that he had lined with sheepskin for just such an emergency.

Coming to his tent, which was pitched as far from Khardan's as was decently possible, the young man angrily jerked open the tent flap. Usti heard Zohra's voice muttering through the folds of The *haik*.

"Unwomanly! . . . Unnatural! . . . Cursed! Hah!"

The djinn cringed, then groaned again as he heard a ripping, slashing sound. Usti risked a look.

"No, madam! Not the cushions!"

Too late.

Drawing her dagger, Zohra stabbed it into a silken cushion, slitting it open from top to bottom. From the look upon her face it was obvious to the djinn that—in Zohra's mind—it was not a cushion that she was murdering. Tossing it into a corner, she caught hold of another and drove the weapon into the fabric flesh, then disemboweled it, yanking out the wool stuffing and throwing it about the tent until it seemed a rare desert snowstorm had struck.

"And we all know who will have to clean this up, don't we, madam," the djinn said to himself gloomily.

Again and again Zohra hurled herself at her enemy, until there wasn't a cushion left alive. Finally, exhausted, she sank back down among the remnants of her rage and gnawed her lip until it bled.

"If this foul marriage does not end soon, I shall go mad!"

she cried. "It is all his fault! I will make him pay. I will make them all pay!"

Zohra's hand closed over the charcoal brazier. Usti, tumbling back into his bathtub, shrieked in despair.

"Madam! I beg of you! Consider what is left of my furniture!"

Zohra, sneering, peered inside the brass brazier. "Why? If it is as worthless as you are, blubbering pile of camel dung, then it can be replaced by a few sticks of wood and the skin of a goat!"

A hissing sound, like air escaping from an inflated bladder, and a wobbly column of smoke emerging from the brazier announced the arrival of the djinn. Assuming his fat and comfortable form, Usti materialized in the center of the tent.

Casting the destruction a bitter, dismal look, the djinn placed his hands together and *salaamed,* bending as low as his rotund belly permitted.

"May the blessings of *Hazrat* Akhran be upon you this morning, delicate daughter of the flowers," said Usti humbly.

"May the curse of *Hazrat* Akhran be upon you this morning, you horse's hind end," returned the delicate daughter with a snarl.

Usti shut his eyes, shuddered, and drew a deep breath. "Thank you, madam," he said, bowing again.

"What do you want?" Zohra demanded irritably. Tossing the brazier down upon the torn cushions, she began pacing restlessly the length of the tent, muttering to herself and twining one long strand of black hair around her finger.

"If madam will recall," the djinn began, carefully repeating what he and Sond had spent last night devising, "she commanded me to come up with a plan by which we could extricate ourselves from the current intolerable situation."

Zohra glared at the djinn. "I commanded you? To come up with a plan! Hah!" Tossing her black mane of hair, she stopped her pacing long enough to pick up a golden jewel box from out of the torn fabric and sheep fluff.

"Per-perhaps I misunderstood madam," Usti stammered.

"Perhaps you did." Madam sneered. "The last command I recall giving you was to—"

"I—I remember!" Usti said, sweat pouring off his face. "And I assure madam that such a thing is physically impossible, even for those of us whose bodies, shall we say, lack material substance. . . ."

Hefting the jewel box in an alarming manner, Zohra eyed the throwing distance between herself and the djinn.

"Please!" gasped Usti. "If you would only listen to me!"

"Is this another of your imbecilic schemes? Flying carpets? Pig's bladders inflated with hot air that sail through the clouds? Or perhaps my personal favorite—putting wings on the sheep so that *they* could fly to us!"

Usti, his eyes on the jewel box, gulped. Drawing forth a silken handkerchief, he began to mop his forehead.

"I . . . I . . ." The djinn's words slipped from him like olive oil from a pitcher.

"Speak!" Zohra raised her hand, the jewel box glinting in the light.

Usti lifted one pudgy arm in defense and closing his eyes, gabbled in a rush: "It seems to me, madam, that if we require horses we should take them!"

The djinn cringed, waiting for the jewel box to career off his head.

Nothing happened.

Hesitantly Usti dared risk a peep at his mistress.

She stood transfixed, staring at him with wide eyes. "What did you say?"

"I repeat, madam," Usti replied, lowering his arm with great dignity, "that if we desire horses we should take them."

Zohra blinked, the jewel box fell from her hand to land unheeded on the wool-covered floor.

"After all, you are the head wife of the Calif," Usti continued, pressing his argument as Sond had suggested. "What is his is yours, is it not?"

"But I asked him for the horses and he refused," Zohra murmured.

"*That* was your mistake, madam," Usti said crisply. "Although we give alms, who among us truly has respect for the beggar?"

For a moment the djinn thought he'd gone too far. Zohra's face flushed a dusky rose color, the flame in her eyes nearly scorched him. Angrily she snatched up the jewel box again, and Usti hurriedly prepared to seek the shelter of his brazier.

But he saw suddenly that Zohra's anger was turned inward, against herself.

Brushing the black hair out of her face, she regarded the djinn with grudging respect.

"Yes," she admitted. "That was my mistake. So you are proposing I take what is mine by right of marriage. I do not think my husband will quite see matters with the same eye."

"Madam," said Usti earnestly, "far be it for me to disrupt a union made in heaven. Your noble husband has many worries. It is of the utmost importance that we do not cause Khardan a moment's anxiety. Therefore I suggest, in order to spare him all discomfort, that we acquire the said horses in the nighttime when his eyes are closed in slumber. When he wakes in the morning, the horses will be gone and it will be no good crying over spilt mare's milk. Then, in order to further spare him pain, we will tell him that the horses were stolen by that son of a she-camel, Sheykh Zeid."

Zohra hid her smile behind the veil of her black hair. "Won't my noble husband discover an inconsistency in our story when he sees my people riding upon the backs of horses that should be a hundred miles away to the south?"

"Is it our fault that Zeid is a notorious idiot and allowed the horses to slip through his fingers? The poor beasts, wandering lost in the desert, appeared in our camp in the foothills and we Hrana—out of the kindness of our hearts and the exhortation of *Hazrat* Akhran that we treat his children with respect—took in the animals, who, noble creatures that they are, did not want us to go to the vast expense of feeding and caring for them without offering their services in return." Usti wheezed for breath, this last statement having completely winded him.

"I see," Zohra said thoughtfully, pressing the cool metal of the jewel box against her cheek as she pondered. "And how am I to convince my father of the merits of this plan? Pious foo— man that he is, he would never permit it."

"Your father, praise his name, is elderly, madam. Care should be taken to make his last days upon this world days of peace and happiness. Therefore I suggest that we do not disturb him with such unsettling matters. I am certain that there are young men within your tribe who would be willing— nay, eager—to take part in such an adventure?"

Zohra smiled grimly. There was no doubt about that! The last dagger-wielding skirmish between the warring tribes had left several young Hrana—including a cousin of hers—lying bleeding and battered in the sand. The Hrana nursed their wounds, praying to Akhran to grant them an opportunity for revenge, and inwardly cursing Jaafar for preventing them from declaring open warfare. These young men would find this raid much to their liking and would have no qualms about keeping it secret from their Sheykh.

"When should this take place?"

"In a week's time, madam. The moon will not smile upon the night and darkness will cover our movements. That will also give me time to contact those you suggest and make them acquainted with our plan."

"I may have underestimated you, Usti," Zohra admitted magnanimously.

"Madam is too kind!" Usti bowed humbly.

Opening the jewel box, Zohra seated herself in a corner of the tent on the one cushion that had escaped her wrath. Lifting a golden sapphire-studded bracelet from the box, she slid it on her arm and studied it critically, admiring the way the jewels caught the rays of the midday sun.

"Now," she commanded leisurely, motioning with her hand at the destruction in the tent, "clean up this mess."

"Yes, madam," said the djinn, heaving a profound sigh.

Chapter 8

The east glowed faint gold with the approach of dawn. South of the Tel there was one cloud in the sky, drifting ever nearer to the camps of the Akar and Hrana. It was a strange cloud, moving leisurely from the south to the north—traveling against the wind currents, which were blowing west to east. On this cloud reclined two djinn, resting comfortably among the ephemeral mists as they might have rested on the finest cushions of the most luxurious couch.

One of the djinn was large, well-built, with skin the color of ebony. He was arrayed in gold cloth, massive gold earrings hung to his shoulders, his arms were encircled with gold enough to ransom a Sultan, and the expression on his face was fierce, for he was a warrior djinn of a warrior tribe. Seated near him, eating figs from a basket and talking animatedly, was the lithe and slender Pukah.

"Yes, Raja, my friend, our God, the Holy Akhran, commanded that the tribes of Sheykh Jaafar al Widjar and Sheykh Majiid al Fakhar join together and live in peace and harmony at the Tel, and that they further symbolize this newly established unity by the marriage of the daughter of Jaafar with the son of Majiid."

"And did they marry?" growled Raja. Lying prone, stretched full length upon the cloud, he hefted a gigantic scimitar into the air, critically appraising the sharpness of the blade by the light of the rising sun.

"Most certainly!" Pukah nodded his head. "It was a wedding that I may truthfully say will be long remem-

169

bered. But surely your master has heard of this from the God?"

"No," said Raja, a dangerous note in his voice. "My master has heard nothing of this . . . miracle."

"Ah!" Pukah sighed sympathetically and placed his hand upon Raja's black-skinned arm. "I know how difficult it must be for you, my friend, to serve such an impious master. If only Sheykh Zeid were more attentive in his service to *Hazrat* Akhran, it might have been your master who was chosen to rejoice in the God's blessings."

"No one knows the pangs I suffer over my master's impiety," Raja remarked, staring at Pukah coldly until the young djinn, with a deprecating smile, hurriedly removed his hand from the huge, muscular arm. The black djinn turned the blade of his weapon this way and that, watching it catch the light. "So you say that the two tribes are living together in the shadow of the Tel? I find this remarkable, considering that they are such bitter enemies."

"*Were*, my dear Raja, *were* bitter enemies," said Pukah. "The wounds of the past have been cauterized by the flame of love. Such hugging and kissing! Such games and revelry, such comradeship we have. It makes one weep to see it."

"I can imagine," said Raja wryly.

"And then the fondness of the Calif for his wife!" Pukah gave a rapturous sigh that ruffled the feathers of a passing flock of startled birds. "From the moment the sun rises and he must leave her arms, Khardan counts the hours until the sun sets and he can rush back to enjoy her numerous charms and endowments."

Knowing the reputation of the lady in question, Raja raised a skeptical eyebrow at this.

"I assure you it is the truth, my dear Raja!" Pukah said solemnly. "But perhaps you doubt my word—"

"No, no, my dear Pukah," Raja grunted. "It is just that I am overcome with joy"—the black djinn brought his sword down suddenly with an alarming swipe that neatly chopped the cloud in two and sent half of it scudding off in the opposite direction—"at this picture of bliss you describe! The thought of peace coming to such bitter enemies overwhelms me. I long to see for myself. . . ."

Pukah did not hesitate. "Precisely why I brought you here. Look, my doubting friend."

Raja, bending over, peered down from the heights of the cloud.

It was just past dawn. Pukah considered this a propitious time to present the camp for inspection, being fairly certain that if there had been any fights last night, the Tel would have attained some semblance of peace if only that the combatants must have dropped from sheer exhaustion.

"See, what did I tell you? The tents of the Hrana standing beside the tents of the Akar!" said the young djinn, proudly exhibiting the camp.

"What is that large splotch of blood there?"

"Where we slaughter the sheep." Pukah's face was innocent and bland as goat's milk.

"I see."

Bent over the rim of the cloud so that Pukah could not see his face, Raja gnawed his lip, scowled, and cast the young djinn a swift, sidelong, angry glance.

"It is the wish of my master, the Calif"—Pukah babbled on happily, noticing nothing of this sudden change of the black djinn's expression—"that your master, Sheykh Zeid, come to us at the Tel and press to his bosom his cousins, Majiid and Jaafar, whose love for Zeid exceeds only the love they bear for each other."

His face once more carefully expressionless, Raja raised his head and looked intently at Pukah. "That is the wish of the Calif?"

"The dearest wish of his heart."

"You may be certain that I will convey this message to my master."

"With all haste?" Pukah prompted.

"With all haste," responded Raja grimly. Good as his word, he disappeared on the spot.

"Ah, I guess he could not contain his eagerness." Pukah leaned back among the feathery cloud. "So much for Sond," he said to himself blissfully. "Let him try to be the hero now! Let him plot his little plots and try to convince *Hazrat* Akhran that *he* was responsible for keeping peace between two tribes. Pukah, you have outdone him! Pukah, *you* will achieve the union of three tribes! Pukah, history will resound with your name!''

Popping a fig into his mouth, the young djinn, arms behind his head, relaxed upon his cloud. Drifting through the sky, he began to mentally lay out the floor plan of the palace a grateful Akhran would bestow upon him, populating the airy rooms of his imagination with supple beauties who danced, sang, and whispered honeyed words of love in his ears.

If, however, at that moment Pukah had looked down from his cloud, he would have seen a sight to make him choke on his fig.

Sond stood with Khardan near the horses, pointing at them and speaking urgently to the Calif.

"This means war!" Khardan shouted.

"Hush, *sidi*, keep your voice low."

The Calif, with a tremendous struggle, did as Sond requested, though his dark eyes glittered with anger. It was dawn. The two were walking near the outskirts of the camp. Khardan's gaze went again to the horses peacefully grazing near the bubbling stream.

"When do they plan their raid?"

"In a week's time, *sidi*. The first moonless night."

"You say that"—Khardan choked on the words—"my—my wife is behind this?"

"Yes, *sidi*. Alas, it grieves me to bring you such news—"

"The woman is a witch!" Khardan clenched his fist. "This ends it, Sond! Akhran himself could not expect me to live with such insult! Stealing my horses!"

If Sond had reported that the Hrana were plotting to steal his children, the fruit of his loins, Khardan could scarcely have been more outraged. In fact, he might have taken that news rather more calmly. As long as there were women and long desert nights, there would be children. But his horses!

According to legend, the magnificent horses of the Akar came by direct lineage from the steed of the God. The nomads likened their horses to the desert itself, the animals' sleek and glistening coats were as black as the desert night or as white as the silver of the shining stars. Their long sweeping tails and manes flowed like the wind across the dunes.

The horses gloried in battle. The smell of blood and the

sound of clashing steel caused ears to prick, eyes to flash, and it was all a *spahi* could do to hold his mount back from charging in where the fray was the thickest. Countless stories were told of horses who continued to attack the enemy even after their own masters had fallen.

Each man in the tribe owned his own stock, whose lineage he could trace back proudly generation through generation. When times were hard, his horses were given first portion of the food and his family made due with what was left. The horses drank first at the oases. A woman whose magic could calm a restless steed was prized above all other women.

Besides raising and breeding these noble animals for their own use, the Akar kept a certain number apart each year to sell to the Sultan in the city of Kich. The sale purchased necessities such as coal and firewood, which were not to be found in the desert; staples such as rice and flour; and luxuries such as coffee, honey, and tobacco. These last were small pleasures, but they made the harsh life of the nomad bearable. In addition, the *souks* of Kich yielded the jewelry so much beloved by the women; the swords, daggers, and scimitars valued by the men; and silks and cottons for the clothing of both.

The Akar's yearly trip to Kich was a momentous event, forming the subject of conversation of the *spahis* for a year after—either recalling fondly the good times they'd had or looking forward to the good times expected. Parting with the horses was the hardest task, and it was not unusual to see some fierce warrior who had literally waded in blood weep unashamedly as he bid good-bye to a beloved animal.

By stealing the horses the Hrana stole the life, the soul, the heart of the Akar. As Sond knew when he suggested it, this was the one crime the Hrana could commit that would cause the Calif to break the commandment of the God.

Sheykh Jaafar could, of course, have argued that—by stealing sheep—the Akar threatened the survival of the Hrana. Sheep provided the wool the Hrana used for their clothing, the meat they ate, the money that bought both necessities and luxuries. So Jaafar might have argued, but he would have argued in vain. Just as each God saw only his own facet of the Jewel of Sul, So Sheykh Majiid and Sheykh Jaafar each saw the light shining on his own Truth. All else around them was darkness.

"What are your orders, Master? Do we attack the sheep-herders immediately?"

Khardan ruminated, his hand stroking his black beard thoughtfully.

"No. They would claim themselves innocent, protesting to Akhran that we had attacked them without cause. We would be the ones facing the wrath of the God instead of those foul bleaters. We must catch them in the act, then we can proclaim to the heavens that it is *we* who have been wronged. I can rid myself of this accursed woman. We can leave this accursed place."

"Your plan is excellent, *sidi*. I myself will relay it to my master—"

"Tell no one, Sond!" Khardan ordered. "Especially not my father! He would be beside himself with fury and might, in his rage, accidentally reveal us to them. I will do what must be done."

"The Calif is wisdom itself."

"I will not forget this, Sond," returned Khardan, choking with emotion. "Your warning has saved us from a dread calamity and will free us at last from the stench of these shepherds. When *Hazrat* Akhran hears the tale of our betrayal, he shall also hear of your devotion to your people from my own lips, and if he chooses to free you of your servitude, no one will be pleased more than I."

Flushing, Sond averted his face from the Calif's eyes. "I beg you will not do that, *sidi*," he said in a low voice. "I—I am not worthy of such honor. Besides, it would devastate me to leave your father . . ."

"Nonsense!" said Khardan gruffly, clearing his throat. He clapped the djinn upon his broad back. "Majiid would miss you, not a doubt of it. You've served this family well, back to my great-great-great-grandfather and probably beyond that. But it is time you left the mortal realm and lived in peace above, with some charming djinniyeh to gladden your days and sweeten your nights, eh?"

Little did Khardan know that he was twisting the dagger in Sond's soul. Flinching with pain, the djinn concealed his anguish by prostrating himself upon his knees before the Calif. Khardan took this as a further touching sign of the djinn's devotion and came near weeping as he returned to his tent.

Long after the Calif had gone, Sond remained crouching on his knees in the desert sand, beating his clenched fists on the windswept rock, striking at it until his immortal flesh bled.

Sond had betrayed not only his people, he had betrayed his God. Akhran the Wanderer was not noted for his mercy; his punishments were swift, harsh, and sudden. There was not a doubt in Sond's mind but that the God would discover his djinn's treachery. True, Sond might plead that he'd done what he had done for the sake of his beloved. But what was the life of one djinniyeh compared to the grand schemes of heaven?

Sond had considered going to Akhran and telling the God that one of his immortals had been taken captive, but the djinn had rejected the idea instantly. The God would be angry, but Akhran's anger would be directed at Quar. The Wandering God would never submit to Quar's demands for Nedjma's safe return nor would he allow Sond to do so either. In his rage Akhran might actually commit some rash act that would cause Sond to lose Nedjma forever.

Reminding himself of this, Sond grew calmer. If anyone was going to save Nedjma, it would have to be him and him alone.

"And if I can do that, I will cheerfully submit to any punishment you mete out to me, O Holy One," Sond vowed fervently, raising his eyes to heaven.

His peace restored, convinced that what he was doing was right, the djinn composed himself and prepared to begin his day's service. On his way to Majiid's tent, Sond passed by the Tel. The djinn cast a glance at the Rose of the Prophet. The cacti looked worse than ever. They seemed dying of thirst; the green fleshy stems had turned a brown and sickly color. Their spines were beginning to fall off.

Well, it will be watered soon, Sond thought grimly. Watered with blood.

Chapter 9

Khardan met secretly with certain of his men, apprising them of the proposed raid by the Hrana and telling them of his plan to thwart it. The Calif's anger was echoed by his *spahis* when they heard of this outrage. It was well that Khardan was present to calm them, or they might have torn down the tents over the Hrana's heads then and there.

Zohra met secretly with her people as well. At first the men of the Hrana had been reluctant to meet with a woman, especially a woman whom they viewed as the enemy. Zohra felt this and it hurt her. Facing the men of the Hrana, many of whom were half brothers, cousins, nephews, she saw their dark faces and suspicious eyes, and flushing deeply in shame, she thought how close she had come to submitting herself to the arrogant Calif, to becoming truly the enemy of her people.

Thank Akhran, that had not happened. Her eyes had been opened.

In a low, passionate voice, she recited the sufferings of her tribesmen at the hands of the Akar. She reminded the men of what they already knew—that lambing season was near: a time when the flocks were most vulnerable to attack by predators. She repeated, word for word, her request for horses and her husband's scathing denial. Then she presented her plan to gain the animals.

The men listened, suspicion losing itself in anger at her eloquent and crafty reminder of their woes, anger deepening to rage at hearing Khardan's insults, rage changing to unbridled enthusiasm over Zohra's proposal. Finally they would have their revenge upon the Akar and a sweet revenge it would be!

A semblance of peace settled over the Tel, both tribes having been instructed by their leaders to commit no rash act that might draw undue attention to themselves. Each settled down to wait out the week, but never had time passed so slowly. Night after night, eyes impatiently watched the moon wane, pouring its pale light down upon the desert, sucking out the colors of all objects. Many noticed that the Rose of the Prophet, curling in upon itself like a dying spider, looked particularly ugly in the moonlight. The withered cacti now gave off a peculiar odor—the smell of rotting flesh.

An impatient people, accustomed to thinking and reacting instantly, the waiting and the need for secrecy was sheer torture. The air around the oasis crackled with undischarged lightning. Both Sheykhs knew a storm was brewing. Jaafar became so nervous he couldn't eat. Majiid demanded of his son outright to know what was going on, but he was only told grimly that everything was under control and that he would be alerted when the time came.

Foreseeing bloodshed, Majiid grinned and sharpened his sword.

The two djinn, Fedj and Sond, were each secretly set by their masters to spy upon the other and did so with such alacrity that they were always to be seen, skulking about the camp, glaring at each other and adding to the overall tension. Thinking he knew what was going on, Pukah enjoyed the game immensely, meanwhile wondering when Sond planned to bring down the wrath of Akhran on the two tribes. Usti, preening himself on his plan, now lived a life of luxury. His brazier stood in an honored place in his mistress's tent. She no longer commanded him to perform menial tasks, never tossed him out the tent, and did not once interrupt his dinner.

The relationship between Zohra and Khardan remained unchanged—at least outwardly. As before, neither spoke when their paths accidentally crossed. Their gazes met, locked briefly, then parted, though it took every ounce of self-control Khardan possessed not to gouge out the black eyes that flashed with secret, triumphant scorn whenever they looked at him. He thought he might well go mad before the week ended.

And then, halfway through the interminable seven days, Pukah brought his master certain information that gave Khardan the opportunity to vent some of his mounting rage. He dared not openly attack his wife; that would give everything away. But he could at least slide a thorn or two into her smug flesh.

Zohra had just returned from her early-morning ride and was in her tent, cleansing her body of sweat and grime and smoothing perfumed oils on her skin, when Khardan suddenly and without warning lifted the tent flap and entered.

"Greetings, wife," he said grimly.

Whirling in alarm, her long black hair flicking over her bare back like a scourge, Zohra caught up a woolen robe and clutched it around her naked body. She glared at her husband with flaming eyes, too furious to speak.

Khardan at first said nothing either. His well-planned speech had been on his lips, but the glimpse of Zohra's lithe figure drove the words from his head.

He stared at the dusky cheeks flushed a deep rose, the tendrils of black hair that swept across her face, the white shoulders visible above the robes Zohra held to her breast. The fragrance of jasmine clung to her, the oil on her body glistening in the sunlight filtering through the tent. One quick grab of that robe with his hand . . .

Abruptly, angrily, Khardan averted his gaze, refusing to let her see his momentary weakness. Why did this woman—of all the women he knew—affect him this way, turning his blood to water? He attempted to salvage his dignity.

"Are you some Pasha's concubine that you appear in such a state in the middle of the day? Clothe yourself, woman!"

The blood of shame and outrage pounded in Zohra's ears and dimmed her vision with a red tide, blotting out Khardan's momentary look of admiration. She saw only that he turned his head from her; obviously in revulsion and disgust. Quivering in fury and hurt pride, she remained standing where she was, her nakedness covered only by the dusty robe she held pressed against her chest.

"Say what you have to say and be gone!" Her voice was low and husky, thick with what in another might have been the desire of love but in her was only the desire to kill this man—of all the men she knew—who continually caught her in some moment of weakness.

Khardan cleared his throat of a sudden huskiness himself and began his prepared speech. "I understand that you have been to my mother to learn the charm that calms horses."

"What if I have? It is no business of yours. Such matters of magic are between women, not meant for men."

"I was only wondering why you are taking this sudden interest in womanly things, wife," Khardan said smoothly, his anger returning to save him as he recalled his wife's scheming. He knew well why Zohra was suddenly so interested in acquiring this magical skill and it pleased him to toy with her.

Zohra heard the odd timbre in his voice, and for a moment her heart quailed. Could he have discovered? . . . No, it was impossible! Every man she had chosen was loyal and trustworthy. Above all, their cause to hate Khardan and his tribe was as great as hers. They would let their tongues be ripped from their mouths before they would reveal the secret.

But she had, unknowingly, revealed herself, Khardan, watching her closely, saw the cheeks swept by a sudden pallor, saw the bright eyes grow dark with fear. Smiling to himself, he added mockingly, with a glance at Zohra's bed, "Perhaps you are interested in other womanly pursuits as well? Maybe this is why you are attempting to entice me with your body?"

"Hah! You flatter yourself!" Zohra laughed contemptuously, fear banished by rage. "I prefer my horse between my legs!"

Her words struck home with the force of a knife. Khardan stared at her in disbelief. No woman he had ever known would dare say such a thing. "By Sul! I could kill you for that insult and not even your father would blame me!"

"Go ahead! Kill me! Killing women, stealing sheep! Pah! Is it not the way of the cowardly Akar?"

Khardan, his blood burning with rage—among other things—sprang forward and caught hold of his wife, grasping her bare arms. His painful grip brought tears to Zohra's eyes, but she did not flinch or struggle. She kept the robe clutched over her body, her fingers curled about the fabric in a deathlike grip. Gazing at Khardan without fear, Zohra's lips curled in disdain.

"Coward!" she said again, and it seemed, from the tilt of her head, so near his, and the slight movement of her tongue across her lips, that she dared him to kiss her.

Furious with himself and the wild thoughts that filled his mind, Khardan flung Zohra away from him. Tossing her backward, he sent her sprawling awkwardly among her perfume bottles and henna jars. "Thank *Hazrat* Akhran for your life, madam!" Turning on his heel, he stalked from the tent.

"I won't thank him!" Zohra screamed after the vanished form of her husband. "I would rather die than be married to you, you— you—"

Her rage strangled her. Choking, she flung herself upon her bed, weeping passionately, still seeing, in her husband's eyes, that look of revulsion and disgust . . . knowing deep within herself that she had offered and been rejected.

Khardan, trembling with anger, stalked through the camp. In his mind he pictured with pleasure the humiliation he would inflict upon this woman. He would drag her before her father, proclaim her a witch, see her cast from her tribe in shame. . . .

And all the time he could smell, lingering upon the skin of his hands, the teasing, tantalizing fragrance of jasmine.

Chapter 10

It was as if Akhran himself extended his blessing upon the Hrana. The day of the raid dawned hot and breathless. During the morning a mass of clouds flowed down from the hills to the west, bringing a damp wind and sporadic, spitting drops of rain that evaporated before striking the hot ground. With the coming of afternoon the rains ceased, though the clouds remained. By night the very air itself seemed to grow thick and heavy. Lightning flickered on the horizon and the temperature plummeted. The *batir* donned curly-haired sheepskin coats over their tunics to protect themselves from the chill of the long ride back to their homes, their heads were covered with black cloth, and they drew the black face cloths over their mouths.

All were well-armed with sword and dagger. Their eyes, barely seen above the face cloths, glinted hard and cold as the steel they carried. Each knew that, if caught, it would be a fight to the death. Each was willing—eager—to take that risk. At last they were striking back at their enemy, hitting him in the heart.

"And I say you should not go, sister!" The whispered voice hissed through the darkness. "It is too dangerous."

"And I say I will go or none of you will stir a step from this place."

"You are a woman, it is not seemly."

"Yes, I am a woman. And which of you men will perform the magic to keep the beasts quiet until we get them away from camp? You, Sayah? You, Abdullah? Hah!"

Wrapping the black mask around her face, Zohra turned away, obviously considering the argument ended. The young men, huddled together in a stand of the tall, tasseled grass growing about the water of the oasis, shook their heads. But none of them continued the argument.

Zohra's magic would undoubtedly be essential to them in handling the horses, particularly since few of these men had ever ridden. Most had spent the week covertly observing the *spahis:* watching to see how they mounted the beasts, listening for what words were used to command them, taking note of how often the animals were fed and watered, what they ate, and so forth. The only question that remained unanswered for the Hrana was how the horses would react to strangers. This was where Zohra's magic could provide help, that and her knowledge of the beasts. They knew her presence was valuable, but—if given a choice—most of the Hrana would sooner have gone forth into the desert with a pouch full of snakes as with the unpredictable, hotheaded daughter of their Sheykh.

"Very well, you can come," came Sayah's grudging whisper. "Are all ready?"

Zohra's half brother, a few months her junior and still unmarried, Sayah had been the Hrana's choice to lead the raid. Cool and calculating, the exact opposite of his impulsive sister, Sayah was courageous as well, having once fought off a starving wolf with his bare hands. Like the other Hrana, he had also been forced to stand and watch in helpless fury as Majiid's raiders swept down on their swift horses and stole the choicest of his flock. Sayah had a few private plans of his own in regard to the horses they were about to acquire; plans he thought best not to mention to his sister, since all of them ended in killing her husband.

Receiving grim, eager replies to his question, Sayah nodded in satisfaction. At his signal the band of thieves crept through the tall grass toward the place where the horses were tethered for the night. Behind them the camp slumbered in a silence that must have appeared unnatural had they stopped to consider it. The night was too still, too calm. No dog barked. No man laughed. No child cried. None of the *batir* noticed, however, or—if they did—they passed it off as the oppression of the coming storm.

The rain had ceased, but its smell was in the breathless,

heavy air. The night was darker than any could believe possible; the raiders could not even see each other as they padded soft-footed over the ground.

"Truly Akhran is with us!" murmured Zohra to her brother.

"You are right, my son," growled Majiid. "The coming of this strange storm is proof that *Hazrat* Akhran is helping us protect our own!"

"*Shhh,* Father. Keep still," hissed Khardan.

His hand reached out to stroke the neck of his trembling horse. The creature shifted restlessly but remained silent, obeying his master's unspoken command. All the horses were nervous and excited, aroused by the presence of the men hiding in their midst, sensing the tension of coming battle. Any experienced horseman approaching the herd would have noted the restless pawing and head-shaking and been on his guard. Khardan was counting upon the fact that Zohra and her *batir* were too inexperienced in the ways of horses to realize something was amiss.

Standing beside his father, surrounded by the other Akar— each man armed not only with steel but with an oil-coated torch—Khardan could feel Majiid's tall, muscular frame quivering with suppressed anger and bloodlust. Khardan had broken the news of the raid to his father only moments before going out to catch the thieves. As his son had foreseen, Majiid flew into such a rage that Sond was forced to hold him by the elbows or the Sheykh would have sped through the camp like an 'efreet and throttled Jaafar on the spot. After much difficulty, Sond and Khardan forced the old man to listen to their plan and he finally accepted it, with the understanding that he alone be allowed to skewer Jaafar.

As to Zohra, Majiid pronounced that she was a witch and should be dealt with summarily, suggesting several fitting punishments, the most merciful of which was having her stoned to death.

Khardan felt his father's hand close over his. It was the silent signal, being passed from man to man, that the scouts had detected the presence of the *batir*. Shaking with eagerness and the excitement of battle, Khardan reached out and squeezed the hand of the man crouched near him, then he readied the flint he would strike to light the torch.

Khardan held his breath, straining to hear the soft swish of feet upon the sandy rock floor. Then his muscles tensed. He had not heard, but he had smelled something.

Jasmine.

Swiftly striking the flint, he shoved it close to the brand. The oil burst into flame. Majiid, wielding his flaming torch, let out a fearful yell and leaped onto the back of his warhorse. Frightened by the sudden fire, the animal reared back, lashing out with its hooves. Scrambling for his own horse, Khardan barely escaped being bashed in the head, and from the sounds of a groan and a dull thud, one of the *batir* wasn't so lucky.

At their Sheykh's signal the rest of the Akar lit their torches and vaulted onto the backs of their horses, their sabers flashing in the firelight. The Hrana, on foot and completely at the mercy of the horsemen, drew their own weapons, striking out at their enemy in bitter anger and disappointment at their failure.

The light and noise drew the attention of the camp, most of whose people had been lying in wait, listening. The djinn Fedj appeared in their midst with a bang, only to be confronted coolly by Sond.

"What are you doing to my people?" Jaafar shrieked, running from the tent of one of his wives, his white nightclothes flapping around his bare ankles.

"I'll tell you what I'm doing! I'm going to roast you over a slow fire, you fornicator of sheep!" Majiid shouted, literally foaming at the mouth. Kicking his excited horse in the flanks, Majiid charged straight for Jaafar, swinging his saber in a blow that would have set the Sheykh to tending the sheep of Akhran had it connected. Due to his own failing eyesight and the flaring torches, Majiid miscalculated, his blade whistled harmlessly over Jaafar's head.

Wheeling his horse, Majiid galloped back for another charge. "You've set your witch-daughter and her demons to stealing my horses!"

"Taste your own poison!" Jaafar cried.

With unexpected nimbleness the wiry old man ducked Majiid's vicious slash. Grabbing the Sheykh's leg as the horse galloped by, Jaafar pulled Majiid from the saddle. The two went over in a tumble, rolling about on the desert floor, fists flailing, seeming in dire peril of being trampled by the wildly excited horses.

Khardan, after the first signal, kept himself clear of the fight. Charging through the crowd, his torch held high, his eyes went from one black-robed figure to another, impatiently lashing out at anyone who got in his way. At last he found the one for whom he had been searching. Slimmer than the rest, moving with an unmistakable grace, this figure—dagger in hand—was grimly facing an opponent whose saber must within seconds slice her in two.

"Mine!" shouted the Calif, urging his horse forward at a gallop. Neatly cutting between the attacker and his black-robed victim, Khardan struck the man's arm down with the flat of his own blade. Leaning over, he caught hold of Zohra around the waist and hoisted her—headfirst, kicking and screaming—up and over his saddle.

"Death will not rob me of my chance to see you humbled, wife!" cried Khardan, grinning.

"Oh, won't he?" Zohra muttered viciously. Dangling head down, fighting to free herself, she raised her dagger.

Khardan saw the blade flash and grappled for it. His horse plunged beneath them, trying to keep its footing.

"Damn you!" the Calif swore, a searing pain tearing through his leg. He could not reach the knife, but a mass of thick, black hair came into his hands. Gripping it firmly, Khardan yanked Zohra's head back. Shrieking in pain, Zohra dropped her knife; twisting, she managed to sink her teeth into Khardan's arm.

Horses surged around them. Swords flared in the torchlight. Flaming brands smashed down on heads; riders were dragged from their steeds; steel blades clashed in the night. Standing on the outskirts of the battle, women wailed and pleaded, their children crying out in fear. Their cries went unheard. Pandemonium reigned, reason was lost in hatred, there was only anger and the lust to kill.

Sond and Fedj fought with gigantic scimitars, stabbing each other's immortal flesh a hundred times over. Majiid was bashing Jaafar's head into the ground. Sayah clashed with Khardan's brother Achmed, neither giving ground nor gaining any, each recognizing the makings of a valiant warrior in his opponent.

In the confusion no one heard the tinkling of camel bells. Only when a brilliant flash of lightning illuminated a *mehariste* did the battling tribes realize that a stranger was in their midst.

At the sight the women hastily grabbed up children and ran for the shelter of their tents. The ringing of steel and the grunts and shouts of the combatants slowly died away as, one by one, the Hrana and the Akar looked around dazedly to see what was happening.

The flames of the torches, flickering in the rising wind of the breaking storm, revealed a short, squat figure swathed in rich fabric seated upon one of the swift racing camels whose worth was known the desert over. The light glinted off the silver and turquoise of a very fine saddle, glistened in the crimson-red silken tassels that hung about the camel's knees, and gleamed brightly in the golden, jewel-studded fringed headdress the animal wore on its head.

"*Salaam aleikum,* my friends!" called out a voice. "It is I, Zeid al Saban, and I have been sent by *Hazrat* Akhran to see what I could not believe—the two of you, bitter enemies, now joined by marriage and living together in peace. The sight of such brotherhood as I witness here at this moment brings tears to my eyes."

Sheykh Zeid raised his hands to heaven. "Praise be to Akhran! It is a miracle!"

Chapter 11

"Praise be to Akhran," muttered Majiid, wiping blood from his mouth.

"Praise be to Akhran," echoed Jaafar glumly, spitting out a tooth.

"Praise be to Pukah!" cried the irreverent djinn, springing up out of the sand in front of the camel. "This is all *my* doing!"

No one paid any attention to him. Zeid's eyes were on the heavens. Majiid's and Jaafar's eyes were on each other. As much as each Sheykh hated the other, each distrusted Zeid more. Leader of a large tribe of nomads that lived in the southern region of the Pagrah desert, the short, squat figure seated elegantly on the *mehari* was wealthy, shrewd, and calculating. Although the desert was his home, his camel trading took Sheykh Zeid to all the major cities of Tara-kan. He was cosmopolitan, wise in the ways of the world and its politics, and his people outnumbered the separate tribes of Jaafar and Majiid two to one.

Mounted on their swift *meharis,* the Aran were fierce and deadly fighters. There had been rumors of late that Zeid—bored with his holdings in the south—had been thinking of extending his wealth by threatening the tribes to the north, force them to acknowledge him as *suzerain*—overlord—and pay him tribute. This was in the minds of both Majiid and Jaafar, and it passed, unspoken, between them as they exchanged grim glances. Two bitter enemies suddenly became reluctant allies.

Elbowing Pukah out of the way, the Sheykhs hastened to pay their respects to their guest, offering him the hospitality of their tents. Behind them their tribes watched warily, weapons in hand, waiting for some sign from their leaders.

Zeid received the Sheykhs with all ease and politeness. Although alone in the midst of those he knew to be his enemies, the Sheykh of the south was not worried. Even if his intentions toward them had been hostile and he had made those intentions known, Zeid's rank as guest made him inviolate. By ancient tradition the guest could remain three days with his host, who must—during that time—show him all hospitality, pledging his life and the lives of his tribe to protect the guest from any enemies. At the end of three days the host must further provide safe escort to his guest the distance of one day's journeying.

"*Adar-ya-yan!*" Zeid ordered, tapping the camel with a slender stick. The beast sank to its knees—first front and then rear—allowing the Sheykh to descend from his magnificent saddle with dignity.

"*Bilhana,* wishing you joy, cousin!" said Majiid loudly, opening his broad arms wide in a gesture of welcome.

"*Bilshifa,* wishing you health, my dear cousin!" said Jaafar, rather more loudly, opening his arms even wider.

Embracing Zeid in turn, the Sheykhs kissed him on both cheeks with the ritual gesture that formally sealed the guest covenant. Then they studied the camel with appreciative eyes, all the while praising the saddle and its fine workmanship. It would never do to praise the camel, for such praise of a living thing invites the evil eye of envy, which was well-known to cause the object thus stricken to sicken and die.

Zeid, in his turn, glanced about in search of something of his hosts' to praise. Seeing, however, one of the Sheykhs clad only in his nightrobes and the other battered and bloodstained, Zeid was somewhat at a loss. He was also intensely curious to find out what was going on. The Sheykh fell back upon an old resource, knowing the surest way to a father's heart.

"Your eldest son, Majiid. What is the young man's name— Khardan? Yes, Khardan. I have heard many tales of his courage and daring in battle. Might I request the honor of his introduction?"

"Certainly, certainly." Bowing effusively, Majiid darted a glance about for his son, hoping desperately that Khardan wasn't covered to the elbows with his enemy's blood.

"Khardan!" the Sheykh's voice boomed into the night.

As the sight of the *mehariste* had put an end to the fight between the fathers, so it put an end to the battle between husband and wife.

"Zeid!" hissed Khardan, hastily pulling the struggling Zohra into a sitting position across the front of this horse. "Stop it!" he said, shaking her and forcing her to look into the ring of torchlight.

Zohra peered out through her disheveled mass of black hair and recognized the camel rider and the danger at the same time. Hastily she shrank back out of the light, hiding her face in her husband's robes. As Sheykh's daughter, Zohra had long been involved in political discussions. If Zeid saw her here, sporting among the men, it would forever lower both her father and her husband in the powerful Sheykh's estimation, giving him a distinct advantage over them in any type of bargaining or negotiation. She must leave quickly, without letting anyone see her.

Swallowing her bitter anger and disappointment, Zohra hurriedly began to wind the men's robes she wore as closely around her as possible. Understanding her intent, Khardan swiftly and silently edged his horse backward into the shadows.

Zohra's hands shook and she became entangled in the garments. Khardan reached out his hand to help her, but Zohra—acutely aware of the firm body pressed by necessity against hers (at least one could assume it was by necessity since both were still on horseback)—angrily jerked away from him.

"Don't touch me!" she ordered sullenly.

"Khardan!" Majiid's voice echoed over the field.

"Coming, my father!" Khardan called. "Hurry!" he whispered urgently to his wife.

Refusing to look at him, Zohra grabbed her long hair and twisting it into a coil, tucked it beneath the folds of the black robe. She was preparing to slip down off the horse when Khardan detained her, sliding a firm arm around her waist. Zohra's black eyes flared dangerously in the flickering torchlight, her lips parted in a silent snarl.

Coolly ignoring her rage, Khardan took off his own headcloth and tossed it over his wife's black hair.

"That beautiful face of yours would never be taken for a man's. Keep it covered."

Staring at him, Zohra's black eyes widened in astonishment.

"Khardan!" Majiid's voice held a note of impatience.

Wrapping the face cloth over her mouth and nose, Zohra slid off the back of the horse.

"Wife," Khardan's voice called out softly but sternly. Zohra glanced up at him. He gestured to the wound in his leg that was bleeding profusely. "I must make a good impression," he said in low tones.

Understanding his meaning, the black eyes—all that were visible of the face hidden by the mask—glared at him in sudden anger.

Khardan, smiling, shrugged his shoulders.

Fumbling for a pouch beneath her robes, Zohra withdrew a green stone streaked with red. Laying it against the knife wound, she bitterly repeated the magic charm that would cause the flesh to close, the blood of the wound to purify. This done, she cast her husband one last look, sharper than a tiger's tooth, and melted away into the shadows of the night.

Khardan, grinning widely, kicked his horse's flanks and galloped up to greet his father's guest. Arriving before the Sheykhs, the Calif caused his horse to go down on its knees, both animal and the man astride it bowing in respect and displaying a nice bit of horsemanship at the same time.

"Ah, excellent, young man, excellent!" Zeid clapped his hands together in true delight.

Jumping off his horse, Khardan was formally introduced to the Sheykh by his father. The usual pleasantries were exchanged.

"And I hear"—Zeid nodded at Pukah, who, blissfully ignorant of the tension in the air, had been beaming upon the assembled company as though he had created them all with his own hands—"that you are newly married and to a beautiful wife—daughter of our cousin."

The Sheykh bowed to Jaafar, who bowed nervously in return, wondering where his unruly daughter was.

"Why are you out here instead of languishing in the arms of love?" Zeid asked casually.

Jaafar shot a swift glance at Majiid, who was eyeing his son worriedly beneath frowning brows. But Khardan, with an easy laugh, made a sweeping gesture with his hand. "Why, Sheykh Zeid, you have come in time to witness the *fantasia* being held in honor of my wedding."

"*Fantasia?*" repeated Zeid in amazement. "This is what you consider a game, is it?"

His eyes went to the men lying groaning on the ground, to their attackers, standing above them, sabers running red with blood. It was the middle of the night. An unusual time for a contest. The Sheykh's eyes, narrow and shrewd, returned to Khardan, studying the young man intently.

The moment Zeid's djinn, Raja, had come to him with news that Majiid and Jaafar had combined forces, Zeid determined to see for himself if this disquieting news was true. The Sheykh had at first discounted it. Zeid did not believe that even Akhran could draw the poison from the bad blood that ran between the two tribes. Traveling north on his swift camel, Zeid had seen, from a distance, the altercation taking place beneath the Tel and he had smiled, his belief confirmed.

"You are mistaken, Raja," he told his djinn, who was concealed in a golden jewel box in one of the Sheykh's *khurjin*. "They have met here to fight, and it seems that we are going to be fortunate enough to witness a good battle."

It struck him as odd, however, that the two tribes should have chosen this remote location—far from their accustomed dwelling places. On riding closer, Zeid was further disconcerted to see the tents of both tribes pitched around the Tel, with the outer signs of having been here for some length of time.

"It appears you may be right, after all, Raja," Zeid had muttered out of the corner of his mouth as he drove his camel forward.

"You play rough, young man," the Sheykh said now in awe, staring at the large patch of blood on the Calif's trousers and the purpling marks of teeth in his hand.

"Boys will be boys, you know, my friend," Majiid said with a deprecating chuckle.

Putting an arm around the Sheykh's shoulder, Majiid turned Zeid away from the sight of churned-up, bloody ground, using slightly more force than politeness dictated.

"Fun is over, young men!" Jaafar shouted. His back to Zeid, he glared sternly at the combatants, indicating by hand gestures that they were to clear the area as rapidly as possible. "Help each other up. That's good men!" he continued in a cheerful, hollow voice.

Reluctantly—eyes on their Sheykhs—the Akar stretched out their hands to the Hrana, assisting those they had been attempting to kill a moment before.

"See if anyone's dead!" Jaafar said in an undertone to Fedj.

"Dead?" Zeid, coming to a halt, twisted out of Majiid's extremely friendly grip.

"Dead! Ha! Ha!" Majiid laughed loudly, attempting to get hold of Zeid once more.

"Ha! Ha! Dead! My father-in-law is such a jokester." Putting his arm around Jaafar, Khardan gave the old man a hug that nearly strangled him. "Did you hear that, men? Dead!"

Scattered laughter rippled through the tribesmen as they hurriedly doused their torches while surreptitiously bending down to check for pulses in the necks of those few who were lying ominously still and quiet on the ground.

"Come, Zeid, you must be hungry after that long ride. Allow me to offer you food and drink. Sond! Sond!"

The djinn appeared, looking grim, dazed, and wild-eyed. If Majiid noticed, he put it down to the interrupted fight and immediately forgot it in the press of other troubles. "Sond, you and Fedj, the djinn of my dear friend Jaafar, go along ahead of us and prepare a sumptuous feast for our guest."

Sond bowed unsteadily, bringing shaking hands to his head, a sickly smile on his lips. "I obey, *sidi*," he said, and vanished.

Majiid heard stifled groans coming from behind him and hurried the Sheykh along until Zeid was practically tripping over his shoes.

"Will your son be joining us?" Zeid asked, turning, attempting once more to see what was going on.

Glaring at Khardan above Zeid's head, Majiid indicated with several urgent nods that the Calif was to remain on the field and keep the fight from breaking out again.

"If you will forgive me, Sheykh Zeid," Khardan said with

a bow, "I will remain behind to take care of this remarkable camel of yours and to make certain everyone finds his tent. Some"—he glanced at a limp Hrana being dragged through the sand by two Akar—"have been celebrating overmuch, I'm afraid."

"Yes," said Zeid, thinking he saw a trail of blood in the sand but unable, because of Majiid's large body blocking his sight, to get a closer glimpse.

"My dear cousin Jaafar will join us, however. Won't you, my dear cousin?" Majiid said, his voice grating.

Jaafar wrenched his gaze from the body being hastily dragged off into the desert and managed to mutter something polite. He fell into step beside them.

"But surely he is not coming to eat dressed in his night-clothes?" Zeid said, glancing at Jaafar in considerable perplexity.

Gazing down at himself, having completely forgotten his state of undress, Jaafar flushed in embarrassment and hurried off to his tents to change, thankful for the chance to regain his composure. But as he went, he heard Majiid loudly telling their guest, "New wife. Wanted to see the fun but didn't want to waste time getting to bed afterward."

Groaning, Jaafar clutched his aching head. "Cursed! Cursed," he moaned as he darted into his tent and hastily pulled out his best robes.

Khardan, standing in the midst of the horses, glaring sternly about to see that his orders were being carried out, heard a step behind him and caught the flash of steel out of the corner of his eye.

"This *fantasia* isn't over, Akar!" came a voice in his ear.

Whirling, Khardan struck his attacker a sharp blow to the stomach with his elbow, hearing the breath leave the man's body with a satisfying whoosh. A well-aimed right to the chin persuaded Sayah that the fun, for him, had ended.

Khardan assisted the groggy young man to his tent and pitched him unceremoniously inside, then hastened back to attend to the dead. Planning to bundle the bodies into hurriedly dug graves, he discovered to his relief that, though several were critically wounded, no one on either side had been killed. Seeing the wounded delivered safely into the care of their wives, hearing laughter and loud talk coming from the tent of his father, Khardan cast a glance at Zohra's tent. It was dark and silent.

Looking at the tooth marks on his hand, the Calif shook his head and smiled, then wearily turned his steps to his own tent and fell, exhausted, into bed.

Teetering on the edge of sleep, the Calif was vaguely conscious of Pukah's voice in his ear.

"This was all my doing, Master! All my doing!"

Chapter 12

The seventy-two hours of the guest period crept along with the slow, dragging steps of a lame and blind beggar. Following the storm, the Tel sweltered beneath a fiery sun that appeared determined to remind them that the unbearable heat of summer was not far off. The tribes themselves sweated in the heat of unresolved anger. They had the taste of blood in their mouths, yet were forbidden to reveal by the least sign, look, word, or deed that all were not the best of friends, the closest of brothers.

This unnatural friendship became such a strain that most of the tribesmen forbore to walk about camp, preferring to skulk about in their tents, plotting dark deeds when the guest period ended. Fortunately the heat of the day gave them the perfect excuse, although the Sheykhs found it difficult to explain why the camp was unnaturally silent and somber during the customary hours of socialization after dark.

Nothing was seen or heard of Zohra during the three days, much to the relief of her father and her husband. This was not unusual, since it was the custom of the tribes to keep their women hidden as much as possible during the visit of a stranger. There was one slight incident: a child, scampering past Zohra's tent, discovered a brass charcoal brazier lying in the sand outside of it. Picking it up to return it to its owner, the child noted with some wonder that the brazier was badly dented and appeared to have been smashed with a rock.

Dinner was the most trying period for everyone concerned. Always an elaborate affair—in honor of the guest a sheep was butchered each night—dinner demanded that Majiid and Jaafar not only exhibit every politeness to their guest but to each other as well. Majiid's forced smile made his face ache. Jaafar was so nervous that the food he ate sat in a lump in his stomach and he was up half the night with belly cramps.

Meanwhile, all feasted on roast mutton; *fatta,* a dish of eggs and carrots; *berchouks,* pellets of sweetened rice; and almond cakes; spread before them on the food carpets by the servants. No one talked during meals, this time being spent in enjoying the food and allowing the digestion to proceed uninterrupted. But after dinner, drinking sweet tea alternated with dark, bitter coffee, nibbling on dates and figs, or sharing the hubble-bubble pipe, the men conversed pleasantly, each keeping his tongue dull and his ears sharp—as the adage goes—hoping to say nothing that would give himself away, hoping to hear something that might be to his advantage.

The burden of conversation fell naturally upon the guest, who was expected to share news of the world with his hosts in exchange for their hospitality. Zeid felt safe in such discussions; the rapidly changing political situation in Tarakan provided him a perfect topic. His first news gave his hosts a shock, however.

"The Amir in Kich—" Zeid began.

"Amir?" Khardan appeared startled. "Since when is there an Amir in Kich?"

"My friends, haven't you heard?" Zeid reveled in the position of being the first to impart important information. "Kich has fallen to the Emperor of Tara-kan!"

"What has happened to the Sultan?" demanded Jaafar.

"Put to death along with his household by the Amir," answered Zeid grimly, "supposedly for refusing to worship Quar. Actually, I don't think the Sultan was offered the choice. He might have been perfectly content to worship Quar, but the Imam needed an example for the remainder of the populace. The Sultan, his wives, concubines, children, and eunuchs were dragged to the top of the cliffs above the city and hurled over the edge; their bodies left to feed the vultures and the jackals. The fortunate ones," he added, chewing a fig, "died in the fall. The less fortunate were rescued and what remained of them turned over to the torturers. Some, it was said, lived for days. As you might imagine, the town's population converted almost to a man; the grandees pooled their funds to build a new temple dedicated to Quar.''

''I trust this will not affect our trading with them,'' said Majiid, frowning, smoke curling from his bearded lips.

''I don't see why it should,'' replied Khardan coolly, lounging back on the cushions and leisurely sipping his coffee. ''In fact, it might just prove more favorable. I presume this Amir is anxious to extend the Emperor's holdings down into Bas. He will undoubtedly be needing horses for his troops.''

''But will he buy them from a *kafir,* an unbeliever?'' queried Jaafar smoothly, delighted at the opportunity to toss cold water on his enemy's fire while maintaining the guise of concerned friendship. ''Perhaps he will throw *you* from the cliffs Majiid.'' Jaafar's unspoken words adding, *May I be there to witness it.*

Hearing that silent comment as clearly as the voiced, Majiid's beard bristled, his eyebrows coming together so alarmingly over his hawk nose that Khardan hurriedly intervened.

''Come, now. The Amir is, after all, a military man. Military men are practical, by and large, and certainly not accustomed to being led around by the nose by priests, no matter how powerful. If the Amir needs horses, he will buy ours and we will have the secret satisfaction of knowing that the horses of *Hazrat* Akhran will bear the followers of Quar into what we devoutly pray is disaster.''

''The Amir, as you say, is a practical man,'' said Zeid cautiously, not wanting to contradict his host impolitely, yet just as eager as Jaafar to thrust a verbal knife into the ribs of his enemies. ''And he is an excellent commander, as you may judge by the fact that he defeated the Sultan's armies in a single battle. But do not underestimate the Imam. This priest is, so I have heard, a charismatic man of great personal beauty and intelligence. He is, as well, a zealot, who has dedicated himself body and soul to the service of Quar. It is rumored that he has great influence not only over the Amir, but—what is more important—over the Amir's head wife, as well. Her name is Yamina and she is reputedly a sorceress of great power.''

''I trust you are not implying that my son will be in danger from the Amir's wife!'' Majiid demanded angrily, nearly forgetting himself.

"Oh, certainly not." Zeid made a graceful smoothing gesture with his chubby hand. "No more than he is in danger from his own wife."

Khardan choked, spilling his coffee. Majiid bit through the pipe stem, splitting it in two with his teeth, and Jaafar swallowed a date whole, nearly strangling himself. Zeid gazed around in perfect innocence, smoothing his beard with his jeweled hand.

Having been commanded by a glum and dour Sond to serve, Pukah hurriedly chose this juncture to pour more coffee. The conversation turned to safer topics, and a friendly argument over the relative merits of horses versus camels allowed the evening to end in harmony.

But before going to his bed that night, Zeid peeped from the guest dwelling, his shrewd eyes following Khardan to his tent—the Calif's tent, *not* the tent where his wife resided.

"Raja was right. It is a marriage of convenience, nothing more," Zeid muttered to himself. "So—I am resolved."

The end of the guest period came at last. The evening of the third day saw Zeid mounting his camel, intending to take advantage of the coolness of the night to make the desert crossing. Khardan offered to serve as escort, taking two of his younger brothers with him.

Zeid left with many protestations of friendship. "It pleases a pious man such as myself that you are carrying out the wishes of our God and living in harmony together. You may rest assured that I will be keeping my eyes on you, cousins. Imbued as you are with Akhran's blessing, you soon might grow as wealthy and powerful as myself."

Seeing Majiid and Jaafar exchanging grim glances, Zeid concealed his smile.

Leaving this barb to rankle in his hosts' flesh, the Sheykh rode off with a flourish, taking the opportunity to exhibit the great speed of his animal. The horses of his escorts galloped along behind.

Following the Sheykh's departure, Majiid saddled his war-horse and went for an hour's gallop in the desert to vent his pent-up rage. Jaafar took to his bed. Pukah, alone in his basket, was relaxing with a plate of sweetmeats when he was surprised to hear a familiar voice asking permission to enter his dwelling.

"Enter and welcome," said Pukah, rising to his feet, somewhat amazed to see Raja. "To what do I owe this great pleasure? Your master and mine are in no danger are they?"

"None, I assure you," Raja replied. Opening his hand, the djinn revealed a lovely little jewel box. "My master sends this to your master, with thanks for his timely 'warning.' "

"Warning?" Pukah's mouth dropped open. "My master gave him no warning. What are you talking about? Are you certain this was intended for the Calif? Perhaps you are seeking Fedj or Sond—"

"No, no," said Raja smoothly, dropping the box into Pukah's limp hand. "It is obvious to Sheykh Zeid that these two tribes have joined together solely for the purpose of attacking him and that he was brought here in hopes that he would be intimidated."

Raja's bland, polite smile changed to a sneer. "Tell your master his plan to frighten Sheykh Zeid al Saban has not succeeded. My master goes now to organize his army, and when he returns, he will crush your tribes into the ground!" The djinn bowed. "Farewell, 'friend.' "

Raja disappeared in a clap of thunder that shook Pukah's basket and set the bowls rattling. The stunned young djinn stood staring at the dark cloud of smoke—all that could now be seen of Raja as he swirled away.

"Sul's blood!" murmured Pukah in despair. "What do I do now?"

Chapter 13

"Wife, wake up!"

A touch on her shoulder roused Zohra from a fitful sleep. Quick as a striking snake, her hand darted to the dagger. Khardan was swifter. His own hand closed over her wrist.

"You have no need of that. I came to tell you that you are wanted in your father's house. We must talk about what has happened."

He was kneeling beside her bed. An oil lamp burned on the floor near him. Holding Zohra's wrist tightly until he felt, from the relaxing of her tense muscles, that she understood what he wanted of her, Khardan stared intently into his wife's flushed face, nearly hidden from view by masses of black hair. The usually fiery black eyes were misty with sleep, confusion, and—deep in their depths—fear. He could guess what she must be thinking. Disgrace, divorce. . . . He smiled grimly.

"What time is it?" Pulling her arm away from Khardan's, Zohra drew the sheepskin blanket close about her body. "Why am I being summoned?"

"Two hours before dawn," Khardan replied tiredly, rubbing his eyes. Standing up, he turned his back upon her, ostensibly out of regard for her modesty, but really in an attempt to forget the softness of her face in sleep, the shadow of her long lashes upon her cheeks, the faint fragrance of jasmine. . . .

"If you want to know why you are summoned, I suggest you dress yourself and come to your father's tent to find out. I have ridden all day and night without rest or food, and I have no energy to argue with you or force you to come if you do not choose. So, wife, you may do as you please.''

Turning on his heel, he left her tent, allowing himself a moment's satisfaction in thinking of the turmoil that must be raging in those soft breasts beneath the sheepskin blanket.

If Khardan had truly known the extent of the agony this mysterious and ominous summons in the dark hours before dawn was causing his wife, he would have felt himself well repaid for the dagger thrust in his leg four nights previous. Once her husband was gone, Zohra shrank back into blankets that had suddenly grown cold and comfortless, her mind a storm of emotion that came near blinding her with its fury.

The three guest days had been difficult for everyone, but torture to Zohra. Accustomed to drowning serious thought in the rushing water of action, she rarely spent a moment in reflection or consideration of her acts. Her self-imposed confinement during the last three days had given her ample and unwelcome opportunity to think. She came to realize the enormity of her crime. Worse, to consider the possible outcome.

The family was an honored and sacred institution for on it rested the survival of the tribe. Divorce—or ''repudiation''— was therefore considered a great evil and came about only following dire circumstances. A divorced woman might be taken back into father's tent, but she was considered disgraced, her children had neither rank nor status in the tribe, and they generally lived worse than the indentured slaves who might—in time—expect to be free.

If the woman had been caught committing adultery, she might further be disfigured in some way—her nose slit, her face scarred—so that she should never tempt a man to sin again. A man caught violating another's wife was treated little better. He was driven from the tribe, his worldly possessions confiscated, his wives and children permitted to enter other families within the tribe or to return to their own parents with honor.

A woman could divorce a man if he failed to provide for her and her children properly or if he mistreated her. A man could divorce a woman if she refused to perform marital duties, just as a woman could divorce a man for the same reason. In all cases of family disputes the matter was taken to the Sheykh, who heard both sides of the story and then made a ruling to which there was no appeal.

Zohra had not only considered the possibility of divorce when she first began planning the wild scheme of stealing the horses, she had welcomed it, looking forward to regaining her precious freedom. Three days of considering what that freedom might cost her, however, had made it seem less and less appealing.

Biting her lip in frustration, Zohra huddled in her bed and considered what to do. She could refuse to go; let them come and drag her out of her tent! That would be humiliating, she realized quickly, and was probably just what Khardan hoped she would do. Far better to go and face him with dignity, she decided. After all, she had as much grounds to divorce him as he had to divorce her. Let him claim she refused to sleep with him. Everyone in the tribe knew he never came near her tent. After all, Zohra realized suddenly, there was the matter of the wedding sheet. If the truth were revealed that she was still a virgin, Khardan would be disgraced before everyone!

As for the incident with the horses, no harm had been done. Well, not much. Not as much as she would have liked! Her decision made, she rose from her bed. Leisurely washing, she dressed herself carefully in her finest clothes, brushed and arranged her long hair, and adorned herself with her favorite jewels. Then she relaxed. Let them wait, she decided. Let them all wait for her pleasure.

When Zohra finally made her way to her father's tent, the first faint rays of the rising sun had drenched the sand in rose pinks and purples. The camp was stirring already, most hurrying to finish their daily work before the intense heat of afternoon drove them to seek the cool shade of their tents. Ignoring the many curious and hostile glances cast in her direction, Zohra left the camp of the horsemen and entered the camp of her own people, where she was accorded almost the same chill reception. Smothering a small sigh, holding her chin rigid, she entered her father's tent.

When she chose, Zohra could make herself beautiful. Generally she did not choose to do so, preferring the freedom of men's clothing. This morning, however, out of a desire to further irritate these men by enhancing her femininity, she had taken extraordinary care with her appearance. She was dressed in a fine silk caftan of a deep rose-red color that became her dusky skin. A veil of the same rose color, trimmed in gold, covered the sleek black hair. Silver bracelets gleamed on her wrists and around her ankles. Her feet were bare—she had rouged the heels and toes with henna. Her black eyes were outlined with kohl, making them appear large and liquid. Her bearing was regal and proud, her face cool and impassive.

It was still dark enough inside the tent for oil lamps to be burning. Within sat—in grim silence—Sheykhs Majiid and Jaafar, the Calif, and their three djinn. Zohra's resolution wavered, the proud gaze faltered. Lowering her eyes, she did not notice the severe, stern expressions on the faces of the men and djinn change as she entered the tent. She did not see Khardan's face—pale with fatigue—soften in admiration. She did not see her father's perennial gloom lift for an instant or see Fedj nod to himself in satisfaction. She might have even seen—had she looked—Majiid's old eyes flash. But Zohra saw nothing except in her mind, and there they were all regarding her with scorn and contempt.

Zohra felt all her disdain seep from her like blood from a knife wound. Truly they considered her crime a heinous one. Some terrible punishment was to be meted out to her. A sudden weakness swept over her. She felt her legs give way and sank down upon a cushion near the entrance. The tent blurred in her vision. Fixing her gaze firmly on a point above the men's heads, she concentrated every fiber of her being on not giving them the satisfaction of seeing her cry. No matter what they did to her, she would face them with pride and dignity.

"Why have I been summoned to my father's tent?" she asked, her voice low.

The men looked to Khardan, who, as her husband, had the right to answer. He was forced to clear his throat before he could reply, but when he did, his voice was cool and smooth.

"Since you have chosen, wife, to meddle in the affairs of men, it has been decided that you be included in this discussion that affects the future and well-being of both Hrana and Akar. It is considered the responsibility of men to deal with matters of politics. Women should be protected from the troubles of this world. You elected to become involved, however, and therefore it is right and fitting that you be forced to accept responsibility for your actions and share in bearing the burden of their consequences.''

Mentally bracing herself for whatever dreadful weapon they intended to hurl at her, Zohra heard Khardan without truly comprehending what he said. When he finished speaking, he regarded her intently, obviously awaiting some response. But his words made no sense. This was not what she had expected. Raising her gaze, she stared at him in perplexity.

''What are you saying, husband?''

Fatigue got the better of Khardan. Dropping the formality, he spoke bluntly. ''I am saying, wife, that you behaved like a damned fool. Because of you, our people came near slaughtering each other. We were saved by the intervention of *Hazrat* Akhran, who sent our enemy to us to act as a mirror in which we might see ourselves reflected. Now that enemy has departed, having gained respect for us, giving us assurances of his friendship—''

''*Yech!*'' A strangled sound came from Pukah.

Khardan, startled, glanced at his djinn in astonishment. ''What? Do you have something to say?''

''N-no, Master.'' Pukah shook his head miserably.

''Then keep silent!'' Khardan snapped.

''Yes, Master.''

The djinn retreated back into the shadows of the tent. Scowling at the interruption, Khardan resumed, now speaking to all those assembled.

''*Hazrat* Akhran is wise as always. This alliance of Akar and Hrana brought the light of newfound respect to the eyes of Zeid al Saban—eyes that once gazed on us with scorn. We can use that respect to bargain as equals with the camel breeder now, instead of coming to him as beggars.'' (Or thieves, the Calif might have added with more honesty, this being the traditional method by which the Akar acquired the few camels they owned.) ''Zeid is a wary old fox, however. He will be watching us, as he warned, and if he sees the tiniest crack in the rock he will smash us with a hammer of steel.''

''*Yrrp!*'' Pukah, huddled in the corner, covered his mouth with his hand.

Khardan glared at him.

"I-I'm not feeling well, Master. If you do not need me—"

"Leave! Leave!" said Khardan, waving his hand.

Pukah dwindled away in a wispy cloud of smoke, appearing as unwell as was possible for an immortal, and Khardan, heaving an exasperated sigh, paused to recall what he had been about to say.

It was slowly occurring to the dazed Zohra that this wild scheme of hers to steal the horses—far from angering her husband—had actually won his grudging respect.

Ah, well, she reflected, what could one expect of a thief?

"Therefore I advise," Khardan was saying, "that we declare an end to the fighting between our two peoples. Further" —the Calif fixed his father with a piercing gaze—"I suggest that we trade the Hrana horses—"

"No!" shouted Majiid. The Sheykh clenched his fist. "I swear I will—"

"—Make no unwise or foolish oath until you have listened to what I propose," Khardan said firmly.

Majiid, glaring fiercely, snapped his mouth shut, and his son continued.

"We trade the Hrana horses in return for a monthly payment of twenty sheep. The Hrana will use the horses for crossing the desert to reach their flocks in the hills. No shepherding." The Calif transferred his piercing stare to Jaafar. "Would that be agreed?"

"Yes! Yes! I assure you!" Jaafar stammered, regarding Khardan with amazement mingled with profound relief.

Ever since the night of the raid the Sheykh had resigned himself to taking his daughter back into his tent and being miserable for the rest of his existence. Now, suddenly, instead of a wayward daughter, he was being given horses! "Praise be to Akhran," the Sheykh added humbly.

By contrast, Majiid's face flamed red, his eyes bulged with anger. He glared at his son with a look that had sent many another man scurrying away in terror. Khardan returned the glare with a calm, steady, unwavering gaze, his bearded jaw firm and unyielding.

Watching from beneath lowered eyelids, Zohra felt a sudden warmth of admiration for her husband. Alarmed and frightened by this unexpected feeling, she told herself she was merely exulting in her victory over him.

"No . . . sheep . . . herding!" The words burst out of Majiid's throat, hissing through his teeth.

"No, no!" Jaafar promised.

Majiid went through a final, agonized internal struggle; saliva bubbled on his lips as though he were being poisoned. "Bah!" he said, rising to his feet. "So be it!"

Ripping aside the tent flap, Majiid started to leave.

"I ask you to listen to me one more moment, Father," Khardan said respectfully.

"Why? What are you going to give him next?" Majiid roared. "Your mother?" He turned to Jaafar, waving his arms. "Take her! Take all my wives!" Yanking his dagger from his belt, he held it out to the Sheykh. "Take my stomach! My liver! Cut out my heart! Rip out my lungs! My son, it seems, wants you to have everything else of value!"

Khardan suppressed a smile. "I merely wanted to suggest, Father, that—in order to allow tempers to cool—I leave for the city of Kich somewhat earlier than when we had originally planned. This will give the hotheads on both sides something to do other than brooding and licking their wounds. We can offer escort to Jaafar's people as far as the hills, then continue on to the city from there."

"Escort him to Sul for all I care!" Majiid snarled, and stalked out of the tent.

Sighing, Khardan looked after him then glanced at Sheykh Jaafar. "My father will keep his word and I will see to it that our people keep theirs." The Calif's voice was cold. "But know this. We are still enemies. However, we pledge by the Holy Akhran that *for the time being*"—he emphasized this—"there will be no more raids, no more insults, not a hand raised by the Akar against the Hrana."

"I pledge to the same. When do we get the horses?" Jaafar asked eagerly.

Khardan rose to his feet. "Undoubtedly my father is handling the matter now. Select those of your men you wish to ride with us and have them ready. We leave with the setting of the sun."

Bowing coldly, Khardan left the tent of his enemy, his dignified bearing an indication that this was only a temporary settlement of their age-old dispute. Zohra lingered a moment after he had gone to cast a triumphant glance at her father, then hastened after the Calif.

News of the agreement was spreading through both camps, bringing reactions of suspicious disbelief in the Hrana's tents and outraged disbelief among the Akar. But as Khardan had planned, there was no time for either side to dispute the matter. The news was also spreading that the Calif intended leaving for the city this very evening, and both camps were thrown into a flurry of confusion—men oiling their saddles and sharpening weapons; women hurriedly mending robes, tucking charms of protection in their husbands' *khurjin*, preparing food for the road, all the while chatting excitedly about the fine gifts their husbands would bring them on their return.

Zohra ignored all of this activity as she hurried through the camps, her one thought to catch up with Khardan, who was walking wearily toward his tent.

Reaching out a hand, Zohra touched his arm.

Khardan turned. The smile on his lips froze, his face darkened. Zohra started to speak, but he forestalled her.

"Well, wife, you have won. You have what you wanted. If you have stopped me with the purpose of rubbing salt in my wounds, I suggest you think twice. I am tired and I see no rest for myself this night. Further, I have much to do in order to prepare for my journey. If you will excuse me—"

Now Zohra *had* planned to gloat over her victory. The sharp words were on her lips, ready to shoot forth and deflate his pride. Perhaps it was the perversity of her nature that made her inclined to do the opposite of what anyone expected of her, perhaps it was the warmth of the admiration she had felt for the Calif in the tent. Whatever the reason, the spears she had ready to cast at her enemy suddenly changed into flowers.

"My husband," said Zohra softly, "I came only to . . . to thank you."

Her hand lingered on Khardan's arm. She could tell by the almost dumbfounded expression on his face that she had startled him, and she tried to laugh at him. His hand closed tightly over hers, however. He drew her near him. The laughter quivered in her throat, disrupted by the rapid beating of her heart.

He was not regarding her with disgust now. His eyes

burned with a fire brighter than the sun, forcing her to lower her gaze before them.

"How deep is the well of your gratitude, madam?" he whispered, his lips brushing her cheek.

The sun's flame kindled in her body. "Perhaps you should cast in your bucket, my lord, and find out," she answered, closing her eyes and lifting her lips.

"Master!" came an agonized voice.

"Not now, Pukah!" Khardan said gruffly.

"Master! I beg an instant only!"

Zohra came to her senses. Glancing around, she saw that they were standing in the center of the camp, surrounded by people laughing and nudging each other. Ashamed and embarrassed, Zohra slipped from her husband's grasp.

"Wait!" He caught hold of her.

Backing away from him, she murmured, "Perhaps, upon your return, my lord, you can plumb the well's depth." Then, breaking free, she fled.

Khardan stared after her, more than half-inclined to follow, when the hand tugged at his arm again.

Turning, he glowered at the djinn. "Well?" he demanded, his voice shaking. "What is it, Pukah?"

"If you do not need me, *sidi*, I beg leave to be gone from your service for a short time. Only the shortest of times, I assure you, *sidi*. An eyeblink will seem long compared to it. You will never miss me—"

"I can guarantee you that! Very well, be gone!"

"Thank you, *sidi*. I am going. Thank you." Bowing, backing up, bowing again, and backing up again, Pukah hastily faded from view.

Khardan turned to follow his wife, the blood throbbing in his temples, only to find that others were crowding around him now, wanting to know who was going to ride with him arguing about whose horses had to be given to the sheepherders, and badgering him with countless other fool questions.

Looking over their heads, hoping for a glimpse of rose-red silk, Khardan saw nothing but the confusion in the camps. Zohra was gone. The moment had passed. He turned back to his men, forcing himself to remember that he was Calif of his people, they had first claim upon him—always.

With an effort the Calif wrenched his mind from thoughts

of rose-red silk and jasmine to deal with the business at hand, answering questions somewhat incoherently, finding that wells and buckets kept getting mixed up in the conversation. The need to settle a fight between one of the Akar and a Hrana effectively cooled his ardor. Then Majiid appeared, demanding to know why his son didn't just rip off his father's head and be done with it, and swearing that he would not give up the oldest nag in his possession to the sheepherders. Patiently Khardan went through his reasoning once again.

His own preparations for the journey took the rest of the day, and before Khardan knew it, the shadows of evening had stretched out their cool, soothing fingers over the sand. It was time to leave. Standing beside his black horse, Khardan glanced around. His *spahis* on their war-horses were gathered in a restless, excitement-laced knot behind him. Further behind them, several Hrana men were seated on their new mounts, their awkwardness and uneasiness on the tall, prancing beasts masked by fierce looks of pride that dared anyone to say they hadn't been born in the saddle.

Trouble would break out before this ride was finished, Khardan knew. He found his gaze straying to Zohra's tent, hoping to catch a glimpse of her.

The other women in camp were bidding good-bye to their husbands, calling out to remember this or that, lifting babies to be blessed. Husbands bent to kiss their wives. Zohra was nowhere to be seen. Thinking suddenly that this trip was a confounded nuisance, Khardan swung himself up into the saddle. Waving to his father, he wheeled his horse. Hooves flashed in the sand, a cheer went up from the men, and the *spahis* galloped after their leader, showing off their riding skills as long as they were within sight of camp.

As he rose past the Tel, Khardan noted with some astonishment that the Rose of the Prophet, previously thought to be dying, seemed almost on the verge of blooming.

Chapter 14

As Khardan's men traveled west over the Pagrah desert to the city of Kich, a slave caravan was traveling eastward over the plains of northern Bas, bound for the same destination. The slaver's journey, unlike that of the *spahis*, was made at a slow and leisurely pace. This was done not out of kindness for the slaves but for reasons of economics. Merchandise put upon the market after being marched halfway across a continent appears to disadvantage and fetches far below its actual worth. The slaves were, therefore, permitted to walk at a relaxed pace and were adequately fed. Not that any of this mattered or was even apparent to Mathew. The young man's misery increased daily. He lived and breathed fear.

Lurching and swaying upon the camel, concealed within the tentlike *bassourab*, he peered despairingly out upon the harsh land. Comparing it to his homeland, he began to wonder if he was on the same planet.

At first they rode through barren plains, the camels walking splay-footed across sandy, flat stretches of rock covered by strange, ugly grasses and flesh-ripping plants. Then the flat plains dipped down into ravines and the camels fought for sure footing along treacherous falls of crumbled stone. Awed by the savage beauty, Mathew stared dazedly at sheer rock walls, streaked with garish colors of reds, oranges, and yellows that soared above him to dizzying heights.

Everything in this land went by extremes, it seemed. The sun either blazed down upon them mercilessly or rainstorms beat at them with incredible fury. The temperature rose and fell with wild abandon. By day the young wizard sweated and suffered from the intense heat. By night he shivered with cold.

And if the land was harsh and the climate cruel, its people were harsher and crueler still. Slavery was unknown in Mathew's country, having been decreed by his God, Promenthas, to be a mortal sin. The concept of slavery was completely alien to Mathew, impossible for him to comprehend or understand. That he and all the rest of these men, women, and children were nothing more to the unseen person in the white palanquin than so much chattel, to be measured in terms not of life but of gold, seemed ludicrous. Mathew could not imagine that one human being could look upon another as he might look upon a horse or a camel.

The young wizard soon learned to think differently. The slaves were not treated like horses. Horses, for example, were never beaten.

What the man's crime was, Mathew never knew. Perhaps he had tried to escape. Perhaps he had been caught talking to another slave—which was forbidden. The *goums* stopped the caravan, threw the unfortunate wretch upon the ground, stripped off the loincloth that was the only clothing the male slaves wore, and beat him swiftly, impersonally, and efficiently.

The blows fell upon the man's buttocks, an area of his body that would remain covered when he was exhibited in the marketplace, thus hiding the unsightly bruises and stripes of the whip. At first the man forbore from crying out, but after three lashes his screams of pain began and soon echoed off the high rock walls.

Mathew, shaking with sick horror, stopped up his ears with his veil. Wrenching his gaze away, he looked at the white palanquin that stood on ground near him, those carrying it taking advantage of the respite to squat down on their haunches and rest. Not a sound came from within the litter, the white curtains did not stir. Yet Mathew knew the man inside looked on, for he saw the *goum* glance at the litter for orders, and he saw that slender white hand come out once, make a graceful motion, then withdraw. The beating ceased. The slave was dragged to his feet and chained back with his fellows, and the caravan proceeded on its way.

Mathew had no fear of being beaten himself. Terrified of

revealing his secret, he kept well apart from the other slaves, never speaking to anyone if he could help it. He had no thoughts of trying to escape. The young wizard knew he would not last twenty minutes in this godforsaken land. For the time being he was safest with his captors—or at least so he assumed.

Evening brought respite from travel. The *goums* assisted Mathew down from the back of the camel—a stupid and vicious beast whose one redeeming feature, so far as Mathew could see, was that it could travel enormous distances through the arid land without requiring water. The guards then escorted the female slaves to a place of privacy where they could perform their ablutions. This moment always brought panicked fear to Mathew, for he not only had to hide himself from the guards but from the women as well. Once this daily terror ended, the *goums* hustled Mathew and the other women into their tents, setting the guards around them for the night, and Mathew could, at last, relax.

Although Mathew never saw the trader, except for that slender white hand, he had the feeling that he was being kept under constant, special surveillance. His tent was always placed closest to the trader's own tent in the evening. The camel he rode was always first in line behind the palanquin. Mathew received his food immediately after the trader received his.

At first this surveillance increased Mathew's fear. Gradually it lulled him into a mindless security, giving him the impression that someone cared about his welfare—a wistful notion, born of desperation, that was soon cruelly dispelled.

On the fourth night of the journey the evening's bowl of food was slipped through Mathew's tent flap. Dully he glanced at it, and without much thinking about what he did, he picked it up and deposited it surreptitiously behind the tent.

One of the *goums* was walking by the tent when he felt something tickle his neck, like feathers touching his skin. Thinking it to be one of the thousand varieties of winged insects in this land, the *goum* slapped at it irritably, but the tickle did not go away. Craning his head in an effort to see what was harassing him, the *goum* saw, instead, Mathew's food bowl slide out of the back of the tent, its contents dumped on the ground.

Scowling, the *goum* forgot about the tickle—that quite mysteriously ceased—and hurried to Kiber to report.

Lying down to try to drown his misery in exhausted sleep, Mathew was scared nearly witless by the sudden entrance into his tent of the leader of the *goums*.

"What is it? What do you want?" Mathew gasped, clutching his women's clothing about him. He was becoming more and more adept at speaking the language—a fact that neither appeared to impress nor surprise his captors. They all had the mentality of animals anyway, and one dog is rarely surprised to hear another bark.

Kiber did not answer him. Grabbing Mathew by the arm, the *goum* hauled him out of his tent and dragged him across the ground to the dwelling of the trader. Kiber apparently had orders already to enter, for he charged inside with Mathew without announcing his presence.

The interior was shadowy and dark; no lamps had been lighted. Half-blinded by the veil over his face, Mathew could see little. He had the general impression of luxury; of fine silken cushions and rich rugs and the glitter of gold and brass. The air was perfumed; there was a smell of food and coffee. He saw a man swathed in white robes, reclining on a cushion. A woman—dressed in black—crouched, head down, some distance away.

At Mathew's entrance the trader raised his head. Despite being indoors he kept his face covered with the face cloth. All that was visible were two eyes, hooded by thick, drooping lids, that glittered above the white mask. Mathew shivered. A ray of cold moonlight, shining through the tent flap, gleamed on the white mask with more warmth than the young wizard saw in those eyes. Not knowing what to expect, Mathew stared back at the man with the frozen calm of despair.

"Down! On your knees, slave!" Kiber twisted Mathew's arm painfully, forcing the young wizard to the ground.

"What is the problem?" the trader asked in a soft voice.

"This one is attempting to starve herself to death."

Mathew gulped. "That—that's not . . . true," he stammered, feeling himself quail beneath the gaze of the cold, hooded eyes.

"Mahad discovered her throwing her food out of the tent, attempting to hide it in the grass. It occurred to him that he had heard animals snuffling in the night near this one's dwelling. Obviously, *Effendi*, your bounty has been feeding the jackals, not this one.''

"So you are using death to escape your fate?" inquired the trader, the eyes gazing at Mathew dispassionately. "You would not be the first," he added in somewhat bored tones.

"No!" Mathew's voice cracked. He licked his parched lips. "I . . . haven't been . . . able to eat. . . ."

His voice trailed away. It had not occurred to the young man to deliberately starve himself to death, yet he suddenly realized he had been doing just that, slowly and surely, without knowing it. Perhaps it had been his unconscious self taking over and carrying out the deed his conscious mind was too cowardly to perform. All Mathew knew was that every time he tried to take a bite, his gorge rose and he could no more have swallowed the food than he could have swallowed sand.

How could he explain this to those hooded eyes? He couldn't. It was impossible. Shaking his head, Mathew tried to say something else, make some lame promise that he would eat, although he knew he couldn't. At least they couldn't force food down him. He was doing to die with dignity perhaps after all. Before he could utter a word, however, the trader made a gesture. The woman who had been kneeling at the rear of the tent came forward and knelt beside him. Putting his hand—the slender white hand—on her chin, the trader lifted her unveiled face so that she looked at Mathew.

Woman! Mathew was appalled. She was a child, no more than fourteen at most. She stared at him with frightened eyes, and he saw that her entire body quivered with fear.

"Your own life obviously means little to you," the trader said softly, "but what about the lives of others?" His hand clenched around the girl's jaw. "When you do not eat, this one will not eat. Nor will she have anything to drink." Dropping his hand to her shoulder, the trader roughly shoved the girl forward, sending her sprawling in a heap at Mathew's feet. "With the heat of the desert ahead, she will last perhaps two—three days." The trader leaned back among the cushions. "When she is dead, there will be another."

Mathew stared at the man, incredulous. His gaze went to

the girl, cowering before him, her thin hands pressed together in a pleading gesture.

"I can't believe you'd do this!" Mathew said in a cracked voice.

"Can't you?" The trader shrugged. "This girl"—he nudged her with the toe of his slipper—"has no value. She is not pretty, she is no longer even a virgin. She will bring a few coppers, nothing more, as someone's house slave. But you, beautiful blossom from across the sea, are worth fifty of her! You see? I am not doing this out of any concern for you, my flower, but out of greed. Does that convince you that I would do it?"

It did. Mathew had to admit that. He also had to admit to himself at last that he was in truth nothing more than marketable goods, merchandise, a thing to be bought and sold. What would happen when this man found out he had been cheated, when Mathew's unsuspecting buyer discovered that he had purchased flawed wares? Mathew didn't dare think of this or he knew he would go mad. As it was, he could only promise, through trembling lips, to eat what food was given him. The trader nodded—the cold, impassive expression in the eyes never changing—and waved Mathew, the *goum,* and the wretched girl out of his sight.

Kiber escorted Mathew and the girl back to the tent. More food was brought. This time Kiber sat inside, watching Mathew expectantly. The girl did the same, except that her eyes were on the food, not on Mathew.

The young wizard wondered how he would be able to choke down the rice that had been mixed with vegetables and greasy meat. He tried to concentrate on the girl, hoping his pity for her would carry him through this ordeal. But he found himself imagining the dreadful life she must lead, the cruel usage to which she had been subjected, the bleak and hopeless future she faced. Gagging, he brought up his first mouthful. Kiber growled in anger. The girl whimpered, clasping her hands.

Resolutely Mathew took another bite. Refusing to let himself think of anything at all, he began to count the number of times he chewed. When he reached ten, he swallowed. Keeping his mind a blank, he grabbed another lump of the substance and shoved it in his mouth. He chewed it ten times as before, his mind thinking of only the numbers. In this way he managed to eat enough to his dinner apparently to satisfy Kiber, who gave the rest to the girl. Grabbing the bowl with both hands, she brought it to her mouth, wolfing it down like a starving dog. She licked out the bowl, getting every last vestige, then prostrating herself before Mathew, she began to weep and pour incoherent blessings down upon his head.

Kiber—evidently feeling his job was finished—jerked the girl to her féet and led her from the tent. Watching through the tent flap, Mathew saw the *goum* take the girl back to the trader's tent and throw her inside.

She is no longer even a virgin. . . .

Mathew heard the cruel voice, saw the cold eyes. Sickened, he lay down upon his cushions, expecting to lose most of what he had eaten. But surprisingly, his body accepted the food. He had not gone without eating long enough to make it reject what it craved, as sometimes happened—so he had heard—to monks who fasted for too long. Closing his eyes, he felt a sense of disappointment that he'd been, once again, cheated of death.

Chapter 15

The flies droned, the sweat trickled down his face, the coolness of a drop felt suddenly startling against his hot skin. Mathew clung to the saddle of the lurching beast on which he rode, half-asleep in the sweltering heat. His body suffered, but he did not notice. He was not truly there. Once more, as he did so often now, he had retreated from reality, taking refuge in the memories of his past.

In his mind he was far away, back in the land that had given him birth. He walked the lush grass of the grounds of the ancient school where he studied. He lunched beneath huge oaks that were older than the school; he and his fellow students discussing in youthful, solemn voices the mysteries of life, chewing on them over cold beef and bread and solving them—every one—before dessert.

Or he was in the classroom, sitting at the tall desk, laboriously copying his first major spell onto the parchment made from the skin of a newborn lamb. His fingers sticky with the lamb's blood used to write the cantrip, he stopped often to wipe them so that he would not drop a blot upon the parchment; the slightest error would negate the magic. He could clearly see the feather of the raven's quill, shining with a black rainbow of color in the mild sunlight filtering through the glass windowpanes. Days and days he worked on that spell, making certain every single stroke of the quill was as perfect as he could possibly make it. His fingers cramped from the strain, his back ached from bending over the tall desk. Never in his life had he been happier.

At last the spell was finished. He sat back and stared at the parchment for an hour, searching for the tiniest flaw, the smallest mistake. There were none. Rolling it carefully, he tucked it into the carved ivory spell case that had been a gift from his parents upon the last Holy Day. Closing the silver lid, he sealed it with beeswax and, carrying it carefully, brought the spell to the desk of his Master, the Archmagus, and laid it before him. The Archmagus, engrossed in reading some moldy, dusty text that literally smelled of arcane knowledge, said nothing but calmly accepted the spell case.

A fortnight later—the longest term of days and nights Mathew had ever spent in his life—the Archmagus called the young man to his private study. Here were gathered several other wizards—teachers of Mathew's. All of them stood regarding him gravely, their long, gray beards brushing against their chests. The Archmagus handed Mathew back the spell case. It was empty. Mathew held his breath. The Archmagus smiled, the other masters smiled. The spell had worked perfectly, they said. Mathew had passed. He was, at last, an apprentice wizard. His reward—to be taken on a journey by sea to the land of Sardish Jardan.

He returned home for a holiday before his trip, spending his time in continued quiet study and meditation with his parents in the candlelit libraries of their castle. The Weslanders lived in what many people of Tirish Aranth considered harsh country. According to popular myth, it was so hilly that one always slept at an angle. The mountainous country was heavily forested, covered with tall stands of pine and aspen. Its soil was rocky, unsuitable for all but subsistence farming. There was no lack of food, however. A wilderness people, the Weslanders had learned long ago to live off the land. They hunted deer and elk in the forest, snared rabbits and squirrels in the valleys, and caught bright-colored trout in the splashing streams.

Lovers of study and of nature, the Weslanders were a solitary people, building their stone dwellings at the top of treacherous paths that only the most adventuresome or loyal of friends dared climb. Here, among their books, the Weslanders lived their quiet lives, raising their children in the slightly preoccupied manner of those to whom the quest for knowledge comes first and all else second.

Because of their slender build, fluting voices, and the physical beauty of both men and women, it was difficult to tell the sexes apart. The Weslanders saw no reason why they should, for that matter. Women and men were one in all they did, from attending schools to hunting. It was this blurring of the sexes that had, over the years—according to the scornful world in general—caused the men to cease to grow facial hair. Having little to do with the world in general, the Weslanders ignored their detractors. They almost never married outside their own race, finding the other people of Tirish Aranth to be boorish and stupid, fonder of the body than the mind as the Weslander axiom ran.

Mathew's family was an old one and had, over the years, amassed a fortune so that they were able to concentrate on their studies to the exclusion of all else. His mother was a philosopher, whose writings on the teachings of Promenthas had received high acclaim from both religious and secular circles. She had been offered chairs at several universities but had always declined. Nothing could ever induce her to leave the hills in which she had been born or the husband to whom she was devoted. Mathew's father was an alchemist—a dreamy man who was never happier than when pottering among his glass tubes and burning blue flames, creating horrendous smells and occasional explosions that rocked the house. Mathew's earliest memory of his father was seeing him emerge from the underground laboratory in a cloud of billowing smoke, his eyebrows burned off, his soot-covered face ecstatic.

Mathew's parents sent him to the finest school for wizards open to young men. He left home at the age of six, returning once a year for Holy Day. Except that his father grew a little grayer and the lines about his mother's eyes grew more pronounced over the years, Mathew always came back to find his parents unchanged. Once yearly they welcomed him home, raising their heads from book or glass tube, smiling at him as though he hadn't been gone over an hour, and calmly going back to their work with a quiet invitation for him to join them. Within moments of his return, Mathew was seated at his own desk, a warm feeling inside him that he had never been away.

He was sitting there now, in the high-backed wooden chair, listening to the scratching of his mother's pen across the page on which she was writing, hearing her murmur to herself, for she spoke aloud while she wrote. A cool breeze, scented with the sharp smell of pine, blew through the open casement. From the laboratory below the house came a muffled thud and then a yell. His father. . . . Strange, he never shouted like that. Mathew raised his head from the book he was perusing. What was wrong? Why this yammering? . . .

With a jolt the young wizard woke up, catching himself just before falling from the saddle. The pain of terrible, bitter knowledge that he had been dreaming twisted inside him. Waking was always agony, the price he paid. But it was worth it to escape this wretched life, if only for a few brief moments. He was just about to try to lose himself in that wonderful haven again when he realized the shouts had not been part of his imagination. Peeping through the fabric of the *bassourab,* Mathew looked to see what the commotion was about. His heart died within him.

They had reached the walls of the city.

Accustomed to the thatched and gabled roofs of the dwellings in his own land, the buildings that he could see rising above the walls appeared as strange and awful to Mathew as the land through which he traveled. Twisting upward in fantastic designs, with spires and towers and minarets that bulged like onions, they seemed to have been built by some insane child.

Mathew could even smell the city from this distance—thousands of unwashed bodies sweating, eating, defecating, beneath the merciless sun. He could hear the noise—a low murmur of hundreds of voices raised in bargaining, praying, fighting. . . . And he would be taken into this city, dragged to the marketplace in chains, made to stand and endure the gaze of countless merciless eyes. . . . Sick with fear, he hung his head down to allay the dizziness that assailed him and waited for the order that would send him into hell.

The only order that came immediately, however, was one which brought the camels to their knees. The white covered palanquin was set upon the ground. A slave came hurrying around with water. Drinking greedily, Mathew peered through the curtains and watched the *goums* forming hastily into ranks. When their lines were dressed to the satisfaction of the leader, they galloped off toward the city walls with a fine display of horsemanship, unfurling banners as they rode. Staring across the plain, Mathew saw riders dash out from the city gates to meet the *goums*. This must be some sort of request for permission to enter the gates, which—as far as Mathew could see—were still closed.

The preliminaries took a long time. A slave came around with food, which Mathew was careful to eat, having the uncanny feeling that the eyes behind the curtains of the litter could see through the camel tent. Although he had watched for her anxiously, Mathew had seen the slave girl only occasionally after that first night. When he did catch a glimpse of her, coming or going from the tent of the trader, she appeared to be as well fed as any of the slaves, and at least she was still alive. She glanced at Mathew once but did not speak to him. Mathew was just as glad. Fearfully guarding his secret, he did not encourage conversation with anyone lest they discover it was a man to whom they spoke, not a woman.

After what seemed like eons, although it was probably only an hour at most, the city riders galloped back to the gates, the *goums* wheeled their horses and returned to the caravan. For the first time Mathew saw the trader actually leave the comfort of his covered palanquin. His white robes billowing around him, he walked out to meet Kiber. Kiber in turn jumped off his horse in mid-gallop and with an ease and grace Mathew found remarkable, ran alongside the animal to come to stand, panting, near the trader.

The other *goums* arrived a few seconds behind, their excited voices shouting to the slaves to come for their horses or calling for water. In an effort to escape the clamor and the dust, the trader and Kiber moved toward the rear of the litter. Their walk brought them close to Mathew's camel. Leaning forward, careful to keep hidden behind the curtains of the *bassourds,* he held his breath so that he could hear their conversation.

"What is the problem?"

"There is a new ruling in effect, *Effendi.*"

"And that is?"

"All magical objects and any djinn we possess must be turned over to the Imam, to be kept in Quar's holy temple."

"What?" Mathew heard the trader's voice grate. "How is

this possible? Did you not tell him I was a loyal and faithful follower of Quar?''

"I so told him, *Effendi*. He said that all who are faithful followers of the God will be happy to perform this act of sacrifice that has been ordered by the God himself.''

"The Imam is a fool! What man will give up his djinn?''

"Apparently many men, *Effendi*. According to the captain, there is not a djinn left in Kich and the people have never lived so well. They go to the Imam with their needs now, and he handles them, dealing with Quar directly. The city is prosperous, says the captain. They lack nothing. There is no sickness, the markets are filled, their enemies fall beneath their feet. Already the people speak of the djinn as remnants of a bygone age, not needed in modern times.''

"So it is true, what we heard. Quar is deliberately getting rid of his own djinn. I do not like this.'' The cold malice in the voice made Mathew shiver despite the heat. "You know the importance of what I carry. What are the chances of getting inside the city without its being detected?''

"Very little, I should think, *Effendi*. The caravan will be thoroughly searched upon entering the city walls. These people are naturally suspicious of outsiders, particularly, it seems, since that band of *kafir* was able to cross the ocean and set foot upon the shores of their land. I told the captain that it was *we* who dispatched the *kafir* in the name of Quar and he seemed impressed.''

"But not impressed enough to let us enter without harassment?''

"No, *Effendi*.''

The trader snarled, a low, growling rumble of anger, like a cat denied its prey. "Would that we had heard this news earlier. It is too late to leave. It would appear suspicious for a trader in slaves to turn back once he reaches the marketplace. And I need the money from their sale to pursue our journey.''

He was silent long moments, lost in thought. Mathew heard Kiber's horse shuffle restlessly. The other horses were being watered and it wanted its share. The leader of the *goums* spoke to the animal softly, and it quieted.

"Very well. Here's what we will do.'' The trader's words were quick and cool. "Gather the magical objects of everyone in camp and put them together with those we took off the slaves when we captured them. Add to that my personal objects—''

''*Effendi!*''

''There can be no help for it! Hopefully this will satisfy them and they will be careless in their search. This and the fact that it was by my orders that the *kafir* died should convince the Imam that I am a loyal follower of Quar. My way will be clear to act.''

''What about—'' Kiber hesitated, as though reluctant to speak.

''I will take care of that, you may be certain. The less you know, the better.''

''Yes, *Effendi.*''

''You have your orders. Proceed.''

''Yes, *Effendi.*''

The two parted, the trader returning to the covered palanquin, Kiber leaving to carry out his master's commands. Mathew, sighing, sat back. He had listened to the conversation hoping to learn what was going to happen. But nothing he heard made any sense. Djinn! He had read of these immortal beings. Supposedly similar in nature to angels, they dwelt on the human plane and were said to live in lamps, rings, and other such silly objects. They talked to men—to all men, not just priests—holding discourse with ordinary humans and performing for them the most trivial of deeds.

Mathew found it astounding that someone as cold and calculating and obviously intelligent as this trader could actually appear to believe in such foolish tales. Perhaps he did so only to humor his men. As for magical objects, the young wizard hungered to know what they might be. For the first time he saw a glimmer of hope in his desperate situation. If he could get his hands on one of these objects . . .

A whispered voice near him made him start in fear.

''Mistress!''

Mathew parted the curtains of the *bassourab* a crack. The slave girl stood beside his camel.

''Mistress,'' she said again, beckoning. ''You come. He want you.''

Mathew shuddered, terror overwhelming him, turning his hot hands ice cold, constricting his throat muscles.

''Come, come!'' The girl cast a swift, fearful glance in the direction of the palanquin, and Mathew realized that *she* would be punished if he was remiss in following orders. Trembling in every limb, he climbed down slowly from the camel saddle.

Glancing around to see if anyone was watching, the girl took Mathew's hand and tugged him after her, guiding him swiftly across the sandy ground to the litter. Mathew noticed that they kept to the outside of the line of camels, steering clear of the crowd that was milling around in the center where some of the *goums* were preparing the slaves for their march into town. Others were collecting the magical items as ordered; still others were seeing to the horses or spreading fodder for the camels. No one paid the least attention to them. The girl led Mathew around to the far side of the palanquin, out of sight of everyone.

"I have her," the girl said to the curtains of the litter.

"Come close, Blossom," came the trader's voice.

His heart pounding so that he could barely breathe for the intense pain, Mathew hesitated, trying to gather his courage. The girl motioned for him to obey, again with the look of fear. Shivering, Mathew stepped closer. The slender hand came out, caught hold of the robes around his neck, and drew him closer still.

"I have just discovered that we are going to be searched when we enter the city. On my person I carry a magical object of rare and immense value. For obvious reasons I do not wish it to be found by these slum dwellers. They will go through my possessions carefully, but they will probably not be too interested in what a slave girl such as yourself carries. Therefore I give this object to you, to keep for me until such time as I may come to claim it."

Mathew gasped. Was it possible? Was he going to come into possession of some arcane relic so easily? The trader could not know he was a wizard; he would suppose him incapable of using the object. It must be powerful. Mathew had seen enough of the harshness of this God, Quar, to understand that the trader was risking his life in defying the orders of Quar's priest. Mathew's hands trembled with eagerness. He needed to gather what information he could about the object in order to use it, however, and hastily searched for some way to do so that would not appear suspicious. At the last moment it occurred to him that a slave girl, such as himself, should probably seem reluctant to take on such a burden.

"I . . . don't understand, *Effendi*." Mathew stammered. "Surely there are others more worthy . . . of—of your trust."

"I don't trust you in the least, Blossom. I give this to you because you will be sold to someone wealthy and important, consequently easy for me to find."

"But what if I should lose it or something should happen to it—"

"Then you will die most horribly," said the cool voice of the trader. "The object is blessed—or cursed as the case may be—so that it cannot be lost or mislaid by accident." The slender hand upon Mathew's robes suddenly tightened its grip, twisting the fabric expertly, cutting off Mathew's breath. "One who attempts to do so deliberately will meet the most excruciatingly painful death that *my* God can devise. And believe me, my dear Blossom, his talents in that area have long been admired."

There was no doubting that voice. Mathew began to strangle, the slave girl stared at him with huge, frightened eyes. At the last moment the hand removed itself from his robes, gliding back into the curtains of the palanquin. Mathew gasped for air. The curtains parted once more. Reaching out, the trader caught hold of Mathew's hand and pressed something inside.

Mathew stared in confusion.

He held a globe of glass. Small enough to fit comfortably in his palm, the globe was decorated on the top and the bottom with the most intricate gold- and silverwork. It was filled with water, and inside the globe swam two fish—one the color of black velvet with long sweeping fins and a fanlike tail; the other a shimmering golden color with a flat body and large, staring eyes.

He had been given a fishbowl!

"I— What—" Mathew could not speak coherently.

"Shut up, Blossom, and attend to me. We haven't much time. You must keep this hidden from sight. The globe itself will help you, for it is naturally loathe to reveal itself to anyone. You need not feed the fish nor care for them, they can fend for themselves. Carry the globe on your person at all times—sleeping or waking. Speak of it to no one. Do not

tremble so, Blossom. You will have this in your possession
for only a few days, if that long. Then I will come to relieve
you of this burden. Serve me well in this matter and you will
be rewarded." The slender hand moved to stroke Mathew's
soft cheek.

"Betray me and . . ."

There was a rustle of curtain, a flash of metal in the
sunlight, and a kind of startled gasp from the slave girl.
Mathew, staring at her, saw her eyes widen with pain, then
slowly drain of life. The girl crumpled to the ground at his
feet, a large red stain spreading over her clothes. The trader's
slender hand, holding a small, silver dagger, was wet with
blood.

Mathew started to recoil in horror, but the trader caught
hold of his wrist and held him fast. "Now no one knows
about this but you and I, Blossom. Return quickly to your
mount." The voice was soft, low. "Remember what you
have seen of my wrath."

The slender hand let loose its grip and disappeared inside
the palanquin. Dazed, Mathew slid the fishbowl beneath the
bodice of his clothing. The glass was cold against his hot
flesh. He shuddered in reaction, as though he had pressed a
handful of ice against his breast. Hardly knowing where he
was or what he was doing, Mathew turned, stumbling blindly
over the hard, sun-baked ground. Instinct alone led him to the
camel.

The rest of the party was preparing to continue to travel.
The slaves removed the halters from the camels' knees, coaxing
them to rise with encouraging shouts and taps of the camel
stick. The *goums* mounted their horses; the litter bearers lifted
their burden to their shoulders; the slaves rose to their feet,
their chains clashing together in an off-key jangle. Two slaves
walked alongside the palanquin, each slave carrying in his
arms a huge rattan basket filled with objects strange and
curious—amulets, charms, jewelry—anything that might
possibly be construed as possessing magic. Kiber galloped up
and down the line, casting his dark-eyed gaze critically over
the assembly. Finally, with a glance at the litter, he nodded
and urged his horse forward. Banners hanging limp in the
hot, breathless air, the caravan set off at a leisurely pace.

Mathew's camel lurched to its feet, grumbling in protest.

Peering through the folds of the camel tent, the young wizard stared down at the body of the slave girl, lying forgotten on the desert sand.

Ahead of him, rising up out of the plains, were the city walls—a prison house of misery and suffering. The city's stench hit his nostrils. The camel picked her way around the body of the slave girl; vultures were already flapping down to the ground.

Twisting in the saddle, Mathew gazed back at the corpse with envy.

Chapter 16

The 'efreet Kaug did not dwell in a sumptuous palace on the plane of the djinn. For reasons best unknown to anyone, he lived in a cave far beneath the Kurdin Sea. Rumor had it that he had, centuries before, been banished to this cave by the God Zhakrin during one of the cycles of faith when that dark God reigned supreme and Kaug's God, Quar, was but a humble licker of boots.

Swimming through the murky salt water of the inland sea, Pukah pondered this story. He wondered if it was true, and if so, what dread deed Kaug had committed to merit this punishment. He also wondered, if Kaug was now so powerful, why he didn't move to a better neighborhood.

Despite the fact that he could breathe water as easily as he breathed air, Pukah felt smothered. He missed the blazing sun, the freedom of the vast, open land. Cutting through the sea with slashing strokes of his arms, the djinn deeply resented having to endure the cold and the wet and what was worse, the stares of goggle-eyed fish. Nasty creatures, fish. All slimy and scaly. No desert nomad ate them, considering them food fit only for city people who could get nothing better. Pukah's skin crawled in disgust as one of the stupid things bumbled into him. Pushing the fish aside, taking care to wipe the slime from his hand on a nearby sponge, Pukah peered through the water, searching for the cave entrance.

There it was, light streaming from within. Good, Kaug was at home.

Kaug's cave stood at the very bottom of the sea, hollowed

out of a cliff of black rock. The light from inside illuminated long, greenish-brown moss that hung from the cliff, drifting about in the water like the hair of a drowned woman. Coral rose in grotesque shapes from the seafloor, writhing and twisting in the constantly shifting shadows. Gigantic fish with small, deadly eyes and sleek bodies and rows of razor teeth flashed past, eying Pukah hungrily at first, then cursing the djinn for his ethereal flesh.

Pukah cursed them back just as heartily—for being ugly, if nothing else. The young djinn was not in the least overawed by his surroundings, beyond a certain repugnance and a desire to gulp a draft of fresh air. Confident in himself and his own intelligence and what he assumed was the correlating stupidity of his opponent, Pukah was actually looking forward to tossing a verbal sack over the head of his enemy.

If Pukah had talked to Sond or Fedj, he would have been on his guard. He would, in fact, have been quaking in his silken slippers, for it was far more likely that—in an encounter with the evil 'efreet—it would be Pukah who would end up in the bag and *not* a verbal one. But Pukah had not discussed his plan with either Sond or Fedj. Still determined to outdo both the other djinn and win Akhran's admiration for himself, Pukah had devised a second scheme to salvage his first. Like many others, djinn and human alike, Pukah mistook a hulking body as an indication of a hulking mind, visualizing himself as being capable of flitting about the older 'efreet's dull intelligence like a teasing bird fluttering about the head of the bear.

Alighting on the seafloor at the entrance to the cave, Pukah stared inside. He could barely see the great bulk of the 'efreet lurking about within, a dark, stoop-shouldered shape against the light that was cast by some kind of enthralled sea urchins, who floated or stood in mournful servitude about the 'efreet's dwelling.

"*Salaam aleikum,* O Mighty Kaug," called out Pukah respectfully. "May I enter your soggy home?"

The black shape paused in whatever it was doing, turning to glare out the entrance.

"Who calls?" it asked harshly.

"It is I, Pukah," said the young djinn humbly, immensely

pleased with his own playacting. "I have come to see Your
Magnificence on a matter of extreme importance."

"Very well, you may enter," Kaug said ungraciously,
turning his back upon his guest, who was, after all, a low-
ranking djinn of little importance.

Nettled at this rudeness, Pukah was doubly pleased to be
able to prick the bubble of the 'efreet's contentment. Glancing
in disgust at the moss-covered boulders that were apparently
meant for chairs, Pukah made his way to the rear of the
water-filled cave. He noticed, in passing, that Kaug had
acquired some particularly lovely objects from the world of
humans. A golden egg, encrusted with jewels, standing in the
center of a giant conch-shell table, attracted the djinn's particular
attention. He'd never seen anything so remarkable.

Firmly Pukah brought his mind back to the business at
hand, making a mental note to come back in half a century or
so, when the 'efreet wasn't home, and relieve him of these
beautiful, delicate objects that were obviously not suited to
the brute's taste.

"Wishing you joy, Great One." Pukah bowed, making a
fluttering gesture with his hand from his turban to his face.

"What do you want?" Kaug demanded, turning at last
from what he was doing to face the young djinn.

Pukah, sniffing, saw that the 'efreet had been bent over a
pot, cooking up something indescribably nasty-smelling. Fearing
he would be invited to stay for dinner, Pukah decided to
launch into his business without preliminary small talk.

"I have come, O Magnificent One, to bring a warning to
your master, the Revered and Holy Quar."

"Ah, yes?" said the 'efreet, staring at Pukah with slit-
eyes, their shrewdness concealed by the narrowing of the
lids. "And why this concern for my Master, little Pukah?"

Little Pukah! The young djinn's anger flared; it was all he
could do to remind himself that he was the wiser, the smarter
of the two, and that he could, therefore, afford to be
magnanimous and overlook this insult.

*But this glob of seaweed will pay for that remark before
I'm finished with him!*

"I come because I do not like to see any of the Gods
humbled and cast down from their high places in the eyes of
the humans, Great One. It gives the petty mortals delusions

of grandeur and makes life difficult for all of us, don't you agree?''

Did you understand that, Chowder Head, or must I use words of one syllable?

"Oh, I agree. Most assuredly,'' said Kaug, lowering his bulk into a chair made from a huge sponge. Thousands of tiny fish darted out from it when he sat down. He gazed up at Pukah comfortably, not inviting the djinn to be seated. "I take it that you foresee some sort of humiliation coming to my Master?''

"I do,'' remarked Pukah.

"Quar will be indebted to you for this timely warning then,'' said Kaug gravely. "Will you be so kind as to describe the nature of this impending disaster, that I may carry the description to my Master and we may prepare ourselves to thwart it?''

"I will tell you, but there is no way you can thwart it. I do this only to spare your Master the shameful end that he will undoubtedly meet should he attempt to fight his fate instead of accepting it.''

There, I guess I told him!

"If what you say is true, then my Master and I will exalt your name, O Wise Pukah. Will you be seated? Some refreshment?''

I'd sooner dine in the Realm of the Dead!

"No, thank you, O Great One, although it smells truly divine. My time is short. I must return to my mortal master, the Calif, who cannot do without me as you must know.''

"Mmmmm,'' murmured Kaug. "Then continue your most interesting conversation.''

"Let us be honest with each other, O Great One. It is no secret that your Holy Master, Quar, is intent upon taking over control of the heavens, and that my Holy Master, Akhran, is equally intent that he—Quar—shall not succeed in this venture. May we agree on that?''

"We can agree on anything you like, my charming friend,'' Kaug said expansively. "Are you certain you won't sit down? Partake of some boiled octopus?''

Boiled octopus! The salt has definitely eaten away at this fellow's brain.

Politely declining the 'efreet's invitation, the young djinn continued, "As you and your Master have no doubt heard, the tribes of Sheykh Jaafar al Widjar and Sheykh Majiid al Fakhar have been joined together, united through the marriage of the Calif, Khardan, and the flower of her tribe, Zohra." Pukah spread his hands, sighing in rapture. "Theirs is truly a marriage made in heaven! Now our blessings have been further increased—may Sul not be envious of our good fortune—by the uniting of yet a third tribe of the desert!"

Pukah's chest swelled with importance, particularly as he noted the 'efreet's grave expression grow considerably graver.

"A third tribe?" Kaug inquired. "And who would that be?"

"The mighty and powerful Sheykh Zeid al Saban!"

Although Pukah never knew it, he did actually manage to astonish Kaug. When one believes someone is meekly eating out of your hand, it is a shock to feel teeth sinking into your fingers. Sond had betrayed him! Kaug's eyes widened in what Pukah took to be fear but what was actually outrage. Then they narrowed, studying the young djinn shrewdly.

"Why are you telling us this?"

"Alas." Pukah heaved a sigh. "I have a soft spot in my heart for city people. The three tribes plan to come together and sweep into Kich, where they will depose the Imam and put him to the sword; take over the palace; and relieve the Amir of the troublesome burden of his many wives and concubines. Perhaps, if they feel so inclined, they will loot and burn the city. Perhaps not. It is whatever suits my master's fancy at the time. I cannot stomach the thought of such violence and bloodshed. And as I stated before, it would be a humiliating defeat for Quar."

"Indeed, it would," said Kaug slowly. "You are right, Pukah. There is a great tragedy in the making here." So there was, but not exactly the one Pukah had in mind. "What do you suggest that we do? What will it take to propitiate this hot-blooded Calif of yours so that he will leave us in peace?"

Smiling charmingly, Pukah appeared to consider the matter. "Khardan is, even now, upon his way to the city of Kich, ostensibly to sell horses to the Amir, but—in reality—to see how he is treated. If he is treated well, he will leave the city untouched, perhaps demanding only several hundred camels, a few sacks of gold and jewels, and a hundred bolts of silk as tribute. If he is in any way insulted or offended, he will level the place!'' Pukah grew quite fierce when expressing this last, making a slashing motion with his hand as of a sword sweeping down upon a bare neck.

Kaug kept his face impassive, though he burned within with such flame that it was a wonder the water surrounding him didn't begin to boil. He regarded Pukah with thoughtful attentiveness. ''If we treat your master as he—no doubt—deserves,'' the 'efreet said smoothly, ''what will he do in return?''

''The Calif will distribute the wealth among the three tribes, then disband them, each going back to the land of his fathers. Quar may keep his city intact and pursue the war to the south in Bas, in whose people we take no interest.''

''Magnanimous,'' said Kaug, nodding.

''That is the Calif,'' said Pukah. ''Magnanimous to a fault!'' The young djinn could tell by Kaug's face that the 'efreet was impressed, even awestruck. His plan was succeeding. Kaug would take news of this to Quar, who would back down and cease to threaten Akhran, who would allow the tribes of Jaafar and Majiid to go back to fighting each other, which would convince Zeid that they weren't going to fight him, which would send Zeid back to his home in the south—all of which would modestly be presented by Pukah as having been his doing and would gain for him the palace in the clouds and the djinniyeh in the bath.

Kaug, anxious to rid himself of his visitor so that he could speed this message to Quar, insisted that Pukah stay to dine, pressing his invitation by reaching into the pot and hauling out dinner by the tentacles.

Pukah, at this point, heard his master calling for him and retired from the 'efreet's premises with ungracious haste.

He had not been gone a second, however, before Kaug rose up out of the water. Able at last to release his rage, the 'efreet surged over the inland sea with the force of a hurricane, the waves foaming and leaping about him, the winds tearing at his flying hair.

In one hand he held lightning, which he hurled at the ground in anger. In the other he held a jeweled egg.

THE BOOK OF QUAR

Chapter 1

The sound of a gong, ringing three times, shivered through the incense-scented darkness. A man, asleep on a cotton pallet that was placed on the cold marble floor in a small alcove, wakened hastily at the sound. At first he stared at the small brass gong that sat upon the altar in disbelief, as if wondering whether he had truly heard its summons or if it had been part of his dream. The gong rang again, however, dispelling his doubts. Dressed only in a white cloth that he wore wrapped about his thin thighs, the man rose from the pallet and hastened across the polished marble floor.

Reaching the altar, which was made of pure gold fashioned in the shape of a ram's head, the man lit a thick beeswax candle, then prostrated himself flat before the altar, his arms outstretched above his head, his belly on the floor, his nose pressed against the marble. He had anointed himself with perfumed oil before retiring, and his brown skin glistened in the dim candlelight. His hair had never been cut—so to honor his God—and it covered his naked back like a black, shining blanket.

The slender body of the Imam quivered as it lay upon the floor, not from the cold or from fear but in eagerness. "It is I, Feisal, your unworthy servant. Speak to me, Quar, O Majesty of Heaven!"

"You have answered the summons swiftly."

Feisal raised his head, staring into the candle's flame. "Do I not—sleeping and waking—live within your Temple, Master, that I may be present to carry out your slightest wish?"

"So I have heard." Quar's voice came from the floor, the ceiling, the walls. It whispered around Feisal; he could feel its vibrations caress his body and he closed his eyes, almost overcome by the holy ecstasy. "I am pleased by this and by the good work you are doing in the city of Kich. Never before has a priest of mine been so zealous in bringing the unbeliever to salvation. I have my eye upon you, Feisal. If you continue to serve me in the future as well as you have served me up to the present, I think the great church of mine that shall one day encompass the world could have no better leader than yourself."

Feisal clenched his fists, a shudder of pleasure convulsed his body. "I am honored beyond telling, O King of All," the Imam whispered huskily. "I live only to serve you, to glorify your name. To bring that name to the lips of the *kafir* of this world is my greatest, my only desire."

"A worthy task, yet not an easy one," said the God. "Even now there comes to your city an unbeliever of the most heinous sort. A devout follower of the Ragged God, Akhran, he and his band of thieves ride to Kich, their intention: to spy upon the city. They plan to attack it and lead the people to the worship of their evil God."

"Akhran!" the Imam cried in a voice of horror such as might have shrieked out the name of a demon rising from the depths of Sul. Stunned by the shock, the Imam sat up, staring around the darkness that was alive with the presence of the God. The sweat that covered his oiled skin trickled down his bare breast. His ribs—all too visible from a lifetime of fasting—constricted, the stomach muscles tightened. "No! This cannot be!"

"Do not look upon this as a catastrophe. It is a blessing, proof that we are destined to win the holy war we fight, that we have learned of their perfidious scheme in time. Consult with the Amir, that you may devise together the best plan to deal with the unbelievers. And so that he knows you act by the command of Quar, you will find a gift from me upon the altar. Take it to the Amir's head wife, Yamina the Sorceress. She will know what use to make of it. My blessings upon you, faithful servant."

Hurling himself flat, Feisal pressed his body into the marble, hugging the floor as though he were physically clinging to his

God. Slowly the rapture within him died and he knew Quar was with him no longer. Drawing a deep, shivering breath, the Imam rose unsteadily to his feet, his gaze going immediately to the altar. A sob choked him. Reverently he reached out his shaking hand, the damp fingers closing around the gift of the God—a small, ebony horse.

Chapter 2

"What is the business of the Akar in the city of Kich?" demanded the gate watchman.

"The Akar bring horses to sell to the Amir," replied Khardan somewhat irritably, "as we have done yearly since before the mud of Kich's first dwellings was dry. Surely you know this, Gate Master. We have always been granted entrance to the city without question before. Why this change?"

"You will find many changes in Kich now, *kafir*," the Gate Master replied, giving Khardan and his men a smug, scornful glance. "For example, before you enter, I must ask that you turn over all magical charms and amulets to me. I will guard them well, you may be certain, and they will be returned to you when you leave. Any djinn you possess you will take with you to the temple, where they will be given up as a show of respect to the Imam of Quar."

"Amulets! Charms!" Khardan's horse, sensing his master's anger, shifted restlessly beneath him. "What do you take us for—women? Men of the Akar do not travel under the protection of such things!" Checking his horse, bringing it once more under his control, Khardan leaned over the saddle, speaking to the Gate Master eye-to-eye. "As for djinn, if I had one with me—which I do not—I would throw it into the Waters of the Kafir before I would give it to the Imam of Quar."

The Gate Master flushed in anger. His hand strayed to the stout cudgel he carried at his side, but he checked the impulse. He had his orders concerning these unbelievers, and he was bound to carry them out no matter how much he might dislike it. Swallowing his rage, he bowed coldly to Khardan and with a wave of his hand, indicated that the nomads could enter.

Leaving the herd of horses outside the walls under the care of several of his men, Khardan and the rest of his *spahis* entered the gate of the city of Kich.

An ancient city that had stood for two thousand years at least, Kich had changed little during that time. Centrally located, built in a pass between the Ganzi mountains to the south and the Ganga mountains to the north, Kich was one of the major trading cities of Tara-kan.

Although under the *suzerain* of the Emperor, Kich was—or had been during most of its history—an independent city-state. Ruled by the family of the Sultan for generations, Kich paid annual rich tribute to the Emperor, expecting in return to be left alone to pursue its favorite pastime—the amassing of wealth. Its people were primarily followers of the Goddess Mimrim—a gentle Goddess, a lover of beauty and money. For centuries the people of Kich led an easeful life. Then matters began to change. Their goddess had never been demanding in the matter of daily prayers and so forth—such solemn things tended to disrupt both business and pleasure. The people began to turn from Mimrim, putting more faith in money than in their goddess. Mimrim's power dwindled and she soon fell victim to Quar.

The people of Kich knew nothing of the war in heaven. They knew only that one day the Emperor's troops, carrying the ram's-head flag—symbol of Quar—swept down on them from the north. The gates fell, the Sultan's bodyguards—drunk as usual—were slaughtered. Kich was now under the Emperor's direct control, the spearhead of an army pointed directly at the throat of the rich cities of Bas to the south.

The city was turned into a military stronghold. Kich was ideally suited for this, being surrounded by a wall seven and a half miles long. Dotted with towers, punctured by loopholes for archers, the wall had eleven gates that were now closed day and night. A curfew was imposed upon its citizens. Movement of any type around the city after eleven at night was forbidden by strict edict, enforced by severe penalty. Cudgel-carrying night watchmen patrolled the streets, banging on the gates of every courtyard they passed, ostensibly in order to frighten away thieves. In reality they were making certain that no fires of rebellion smoldered behind closed doors.

There were, in addition to these watchmen who walked the street, those who walked the roofs of the bazaars. Covered to protect them from the sun, the boothlike shops were provided with skylights every hundred feet or so. The watchmen patrolled these roofs, beating a drum and peering down through the skylights to see if there was any suspicious movement below.

There was no rebellion brewing in Kich, however. Although the people resented these measures at first, they soon found compensation. Business increased threefold. The roads to the north, previously too dangerous to travel because of raiding *batir,* were now guarded by the Emperor's troops. Trade between Kich and the capital city of Khandar flourished. The people of Kich began to look upon their new God, Quar, with a friendly eye and did not begrudge him his tribute or his demands for strict obedience.

By day, the *souks* of Kich were crammed with people. The jabbering and shouting and yelling of their bargaining mingled with the cries of the sellers enticing would-be customers. Shrieking, shrill-voiced children darted about underfoot. The air rang with curses, cajolings, and the laments of beggars, all tangled up in a confusion of growling, snorting, bleating, barking animals.

Space within the city was at a premium, for no one was foolish enough to dwell outside the protective walls. The streets were cramped and narrow, laid out in a crazy labyrinth in which a stranger was instantly, invariably, and irrevocably lost. Windowless houses made of clay covered over with plaster piled up against each other like ships run aground, facing any and every direction along streets that wound around and in and over and upon themselves, sometimes ending inexplicably in a blank wall, sometimes wandering up or down stairs that appeared to have been carved out of the houses themselves.

Entering the city, Khardan glanced about uneasily. Before, he had always found the noise and the smells and the excitement exhilarating. Now, for some reason, he felt trapped, stifled.

Dismounting, the Calif motioned to one of the older men riding with the group.

"Saiyad, I don't like this talk of changes," Khardan said in a low voice. "Keep everyone together until my return and wait for me here."

Saiyad nodded. A cleared area inside the gate was used as a standing place for carts that had been brought into the city by traders. Seeing his men and their horses settled there and trusting to Saiyad to keep them out of trouble, Khardan and his younger brother Achmed turned their footsteps toward the Kasbah.

They did not have far to go. Combination palace and fortress, the Kasbah stood near the northern end of the city wall. The graceful minarets, tall spires, and cupola of the late Sultan's palace could be seen rising above its own protective wall that kept the palace aloof from the city. Made of crystalline quartz, its bulbous domes capped with gold, the palace itself shone like a jewel in the bright sunlight. Delicate, lacy latticework decorated the windows. The waving fronds of palms, visible above the walls, hinted at the pleasure gardens within.

It was Achmed's first visit to the city, and his eyes were wide with wonder.

"Watch where you are going," Khardan remonstrated, pulling his brother out of the path of a donkey, whose rider lashed out at them with his long stick. "No! Don't trouble yourself! Ignore him. He is beneath your notice. Look, look there."

Distracting his brother, who was glaring threateningly after the donkey rider, Khardan pointed to an octagonal-shaped stone building that stood on their left, opposite the walls of the Kasbah.

"That must be the new Temple they have built to Quar," Khardan said grimly, eyeing with disfavor the golden ram's head that gleamed over the entryway. "And over there"—he gestured to a tall minaret, the tallest in the city—"the Tower of Death."

"Why is it called that?"

"Thus do they deal with condemned criminals in Kich. The offender is bound hand and foot, then tied up in a sack. He is dragged to the top of the tower and hurled alive over its balcony, plummeting down into the street below. There his body lies unburied as a warning to all who would break the law.''

Achmed gazed at the Tower of Death in awe. ''Do you suppose we will get to see such a thing?''

Khardan shrugged, grinning. ''Who knows? We have all day.''

''Where do we go now? Don't we want to visit the palace?'' Achmed asked in some confusion, noting that they seemed to be walking away from it.

''We must enter through the front gate, and that stands across the city, on the other side of this wall. To get there, we must go through the bazaars.''

Achmed's eyes glistened with pleasure.

''Careful,'' added Khardan teasingly, ''you keep swiveling your head like that, you'll break your neck.''

''I want to see everything!'' Achmed protested. Gasping, he grasped Khardan by the arm and pointed. ''Who is that?''

Moving with sublime calm through the chaos and turmoil that swirled around him like seawater around an 'efreet was a man who outshone the sun. Dressed in bright yellow velvet robes—every inch of which was covered with golden embroidery and studded with jewels—the man wore loops of heavy gold chains about his neck. Silver and golden bracelets covered his arms; his fingers could not be seen for the rings that adorned them; his earlobes had been disfigured by the weight of the gold that hung from them. His skin was an olive color, his eyes slanted and painted with bright colors, outlined by stripes of black that ran from the lids to his ears. Behind him scurried a servant, holding a huge palmetto leaf over the man's head to shade him from the sun. Another servant walked beside him, cooling him with the constant breeze of a feathered fan.

''He is a moneylender, a follower of Kharmani, God of Wealth.''

''I thought everyone in Kich worshiped Quar.''

''Ah, even Quar dares not offend Kharmani. The economics of this city would come to a sudden halt if he did. Besides, the followers of Kharmani are few in number and probably not worth Quar's attention. They have no interest in wars or politics, being concerned only with money.''

Achmed gazed at the man, who strolled along through the crowd with grand aplomb, seeming to thrive on the glances of envy and lust that were cast at him.

"Do they ever ride alone into the desert, these followers of Kharmani?" Achmed whispered to his brother. "One of those bracelets would support a man and three wives—"

"Don't even think such thoughts!" Khardan returned hastily. "You will bring down the wrath of the God on all of us! None dare rob one of Kharmani's chosen! The last time I was in Kich I saw a follower of Benario, God of Thieves, who had tried to pick a moneylender's pocket. The moment he touched the man's purse, his hand froze to it, and he was forced to spend the rest of his life trudging after his victim, his hand always in the man's pocket, never able to free himself."

"Truly?" Achmed appeared skeptical.

"Truly!" Khardan averred, hiding his smile.

Achmed was gazing regretfully after the moneylender when a strange, clanking sound coming from the opposite direction drew the young man's attention. Looking over his shoulder, he tugged at the sleeve of his brother's tunic. "Who are those poor wretches?"

Khardan's lip curled in disgust. "Slaves being taken to the slave market." He pointed to a row of tents standing a few feet from them. "I detest that part of the city. The sight leaves a bad taste in my mouth for days. See the white palanquin being carried behind them? The slave trader. Those men riding around him are *goums*, his bodyguards."

"Where do the slaves come from?"

"These are from Ravanchai, most likely." Khardan glanced coolly at the line of men and boys chained together, shuffling through the streets, heads bowed. "The people of that land are farmers"—he spoke with disdain—"living in small tribes. A peaceful people, they are easy prey for the traders and their bands of *goums*, who periodically sweep down on them, round up the strong young men and the comely young women, and carry them off to sell here in Kich."

"Women? Where are they?" Achmed studied the line of slaves with renewed interest.

"Probably in that covered cart, right in front of the palanquin. See how closely guarded it is? You can't see them, of course.

They will be veiled. Only when they get to the selling block will the dealer remove their veils so that the buyers can see what they are purchasing."

Achmed licked his lips. "Perhaps with my share of the money I could—"

Khardan, with a quick, easy motion, cuffed the young man on the side of the face.

Putting his hand to his stinging cheek, his skin burning with embarrassment and pain, Achmed glared at his older brother. "What did you do that for?" he demanded, stopping in the middle of the street, where they were immediately surrounded by a group of half-naked children, begging for coins. "Father owns slaves. So do you—"

"Indentured servants!" Khardan rebuked him sternly. "Men who have sold themselves to pay back a debt. Such slavery is honorable, for they work to buy their freedom. This man" —making an angry gesture toward the palanquin—"trades in humans for personal gain. He captures them against their will. Such a thing is forbidden by Akhran. Besides"—Khardan smiled, cuffing his brother on the cheek again, this time playfully—"the women you could afford you wouldn't want, and those you would want you couldn't afford."

They started on their way again, the beggar children setting up a wail of protest.

"Here," said Khardan, turning down a street to his right, "are the bazaars."

Gaping in wonder, Achmed immediately forgot his pain. He had never imagined such wealth and splendor, such an array of goods for sale, such a confusion of noise. Walking along, he looked down street after street of covered booths surrounded by gesticulating buyers.

Sections of the bazaars and sometimes entire streets in Kich were dedicated to selling specific types of merchandise. Directly across from the palace wall, on the southern side, was the Street of Copper and Brass—dazzling to the eye as sunlight glinted off its wares. Next to that stood the Baker's Bazaar, the smells from this street causing Achmed's stomach to rumble loudly. Canting away at an angle from this row of covered booths was the Carpet Bazaar—a blur of fantastic colors and designs that made one dizzy to look into it.

"Down that street," Khardan said, indicating a branching

road that traveled farther south, "is the Silk and Shoe bazaar. We will buy presents for our mothers there."

"And something for your wife?" Achmed said slyly, to pay for the blow.

"Perhaps." Khardan flushed and fell silent.

This not having been the answer Achmed expected, the young man glanced at his brother in some astonishment. Khardan saw rose-colored silk in his mind's eye. Smelling again the fragrance of jasmine, he hurriedly continued pointing out the sights. "Beyond that is the Wood and Straw sellers, then the Street of the Dyers and Weavers, the Street of the Rope-makers, the Potter's Bazaar, the Goldsmith's and Jeweler's, the Moneylenders, the Tobacco and Pipe dealers, and the Teahouses and the *arwat*—the rest-houses. Down that direction are streets where you may purchase magical charms and amulets, salt, sweetmeats, furs, ironware, and weapons."

"Weapons!" Achmed's eyes shone. His father had promised him a sword with a share of the money. He peered down the crowded street in a vain effort to catch a glimpse of shining steel. "We will go there first."

"Undoubtedly. Watch out." Khardan caught his brother just as the young man was about to stumble into a huge pool of water standing between the street and the Kasbah wall.

"What is that?"

"A *hauz*. There are many such artificial ponds in the city. The water comes from the mountains, carried by *ariqs*. It has many uses. . . ." Khardan nudged Achmed, pointing out a man washing camel dung from his hands in the pool while a veiled woman filled a drinking jug not half a yard away. "Thirsty?"

"Not now!"

"City dwellers," Khardan said in the same tone in which he might have said "jackals." Achmed nodded, his young face solemn with newly acquired wisdom.

Mindful of the importance of their errand and knowing that the Amir's audience hours lasted only during the cool of the morning, Khardan hurried his brother along, keeping him from falling into the clutches of the vendors, who soon would have relieved the young man of the ten silver *tumans* he had brought with him. Seeing that the sun was nearing its zenith, the brothers left the bazaars and made their way to the great entrance of the Kasbah.

Two stalwart towers of stone flanked the massive wooden doors that stood open beneath an arched passage. Above the door, on the second story between the towers, ran a colonnaded porch. A third story, open to the air, was atop that. From the roof of this third story, directly above the door, hung a gigantic sword.

Suspended by strong iron chains, the magnificent sword was the symbol of the Amir, a powerful symbol that reminded all who looked upon it that they were under his iron rule. The sword was so large and so heavy that it had taken a veritable army of men and seven elephants to move it over the mountains from the capital city of Khandar.

The day the sword arrived in Kich had been a day of ceremony in the city, marking the ascension of the Amir to the throne. The 'efreet Kaug had hung the sword himself, the immortal's hands easily lifting the heavy weapon from the huge cart on which it traveled. The Imam blessed the sword, prophesying that it would hang there to glorify the new order of Quar, whose reign would last until the sun, the moon, and the stars fell from the skies. The people of Kich had, needless to say, been impressed.

Khardan was not. Staring grimly at the sword suspended above his head, he remembered regretfully how things had been in the past.

A solid-silver crescent moon had hung there in the days of the Sultan—a simple, pleasure-loving man who paid his annual tribute to the Emperor at Khandar and then promptly did his best to forget about politics for another year. There had been no questions asked at the gate under the Sultan's rule, no nonsense about bringing djinn to the Temple of the Imam. The guards in the tower that stood to the right of the great gate had languished half-asleep in the afternoon sun. There had been no curfew. Every night the city's men gathered around the *hauz* outside the great gate, coming there to relax, share the day's gossip in whispers, or listen to storytellers recalling days gone by. The soldiers in the barracks, located in the inner court to the gate's left, had lounged about, gambling, eyeing the veiled women who came to the *hauz*, or indulging in swordplay.

Now the guards in the tower were alert, scrutinizing all who entered. People still came to the *hauz* for water, but they did not linger long under the baleful gaze of the guards.

The wooden doors stood open, but there were guards here, too, who insolently questioned Khardan about everything from the lineage of his horses to his own—at which point the Calif nearly forgot himself. Only the remonstrating hand of his younger brother on his arm made Khardan—literally— bite his tongue to keep back the angry words.

Finally the guards ungraciously let them pass. They entered the cool shadows of the Kasbah; Achmed stumbled over the paving stones, his head craned at a painful angle to view the gigantic sword. Khardan strode beneath it without a glance, his face grim and stern and dark with suppressed anger.

The price of horses was going up.

Chapter 3

"The nomad and his men have arrived in the city, O King."

"Very well. Inform the Imam."

Bowing low, hands folded together, the servant retired, backing out of the audience room with silent steps. The Amir glanced at the Captain of the Guard, who lingered near the throne and who was not only second-in-command but chief Wazir. Civilian ministers had held this exalted position in the city of Kich in the past, but Kich was under military rule now; the Amir considered himself a general first and a reluctant king second.

Amir Abul Qasim Qannadi did not trust civilians. The last Wazir met the same fate as did his Sultan, having the distinct honor to be hurled over the cliff while the screams of his ruler could still be heard echoing among the jagged rocks below. When Qannadi took control of the city, the Amir replaced all civilian personnel with his own military men. A practical soldier, the Amir would have killed the minor officials as well, or at the very least thrown them into the dungeons. But the Imam, Feisal, as spiritual leader, demurred over this unnecessary bloodshed.

At Feisal's insistence the minor officials were given the choice of serving Quar in this life or serving their former God in death. Needless to say, one and all experienced a sudden religious transformation and were allowed to live, though dismissed from their posts. A few of those known to have been most loyal to the Sultan had later met with unfortunate accidents—all of them being waylaid and beaten to death by, so it was presumed, followers of Benario. Eyewitness reports that the followers of Benario were wearing the uniform of the Amir beneath their black cloaks were instantly discounted.

The Amir appeared grave when the families of these men protested. Qannadi expressed his regret, denied the rumors, and told them to thank Quar that Kich was now in the hands of someone who could restore law and order and make it safe for decent citizens. The Imam appeared graver still and comforted the relatives with the thought that their late fathers or husbands or brothers had found the true faith before departing this world.

What words Feisal—the Imam, and Qannadi—the Amir, exchanged over this matter in private were not known, but sharp-eyed court observers remarked that the next day the Amir's face was white with fury and he avoided the Temple, while the Imam appeared long-suffering and martyred. The quarrel between the two was patched up, according to whispers, by Qannadi's head wife, Yamina—a sorceress of great skill and power, who was also extremely religious and devout.

This was mere rumor and speculation. What was known for certain was that, following this incident, the Amir handed over the running of the city to the Imam and Yamina.

It turned out to be a providential arrangement for all concerned. The Amir, who detested the petty bureaucratic day-to-day affairs of state, was able to devote his entire attention to extending the war to the south. The Imam was able to exert the God's influence over the daily lives of the people, thus coming a step nearer his dream of establishing a city devoted to spreading the glory of Quar. As for the Amir's wife Yamina, it brought her two things she desired most: power and daily contact with the Imam.

When the Imam received word from his God that the *kafir* who dwelt in the Pagrah desert were making warlike, threatening gestures, the priest took the matter straight to the Amir.

The Imam expected Qannadi's reaction to this threat to be the same as his. Feisal's eyes shone with the scorching flame of holy zeal as the two walked together in the pleasure garden.

''We shall sweep down on them with our armies and show

them the might of Quar. They will fall to their knees in worship as did the people of Kich!''

"Who? The Desert Dwellers?" Grinning, the Amir scratched his graying black beard with a small forked twig he had broken off an ornamental lemon tree. "A few bloody and broken bodies won't cause them to convert. They may not appear to be devout followers of their Ragtag God, but I'll wager you could throw each and every Akar off the highest cliff in the world and not a one would even spit in Quar's direction.''

The Imam, shocked by such crude talk, reminded himself that the Amir, after all, was a soldier.

"Forgive my blunt tongue, but I think you underestimate the power of *Hazrat* Quar, O King," Feisal rebuked. "What's more, you overestimate the power this Wandering God exerts on his people. After all, what has he done for them? They live in the most appallingly desolate place in the known world. They are forced to roam the land in search of water and food, their lives are a constant struggle for survival. They are wild, uneducated, uncivilized, barely classifying as human beings at all. If we brought them into the city—"

"—They would rise up in the night and slit your throat," said the Amir. Plucking an orange off a tree and biting through the flesh with his strong teeth, he spit the peel out onto the walkway, to the disgust of several palace eunuchs.

"You border on sacrilege!" The Imam spoke in a low voice, breathing heavily.

Qannadi, glancing at the black eyes burning in the priest's gaunt face, suddenly deemed it wise to end the discussion. Stating that he would consider the matter from a militarily standpoint and let the Imam know of his decision, he abruptly turned on his heel and left the garden.

Feisal, fuming, returned to his Temple.

The next day Qannadi called the Imam to the *divan*—the audience chamber—and proposed a plan for dealing with the upstart Calif of the Akar. Feisal listened to the plan and expressed his concerns. He did not like it. The Amir had not expected he would. But Qannadi had sound reasons—militarily if not spiritual—for pursuing a more cautious course of action than the one the Imam proposed.

Feisal continued to press his arguments daily, hoping to

persuade Qannadi to change his mind—all without result. Still the priest persisted, even to the last moment. Upon receiving word that Khardan was on his way to the palace, the Imam hurriedly left the Temple, and entering the Kasbah by a secret, subterranean passage built beneath the street, he hastened to Qannadi, hoping to make one final appeal.

"I understand that the nomad Khardan is on his way here, O King," Feisal said, approaching the rosewood throne where Qannadi sat dictating to a scribe a letter to the Emperor.

"We will conclude after luncheon." The Amir dismissed the scribe, who bowed and left the *divan*. "Yes, he is on his way. The guards have orders to let him pass, after a certain amount of harassment. My plans are in readiness. I presume"— Qannadi regarded the Imam with a cool glance from beneath white-streaked black brows—"that you still do not approve?"

Abul Qasim Qannadi was in his early fifties, tall and stalwart, with a face tanned by sun, burned by wind, lashed by rain. The Amir kept himself in prime physical condition, riding his war-horse daily and taking strenuous exercise with his officers and men. He detested a "soft" life, and his disgust at the excesses and luxuries indulged in by the late Sultan had been so great that—if he'd had his way—the palace would soon have been altered to resemble a barracks.

Fortunately the Amir's wives—led by Yamina—intervened. The silken tapestries remained in place, the ornately carved rosewood throne had not been hacked to kindling, the delicate vases were not crushed like eggshells. After much arguing, pouting, and sulking, Yamina, who—as head wife—could see to it that her husband's nights were extremely cold and lonesome, even persuaded the Amir to replace his comfortable military uniform with the silken, embroidered caftans of a ruler. He wore them only around the palace, however, never appearing in them before his troops if he could help it.

Bluff, sharp-tongued, quick to mete out discipline, Qannadi was the terror of the servants and the palace eunuchs, who had previously led an idyllic existence under the pleasure-loving Sultan and who now fled to Yamina for comfort and protection.

A djinn might have flown the world round and not found another human who contrasted more sharply with Qannadi than the Imam. In his middle twenties, yet already a power in the church, Feisal was a small-boned man whom the powerful Qannadi might have tucked under one arm and carried around like a child. But there was that about the Imam which made people, including the crusty old general, leery of crossing him. No one truly felt comfortable around Feisal. Qannadi often wondered, in fact, if the rumors were true that the Emperor had given the priest control of the church in Kich simply to be rid of him.

It was the presence of the God in the Imam that made other mortals tremble before him. Feisal was a handsome man. His liquid, almond-shaped eyes were set in a fine-boned face. The lips of the mouth were sensuous. His long-fingered hands, with their gentle touch, seemed made for the pleasures to be found behind silken, perfumed curtains. Yamina was not the only one of the palace's wives and concubines to discover their interest in their religion renewed when the Imam took over as head of the church. But the women sighed for him in vain. The only passion that burned in the almond eyes was a holy one; the lips pressed their kisses never on warm flesh but only upon the cold and sacred altar of Quar. The Imam was devoted body and soul to his God, and it was this, Qannadi recognized, that made the priest dangerous.

Though the Amir knew his plan for dealing with the nomads was militarily sound and he had no intention of renouncing it, he could still not help but glance at the priest out of the corner of his eye. Seeing the thin face become too smooth, that look of martyred tolerance in the almond eyes, Qannadi's own expression hardened stubbornly.

"Well?" he prompted, irritated at the Imam's silence. "You disapprove?"

"It is not I who disapprove, O King," the Imam said softly, "but our God. I repeat my suggestion that you should act now to stop the unbelievers before they become too powerful."

"Bah!" Qannadi snorted. "Far be it from me to offend Quar, Imam, but he seeks only more followers. I have a war to fight—"

"So does Quar, O King," interrupted the Imam with unusual spirit.

"Yes, I know all about this war in heaven," Qannadi replied wryly. "And when Quar has to worry about His lines of supply being severed, His right flank being menaced by these hotheaded nomads, then I'll listen to His ideas on military strategy. As for the notion of calling up my troops from the south, marching them back five hundred miles, and sending them out in the desert chasing after an enemy that will have scattered to the four winds once they get there, it's ludicrous!''

The Amir's graying brows bristled. Closing over the beaked nose, they gave him the formidable glare of a fierce old bird of prey.

"Pull back and we give the southern cities time to strengthen. No, I will not be drawn into fighting a war on two fronts. I do not believe it necessary, for one thing. The idea that these tribes have united! Hah!''

"But our source—''

"A djinn!'' Qannadi scoffed. "The immortals work always for their own ends and be damned to either man or God!''

Seeing, from the swift flare of the almond eyes and the sudden pallor of the Imam's smooth skin that he had ridden near a deadly quagmire, the Amir retreated back to firmer ground, neatly turning his enemy's own weapon against him.

"Look here, Feisal—Quar himself professes as much. The wisest thing the God ever did was to order you to remove the djinn from the world. This is a military matter, Imam. Allow me to handle it my own way. Or''—he added smoothly— "will you be the one to tell the Emperor that his war to gain control of the rich cities of Bas has been halted to chase after nomads who will send their tribute to him in the form of horse manure?''

The Imam said nothing. There was nothing he could say. Feisal knew little of military matters, but even he could see that turning the spear point away from the necks of the south would give them a chance to draw breath and perhaps even allow them time to find the courage they seemed to have, for the moment, mislaid. Though devoted to his God, Feisal was not a fanatical fool. The Emperor was known as Quar's Chosen for good reason, possessing a power that even a priest dare not cross or thwart.

After a moment's thought Feisal bowed. "You have persuaded me, O King. What is it that I may do to assist you in your plan?''

The Amir wisely refrained from smiling. "Go to Yamina. Make certain all is in readiness. Then return to me here. I assume you want a chance to try to talk the *kafir* into transferring his faith to Quar?"

"Assuredly."

The Amir shrugged. "I tell you again, you waste your breath. Steel is the only language these nomads speak."

Feisal bowed again. "Perhaps, O King, because that is the only language they have ever heard spoken."

Chapter 4

Khardan and Achmed crossed the courtyard of the Kasbah, heading for the palace. To their right, standing just inside the great entryway, were the soldiers' barracks. There appeared to be an unusual amount of activity among the soldiers, activity that Khardan put down to preparations for the war in Bas. The uniformed men—dressed in their stiff-collared, waist-length red coats adorned on the back with the gold ram's head—stared at the nomads, dressed in their long, flowing black robes. There was enmity in the stares, but there was respect as well. The reputation of the nomads as a superb fighting force was well-known and well-deserved. Legend had it that an outpost in Bas had surrendered without a blow on just hearing the rumor that the tribes of Pagrah were going to sweep down upon them.

Blissfully unaware of Pukah's wild tale, completely ignorant of the fact that they were—according to the djinn—here as spies, Khardan and Achmed noticed the soldiers' dark gazes but simply accepted them as a natural compliment to their fighting prowess.

"Shut your mouth; you'll swallow a fly." The Calif nudged his younger brother in the ribs as they approached the palace. "It's only a building, after all, built by men. Who are we to be impressed with such human creations? We have seen the wonders of Akhran."

Having lived with the sandy wonders of Akhran all of his seventeen years, and never having seen anything so splendid and beautiful as the palace with its golden domes and shimmering lacework and graceful minarets glittering in the sun, Achmed felt rather resentfully that he had a right to be impressed. Nevertheless, his respect and love for his elder brother was such that he immediately closed his gaping mouth and hardened his features, attempting to appear bored. Besides, he had his dignity to uphold among these soldiers, and he wished devoutly that he had a sword hanging at his side as Khardan wore his.

Entering the palace, under the scrutiny of more guards, Khardan was surprised to find the vast waiting room, which had—in the days of the Sultan—been packed with supplicants and grandees and ministers, now virtually empty. Their boots made a hollow sound, echoing beneath the ceiling whose wood beams were made of juniper and rosewood and whose intricate designs supposedly took a team of artisans thirty years to carve. Struck dumb by the beauty of the marvelous ceiling, the gorgeous tapestries lining the walls, the fantastic-patterned tiled floor beneath his feet, Achmed came to a complete standstill, staring about him in wonder.

"I like this less and less!" Khardan muttered, catching hold of his dazed brother and thrusting him forward. A silk-caftaned servant, gliding toward him, inquired his name and his business. Acting on Khardan's reply that he was expected, the servant led the nomads to an antechamber outside the *divan*. Khardan immediately removed sword and dagger, handing both weapons to a captain of the guard. Achmed turned over his dagger, then spread his robes to show that he wore no sword. The brothers started toward the door that led to the audience room when the captain stopped them.

"Wait. You may not proceed yet."

"Why not?" Khardan looked at the man in astonishment. "I have given you my weapons."

"You have not been searched." The captain made a gesture. Turning, Khardan saw a eunuch step toward him.

"What is the meaning of this?" Khardan demanded angrily. "I am Calif of my people! You have my word of honor that my brother and I carry no weapons!"

"It is not the Amir's intention to insult the Calif of the Desert," the captain said with a sneer, "but it is now the law of Quar, as given to us through his most holy Imam, that the persons of all *kafir* are to be searched before being admitted into the presence of the Amir."

This is it, Achmed thought, tensing. Khardan won't stand for much more. And at first it seemed that this was Khardan's thought as well. His face pale with fury, the Calif fixed the eunuch with a stare so ferocious that the huge, flabby man hesitated, looking to the captain for counsel. The captain snapped his fingers. At this signal two guards, who had been standing on either side of the entrance to the *divan*, their sabers at their sides, drew the flashing blades and held them crossed before the door.

Khardan's inner mental battle was visible to Achmed. The Calif longed to walk from the place and kick the dust from his boots in the faces of everyone present, but his people needed the money and the goods it would buy to survive another year. It was they who would pay for any prideful act, no matter how satisfying. Quivering with anger, Khardan submitted to the search that was offensive and humiliating in the extreme, the eunuch's fat fingers, thrust inside the Calif's robe, poking and prodding, left no part of Khardan's body untouched.

Achmed, nearly dying of shame, was searched as well. Finding no hidden weapons, the eunuch nodded to the captain.

"Now may we enter?" Khardan demanded, his voice taut.

"When you are wanted, *kafir*, not before," replied the captain coolly, sitting at a desk and calmly preparing to eat his lunch—an act of extreme rudeness to the nomads, who never ate in anyone's presence without offering food first to the guest.

"And when will that be?" Khardan growled.

The guard shrugged. "Today, if you are lucky. Next week, if you are not."

Seeing Khardan's face flush darkly, Achmed cringed, waiting for the storm. But the Calif mastered his rage. Turning his back on the captain, folding his arms across his chest, Khardan strode over to examine other weapons that had been confiscated from those entering the Amir's presence. The ominous fact that the weapons were here, whereas their owners were not, might have spoken much to Khardan, had he been attentive. But in reality he wasn't even seeing the weapons. Fists clenched beneath his robes, he stared blindly into a blood-red tide of rage that was washing over him.

"Never again," he muttered, his lips moving in a silent vow. "As Akhran is my witness, never again!"

A servant entered from the *divan*. "The Amir will see the *kafir* Khardan, who calls himself Calif."

"Ah, you are lucky, it seems," the captain said, munching on a crusty hunk of bread.

The guards at the door stepped back, their blades held once more at their sides.

"I *am* the Calif. I have been Calif longer than this upstart has been Amir." Khardan glowered at the silk-clad, mincing servant, who raised his feathery eyebrows and looked down his long nose in disapproval of this speech.

"Go straight ahead," the servant said coldly, standing as far back as possible to permit the nomads to walk past.

His long robes sweeping around him, Khardan entered the *divan*. Achmed, following, noted that the servant's nose wrinkled at the strong smell of horse that clung to them both. Head held high, Achmed deliberately brushed up against the elegant servant. Glancing back behind him to enjoy the man's reaction of disgust, Achmed saw something else.

The captain, lunch forgotten, had risen from the table and was loosening his sword in his belt. Gesturing, he gave an order in a low voice. The doors they had entered, doors that led to the outside of the Kasbah, swung shut on silent hinges. Two more guards, swords drawn, slipped quietly into the room and took up positions before the barred doors.

Achmed reached out for his brother. Their way out of the palace had been sealed off.

Chapter 5

"Not now, Achmed!" Khardan snapped nervously, brushing away his younger brother's hand that was urgently tugging at the sleeve of his robe. "Do as I told you. Bow when I bow and keep your mouth shut."

Crossing the colorful mosaic-tiled floor of the *divan*, Khardan glanced about the audience chamber, noting a great many changes since the Sultan's time. In bygone days the divan would have been filled with people standing about, discussing their dogs or their falcons or the latest court gossip, waiting for the Sultan's eye to fall upon them that they might curry his favor. Poorer supplicants, herded into a corner, would have waited humbly to present cases as important as a murdered relative or as trivial as a dispute over the rights to a stall in the bazaar. Numerous servants, scurrying here and there on bare feet, kept all in order.

The *divan* today, by contrast, was empty.

"On entering the front, always look to the back." Thus goes the old saying. Acting with the instincts of a seasoned warrior, Khardan quickly studied the chamber that he had not visited in over a year. Closed on three sides, the high-ceilinged, rectangular-shaped room was open on a fourth—a columned balcony looked out over the beautiful pleasure garden below. Khardan glanced longingly in that direction without even realizing that he did so. He could see the tops of ornamental trees at a level with the balcony. A breeze scented with the perfume of exotic flowers drifted through the *divan*, sunlight streamed in between the columns. Huge wooden partitions, standing near the walls, could be pulled across the floor to seal shut the *divan* when the weather was inclement or if the palace was under attack.

Doors led from the chamber to various other parts of the palace, including the Amir's private living quarters. The Amir's bodyguards stood at these, two more flanked his throne. Khardan glanced at them without interest. Now that he had familiarized himself with the room, his attention turned upon the man—Abul Qasim Qannadi, the Amir of Kich.

Two men stood near the rosewood throne that had been the Sultan's. Khardan examined each closely, and had no trouble determining which was the Amir—the tall man with the straight, broad shoulders, who moved awkwardly in the richly embroidered silken caftan. Hearing Khardan approach, the Amir gathered the long sweeping folds of silk in his hand and stiffly climbed the stairs leading up to the rosewood throne. Qannadi grimaced as he sat down, he obviously found the throne uncomfortable. Khardan—noting the deeply tanned, weathered face—guessed that this was a man who would be much more at home seated in a saddle. The Calif felt his anger slip away from him; here was a man he could understand. Unfortunately it did not occur to Khardan that here was a man he should fear.

The other man moved to stand beside the throne. Noting he was a priest by the plain white robes that hung straight from the shoulders, Khardan barely spared him a glance. The Calif wondered idly what interest a priest could have in the selling of horses, but supposed only that perhaps he and the Amir had been conferring and that the arrival of Khardan had interrupted their talk.

Reaching the foot of the throne, the Calif made the formal *salaam*, bowing, his hand moving in the graceful gesture from forehead to breast as he had been accustomed to performing before the Sultan. Watching out of the corner of his eye in order to make certain Achmed was imitating him and doing nothing to disgrace them both, Khardan missed the shocked expression that crossed the Imam's face and the man's furious hand gesture. Straightening, the Calif was considerably surprised to find an armed guard stepping between him and the Amir.

"What do you mean by this lack of respect, *kafir*?" the guard said. "On your knees to the representative of the Emperor—Quar's Chosen, the Light of the World."

Khardan's temper flared. "I am Calif of my people! I go on my knees to no one, not to the Emperor himself were he here!"

"Worm!" The guard raised his sword threateningly. "You would be on your belly if the Emperor were here!"

Khardan's hand went for his weapon, only to close over empty air. Frustrated, his face flushing dark, he took a step toward the guard as if he might challenge him bare-handed, but a deep voice came from the throne.

"Leave him be, Captain. He is, after all, a prince."

Khardan, his blood throbbing in his ears, did not hear the subtle mockery in the man's voice. Achmed did, and his heart was in his throat. The strange, chill emptiness of this huge chamber made him uncomfortable; he distrusted the man on the throne with his cold, impassive expression. But it was the priest with his thin, wasted face that made the hair on the young man's neck prickle and rise as does that of an animal who senses danger yet cannot find the source. Achmed wanted to look anywhere else in the chamber except into those burning eyes that seemed to see nothing of any consequence in this world, only in the next. But he couldn't. The almond eyes caught him and held him fast, a prisoner of the Imam's more surely than if the priest had bound the young man in chains. Frightened, ashamed of his fear, Achmed was helpless to speak it. He could do nothing except obey his brother's instructions and pray that they escaped this terrible place alive.

"Let me introduce myself," the Amir was saying. "I am Abul Qasim Qannadi, General of the Imperial Army and now Amir of Kich. This"—he gestured to the priest—"is the Imam."

The priest did not move but remained staring at Khardan, the holy fire rising in him, burning hotter and hotter. Khardan, glancing at the priest, was touched by the flame. He found that, like his brother, he could not easily withdraw his gaze.

"I . . . trust we can conclude our business swiftly, O King." Khardan appeared somewhat disconcerted. "My men wait for me near the Temple." Wrenching his gaze from the

Imam's hold with what seemed an almost physical effort, he glanced uncomfortably about the chamber. "I do not feel at ease within walls."

Beckoning to a scribe, who came forward with a sheaf of papers, the Amir referred to them briefly, then looked back at Khardan. "You come here to offer your tribe's horses for sale as you have done annually according to the records," said the Amir, his dark eyes regarding the Calif coolly.

"That is true, O King."

"Did you not know that much has changed since your last visit?"

"Some things never change, O King. One of these is an army's need for good horses. And ours"—Khardan lifted his head proudly—"are the best in the world."

"So it does not disturb you to sell your horses to enemies of the late Sultan?"

"The Sultan was not my friend. He was not my enemy. His enemies, therefore, are neither my friends nor my enemies. We did business together, O King," said Khardan succinctly. "That is all."

The Amir raised an eyebrow; whether he was startled at the answer or impressed with it was impossible to tell. The impassive face was unreadable. "What price do you ask?"

"Forty silver *tumans* a head, O King."

The Amir referred again to the paper. The scribe, whispering something, pointed to a row of what looked to Khardan to be bird tracks on the sheet.

"That is higher than last year," the Amir said.

"As you said," remarked Khardan coolly with a glance toward the antechamber where he had been searched, "some things have changed."

The Amir actually smiled—a smile that drove one corner of his mouth deeper into his beard—and went back to studying the paper, his hand stroking his chin meditatively. Khardan remained standing before him, arms folded across his chest, looking anywhere but at the Imam. Achmed, unnoticed and forgotten, glanced continually at their exit that was an exit no longer and wished himself back in the desert.

"May I ask you a question, Calif?" The Imam's voice flicked like a flame. Khardan started, as though it had burned his skin. Glancing at the Amir and seeing him apparently absorbed in studying the figures on last year's sale of the horses, Khardan—his eyes dark and shadowed—reluctantly faced the priest.

"You are a *kafir,* an unbeliever, is that not true?"

"No, it is not true, Holy One. My God and the God of my people is Akhran the Wanderer. Our belief in him is strong."

"Yet thankless, is it not, Calif? I mean"—the Imam spread his long-fingered hands—"what does he do for you, this Wandering God? You dwell in the cruelest of lands, where every drop of water is counted as precious as a jewel, where the sun's heat can boil the blood, where blinding storms of sand flay the flesh from the bone. Your people are poor, forced to live in tents and to roam from place to place to find food and water. The meanest beggar in our streets has at least a roof over his head and food to eat. You are uneducated, neither you nor your children"—his gaze went to Achmed, who immediately looked somewhere else—"can read or write. Your lives are unproductive. You are born, you live, you die. This God of yours does nothing for you!"

"We are free."

"Free?" The Imam appeared puzzled.

Achmed noticed that the Amir, though seemingly involved in reading the document, was listening and watching intently out of the corner of his eye.

"We are under the rule of no man. We follow no one's laws but our own. We move freely as the sun, taking what we need from the land. We work for ourselves. Our sweat is not another's profit. We cannot read"—he gestured toward the Amir's document—"scratches drawn on paper. But why should we? What need is there?"

"Surely there is need to read the sacred writings of your God!"

Khardan shook his head. "The text of our God is written on the wind. We hear his voice singing in the dunes. We see his words in the stars that guide our way through the land. Our sacred credo soars on the wings of a hawk, it beats in the hooves of our horses. We look into the eyes of our wives and see it there. We hear it in the cry of every newborn child. To capture that and commit it to the bondage of paper would be an evil thing. Our God forbids it."

"So"—the Imam smiled—"your God *does* give you commands and you obey them?"

"Yes."

"Then you are not truly free."

"We are free to disobey," remarked Khardan, shrugging.

"And what is the punishment for disobedience?"

"Death."

"And what is the reward for leading a virtuous life?"

"Death."

A noise came from the Amir, a sort of low chuckling sound that immediately became a clearing of the throat when the Imam cast him an irritated glance. Qannadi turned his gaze back on Khardan, who was becoming increasingly impatient at what he considered childish ramblings. Adults did not waste their time speaking or thinking of such obvious things. Achmed saw the flickering fire in the priest's eyes and wished his brother were taking this more seriously.

"So you are free to lead a harsh life and die a cruel death. These are the gifts of this God of yours?"

"The life we live is our own. We do not ask you to live it or understand it. As for death, it comes to all, unless you have discovered some way for city walls to shut it out."

"Those who have been blind from birth, who walk in perpetual darkness, are said not to be able to comprehend light, having never seen it." The Imam's voice was gentle. "One day your eyes will be opened to the light. You will walk in Quar's radiance and you will realize how blind you have been. You will leave off your aimless wandering and come here to the city to glory in the gifts of Quar to his people and to show your thankfulness to him by leading productive, useful lives."

Khardan cast a glance at his younger brother, rolling his eyes significantly. Among the nomads the insane are well treated, for all know that they have seen the face of the God. One did not listen to their ravings, however. The Calif pointedly turned his attention back to the Amir.

Clearing his throat again, Qannadi handed the paper to the scribe, dismissing the man with a wave of his hand.

"I am pleased to hear your people have such a philosophical outlook, Calif." The Amir regarded Khardan with cold eyes.

"For a harsh life is about to become harsher. We have no need for your horses."

"What?" Khardan stared at the Amir in amazement.

"We have no need of your horses now, nor is it likely that we ever will in the future. You must return to your people empty-handed. And much as you despise the city, it does supply you with certain necessities of life without which you may find it difficult to survive. That is," he added with heavy irony, "unless your God has seen fit to rain down rice and wheat from the heavens."

"Do not take me for some rug merchant, O King," Khardan said grimly. "Do not think you can make me run after you, offering you a lower price because you first turn away. You may go to a hundred rug merchants, but you will find only one man who sells the horses you need to carry you to victory. Animals bred to war who will not shy at the smell of blood. Animals who prick their ears to the call of the trumpet, who lunge forward into the heart of the battle. Animals descended from the horse of the God! Nowhere—nowhere on this world—will you find such horses!"

"Ah, but you see, Calif, we are no longer limited to this world," the Amir said. "Send for my wife," he instructed a servant, who bowed and ran to do his bidding.

"Perhaps this is the light of which you spoke, Imam," continued the Amir conversationally in the tense silence that followed. "Perhaps hunger will open their eyes and lead them to the city walls they despise."

"Quar be praised if this is so," the Imam said earnestly. "It will be the saving of their bodies, the salvation of their souls."

Khardan, scowling, said nothing but glowered at them both. He had taken an involuntary step backward on hearing the Amir send for his wife. Zeid's words came back to him. The Amir's head wife—*reputedly a sorceress of great power.* Khardan did not fear magic, considering it a woman's province, suitable for healing the sick and calming horses during a storm. But—as something he could not control—he did not trust it. He had heard stories of the powers of the ancients, stories of the power to be found in the *seraglios* of the city dwellers. He had scoffed at these, despising men who let their women become too strong in this arcane art. Looking at the powerful Qannadi, however, it occurred to Khardan—rather late—that he may have misjudged the matter.

A woman entered the *divan*. She was clothed in a *chador* of black silk, embroidered with threads of spun gold that had been stitched to form dots like small suns over the surface of the fabric. Though her figure was completely hidden, the woman moved with a grace that spoke of the beauty and symmetry of her form. A black veil rimmed in gold covered her face and head, leaving only one eye visible. Outlined in kohl, that one staring eye regarded Khardan boldly, penetrating him, as though the focus of her two eyes had been combined and were thus made stronger in just one.

"Yamina, show this *kafir* the gift of Quar to his people," ordered the Amir.

Bowing before her husband, her hands pressed together to her forehead, Yamina turned to face Khardan, who stared at her coldly; the ever-shifting dunes revealed more expression than his face.

Slipping jeweled fingers into the filmy folds of the *chador*, Yamina withdrew an object. Placing it in the palm of her hand, she held it out before Khardan.

It was a horse, wonderfully carved, made of ebony. Perfect in every detail, standing about six inches tall, the animal's nostrils were two fiery red rubies, and topaz gleamed in the eyes. Its saddle was of fine ivory with gold and turquoise trappings. Its hooves were shod with silver. Truly it was an exquisite work of art, and Achmed, looking at it, sighed in longing. But Khardan remained unimpressed.

"So this is Quar's gift to his people," the Calif said scornfully, glancing swiftly at the Amir to see if he were being made sport of. "A child's toy."

"Show him, Yamina," the Amir ordered gently, by way of answer.

The sorceress placed the horse upon the floor. Touching a ring she wore upon her hand, she caused the setting of the jewel to spring open. From inside the ring Yamina withdrew a tiny paper scroll. Prying open the horse's mouth, she tucked the scroll inside, clamping the statue's teeth over it so that it held it firmly. As she knelt beside the toy horse, the single, visible eye of the sorceress closed; she began to whisper arcane words.

A puff of smoke came from the horse's mouth. Catching hold of Achmed's hand, Khardan drew back away from the animal, his face dark with suspicion. The Imam murmured to himself in a low voice—prayers to Quar undoubtedly. The Amir watched with amused interest.

Khardan drew a shivering breath. The horse was growing! As the sorceress spoke, repeating the same words over and over, the animal gained in height and width; now it was a foot tall, now it came to Khardan's waist, now it was as tall as a man, now as tall as the Calif's own warhorse. The sorceress's voice hushed. Slowly she rose to her feet, and as she did so, the ebony horse turned its head to look at her and it was ebony no more!

The horse was flesh and blood, as real and alive as any steed that ran free in the desert. Khardan stared at it, unable to speak. Never had he seen magic such as this, never believed it possible.

"Praise be to Quar!" breathed the Imam reverently.

"A trick!" Khardan muttered through clenched teeth.

The Amir shrugged. "If you like. It is, however, a 'trick' that Yamina and the rest of my wives and the wives of the grandees and nobles of this city can all perform." Rising to his feet, the Amir descended from the rosewood throne, coming to stroke the horse's neck. It was, Khardan could plainly see, a magnificent animal—restive, with a spirit to match the fiery ruby red of its nostrils. The horse's eyes rolled round to view its strange situation, its hooves dancing nervously on the tiled floor.

"This fine animal is, as I said, a gift from the God," the Amir remarked, stroking the velvety black nose. "But the spell will work on any object made into a likeness of a horse. It may be carved of wood, shaped of clay. One of my own sons, a lad of six, fashioned one this morning."

"Do you take me for a fool, O King?" Khardan demanded angrily. "Asking me to believe women can perform such magic as this!"

But even as he spoke, Khardan's eyes went to Yamina. The single, staring eye of the sorceress was on him, its gaze unblinking, unwavering.

"It doesn't matter to me what you believe, Calif," the Amir said imperturbably. "The fact remains that I do not need your horses, which places you and your people in a desperate situation. But Quar is merciful.'' The Amir raised a hand to prevent Khardan from interrupting. ''We have room in the city to house you and your tribesmen. Bring your people to Kich. Work will be found for you. The men of your tribe can join the ranks of my own armies. Your reputation as warriors is well-known. I would be honored''—his voice changed subtly, his sincerity on this point was obvious—''to have you ride among us. Your women can weave rugs and make pottery to sell in the bazaar. Your children will go to school in the Temple, learn to read and to write—''

''—And the ways of Quar, O King?'' Khardan concluded coldly.

''Of course. No one may live within these walls who is not a devout follower of the one, true God.''

''Thank you, O King, for your generosity,'' said Khardan, bowing. ''But my people and I would sooner starve. It seems we have wasted our time here. We will be leaving—''

''There, you see!'' said the Imam quickly, coming forward. His thin arm raised, he pointed a trembling finger at Khardan. ''Now do you believe, O King!''

''So!'' thundered the Amir in a voice that caused the horse to neigh shrilly, thinking it heard the call to battle. ''It is true! You are spies, come to scout the city so that you and your murdering devilmen may sweep out of the desert and attack us. Your attempt has failed, Calif! Our God is all-knowing, all-seeing, and we have been warned of your treacherous plans!''

''Spies!'' Khardan stared at the man in amazement.

''Guards!'' shouted the Amir above the horse's whinnyings, the commotion causing it to rear up on its hind legs. ''Guards! Seize them!''

Chapter 6

Forced to hold on to the bridle of the plunging, excited horse, the Amir called loudly for the guards, who began running from all corners of the room. Gliding out of the way of the flashing hooves, moving near the rosewood throne, the Imam watched intently, his face grave. Beside him stood Yamina, her hand resting lightly on the priest's bare arm, the single, visible eye staring out from the shimmering black fabric of her robes. The Amir's bodyguards, who had been flanking the throne, ran toward Khardan and Achmed, sabers flashing.

Thrusting Achmed behind him, Khardan kicked out at the guard nearest him. The Calif's black riding boot struck the guard's swordhand. Bone crunched, and the saber went flying, falling to the tile floor with a clatter.

"Get it!" Khardan cried, shoving Achmed toward the blade skidding over the floor.

Stumbling in his haste, Achmed dove for the saber. The other bodyguard swung his blade in a vicious stroke that would have parted Khardan's head from his shoulders had not the Calif ducked down beneath it. Rising again swiftly, Khardan blocked the guard's follow-through stroke with his forearm, seized the man's wrist with both hands, and twisted.

Bones cracked, the guard screamed in pain, his sword fell from limp fingers. Shoving the guard backward into another, Khardan picked up the sword. Achmed stood at his back, his own weapon raised.

"That way!" Khardan shouted, jumping toward the antechamber through which they had entered.

"No, it's sealed off!" Achmed gasped. "I tried to tell you—"

But Khardan wasn't listening. His eyes swept the *divan*, searching for a way out.

"Shut the partitions!" the Amir bellowed. "Shut the partitions!"

The partitions! Turning, Khardan saw the balcony, the tops of the trees visible in the pleasure garden below. The garden was surrounded by a wall and beyond that wall was the city and freedom. But already servants were scurrying in a panic to obey the Amir's command. The partitions, scraping against the tile floor, were hastily being dragged shut.

Khardan shoved his brother toward the balcony. A guard leaped at the Calif, but a slicing swing of Khardan's saber caused him to fall back, clutching his arm that had been nearly severed from his body. Turning, Khardan ran after his brother, his robes swirling about him as he raced toward the partitions.

They were almost shut, but the servants—seeing the two desert nomads hurtling down on them, weapons flashing in the sun—broke and ran, shrieking, for their lives. The Amir's voice echoed throughout the *divan*, cursing them all for cowards.

Squeezing between the partitions, Khardan and Achmed ran out onto the balcony.

"Shut those!" Khardan ordered Achmed while he hurried to look over the smooth stone balustrade. It was a twenty-foot drop, at least, into the garden below. Hesitating, he turned around. Behind him could be heard the stomping of feet; he could see the partitions being forced apart again. There was no help for it.

Grabbing hold of Achmed, he helped his brother over the stone railing.

Keeping one eye on the slowly parting partition, Khardan climbed over the balustrade, perching precariously on the narrow lip of stone.

"The flower bed! Jump for it!" he ordered.

Dropping his sword down first, Achmed prepared to follow. He couldn't make himself jump, however. Clinging to the railing with both hands, his face white and strained, he stared down at the garden that seemed miles beneath him.

"Go!"

Khardan shoved his brother with his boot. Achmed's hands slipped, he fell with a cry. Tossing his own sword down into the flowers, the Calif leaped after him, falling through the air and landing in the flower bed below with the grace of cat.

"Where's my sword? Are you all right?"

"Yes," Achmed managed to answer. The heavy fall had jarred him, leaving him dazed and shaken. Blood trickled from his mouth; he'd bitten his tongue on landing and wrenched his knee painfully, but he would die before admitting this to his elder brother. "Your sword's there, by those pink things."

Seeing the hilt flash in the sunlight, Khardan swiftly bent down and caught hold of it. He glanced around, getting his bearings, trying to remember what he knew of the palace and its environs. He had never, of course, been in the pleasure garden before. Only the Sultan, his wives, and his concubines were allowed here, spending the heat of the day relaxing amid the shade trees and orange blossoms, dabbling in the ornamental pools, playing among the hedgerows. Located at the eastern end of the palace, far from the soldiers' barracks and surrounded by a high wall, the garden was private and effectively cut off from the city noises and smells.

"If we climb the northern wall, we should come out near our men," Khardan muttered.

"But which way leads north?" Achmed asked, staring helplessly at the maze of hedges and branching paths.

"We must pray to Akhran to guide us," the Calif said.

At least there weren't any guards here, he thought, knowing that only the eunuchs were allowed in the pleasure gardens with the women. But he could hear shouts and orders being issued. That would undoubtedly change. They hadn't much time.

Plunging out of the flower bed, he jumped onto a path, startling a gazelle that bounded off in fright. Glancing back, he motioned for his brother to come behind him. The boy's face was pale but grim and resolute. Khardan saw him limping.

"Are you sure you're all right?"

"I'm fine. Just get us out of here."

Nodding, Khardan turned and selected a path that appeared to lead toward the north. He and Achmed followed it until it

opened into a wide patio around a pond. Achmed was about
to step out, but Khardan pulled him back into the bushes.

"No! Look above!"

Archers lined the balcony, their bows ready, their arrows
aimed into the garden below.

Keeping himself and his brother hidden as best he could
among the hedgerows, daring to raise his head only now and
then to see if he could locate the wall, Khardan tried first one
path, then another, becoming increasingly frustrated as each
seemed to lead him deeper and deeper into the garden's
sweet-smelling labyrinth. Achmed kept up, never complaining.
But Khardan knew the boy was nearly finished; he could hear
Achmed's breath come in in painful gasps, his limp was
worsening.

Rounding a corner, the Calif finally caught a glimpse of
the wall and he breathed a sigh of relief. By this time he was
so disoriented he didn't know if it would bring him out to the
right place or not, but he didn't care. Once he was in the
open, he would take on the Amir's army if he had to.

But as he drew nearer the wall, Khardan's heart sank. It
was over twenty feet high, smooth and sheer, without a
handhold or foothold visible. Vines that might have grown
over it had been cut away. The trees that stood near it had all
been pruned to prevent any branches from overhanging the
wall. Obviously the Sultan had been careful of his wives,
making certain that no would-be lovers had easy access to his
garden.

Gnashing his teeth in frustration, Khardan ran along the
base of the wall, hoping desperately to find a crack in the
surface, a vine some gardener might have overlooked, anything!
The whiz and thud of an arrow near him let him know that
even if they couldn't be seen plainly, their movements through
the foliage were easily detected. Already guards must be
pouring through the gates. . . .

"No! Please, let me go!" begged a voice. "I'll give you
my jewels, anything! Please, please don't take me back there!"

Khardan stopped. It was a woman's voice and it sounded
very near him. Holding up his hand, warning Achmed—coming
along behind him—to stop, the Calif peeped cautiously through
a stand of rose trees. Thankful for the rest, Achmed leaned

dizzily back against the wall, massaging his leg that throbbed and burned with each move.

About five feet from Khardan a woman was struggling with two of the palace eunuchs—big men, their bodies had run to flab as often happens among their kind, but they were strong nevertheless. Holding the woman's arms, the eunuchs were dragging her down a path, presumably toward the palace. The woman was young, her clothes were disheveled and torn, and her veil had been ripped from her head, leaving her face and head visible. Khardan—even in the midst of his own danger—gasped in awe at her beauty.

He had never in his life seen hair like that. Long and thick, it was the color of burnished gold. When she shook her head in her pleadings, it billowed about her in a golden cloud. Her voice, though choked with tears, was sweet. The skin of her arms and breasts, plainly visible through the torn fabric of her clothes, was white as cream, pink as the roses that surrounded him.

That she had been ill-treated was obvious. There were bruises on her arms, and—Khardan sucked in his breath in anger—marks of a lash could be seen on her bare back.

"Stay here!" Khardan ordered Achmed. Running out onto the path, his sword drawn, the Calif accosted the eunuchs.

"Let her go!" he demanded.

Startled, the eunuchs turned, their eyes opening wide at the sight of the desert nomad in his long robes and riding boots, the saber in his hand.

"Help!" cried one of the eunuchs in quavering, high-pitched squeaks, still holding firmly to the girl. "Intruders in the *seraglio*! Help! Guards!"

His captive turned a lovely face toward Khardan, peering up at him through a golden shower of hair.

"Save me!" she begged. "Save me! I am one of the Sultan's daughters! I have been hiding in the palace, but now they have discovered me and are taking me to cruel torture and death! Save my life, bold stranger, and all my fortune is yours!"

"Shut up!" One of the eunuchs slapped the girl with the back of his fat hand.

He screamed in pain himself the next moment, staring

stupidly at the bloody gash that had split his arm open from shoulder to wrist.

"Let her go!" Khardan leaped menacingly at the other eunuch, but he already let loose of the girl's arm.

"Guards! Guards!" The eunuch cried in panic, backing away from Khardan and finally turning and running down the path, the flesh of his flabby body jiggling and bouncing ludicrously. The other eunuch had fainted dead away and lay with his head in a pool, his blood staining the water red.

"How do we get out of here?" Khardan demanded, catching hold of the girl as she threw herself into his arms. "Quickly! There are guards hunting for me as well! My men are outside the wall, by the slave market. If we can just get to them—"

"Yes!" she panted, clinging to him. "Just give me a moment."

Her breasts, pressed against Khardan's chest, heaved as she sought to catch her breath. Her fragrance filled his nostrils, her hair brushed against his cheek, shining as silken web. She was warmth and roses and tears and softness, and Khardan put his arm around her, drawing her closer still and soothing her fright.

She was as courageous as she was beautiful, apparently, for she drew a quivering breath and thrust herself away from him. "There is . . . a secret way . . . through the wall. Follow me!"

"Wait! My brother!" Khardan darted back into the bushes, coming out with Achmed behind him.

Beckoning with a hand so slim and white it might have been the petals of the gardenia blooming around them, the girl motioned Khardan and Achmed to follow her down a path that neither of them would ever have seen, so cunningly hidden was it by the twists and turns of the maze. No more arrows fell around them. They could hear questioning shouts of deep voices, however, and the shrill piping of the eunuch.

The girl did not hesitate but led them confidently through a veritable jungle of foliage in which both of them must immediately have been lost. Khardan could no longer see the wall; he couldn't see anything through the tall trees, and the vaguest suspicion of doubt was starting to form in his mind when suddenly they rounded a corner and there was the wall, a stand of bushes with long, wicked-looking thorns backed up against it.

Khardan stared at it gloomily. They might use the bushes to climb the wall, but their flesh would be in shreds by the time they reached the top. He wondered, too, if the thorns were poisonous. A drop of something waxy glistened at the tip of each. Still, it was better than languishing in the Amir's prison. He started to shove the girl behind him, planning to climb the bush, when—to his surprise—she stopped him.

"No, watch!" Hurrying to the wall, the girl pulled out a loose rock. There was a grinding sound, and to Khardan's astonishment, the thorn bush slowly moved aside, revealing an opening in the wall. Through it, Khardan could see the marketplace and hear the babble of many voices.

Other voices behind them—the guards'—were growing louder. The girl darted out into the street. Grasping hold of Achmed, Khardan thrust his brother through the hole in the wall and followed after him.

He found the girl kneeling down beside a blind beggar who happened to be sitting just near the wall's opening. She was talking to him hurriedly. Khardan, watching in amazement, saw her draw a golden bracelet from her wrist and drop it into the beggar's basket. The blind beggar, with amazing dexterity for one who couldn't see, snatched up the bracelet and hurriedly stuffed it down the front of his rags.

"Come!" The girl grasped Khardan's hand.

"What about the opening in the wall?" he asked. "They'll know we've escaped. . . ."

"The beggar will take care of it. He always does. Where did you say your men are waiting?"

"By the slave market."

Khardan glanced around the streets. Achmed was looking at him expectantly, waiting for orders, but the Calif had no idea which way was which. The bazaars all melded into one another; he was completely lost. The girl, however, seemed to know exactly where she was. Hurriedly she drew Khardan and his brother into the crowd around the colorful stalls. Looking backward, the Calif was astonished to see the wall smooth and unbroken, the beggar sitting there, his milk-white eyes seeing nothing, a basket with a few coppers on the ground before him.

No one else seemed to be paying any attention to them.

"The soldiers will suppose they have you trapped in the garden!" The girl, holding on to Khardan tightly, pointed. "There is the slave market . . . and . . . are those your men?" She faltered. "That . . . rough-looking group. . . ."

"Yes," said Khardan absently, thinking. "You believe the soldiers will concentrate on searching the palace?"

"Oh, yes!" The girl looked directly at him, her eyes wide, and he suddenly noticed that they were blue as the desert sky, blue as sapphires, blue as cool water. "You will have time to flee the city. Thank you, brave one"—she flushed, her eyes lowering modestly before his gaze—"for rescuing me."

Khardan saw the girl swaying on her feet. Catching hold of her in his arms as she fell, he cursed himself for not having realized she must be weak and dazed from her terrible ordeal.

"I'm sorry," she murmured faintly, her breath soft as the evening wind against his cheek, "to be so much trouble. Leave me. I have friends. . . ."

"Nonsense!" Khardan said harshly. "You will not be safe in this city of butchers. Besides, we owe you our lives."

Opening her blue eyes, the girl looked up at him. Her arms stole around his neck. Khardan's breath came fast. Her hand with its cream-and-pink fingers raised to touch his bearded cheek. "Where will you take me . . . that I will be safe?"

"To my tribe, to the desert where I live," he answered huskily.

"That means you are a *batir*, a bandit!" Her face paled; she averted her eyes from his. "Put me down, please! I will take my chances here." Tears glistened on her cheeks. She pressed her hand against his chest. Such gentle hands, they could not have torn the petals from a flower, Khardan thought. His heart melted in his breast.

"My lady!" he said earnestly. "Let me escort you to safety! I swear by *Hazrat* Akhran that you will be treated with all respect and honor."

The lovely eyes, shimmering with tears, raised to his. "You risked your own life to save mine! Of course I believe you! I trust you! Take me with you, away from this terrible place where they murdered my father!"

Overcome by weeping, she hid her face in his chest.

The blood beating in his ears so that he was wholly deaf, Khardan held the girl close, his soul filled with her perfume, his eyes dazzled by the radiance of the sunlight on her hair.

"What is your name?" he whispered.

"Meryem," she replied.

Chapter 7

"Brother!" said Achmed urgently. "Let's go!"

"Yes! We should not linger," Meryem said, glancing around nervously. "Though the soldiers are not out here, there are spies, who may report us to the Amir. You can put me down now," the girl added shyly. "I can walk."

"Are you certain?"

She nodded, and Khardan set her upon her feet. Seeing his admiring eyes on her, Meryem realized she was half-naked. Blushing, she gathered up the torn shreds of her clothing, trying to draw them together to preserve her modesty and succeeding only in revealing more than she covered.

Glancing about quickly, Khardan saw a silk merchant's stall. Snagging a long scarf, he tossed it to the girl.

"Cover yourself!" he ordered harshly.

Meryem did so, winding the silk around her head and shoulders.

"Where is my money?" the merchant screamed at them.

"Collect from the Amir!" Khardan thrust the small man aside. "Perhaps his wife will conjure it up for you!"

"This way!" Taking hold of the Calif's hand, Meryem led Khardan and Achmed through the bazaars, pushing past vendors, customers, donkeys, and dogs.

"Saiyad!" Khardan called once they were in sight of his men.

The *spahi* ran up to them. "By Sul, Calif! What has happened? We heard a great shouting coming from the palace . . ."

Saiyad stared at them in wonder—the strange girl wrapped up in a stolen scarf, Achmed white-faced and limping, Khardan's robes spattered with blood.

"It is a long story, my friend. Suffice it to say that the Amir will not be buying our horses. He accused us of being spies and tried to have us arrested."

"Spies?" Saiyad's mouth gaped open. "But what—"

Khardan shrugged. "They are city dwellers. What do you expect? Their brains have rotted in this shell."

The rest of the men, crowding around, were muttering among themselves.

"No, we're not leaving empty-handed," the Calif called out, raising his voice. "And I'm not running from these dogs! We will leave the city when and how we choose!"

The *spahis* cheered raggedly, swearing bitter oaths of revenge. Gazing at them fearfully, Meryem shrank back next to Khardan. He put his arm around her, and drew her close. "We came to deal fairly, but we have been insulted. Not only that, our God has been insulted as well." The men glowered, fingering their weapons. Waving his hand at the stalls, Khardan shouted, "Take what you need to live on this year!"

The men cheered and began running for their horses.

Khardan grabbed hold of Saiyad's bridle to detain him. "Watch for the soldiers."

"Aren't you coming?"

"Achmed is hurt and there is the woman. I will wait for you here."

"Anything I can get you, my Calif?" the grinning Saiyad asked.

"No. I have already acquired more treasure than I came with the intent to buy," Khardan replied.

Saiyad glanced at the girl, laughed, and dashed off.

Yelling wildly, brandishing their swords in the air, the *spahis* rode straight for the stalls of the bazaars. People scattered before them like terrified chickens, screaming in panic at the sight of the lashing hooves and flashing steel.

Saiyad guided his horse straight into a silk merchant's stand. The stall toppled. Its owner hopped about the street in rage, cursing the nomads at the top of his lungs. Roaring with laughter, Saiyad speared several fine silks with his sword blade and began waving them in the air above his head like a flag.

Across the street, Saiyad's brother—with a few well-aimed blows of his scimitar—cut down the shelves of a brass merchant's stall. Pots, lamps, and pipes crashed to the street with ringing clangs like a hundred bells. Snatching up a fine lamp, the nomad stuffed it into his *khurjin* and galloped off in search of more plunder.

"Someone will be killed!" said Meryem, shivering with fear and crowding close to Khardan.

"They will if they try to stop us," said the Calif.

Eyes gleaming with pride, he was watching his men wreaking havoc among the stalls when a push from behind him nearly knocked him over. Turning, he saw his war-horse. Dancing restively, the animal nudged him again with its head, urging him in the direction of the fray.

Laughing, Khardan patted his horse's nose, soothing the excited beast.

"Khardan, the guards. Don't you think we should go?" Mounted on his own horse, Achmed looked back worriedly toward the palace.

"Relax, little brother! They probably think we're still running around in the garden. But you are right, we should be ready, just in case."

Grasping Meryem around her waist—such a small waist, his hands almost completely encircled it—Khardan started to lift her up onto the back of the horse when a sudden tickling sensation, like feathers brushing against the back of his neck, caused him to turn his head.

The slave market—set apart from the rest of the bazaars in the *souk*—was conducting business as usual. Riots in the bazaars were commonplace. The slave buyers were far more interested in the merchandise being exhibited on the block, and at that moment a young woman was being put up for sale—a woman, it seemed, remarkable for her beauty, for a low murmur of anticipation was rippling through the crowd when the auctioneer dragged the veiled woman before them.

Having rescued one helpless person from the clutches of this city of devils, Khardan felt his heart swell with pity and anger at the sight of another, who probably faced a similar, cruel fate. Grasping hold of her veil, the dealer tore it from the woman's head. The crowd gasped in wonder and even Khardan blinked in astonishment. Hair the color of fire caught the rays of the noon sun. It seemed that blazing red flame tumbled down around slender shoulders.

But it was not the woman's beauty that struck Khardan. Indeed, she was not particularly beautiful at the moment. Her face was thin and wasted, there were dark shadows beneath her eyes. It was the expression on the woman's face that drew Khardan's attention, a look such as the Calif had never seen before—the despairing look of one who has lost all hope, who sees death as the only salvation.

"The trip was a hard one for such a delicate blossom," the auctioneer was shouting. "With some food and drink, however, she will soon be a prize flower, ready for any man to pluck! What am I bid?"

Anger swept over Khardan, a white-hot rage. That one human being should be able to buy another and thereby acquire the power of a God—the power of life and death—was true evil.

Turning, he lifted Meryem up onto a horse, but it was Achmed's mount, not his.

"Take care of her," he ordered his younger brother, who was staring at him in astonishment. Shrieks and crashes were audible from the bazaar, an indication that the *spahis* were still having their fun. Another sound rose above it, however—the blare of trumpets, coming from the Kasbah.

"The soldiers!" Meryem cried, her face pale. "We must leave!"

Swinging himself into his saddle, Khardan glanced coolly in the direction of the trumpet calls. "It will take them some time to get organized, still longer to get through the crowds. Do not worry. Saiyad hears them as well as we do. Wait for me. I won't be long."

A single word of command caused the Calif's horse to leap forward. Deadly silent, without a yell or word of warning, Khardan rode straight into the mass of slave buyers. Wild-eyed faces stared up at him. The men either got out of his way or were ridden down. Shouts and curses and yells rose into the air. Someone grabbed hold of his boot, trying to drag him from his steed. A blow from the flat of Khardan's sword sent the slaver crashing to the ground, blood streaming from his head.

The mob surged around the Calif, some trying to escape, others trying to attack him. Striking out to the right and left with his sword, Khardan—his eyes on the slave block— continued to urge his horse forward. The auctioneer suddenly became aware of Khardan's purpose. Frantically calling for his bodyguards, he tried to save his sale by hustling the woman from the platform.

A blow to the head from Khardan's boot sent the auctioneer tumbling over backward into the arms of his guards.

"Here, I've come to save you!" Khardan shouted.

The woman on the block looked up at him with that same hopeless, despairing expression. Whether he meant to drive his sword through her body or carry her away to safety seemed all one to the wretched creature.

Fury burning in his heart that one human could so reduce another to this pitiable condition, Khardan leaned down from the saddle. Sliding his arm around the woman's waist, he lifted her easily, hauling her up behind him on the horse's back and clamping her hands around his chest.

The woman's arms slipped nervelessly from around him. Turning, Khardan saw that she was staring at him with dull, uncaring eyes.

"Hold on tightly!" Khardan commanded.

For an instant he wondered whether or not she would obey him. If she didn't, she was lost, for the Calif could not both hold her and guide his horse back through the raging mob.

"Come alive, damn you!"

Khardan was battling to keep the horse standing amid the attacking mob, he had no real idea what he was saying. Beating and kicking and lashing out at those trying to grab his horse's bridle, the Calif knew only that saving this young woman had suddenly become extremely important to him—a symbol of his victory over these foul city-dwellers.

"Come back to life!" he shouted. "Nothing is that bad!"

Perhaps it was his words or perhaps it was the fear of falling from the plunging, rearing horse, but Khardan felt the arms around him tighten. Slightly amazed at her strength— unusual for a woman—Khardan did not have time to wonder at it. A group of mounted *goums* belonging to one of the slave traders was endeavoring to make its way through the mob to get at Khardan.

At a command from its master, Khardan's horse reared into the air, lashing out with deadly hooves. The mob scattered, more than a few fell to the ground, blood streaming from broken heads. Seeing their fellows fall, the slavers turned and ran. The *goums* and their horses became entangled in a mass of people milling about in panic.

Grimly triumphant, Khardan galloped out of the slave market just as a few of the trader's *goums* were able to make their way through the mob. Heading back to where his brother awaited him, Khardan rode past a white palanquin.

At the sight the woman behind him gave a slight gasp, her grip on Khardan tightening. Glancing down, the Calif saw the litter's curtain being held back by a slender hand, a man's face looking out. Cruel and malevolent, the man's eyes went through Khardan like cold steel.

His very soul chilled, Khardan could not withdraw his gaze. He actually checked the horse and paused, staring at the man in the palanquin with awful fascination. The whistle of a sword slashing by his head recalled him to his senses. Whirling, he struck out with the hilt of his sword catching the *goum* on the chin and knocking him from his horse. But the other *goums* were catching up with him now, too many to fight.

"We're going to run for it!" he shouted to the woman. "Hold on!"

Kicking the horse's flanks, Khardan urged the animal ahead at a gallop. The street was clear now, the people having fled for safety. Out in the open at last, the desert horse ran with the speed of the wind that was its grandsire. Khardan risked a glance back at his prize. Her red hair streaming behind her like a fiery banner, the woman was holding on to him for dear life; her head pressed against Khardan's back, her arms gripping him with a panicked strength that was nearly squeezing the breath from his lungs.

The *goums* pounded behind them. Khardan's horse, exhilarated at this wild race and the yells and shouts of encouragement from the waiting Akar, unleashed all its energy. Few horses in the tribe could keep up with Khardan's stallion. One by one the *goums* fell behind, shaking their fists and calling out curses.

Intoxicated with the danger and excitement, the *spahis* rode up around their leader, shouting and yelling and clapping him on the back. Festooned with stolen bolts of silk and cotton, their saddlebags bulging with filched jewelry, their sashes bristling with newly appropriated weapons, the nomads carried huge sacks of purloined flour and rice slung across their saddles.

The soldiers of the Amir were in sight now, but their progress through the stalls of the bazaar was being hampered by the wreckage the *spahis* had left behind.

Gathering his men around him, Khardan raced for the city gates, which were standing wide open to permit a long camel caravan to enter.

The last building the *spahis* passed was the Temple of Quar. Wheeling his horse, heedless of the rapidly gaining soldiers, Khardan guided the animal up the Temple stairs.

"Here is how we pay homage to Quar!" he shouted.

Lifting the sword he had taken from the Amir's guard, Khardan plunged it through one of the priceless windows. The stained glass, which had been made in the image of a golden ram's head, shattered into a thousand sparkling shards. Minor priests ran screaming from the Temple, shaking their fists or wringing their hands.

Turning, Khardan's horse cleared the stairs in a single jump. The Calif and his spahis swept out of the city gates, riding down the few guards who made a halfhearted attempt to stop them.

Once out of arrow range but still in sight of the city walls, Khardan called a halt.

"Some of you round up the horses!" he instructed. "Make certain you get them all! I'll leave nothing behind for these swine!"

"Will the soldiers come after us?" Saiyad shouted.

"City dwellers? Out into the desert? Hah!" Khardan laughed. "Here, my friend, take this girl, will you?"

"With pleasure, my Calif!" Grinning from ear to ear, Saiyad caught hold of the red-haired slave girl and transferred her from the Calif's horse to the back of his own.

Riding over to Achmed, Khardan held out his hands to the

Sultan's daughter. "Will you ride with me, my lady?" he asked.

"I will," Meryem said softly, flushing as Khardan lifted her in his arms.

Flinging one final, defiant shout of triumph at the city walls, the *spahis* wheeled their steeds and dashed off into the desert, their black robes swirling around them.

At the city gates the captain of the soldiers sat upon his horse, watching the nomads go, his men lined up in silent ranks behind him. The leader of the *goums* was arguing violently with him, pointing at the rapidly disappearing *spahis* and raving at the top of his lungs. But the captain, with a shake of his head, simply turned his horse and rode back into the city, his men following behind him.

In the palace the Amir and the Imam stood on the balcony overlooking the pleasure garden, watching as the servants rolled the injured eunuch onto a litter.

"All went as you planned," said the Imam. (The priest did not yet know of the desecration done to his Temple, or he might have been less conciliatory.)

The Amir, detecting a grudging note in Feisal's voice, smiled inwardly. Outwardly his face maintained its stern, military calm. "Of course." He shrugged. "Although I thought for a moment we were going to capture the arrogant young whelp accidently. I thought I would have to pick him up and hurl him into the garden myself, but fortunately he caught my hint about the partitions."

"He has taken the viper to his bosom," said the Imam in a soft voice. "Are you certain of its fangs?"

The Amir glanced at Feisal irritably. "I grow tired of your doubting, Imam. My wife handpicked the girl from among my concubines. Yes, I am certain of her. Meryem is ambitious, and if she succeeds, I have promised to marry her. She should have no trouble. These nomads, for all their bluster, are naive as children. Meryem is skilled in her art—" The Amir paused, his eyebrows raised. "She is skilled in many arts, as a matter of fact, not the least of which is the art of giving pleasure. The young man should have an interesting time of it."

He turned back, gazing out over the city walls into the desert. "Enjoy your nights well, *kafir*," Qannadi murmured. "If the reports of your tribes uniting are true, those nights are numbered. I cannot allow you and your Ragtag God to stand in the way of progress."

Chapter 8

Although Khardan truly believed that the Amir's soldiers would not be so foolish as to pursue them, the Calif deemed it wise to ride homeward as swiftly as possible. It wasn't fear of the Amir that drove him. It was the memory of the cruel face in the palanquin. There had been more than a threat of revenge in the malevolent eyes, there had been a promise. Khardan found himself starting awake the first night away from the city. Bathed in cold sweat, he had the feeling that something was creeping up on him.

He would sleep better in his own land, and he knew his men were as eager to return home as he. No one complained at riding all night and into the cool hours' of the day, switching horses often to keep the worms from tiring. They ate their meals in the saddle, managed to snatch a few hours' sleep burrowed like worms in the sand, the horses' reins tied around their wrists. The *spahis* were in good spirits, far better than if their journey had been successful, for they loved nothing better than raiding. This moment would stand out forever in their lives, and already they were reliving it, enlivening the long journey with repeated tales of their victory in the city of Kich, tales that were expanding like bread dough with the yeast of their telling.

At first Khardan was silent during these sessions, inclined to brood on nagging questions that rankled like thorns in his flesh. What had the Amir meant about Quar's warning them of the Akar's coming? Where had Qanndi gotten the notion that the Akar were spying on the city so that they could conquer

it? Nothing that mad would ever occur to Sheykh Majiid—
any of the sheykhs of the desert for that matter. Not only did
they know it would be foolhardy in the extreme to attack such
a fortification as the walled city of Kich, why in the name of
Sul would anyone want such a place anyhow?

Then there was the man with the cruel eyes in the palanquin.
A slave trader, obviously, but who was he and where did he
come from? Khardan found himself unpleasantly obsessed
with the memory of that man, and he endeavored to find out
more about him during the rare times when he was able to
talk to the slave woman he had rescued.

But the woman proved to be no help. Silent, reclusive, she
kept by herself whenever possible, shrinking even from the
company of Meryem, who would have been happy to have
another woman go with her to perform the private ablutions prohibited to the eyes of men. So quiet was the red-haired woman
—never talking, never answering questions spoken to her—that
Khardan began to wonder if she was deaf and dumb.

Saiyad reported to Khardan that the woman never said a
word to him. She ate and drank what was given her but took
nothing on her own. If no one had brought her food, she
probably would have starved. The hopeless look in the eyes
had not gone away; if anything, it was intensified. It became
apparent to Khardan that the woman would just as soon lie
down and die in the sand as to be kept clinging to this life,
and he wondered more than once what dreadful thing had
happened to her. Recalling the cruel, cold eyes of the man in
the palanquin, the Calif did not think he needed to search far
to find an answer.

Eventually, as the days passed and the Akar drew nearer
their own land, leaving behind the city with its walls and its
noise and its stench, the Calif's spirits rose. He not only
began enjoying hearing the stories of his men, but he told his
own as well, elaborating with parental fondness on the courage
of his younger brother in the palace escape until Achmed's
ears were red with embarrassed pleasure. The men listened in
admiration as Khardan recounted with all due modesty the
discovery and rescue of the Sultan's daughter, enlivening the
tale with shrill imitations of the eunuchs' squeals that caused
the men to roar with laughter.

The Sultan's daughter was another cause for the rise in the

Calif's spirits. True to his word, Khardan treated her with the respect and reverence he would have accorded his own mother. He even offered her a horse of her own to ride—something completely unheard of—but she shyly refused, saying she knew nothing of the beasts and was terrified of them. She would continue to ride with him, if she wasn't too great a burden.

Too great a burden! Khardan's heart sang like the wind among the dunes as he galloped over the sands, the lovely creature clinging to him, her hands entwined about his chest, her head leaning against his back when she grew weary. He did not know by what art she managed it, but not even the strenuous ride diminished her beauty. He and the others smelled of sweat and horse; she smelled of rose and orange blossoms. She kept carefully veiled, her white body completely covered to protect her from the sun and from the eyes of men. She rarely lifted her blue eyes when in the presence of men but kept them lowered as was considered proper in a woman, her long, black lashes brushing her cheeks.

The modesty that bespoke the virgin was all the more enchanting to Khardan because of the closeness they experienced riding together. It was her fear of the horse—which seemed to her a great and powerful beast, so Meryem said—that made her sit so near Khardan. Tears glistened in her eyes. He must think her shameless! Wiping away those tears, Khardan assured her that he didn't think her shameless at all. He barely knew she was with him. Meryem smiled sweetly and held him all the tighter. Khardan, feeling her warm and soft against his flesh, their bodies moving together in time to the rhythm of the horse's motion, sometimes ached with a passion that it took all his self-command to conquer.

The Calif comforted himself with the thought that this pleasure would not be long deferred. Every time he looked into Meryem's blue eyes, he saw love and admiration blooming there. When he reached the Tel, the first thing he would do would be to make the Sultan's daughter his wife. Soon he would sleep in her arms, laying his head upon the trembling bosom that pressed so often against his back.

Thoughts of Zohra flew from his mind on the wings of this new passion, with only the briefest wonder at how she would react to the introduction of a new wife into the *harem*.

"Ah, well," Khardan told himself, thinking of their final moments together in camp, "Zohra is tame now, at least. That last episode has frightened her into submission. I will do what I must to keep her happy and find true joy with another." (Which only went to prove the Amir's statement that, despite their bluster, the nomads were as naive as children.)

Meryem's conversation enlivened the long, dark hours of the night ride across the desert. She told Khardan tales of life in the Sultan's palace—tales that the Calif found incredible.

She spoke of the enclosed, marble baths where the wives and concubines went daily to bathe and play in the heated, perfumed water, always conscious—though they were never permitted to show it—of the small hole in the wall through which the Sultan watched, selecting his choice for the night.

She described the elaborate maze the Sultan had ordered specially built within the palace walls so that he could have the pleasure of chasing the selected favorite until he caught her and forced her to surrender. She told about the dinners during which the Sultan would invite the girls to dance. Stripping off their veils and their clothes, the women stepped lightly to music played by musicians whose eyes had been gouged out that they might not look upon the beautiful bodies moving gracefully before them.

Meryem spoke, too, of the secret passage through the garden wall; how those women not chosen by the Sultan used it to admit lovers into the garden, paying the blind beggar well to keep his mouth shut and conceal their transgressions, for it would be as much as their lives were worth if the eunuchs discovered them.

Khardan listened in amazement, his blood tingling in his veins. He asked if the Amir was indulging in the same style of life. Remembering the stern face, the rigid military posture, the Calif could not believe it of the man.

"No," Meryem replied. "Qannadi has no heart. He sees beauty in nothing but war and bloodshed. Oh, he has his *harem*, his wives. But he keeps them for the power of the magic they bring him. The *seraglio* is a witches' coven, not a place of love. The women speak only of magic, of their skills in *that* art, not in the art of loving. They go to the baths to bathe, not to show themselves. I even heard that the Amir ordered the spy hole closed up. There are no more intimate

dinners. The Amir sent the musicians to play for his soldiers.
The garden might be filled with the lovers of his wives, for
all the Amir cares.''

Realizing she was speaking more bitterly than might seem
right for a Sultan's daughter, Meryem hastily changed the
subject.

''That was how I managed to escape detection for so long.
When the soldiers of the Amir seized the palace, they easily
caught my father. His bodyguards fled—the cowards—and
left him to his cruel fate. There are secret hiding places built
into the palace, with a tunnel that runs below ground to the
soldiers' barracks. The Sultan did not have time to avail
himself of this; the Amir made certain of that, sending his
troops in to capture the palace before they had even conquered
the city. I was able to hide myself in one of these secret
places, however. It was little larger than a closet. I stayed
there for I don't know how long, crouched in the darkness,
thirsting and starving, but too scared to leave. I heard the
screams''—she shivered—''and I knew what was happening
out there. Later I overheard the eunuchs talking about my
father's death.''

Her voice broke. With a great effort she managed to control
her tears and continue with her story.

''At last I knew I must leave the closet or die there. I crept
out. My plan was to hide myself among the numerous
concubines of the Amir. I would be safe, I hoped, unless he
sent for me. My plan worked, at least so I imagined. I told
the other girls and the eunuchs that I was new, a present from
one of the grandees. I thought I had fooled them, but as it
turned out, they knew me all along. The Amir, it seems,
thought I was part of a plot of one of the nobles to overthrow
him and so he had me watched. I waited for my opportunity
to escape, and when you created the commotion in the *divan*,
I thought I had my chance.

''I hurried to the garden, intending to slip out the hole in
the wall. But the eunuchs caught me and beat me, trying to
make me reveal the name of the man for whom I worked.
They were going to drag me back to the Amir's torture
chambers when you saved me.''

She hugged Khardan close, her body shivering with her
emotion. The Calif did what he could to comfort her, although

what comfort he could offer was of necessity limited by the fact that they were riding horseback at the head of a troop of his men. This was, perhaps, just as well, or his resolution to wait and make the girl his wife might have vanished there in the night in the desert sand.

To take his mind off the aching of desire, he gruffly asked another question, this one about the Imam. Meryem readily answered, although it was some time before the infatuated Khardan could fully attend to what she was saying.

"—a result of the Imam's teaching, for he believes that passions of the body, while necessary to . . . to"—Meryem flushed prettily—"produce children, take the mind away from the worship of Quar.

"If you can believe the eunuchs," she whispered in Khardan's ear, embarrassed to discuss the matter aloud, "the Imam is said never to have slept with a woman. That is something Yamina would very much like to change, if you credit gossip."

Khardan recalled the holy zeal he'd seen burning in the priest's liquid eyes and could well believe this to be true. But the subject of Yamina brought another question to his mind.

"The magic of the horse," he asked Meryem, "is that true magic or was it a trick such as one performs for gullible children?"

"It is true magic!" Meryem said, her voice tinged with awe. "And that is not the greatest of Yamina's powers."

"Are you yourself this . . . skilled in the art of magic?" Khardan asked abruptly and somewhat uneasily.

"Oh, no!" Meryem replied glibly, guessing at the nomad's fear. "I have the usual women's talents, of course. But magic was not considered important in my father's court, nor was it considered seemly that I—as his daughter—should be taught such a common art." She spoke haughtily, and Khardan nodded in grave approval. "Certainly I am far from being as powerful as Yamina. She can enchant the weapons of the Amir's soldiers so that they never miss their target—"

"She must have slipped up on that one," interrupted Khardan with a grin, thinking of the inept guards who had tried to stop them at the palace.

He felt the girl's body tense. Imagining she must be reliving once again those few terrible moments of her capture, he turned and gave her a reassuring smile. She had an answering smile ready for him behind the veil, but it vanished the moment he looked away from her again, and he did not notice her biting her red lips in anger at herself for having used them too freely. The Calif must not guess that the soldiers had missed on purpose!

There was no more talk between them that night. Meryem—resting her head against Khardan's strong back—pretended to sleep. Guiding his horse across the sands as carefully as possible, keeping a sharp watch for any irregularity in the path that might cause the horse to slip and thus jostle the girl and waken her, Khardan let his mind roam among the stories he had heard as he might have roamed among the many rooms of the Sultan's palace. The sun rose, a ball of fire burning in the pale blue sky. Khardan did not see it. He was lost in a sweet dream of blind musicians, playing at his command.

After days of hard riding the Akar reached the foothills where the tribesmen of Sheykh Jaafar al Widjar received them with sullen hospitality. Having ascertained that the horses given the sheepherders were being well cared for, Khardan accepted the freshly butchered carcasses of several sheep in return, and refusing the grudgingly offered three days of guest hospitality, the *spahis* continued their ride.

Another day and a night of hard riding brought them to the Tel, brought them home.

Chapter 9

Every man, woman, and child of both tribes camped around the Tel turned out to meet the *spahis,* who could be detected some distance away by the cloud of dust they raised. Standing at the edge of the camp, his eyes peering into the late afternoon sun, Majiid thought the dust cloud looked bigger than it should. His brow creased in worry. He'd had the uncomfortable feeling for days that something was wrong. He had summoned Sond, intending to send him to find Khardan and make certain he was safe, only to discover that the djinn had vanished. This unusual disappearance on the part of the immortal added to Majiid's nagging worries. Something had gone awry; Majiid knew it.

Now, seeing the dust cloud, he knew what it was. They were bringing back the horses. The sale had fallen through.

The *spahis* made a fine entrance into camp. Showing off their riding skills, they drew their horses up in a line before Majiid, and led by Khardan, each man had his horse kneel to the Sheykh. Despite his misgivings, Majiid's heart swelled with pride. He could not resist a triumphant glance at Jaafar. Let your sheepherders do this!

Majiid discovered Jaafar staring not at the horsemen but at the horses that they had brought back with them, and now it was Jaafar's turn to look at Majiid with raised eyebrows. Scowling, Majiid turned away. Hurrying over to talk to Khardan and determine what had gone wrong, the Sheykh's gaze went balefully to the Sultan's daughter. Women! Majiid had the instinctive feeling that this female was going to be the root of the trouble.

Other eyes saw the Sultan's daughter; other eyes frowned at the sight. Dressed in her finest gown, her black hair brushed until it glistened like a raven's wing, her body perfumed with jasmine, Zohra had been about to step from her tent and greet her husband when she caught a glimpse of the heavily veiled woman riding behind him. Who was she? What was he doing with her? Stepping back quickly into the shadows of her tent, Zohra watched the meeting between father and son, listening carefully to all that was said.

Jumping down from his horse, Khardan embraced his father.

"Welcome home, my son!" Majiid clasped his arms around Khardan, true emotion apparent in the slight quiver of his voice.

Around them rose a hubbub of voices, the other tribesmen joyfully greeting friends and family, pulling booty from the *khurjin* and distributing it to laughing wives and children.

Looking at the spoils, Majiid glanced questioningly at his son. "It appears your trip was successful?"

Khardan shook his head, his face grave and serious.

"What happened?"

"Yes, tell us, Calif, why you failed to sell the horses," said Jaafar loudly to Majiid's extreme irritation.

In a few words Khardan repeated his story. Aware that others were listening, he kept it brief, saving the details and his own private concerns for a later talk in his father's tent. It was not difficult for the Sheykh to hear his son's unspoken words, however, and a sidelong glance at Jaafar's darkening face showed him that the sharp mind of the Hrana had picked them up. Zohra, standing unnoticed within the shadows of her tent, heard them, too.

"Well, well," Majiid said with forced gaiety, slapping Khardan on his shoulders and embracing him again. "It must have been a glorious victory! I wish I had been there! My son, defying the Amir! My men, looting the city of Kich!" The Sheykh laughed boisterously. The *spahis* who heard his words exchanged glances of pride. "And are these some of the treasures of the city you have brought back with you?" Majiid asked, strolling over to the horses where sat the two women Khardan had freed.

Handling her as carefully as if she were made of fragile porcelain, Khardan grasped Meryem around her waist and lifted her down from the saddle. He led her by the hand to the Sheykh.

"Father, this is Meryem, daughter of the late Sultan of Kich."

Falling on her knees in the sand, Meryem prostrated herself before Majiid. "Honored father of my savior. Your son risked his life to save me, unworthy orphan of cruelly murdered parents. I was discovered, hiding in the palace. The Amir would have tortured me, then killed me as they did my father, but your son rescued me and carried me from the city." Raising her head, Meryem looked at the Sheykh earnestly, clasping her white hands together. "I cannot repay his kindness in wealth. I can repay it only by becoming his slave, and this I will gladly do, if you will accept a pitiful beggar such as myself into your tribe."

Touched by this pretty speech, enchanted by its deliverer, Majiid glanced up at Khardan. He saw his son's eyes aflame with a passion that any man must have felt. Although the Sheykh could not see the woman, veiled as she was, he caught a glimpse of the golden hair glistening in the sun. He saw the blue eyes sparkling with grateful tears and could witness the grace of the slender figure hidden by the folds of the *chador*. Majiid was, therefore, not surprised when Khardan, leaning down, gently raised up Meryem to stand beside him.

"Not a slave, Father," Khardan said, his voice husky, "but my wife. I pledged her my honor that she would be treated with all respect in this camp, and therefore, since she no longer has a father or mother of her own, I ask that you take her into your dwelling as your own daughter, my father, until such time as arrangements can be made for our wedding."

Black eyes, hidden in the shadows, flashed in anger. Feeling half-suffocated, Zohra drove her nails into the flesh of her palms and struggled to compose herself. "What do I care?" she demanded, gasping for breath over the terrible pain in her chest. "What does it matter to me? Nothing! He is nothing to me! Nothing!"

Growing calmer with this remembrance, repeating the words to herself, Zohra was able, after a few moments, to continue to watch and listen.

Majiid had welcomed his newest daughter and turned her over to his wives, who gathered around the girl, murmuring sympathetically over her cruel fate. Khardan's mother led the Sultan's daughter by the hand to her own tent. The Calif watched proudly, his eyes burning with a love visible to everyone in the camp.

"And what of this one?" Majiid questioned, looking at the silent woman shrouded in black.

The slave had not moved from her place on Saiyad's horse. She did not look around her. Neither interest, curiosity, nor fear was visible in the eyes above the black veil. Their gaze held only that same hopeless despair.

In a grim and angry voice Khardan told his father of the slave market and how he had rescued the woman as she was about to be auctioned off. The Calif told his exciting tale about outriding the *goums,* but he kept quiet about the cruel-eyed man in the white palanquin. Khardan had not mentioned him to anyone, nor did he intend to, having a sort of superstitious dread that—like a demon of Sul—speaking of the man might somehow summon him.

"Saiyad has offered to take the woman into his *harem,*" Khardan added. "This is a noble gesture on Saiyad's part, Father, since the woman is dowerless."

Majiid glanced questioningly at the *spahi*. Saiyad, coming forward, bowed to the Sheykh to indicate that Khardan spoke the desire of his heart. Majiid turned to his son. "The woman's life is in your hands, Calif, since you are her savior. Is this your will?"

"It is, O Sheykh," answered Khardan formally. "This man was leader in my absence and performed his duties with exemplary skill. I can think of no more suitable reward."

"Then so shall it be. Woman, attend to me."

The Sheykh looked up at the female, who still sat unmoving upon the horse. "Woman?"

The slave did not respond but stared straight ahead with a face so white and rigid that Majiid was reminded uncomfortably of a corpse.

"What's the matter with her?" he demanded, turning to Khardan.

"She has suffered a great shock, Father," Khardan replied in a low voice.

"Um, well, Saiyad will soon comfort her," Majiid said
with an attempt at a laugh that failed beneath that frozen face,
glimmering pale like a waning moon. Majiid cleared his
throat. "Woman, you will henceforth belong to this man,
who, in his mercy, has deigned to take you dowerless into his
family. You will submit to his will in all things and be a
dutiful servant, and you will be rewarded by his caring and
compassion."

Saiyad, bowing again, grinned broadly at Khardan. Reaching
up his hands, he grasped hold of the woman and brought her
down—limp and unresisting—from the horse's back.

"If there is nothing else I can do for you, my Sheykh,"
Saiyad began, licking his lips, his hungry gaze fixed upon the
woman, "it has been a long ride. . . ."

"Yes, of course!" Majiid smiled. "No doubt you are tired
and desire some rest. Go ahead!"

Taking hold of the woman by the arm, Saiyad led her to
his tent.

Watching her go, her head bowed, her feet stumbling as if
she did not see the ground on which she walked, Khardan
quieted the misgivings stirring in his heart. Irritably he told
himself that it was all for the slave woman's own good. Why
couldn't she be grateful? If Khardan had not rescued her, she
might now be in the clutches of some brute, who would use
her for his foul pleasures, then cast her to his servants when
he grew tired of her. Saiyad was rough and certainly not
handsome. A poor man, he had only one wife, so this addition
to his household would be a welcome one. The slave woman's
life would be hard, but she would be fed and sheltered.
Saiyad would not beat her. Her children, if she bore him any,
would be well-cared for. . . .

Saiyad and his new woman disappeared into his tent.
Khardan's father asked his son a question about the situation
in Kich, and with relief, the Calif turned his attention to other
matters. Deep in discussion, the two walked together to the
Sheykh's tent. Noticing Jaafar watching them intently, Khardan
glanced at his father and received a grudging nod to include
the other Sheykh in their talk. The three men disappeared
inside Majiid's tent; Fedj, the djinn, came along to serve
them.

The other *spahis* went to their tents, accompanied by their families, the women exclaiming excitedly over lovely silks or new brass lamps or showing off sparkling bracelets. Unnoticed, forgotten, Zohra crept back inside her own tent. Pressing cold hands to feverish cheeks, she sank down upon silken cushions, biting at her veil in her frustration.

All was silent in the camp. The sun, sinking down in the west, brought an eerie beauty to the harsh land, painting the sands with rose pink, deepening to purple. The first cool breeze of coming night was drifting among the tents with a soft sigh when the sound of a hoarse yell split the air.

So ferocious was the sound, so filled with rage, that everyone in camp thought they were under attack. Weapons in hand, men dashed from their tents, looking about wildly and demanding to know what was happening. Women clasped children to their breasts and peered fearfully from the entrances. Khardan and the Sheykhs rushed from Majiid's dwelling.

"What is it? What in the name of Sul is going on?" Majiid thundered.

"This, O Sheykh!" yelled a voice. Choked with fury, it could hardly be understood. "Witness this!"

Expecting nothing less than the Amir's army galloping down upon him, Majiid turned with astonishment to see Saiyad emerging from his tent, dragging the slave woman by the back of her robes. She was unveiled, her red hair tumbling about her in a brilliant mass. With a vicious snarl Saiyad hurled her across the compound. The woman fell forward on her stomach, hands outspread, to lie face down, unmoving, at Majiid's feet.

"What is this, Saiyad?" the astounded Sheykh demanded, angry at being alarmed over nothing. "What's the matter? Isn't the girl a virgin? Surely you didn't expect as much—"

"Virgin!" Saiyad drew a seething breath. Reaching down, he grasped hold of a handful of the red hair and yanked the woman's head up, forcing her to face Majiid.

"Virgin!" Saiyad repeated. "She isn't a virgin! She isn't even a woman! She is a man!"

Chapter 10

Jaafar, staring at Saiyad, burst into raucous laughter.

Saiyad flushed an angry red. Reaching out, he grabbed Khardan's scimitar, snatching it from the Calif's hand.

"I have been shamed!" Saiyad cried. "Defiled!"

He dragged the disfigured man to his knees. Raising the sword, Saiyad held it poised above the kneeling, shivering figure. "I will have my revenge by cleaving this unclean head from its neck!"

The man raised his head. Khardan saw the expression on the pale face undergo a swift and horrifying change, the eyes reflecting stark terror and fear such as he had never seen in the eyes of another human before. It was not terror at the blow coming, it seemed, but at a memory of something so horrible it blotted out the threat of death. Staring aghast into the white face, Khardan realized with a riveting shock that this was no man—it was a youth, not much older than Achmed. A boy, frightened and alone.

Once again Khardan saw the woman . . . the boy . . . standing upon the slave block, saw the look of hopeless despair. Now he understood. Who knows how or why the young man came to be dressed as a woman, but he had foreseen as surely as he drew breath that he must be discovered and that his end would be a terrible one. This sword blow, at least, would be swift and painless, the misery that was traced upon the face soon ended . . .

Saiyad's arms tensed, ready to deliver the killing stroke.

Moving swiftly, without stopping to consider why, Khardan

caught hold of Saiyad's hands, wrested the sword from the man's grasp.

"Why did you stop me? Why?" Foam flecked Saiyad's lips, his eyes were bloodshot and bulging from his head.

"I saved this life," Khardan said sternly. Retrieving his scimitar from the sand where it had fallen, he thrust it into his belt. "Therefore, the life is mine alone to take."

"Then you kill him! You must. I demand it! I have been shamed!" hissed Saiyad, breathing heavily and wiping his hands repeatedly upon his robes as though to rid himself of some filth. "You cannot let him live! He is foul, unclean!"

Ignoring Saiyad and ignoring, too, the swift angry glance his father shot him, Khardan turned to face the youth. People crowded near, pushing, shoving, and craning their necks to get a better view.

"Back off!" the Calif commanded, glaring around him.

Scowling, still rubbing his hands against his tunic front, Saiyad remained standing where he was. No one else moved.

"Father, is this not my right?" Khardan demanded.

Majiid nodded wordlessly.

"Then let me talk to the . . . this man!"

His face grim, Majiid moved some distance away, dragging Jaafar with him. One by one the other members of the tribe backed away, forming a large half-circle. Khardan stood in the center, the young man remaining kneeling before him, head bowed.

The Calif stared helplessly at the youth, completely at a loss as to what he should do. By law, this man who had disguised himself as a woman and who had apparently used this disguise to entice another man to lay hands upon him must surely die. Khardan would be unworthy of his standing as Calif of his people if he defied the law. Slowly the Calif drew his sword.

And yet . . . there had to be some other explanation!

The youth's face had regained its terrible composure. Crouched on his knees, his hands clasped tightly together as though clutching every bit of courage he possessed, he looked up at Khardan with empty eyes, facing death with a despairing calm that was dreadful to see.

Khardan's palms began to sweat. He flexed them around the sword's hilt. He had killed men before, but never one

kneeling, never one who was defenseless. The Calif felt
sickened at the thought, yet he had no choice. Shifting nervously
in his stance as though to better position himself to deliver the
killing blow, Khardan glanced swiftly around the camp, seeking
inspiration.

He received it, from an unexpected source.

Movement in the shadows of a tent caught his eye. Coming
forward noiselessly so that she stood within the failing twilight,
Zohra mouthed a word, at the same time tapping her head as
though there were something wrong with it.

"Mad!"

Khardan stared at her, the sudden rush of thoughts confusing
him. How had she known the reluctance he felt? Stranger
still, why should she care about this boy one way or another?
No matter, the Calif supposed. He had his answer now. He
knew the beginning, if not exactly where all this would end.

Lowering his sword, Khardan cast a grim glance around
the assembled tribes. "I have remembered that Akhran gives
everyone the right of speaking in his own defense. Does
anyone question this?"

There was some muttering. Saiyad snarled angrily, mumbling
something inaudible, but he said nothing aloud.

Khardan turned back, regarding the youth grimly. "You
may speak. Tell why you have done this thing."

The youth did not answer.

Khardan checked a sigh. Somehow he had to force him to
talk.

"Can you answer me?" he asked suddenly. "Are you dumb?"

Wearily, as though longing for sleep that was denied him,
the young man shook his head.

"From your look, you are not of this land," Khardan
continued patiently, hoping to force the young man to respond.
"Yet you understand our language. I saw your face. You
understood Saiyad's words when he threatened to kill you."

The youth swallowed, and Khardan could see the knot in
the young man's throat that marked the true nature of his sex.

"I . . . I understand," the young man said in a voice that
was like the music of the flute. They were the first words he
had spoken since Khardan had rescued him. The empty eyes
looked up at the Calif.

"Why these questions?" the youth continued in a dulled, uncaring tone. "End it now."

"Damn it, boy! Don't make me kill you!" Khardan shot back in a vehement whisper, meant for the youth's ears alone.

Startled, the young man blinked, as though awakening from some terrible dream, and stared at Khardan dazedly.

Walking over to the youth, the Calif grasped hold of the young man's chin, turning his face roughly to the light. "You have no beard." With the blade of his sword he parted the robes. "No hair upon the chest."

"It . . . is the manner of . . . men of my . . . land," the youth said in a strained voice.

"Is it also the manner of men of your land to dress as women?"

Bowing his head, flushing in shame, the young man did not reply.

"What did you do in this land of yours?" Khardan persisted.

"I . . . I was a wizard—a 'sorcerer' in your tongue."

Khardan relaxed. Behind him he heard excited, wondering whispers.

"Where is this land?" Khardan continued, praying to *Hazrat* Akhran to grant him wisdom and a certain amount of luck.

The God heard his prayers. Or at least some God heard.

"Across the Hurn sea," the boy mumbled.

"What?" Khardan gripped the young man painfully by the chin, raising his head. "Repeat your words, that all may hear!"

"Across the Hurn sea!" the youth cried in desperation.

With a grim smile Khardan thrust the young man roughly away from him. The Calif turned to face his tribe.

"There, you hear? He claims to be a sorcerer! All know only women may practice magic. Not only that, but he claims to come from a land across the Hurn." The Calif waved his arms. "All know that there is no such land! All know that the Hurn empties into the abyss of Sul. It is as I thought. The young man is mad. By the laws of *Hazrat* Akhran, we are forbidden to harm him."

Khardan gazed about defiantly. Victory was within his grasp, but he hadn't won. Not yet. Accustomed to either obeying or disobeying the laws of their God as they saw fit, the nomads weren't going to give up the excitement of an execution so easily.

Saiyad—his honor unsatisfied—took a step forward and turned to face the tribes.

"I say he is not mad! I say he is a perversion and should, by the laws of *Hazrat* Akhran, be put to death."

Khardan glanced at his father. Majiid said nothing, but it was obvious that the Sheykh agreed with Saiyad. Arms folded over his massive chest, eyebrows bristling, the Sheykh regarded his son with anger, mingled with concern.

Khardan realized that his leadership in the tribe was balanced on a knife's edge. He cast a swift glance at Zohra, still hidden in the shadows. He could see her eyes, black, fiery, watching him intently, but he had no idea what she might be thinking.

If it is your will that this young man live, then help me, Akhran, Khardan prayed silently.

And suddenly, whether from Akhran or from within himself, the Calif had his answer.

Khardan turned back to face the youth. "You yourself will make the decision whether you live or die. I give you a choice. If you are sane, you will choose to die bravely as a man. If you are mad, you will choose to live—as a woman."

A murmur of appreciation and awe rippled through the tribe. Majiid glanced about proudly now, defying anyone to argue with such godlike wisdom.

"Will that satisfy you?" Khardan looked at Saiyad.

Head to one side, Saiyad considered. If the young man was sane, he would pay with his life for his crime and Saiyad's honor would be avenged. If the youth were mad—and what sane man would choose to live life as a woman—then it would be understood by everyone that the boy had seen the face of Akhran and no shame could come to Saiyad. Either way, his honor would be appeased. Saiyad nodded once, his brow clearing.

Raising the sword, the blade flashing red in the light of the setting sun, Khardan held it poised, flexing his hands on the hilt to get a firmer grip. "Well?" he prompted harshly.

His eyes stared into the eyes of the youth. For a brief instant there was just the two of them, poised upon the turning world. No one else was present, no one at all. Khardan could hear the beating of his own heart, the whisper of his own breath. The sun was sinking, deepening to blood red, the sky to the east was black, glittering with the first faint stars. He could smell the scents of the desert—the tamarisk and sage, the sweet scent of the grass around the oasis, the acrid odor of the horses. He could hear the rustling of the palm leaves, the song of the wind across the desert floor.

"Live!" he pleaded softly, almost reverently with the boy. "Live!"

The eyes looking into his flooded with tears. The head drooped, the red hair fell around the shoulders like a veil. A sob burst from the young man's throat, his shoulders heaved.

Weak with relief, Khardan lowered the sword. His impulse was to take the young man by the shoulders and comfort him, as he might have comforted one of his younger brothers. But he dared not. He had his standing to maintain. Scowling darkly therefore, he turned back to face the tribes.

"I will not kill a woman!" He thrust his sword into his belt.

"That is all very well," said Jaafar suddenly, stepping forward and pointing at the wretched figure huddled on the sand. "And I admit that the boy is undoubtedly mad, touched by the God. But what is to become of him? Who will take care of him?"

"I will tell you!" came a clear voice.

From out of the shadows of her tent stepped Zohra, her silken *caftan* rippling with the rising wind, her jewelry sparkling in the dying light. "He says he has the power of magic. Therefore he will enter the *harem*—as Khardan's wife!"

Chapter 11

The sun sank behind the far western hills. The afterglow lit the sky and was reflected back by the crystals of desert sand. There were a few startled gasps from some of the women, a flurry of whispers and silken rustling as wives crowded together like flocks of birds, and here and there a low voiced command from a husband to hush.

Silence, thick and heavy with amazement, fell over the tribesmen. All looked to Khardan, awaiting his reaction.

The Calif both looked and felt as though he'd been riding his horse at a mad gallop when the animal suddenly dropped dead beneath him. The breath left his body; his skin flushed red, then went deathly white; his frame trembled.

"Wife, you go too far!" he managed to gasp out, nearly strangling.

"Not at all," Zohra replied coolly. "You have stolen two—shall we say—'women' and carried them far from their homes. By the law of Akhran you are, therefore, required to provide for them, either by establishing them in your tent or seeing them established in another—"

"By Sul, wife!" Khardan swore viciously, taking a step nearer Zohra. "I saved their lives! I didn't carry them off in a raid!"

Zohra made a fluttering motion with her hands. Her face was unveiled, and it was smooth and grave and solemn. Only Khardan, looking into the black eyes, saw smoldering there coals he had fondly thought quenched. What could have touched off this fire, the Calif couldn't imagine. In another woman he might have said it was jealousy, but jealousy implies a certain amount of caring, and Zohra had made it clear countless times that she would as soon give her love to the meanest creature that walked as to give it to him.

He had thought her changed, but apparently not. No, this was just another attempt to humiliate him, to shame him before his people and to elevate herself in the eyes of her own. And once again, as in the matter of the bridal sheet, Khardan was helpless to fight her, for she stood solidly on her own ground—magic, a woman's province, inviolate by men.

"I will give each of these 'girls' the ritual tests, of course," Zohra said.

Her proud gaze swept over everyone to light upon Meryem, who shrank into the arms of Khardan's mother.

"What about it, child?" Zohra asked of her with mocking gentleness. "Are you—a Sultan's daughter—skilled in the art of magic?"

"I—I am not . . . very good," the girl admitted timidly with a sidelong glance at Khardan from beneath her long lashes. She appeared confused, yet confident. She did not yet understand her danger. "But I would do my best to please my husband. . . ."

"I'm sure you would," murmured Zohra with the purring sound a lioness makes before tearing the throat from her victim. "And I'm sure there will be many men here who will come to 'your father' "—Zohra smiled placidly upon the glowering Majiid—"and will offer to take you to wife despite your lack of skill in magic. For I am certain that you have talents in other areas. . . ."

"But I am to be Khardan's wife," Meryem began innocently, then stopped, realizing something was wrong.

"Ah, I'm afraid not, poor child." Zohra sighed softly. "Not if he takes this other 'woman' into his tent. Are you skilled in magic?"

Turning, she glanced at the youth, who had no idea what any of this was about and who knew only that—once again—his fate was being held in balance. Still crouched on the ground, the young man's sobs had ceased. He stared from Khardan to Zohra in blank confusion.

"Yes, I am . . . skilled. . . ." He faltered, not knowing what else to say.

Truly mad! Zohra thought. But—mad or sane—he serves my purpose.

Zohra had taken a gamble on her course of battle. Armed with knowledge of her husband and a woman's knowledge of other women, she had ridden forth, confident of victory, and she had just achieved it. Like all men, Khardan distrusted magic, since it was something he could not control. No matter how proficient in the art Meryem truly was—and Zohra, thinking of the soft life in the Sultan's court, did not believe this could be very proficient at all—the girl would surely play down her talent in this area in favor of others that Khardan was certain to find more to his taste. As for the madman, whether he was skilled or not didn't matter. After all, it was Zohra who gave the tests and they were always given in secret. . . .

"You see, my child," Zohra continued, her limpid-eyed gaze turning back to Meryem, "Khardan has a wife already. This will make his second. It is a law that a man can take no more wives than he can support, and since the failure to sell the horses, it will be all my husband can do to keep the two of us. He cannot provide for a third."

Had Zohra been watching Meryem closely, she would have seen the blue eyes go suddenly cold as blue steel, she would have felt their sharp, cutting edge, and she would have known that she had created an enemy—a deadly one, who could fight her on her own level. Exultant in her victory, enjoying the sweet fruits of vengeance against her husband, Zohra did not see the dagger in Meryem's gaze.

One person saw it, however—the young man. But he was so lost in confusion that though he saw the girl's deadly, darting gaze, he soon lost the memory in the turmoil of his mind.

"Father!" said Khardan, turning to the Sheykh. "I put this to you! Give me your judgment and I will abide by it."

It was obvious from Majiid's lowering brow and quivering mustache that he would have sided with his son. But he had the law to uphold, justice must be served.

Shaking his head, he said sternly, "We cannot leave the madman to starve; that would anger *Hazrat* Akhran. You have accepted responsibility for the madman. If you had not intervened, then he would be dead now—purely by accident''—the Sheykh looked up deprecatingly into the heavens—''since we would have had no way of knowing he was mad, in which case we would have been forgiven his death due to our ignorance, and you, Khardan''—Majiid glowered at his son—''would be making wedding plans. Let this be a lesson!''

He gestured at the girl. ''I have accepted Meryem into my family. She will be well cared for until such time as a suitor comes who can claim her hand.''

The judgment given, the Sheykh's lips snapped tightly shut. Folding his arms across his chest, he turned his back upon the supplicant, a sign that there was to be no further discussion.

''Now wait just a minute!'' The voice was that of Badia, Khardan's mother.

Stepping forward, she faced Majiid. A diminutive woman, she did not come to her tall husband's shoulder. Generally meek and docile, knowing and accepting her place as head wife and mother, Badia had her limits, however, and these had just been reached. Hands on her hips, she faced her astonished husband, casting a glance around the assembled tribes.

''I think you have all lost your wits! You are as mad as this wretched creature!'' she said with a scathing gesture at the youth. ''A man in the *harem*! Such a thing is not done unless he is . . .has been . . .'' She flushed deeply but was not embarrassed enough to be swerved from her course. ''Has had his manhood cut away,'' she said finally, ignoring her husband's shocked look.

Other women in the tribe nodded and murmured in agreement.

''The poor young man is mad. You're not going to make a eunuch of him, too,'' Khardan said coldly. ''A beardless chin, a hairless chest. What harm can you fear he will do? Especially in my *harem*.'' He cast a bitter glance at Zohra. ''My wife is more of a man than this one! But—if it will please you, Mother—I will set a guard at his tent. Pukah shall watch over him. There is probably wisdom in that anyway, lest he—in his madness—chooses to do harm to himself or someone else. And now there is one more thing I will say before the matter closes."

Leaving the center of the compound, Khardan walked over to stand before Meryem. He took hold of her hands in his, looking down into the adoring, tear-filled eyes. "By day, you are more radiant than the sun. By night, you brighten my darkness like the moon. I love you, and I swear as *Hazrat* Akhran is my witness that no man will possess you except myself, Meryem, if I have to steal the wealth of the Amir's treasury to do it."

Leaning down, he kissed the girl's forehead. Weeping, Meryem nestled against him. He felt her body, soft and warm, trembling in his grasp. Her fragrance intoxicated him, her tears inflamed his heart. Hurriedly his mother came to take the girl and lead her away.

Breathing as though he had been fighting a battle with ten thousand devils, Khardan left as well, walking rapidly into the deepening darkness of the desert. If he went to find some glimmer of hope in the Rose of the Prophet, it was not there. Green and almost healthy looking when Khardan had left for his journey to the city, the plant was—once again—brown and shriveled.

One by one the other members of the tribes melted away, hurrying to their tents to discuss the day's events in excited whispers. Only two were left standing in the compound, Zohra and the youth.

Zohra had won, but for some reason the sweet fruit of revenge had changed to ashes in her mouth. Hiding her wounds, she made her way with haughty demeanor back to her tent.

The young man remained behind, crouched on his knees on the hard granite of the desert floor. Many gave him sidelong glances as they scurried past. None came to him. He did not know what to do, where to go. If it had been his headless corpse lying there, he could not have experienced more bitterly the taste of the loneliness of death than he did now, surrounded by the living.

John had died once, his life severed by the blade.

"How many times have I died?" Mathew asked himself miserably. "How many times must I go on dying?"

His strength gave way and he sank down onto the warm, hard ground, his senses slipping from him. He never noticed the soft feathers of the angel's wing drawing over him or felt the light touch of the angel's tear, falling like dew upon his skin.

Chapter 12

"Who are you?" asked Pukah in astonishment.

The woman who had been hovering over the young man whirled in fear. At the sight of Pukah, she instantly disappeared.

"Wait! Don't go!" Pukah cried. "Beautiful creature! I didn't mean to frighten you! Don't leave! I— She's gone." The djinn gazed around disconsolately. "What was she? An immortal, of course, but like none I've seen in all my centuries!"

Coming nearer the unconscious youth, Pukah felt about in the air with his hands. "Are you here, lovely being? Show yourself. You needn't be afraid of Pukah. Gentle Pukah, I am called. Harmless as a human babe. Come back, dazzling enchanter! I want only to be your adoring slave, to worship at your feet. Such small, white feet, peeping beneath your white gown, hair the silver of starlight, wings like a dove. . . . Wings! Imagine that! And eyes that melt my heart! . . .

"Nothing. She's gone." Pukah heaved a sigh, his shoulders slumped. "And I am desolated! I know what you are going to say." He raised his hand to forestall any argument that might be forthcoming from his other half. "You, Pukah, are in too much trouble already. The last thing you need is a female— even if she did have wings. Because of you, Sheykh Zeid and twenty or so thousand mad *meharistes*—give or take several thousand—are going to sweep up out of the south and murder us all. Thinking to right this by trying to bring about peace between Quar and Akhran so that the tribes can separate and no longer prove a threat to Zeid so that Zeid would go back to

314

his camels and leave us in peace, I went to Kaug—may sting rays swim into his *pantalons*—and told him that all three tribes were gathering together to strike out at the city of Kich.''

Shaking his head sadly, Pukah lifted the unconscious youth. ''And it should have worked! Kaug was terrified, I swear it! Well, you know! You saw him!'' This to Pukah's alter ego, not the young man. ''It was Quar, that archfiend of a God, who stirred up trouble. How was I to know the Amir was such a powerful general? How was I to know he had magical horses? How was I to know he would try to arrest my poor master and nearly get us all killed? I—''

''So it was *you*!'' came a ferocious voice from out of the darkness.

Pukah nearly dropped the young man he was carrying over his shoulder. ''Pukah,'' he muttered to himself, glancing around swiftly, ''will you never learn to keep your mouth shut? Who . . . who is there?'' he called.

''Sond!'' came the terrible voice.

The large, muscular djinn took shape and form, standing before Pukah, his strong arms folded before his broad chest, and a dark expression on his face.

''Sond! Honored friend! I would bow, but as you see, I am rather discommoded at the present time—''

'' 'Discommoded!' '' said Sond, his voice swelling with his rising passion. ''When I am through with you, swine, you will not only be discommoded, you will be disembodied, disemboweled, disexcruciated, disenchanted, and dis-anything else I can think of!''

The young man, hanging upside down, his head and arms dangling across Pukah's shoulders, groaned and began to stir. Wondering why Sond was in such a towering rage, and also wondering, uneasily, how much the elder djinn had overheard, and further wondering how he could escape with his skin and his ambition both intact, Pukah gave Sond a meek smile.

''I am honored that you take such an interest in me and my unworthy doings, Sond, and it would please me no end to be able to discuss them with you, but—as you see—my master has ordered me to tend to this poor madman, and of course, I must obey, being the dutiful servant that I am. If you will wait for me here, I will deposit the madman in his bed, then return. I swear, I will be back in two barks of a dog—''

"Two barks of a *dead* dog," Sond interrupted grimly. "Don't think you can escape me so easily, worm."

The djinn clapped his hands together with a sound like thunder. The young man hanging over Pukah's shoulders disappeared.

Pukah nervously began to back up.

"My poor madman!" he cried. "What have you done with him?"

"Sent him to his bed. Weren't those your orders?" Sond said through clenched teeth, advancing one step forward for each step Pukah retreated. "I have done your work for you. Are you not grateful?"

"I—I am!" Pukah gasped, inadvertently putting his foot into a brass pot and nearly falling into a tent. "Dee-deeply grateful, friend S-s-sond."

Catching his balance, Pukah hopped along, trying desperately to extricate his foot from the pot. Sond, shoulder muscles bulging, veins popping, eyes flaming, continued to stalk the unfortunate young djinn.

"Therefore, since you are so grateful to me, 'friend' Pukah, do continue your most interesting conversation. You went to Kaug, you say, and told him—told him what?"

"That . . . uh . . . that the two tribes of Sheykhs Majiid al Fakhar and Jaafar al Widjar were united at last and that . . . uh . . . we were now rejoicing that a third tribe—that of the powerful Sheykh Zeid al Saban—would soon be united with us as well and . . . and''—Pukah thought swiftly—"I told Kaug that this was all *your* doing, O Great Sond, and that truly this is proof of your high intelligence—"

Thinking to flatter the elder djinn (also thinking that if Zeid did attack them it would be best to start laying the groundwork for casting the blame onto someone else's shoulders), Pukah was astounded beyond measure to see Sond—upon hearing these words—go livid.

"You . . . what?" The djinn choked, near strangling.

"I gave you all the credit, friend Sond," Pukah said humbly. Finally kicking the pot off his foot, he straightened and held up his hands deprecatingly. "Do not thank me. It was nothing but your due. . . ."

Pukah's voice died. Sond, bellowing terrifyingly, had soared to nearly twenty feet in height. His great arms lifted above his head as though he meant to tear the stars, one by one, from the sky. Pukah saw instantly, however, that the stars were not the target of Sond's wrath. Plunging down like a meteor, the djinn descended upon Pukah.

Panic-stricken, the young djinn had time only to hide his head in his arms and regret his young life, tragically ended, visualizing himself stuffed in an iron money box, locked and sealed and buried one thousand feet below the surface of the world. A gigantic wind hit him, blew all around him, completely uprooting two palm trees. . . .

Then the gale stopped.

This is it, the end, thought Pukah grimly.

But there was nothing.

Fearfully he waited.

Still nothing.

Keeping his arms covering his head, his eyes squinched tightly shut, Pukah listened. All he heard was a pitiful moaning as of a man having his guts wrenched out. Cautiously Pukah opened half an eye and peered out over his elbow.

Bent double, his arms clasped around his stomach as though he were holding himself together, was Sond—sobbing bitterly.

"Ah, my dear friend," said Pukah, truly touched and feeling more than a little guilty that he hadn't spoken the truth. "I know that you are grateful to me, but I assure you that this display of emotion is completely—"

" 'Grateful' !"

Sond lifted his face. Tears streaked the djinn's cheeks, foam frothed on his lips, blood dripped from his mouth. Teeth gnashing, hands outstretched, Sond leaped for Pukah's throat.

"Grateful!" Sond screamed. Knocking Pukah to the ground, he grabbed the young djinn around the neck and began bashing his head into the desert floor, driving it deeper with each word he spoke. "She is lost! Lost to me! Forever! Forever!"

Bash, bash, bash . . .

Pukah would have screamed for help, but his tongue was so tangled up with everything else rattling around in his head that all he could do was gasp "Uh! Uh! Uh!" at each blow.

Eventually Sond's strength gave out, or he might have

bashed Pukah clear through the world, where the djinn would have come out on the other side and discovered that Mathew wasn't mad after all. Exhausted by his grief and his rage, Sond merely gave Pukah a final shove that sent the young djinn down through six feet of solid granite. Then Sond fell over backward, moaning for breath.

Dizzy, disoriented, and thoroughly shaken, Pukah at first considered staying in his hole and—not content with that hiding him from Sond—pulling the desert in on top of him. But as his head cleared, he began to consider the elder djinn's words: *She is lost. . . . Lost to me forever. . . .*

She who? Lost how? And why was it apparently all his— Pukah's—fault?

Knowing he would never rest content—not even locked in an iron money box—without the answer to these questions, Pukah peered up out of his hole.

"Sond?" he said timidly, preparing to dive back down if the elder djinn showed signs of renewed hostility. "I don't understand. Tell me what's wrong. Something *is* wrong, I take it."

Sond groaned in answer, flinging his head about from side to side, his face contorted in a grief most awful to witness.

"Sond," said Pukah, beginning to have the feeling now that something was really, really wrong and wondering if it was going to further compound his own troubles, "if you'd . . . uh . . . tell me, perhaps I could help—"

" 'Help'!" Sond propped himself up on his elbows, gazing at Pukah with bloodshot eyes. "What more can you do than you've done already except to take my sword and slice me in two!"

"I would be honored to do that, of course, if it is what you truly desire, O Sond," began Pukah humbly.

"Oh, shut up!" Sond snarled. "There is nothing you can do. Nothing anyone can do, not even Akhran."

Upon hearing the name of the awful God, Pukah glanced nervously up into the heavens and scrunched back down into the hole.

"You . . . spoke to Holy Akhran?"

"Yes. What else could I do?"

"And . . . what did you tell him?"

"I confessed my guilt to him."

Pukah heaved a sigh of relief. "For which guilt I am certain the merciful God has forgiven you," he said soothingly.

"That was, of course, before I knew anything about the hand you had in this!" Sond growled, glaring at Pukah. He sighed bleakly. "Not that it matters anyway, I suppose."

"I'm sure it doesn't!" Pukah said, but Sond wasn't listening. "I lost Nedjma the night Kaug stole her from the garden. Akhran made me see this. I was a fool to believe that anything I did would induce Kaug to give her back. He was using me. But I was desperate. What else could I do?"

In a few bitter words Sond related the story of Nedjma's capture by the 'efreet and Kaug's demands that Sond separate the tribes or lose Nedjma forever.

"I tried to split them apart. It didn't work. You saw that," Sond continued miserably. "Everything was against me! Zeid coming out of nowhere like that"—Pukah squirmed uncomfortably—"and forcing the Akar to make friends with the Hrana. I went to Kaug to try to explain and beg him to give me another chance, but he only laughed cruelly. He asked if I truly thought myself clever enough to thwart him. Nedjma was gone, he said, and I would never see her again—until the day I myself was sent to join her."

Pukah's brow wrinkled in thought. "That's an odd statement. What did he mean by it?"

Sond shrugged wearily, letting his head lapse into his hands. "How should I know?" he mumbled.

"And what did *Hazrat* Akhran say?"

"After I finally found him," Sond said, looking up, his face drawn, "a search that took four days and four nights, he told me that he understood why I had done what I had done. He said that next time I was to come to him directly, then he gave me a stern lecture on attempting to subvert the ways of the Gods and reminded me that he himself had ordered *us* to find out what was happening to the vanishing immortals—"

"Why, that's it!" Pukah cried.

"That's what?"

"That's what happened to Nedjma! Kaug's sent her to wherever the lost djinn are. From what he said about your going to join her, we're next, seemingly," Pukah added after some reflection.

"Do you truly think so?" Sond looked up, hope illuminating

his face so that it glowed in the dark with a pale, white radiance.

Pukah looked at him in amazement.

"Honored Sond, I am pleased beyond measure that you have recovered your spirits and that any poor words of mine have performed this transformation, but I can't help wondering why this dread news of Nedjma's being banished to the Gods know where—no, on second thought, to someplace of which *they* don't even know—fills you with such joy?"

"I . . . I feared . . . she was . . . that Kaug had . . ." Sond's voice trailed off huskily, his face growing dark and brooding once more.

"Ah!" said Pukah in sudden understanding. "Kaug?" He scoffed. "You say Nedjma is delicate and beautiful? Then she will not arouse Kaug's interest. He ruts with sea cows. I'm serious! I have it on very good authority. . . . Now, come, my friend."

Pukah felt confident enough to climb out of his hole. Going over to Sond, he respectfully assisted the djinn to his feet. "I am always thinking, you know. It is my curse to have a fertile brain. And I have the beginnings of a plan. No, I can't say anything yet. I must do some research, some investigating," the djinn continued importantly, brushing the sand off Sond's shoulders and putting the djinn's rumpled clothing to rights. "Don't say a word to anyone yet about . . . well, what you overheard me discussing with myself tonight, particularly to the master. All this is part of the plan. You might spoil it.

"And now," continued Pukah, as Sond stood gazing at him in bewilderment, "I must go and tend to the madman as my master ordered. As if I didn't have enough to do!" He sighed a long-suffering sigh. "Be of good hope, O Sond!" Pukah clapped the djinn on the shoulder. "And put your faith in Pukah!"

With that, he vanished.

Chapter 13

Waking from the strangest dream he'd ever experienced, Mathew sat up suddenly, shivering in fear. He'd been lying in the sand when a young man wearing a white turban and flowing silken pants appeared out of nowhere and—with an unbelievable strength—lifted him up onto his shoulders. This young man had been talking to himself—at least so Mathew thought, until another man appeared. His face was dreadful to behold. He made a sound like thunder, and then both men were gone and the young wizard was alone inside a tent that smelled strongly of goat.

Glancing around in the darkness, Mathew began to realize that at least that part of his dream hadn't been a dream. He *was* lying in a tent, it *did* smell as if a goat had been its former inhabitant, and he was alone in the night. The air was bitterly cold, and he groped about in the darkness for something to cover himself. Finding a soft woolen blanket, he wrapped it around his body and lay back down upon the cushions.

Suddenly, with a pang of fear, he started back up. Thrusting his hand deep inside his robes, he felt frantically for the fishbowl. His fingers closed over its cold surface, the edges of the gold and silver metalwork biting into his skin. Gently he shook it and was reassured by the feeling of motion within the globe. At least the water was still there; presumably the fish were safe and unharmed.

A light step from outside the tent caused Mathew to hastily thrust the bowl back inside his robes. His heart pounding, wondering what new terror he was going to have to endure, the wizard stared at the tent entrance.

"Are you awake, mast—er, mistress?" The voice seemed a bit confused.

"Yes," Mathew answered after a moment's hesitation.

"May I enter?" the voice continued humbly and servilely. "My master has instructed me to make you comfortable for the night."

"Are . . . are you from Khardan?" Mathew asked, daring to breathe a little easier.

"Yes, mas—er, mistress."

"Then please, come inside."

"Thank you, mas . . . mistress," said the voice, and to Mathew's astonishment one of the figures came out of his dream and stepped inside the tent.

It was the young one, the one who had picked him up with the ease of a man lifting a puppy. Hands folded before him, his eyes cast down, the young man in the white turban performed the *salaam,* politely wishing Mathew health and joy.

Mathew stammered out a suitable reply.

"I have brought a *chirak,* an oil lamp," the young man said, producing one out of the night. Setting it down carefully upon the tent floor, he caused it to light with a wave of his hand. "And here is a brazier and charcoal to burn to warm yourself. My master tells me that you are not of this land"— the young man spoke carefully, with elaborate politeness as though fearing to unduly upset Mathew—"therefore I assume you are not familiar with our ways?"

"N-no, I'm not."

The young man nodded solemnly, but—when he thought Mathew wasn't watching—he rolled his eyes to the heavens.

"Make certain that you set the brazier here, beneath the opening in the tent, so that the smoke may rise up and out. Otherwise you will not wake up in the morning, for the smoke of the charcoal is poisonous. If you will allow me to arrange your bed"—the young man gently but firmly crowded Mathew into a corner of the tent, out of the way—"I would suggest that you be careful to keep the cushions on the felt rug when you sleep. Neither the scorpion nor the *qarakurt* will cross felt, you know."

"No, I didn't," Mathew murmured, gazing in awe at this remarkable young man. "What is a *qarakurt*?"

"A largish black spider. You are dead within seconds of its bite."

"And . . . you say it won't walk on felt? Why not?" Mathew asked nervously.

"Ah, only *Hazrat* Akhran knows the answer to that one," the young man said piously. "All I know is that I have seen a man sleep soundly, though surrounded by an army of such spiders, all thirsting for his blood. Yet they would not set one black leg upon his felt blanket. And you must also remember to shake your clothes and especially your shoes out every morning before putting them on, for though the scorpion will not cross felt, he is smart and will wait for his chance to sting by hiding in your garments."

Remembering the past nights when he had not cared where he lay and thinking of how he had heedlessly slipped on the women's shoes each morning, Mathew felt his throat constrict as he vividly imagined the stinging tail of the scorpion thrusting itself into his flesh. To turn his thoughts from these horrors, he questioned the young man.

"You are a remarkable wiz—sorcerer," Mathew said earnestly. "How long have you studied the art?"

To Mathew's astonishment, the young man drew himself up very straight and regarded the wizard with a cold eye.

"I know you are mad," the young man said, "but I cannot see that this gives you the right to insult me."

"Insult you? I never meant—"

"To refer to me as a sorcerer! To imply that I dabble in that woman's art!" The young man appeared highly offended.

"But—the lamp you conjured. And the light. I assumed—"

"I am a djinn, of course. I am called Pukah. Khardan is my master."

"A djinn!" Mathew gasped and shrank back. Apparently he wasn't the only madman in this camp. "But . . . there are no such things as djinn!"

Pukah gave Mathew a pitying glance. "Mad as a foaming-mouthed dog," he muttered. Shaking his head, he continued to plump up the cushions. "By the way, mas-mistress. When I came to find you this night and discovered you lying

senseless upon the ground, there was an immortal—one of
my kind—bending over you.''

Eyes glowing with the memory, Pukah forgot what he was
doing and slowly sank down upon the cushions. "Yet she
wasn't of my kind, either. She was the most beautiful creature
I have ever seen. Her hair was silver. She was dressed in long
white robes, soft feathery white wings grew from her back.
spoke to her," the djinn said sadly, "but she vanished. Is she
your djinniyeh? If so," he continued eagerly, "could you tell
her that I truly mean her no harm and that I want just one
moment, one second with her to speak of my adoration—"

"I don't know what you're talking about!" Mathew
interrupted. "Djinniyeh! That's ridiculous! Although"—he
hesitated—"what you describe sounds very much like a being
we know as an angel. . . .''

" 'Angel'!" Pukah sighed rapturously. "What a beautiful
word. It fits her. Do all in your . . . uh . . . land have such
creatures to serve you?"

"Angels! Serve us!" Mathew was shocked at the sacrilege.
"Absolutely not! It would be our privilege to serve them if
we should ever be fortunate enough to see one."

"That I can believe," said Pukah gravely. "I would serve
her all my life, if she were mine. But then, if you never see
these beings, how do you communicate with your God?"

"Through the holy priests," Mathew said, faltering, his
thoughts going painfully to John. "It is the priests—and only
the highest ranking of their Order—who talk with the angels
of Promenthas and so learn His Holy Will."

"And that is all these angels do?"

"Well"—Mathew hesitated, suddenly uncomfortable—
"there are such beings known as guardian angels, whose duty
it is to watch over the humans in their care, but . . ."

"But what?" Pukah prodded inquisitively.

"I—I never really believed . . . I mean, I still don't. . . .''

"And you do not believe in me, either!" the djinn said.
"Yet here I stand. And now"—Pukah rose gracefully to his
feet—"if there is nothing further I can do for you, I must
return. My master undoubtedly needs me. He attempts nothing
without my advice and counsel."

"No, that—that is all," Mathew mumbled, his thoughts in
confusion. "Thank you . . . Pukah. . . .''

"Thank *you*, mas—mistress," rebuked the djinn, bowing, and melting into smoke, he disappeared as if sucked out the tent flap.

Catching his breath in amazement, Mathew stared blankly at where the djinn had been standing. "Maybe I *am* mad," he muttered, putting his hand to his head. "This isn't real. It can't be happening. It is all part of a dream and I will soon waken—"

Someone else was outside his tent. Mathew heard a clashing of jewelry, a silken rustle, and smelled the sudden sweetness of perfume. "Are you awake?" came a soft whisper.

"Yes," Mathew answered, too dazed to be frightened.

"May I enter? It is Zohra."

Zohra? He had a dim impression that this was the woman who had announced that he was to be taken into the *harem*. He vaguely remembered hearing someone refer to her by that name. This meant, from what he'd gathered, that she was Khardan's wife. "Yes, please do. . . ."

The tent flap darkened, a figure shapeless in a silken *caftan* entered. The lamplight gleamed off bracelets and rings, its flame reflected in black, flashing eyes barely visible above her veil. Entering swiftly, Zohra carefully shut the tent flap behind her, making certain that no chink of light escaped. Satisfied, she seated herself upon the cushions, kneeling with easy grace, staring at Mathew, who remained crouched in the corner of the tent where he had been driven by the djinn.

"Come within the light," Zohra ordered, making a commanding gesture with her arm, her bracelets clinking together musically. "There, sit across from me." She pointed to a pile of cushions opposite her, keeping the charcoal brazier and the oil lamp between them.

Doing as he was bidden, Mathew came to sit on the cushions. A pool of warm yellow from the flame of the lamp encircled them both, illuminating their faces, setting them against a backdrop of shadows that moved and wavered with the flickering of the flame. Slowly Zohra lowered the veil from her face, her eyes, all the while studying Mathew intently.

He, in turn, looking at her, thought that he had never before seen a woman so beautiful or so wild.

My wife is more of a man than this one!

Khardan's bitter words came back to Mathew, and—looking into the face of the woman who sat opposite him—he could well understand them. There was something masculine about the face in its unbending pride, the fierce anger that he could sense smoldering beneath the surface. Yet he had the feeling that the lips could soften, the eyes could be tender if she chose.

"I want to thank you, madam," Mathew said evenly, "for the part you played in saving my life."

"Yes," was the woman's unexpected reply, her eyes never leaving Mathew's face. "I came to find out why I did. What is there about you that moved me to intercede in your behalf? What is your name?"

"M-Mathew," the young man answered, startled at the abruptness of the question.

"M-Mat-hew." Zohra stumbled over it, her lips forming the unusual sound awkwardly.

"Mathew," Mathew repeated, feeling a certain joy at hearing his name spoken by another human being. It was the first time anyone had asked him.

"That is what I said. Mat-hew," Zohra replied loftily. "And so, Mat-hew, can you tell me why I saved your life?"

"N-no," replied the young man, startled at the question. Seeing that Zohra obviously expected an answer, he fumbled for words. "I . . . can only assume that your woman's heart, feeling pity . . ."

"Bah!" Zohra's contempt burned brighter than the lamp. "Woman's heart! I have no woman's heart. And I do not feel pity. If anything"—she cast him a scornful glance—"I feel contempt!" Angrily she tore at her gown, her sharp fingernails rending the fragile fabric. "If I had a man's body, I would never hide in this . . . this winding sheet!"

"And you would not have done what I did to save my life," Mathew said. Ashamed, he lowered his head before her scathing gaze. "And neither would he," he added softly, so softly he did not think she heard. But Zohra caught the words, pouncing on them like a diving hawk.

"Khardan? Of course not! He would die the death of a thousand daggers before hiding in woman's clothing. As for me, I am trapped in them. I die the death every morning when I wake and put them on! Perhaps"—now it was she who was speaking to herself—"perhaps that is why I saved you. I saw them looking at you, saw them staring at you the same way they stare at me. . . ."

Mathew, with a flash of insight, suddenly understood. The pride in the handsome face masked a gnawing pain. But why? What is wrong here? He did not understand, he had no way of knowing about the age-old enmity between the two tribes, of the marriage forced upon them by their God, of the brown and dying plant upon the Tel. He knew only because he saw it in her face that this woman was—like himself—surrounded by people and desperately lonely.

Now it was he who pitied her, pitied her and longed to help. And for the first time, the fear he had lived with for those torturous weeks since his capture began to fade to the back of his soul, replaced by a feeling more blessed—a feeling of caring. Yet he was wise enough to know that he must guard against revealing this feeling to her or endure the stinging lash of her pride.

"I do not believe you are mad," she said suddenly, and Mathew felt the fear return. "Yes," she added, seeing it flare in his eyes, "you must continue to make others believe you are insane. I shouldn't imagine that will be too difficult." Her lips twisted. "They are, as you have seen, fools."

"What . . . about Khardan?" Mathew hesitated, feeling his face flush. "Does he . . . think me mad?"

Zohra shrugged her slender shoulders, causing the silk to rustle around her, the perfume to drift lightly on the warmth spreading through the tent. "Why do you suppose I should know—or care—what he thinks?" Her eyes challenged Mathew to answer.

"No reason, except"—the young man faltered, uncomfortable at this discussion of intimate affairs between man and woman— "except that you are . . . his wife. I thought that he must—"

"Spend his nights in my company? Well, you are wrong." Zohra drew her robe around her as if chilled, though the heat radiating from the charcoal brazier was rapidly becoming stifling in the small tent. "We are man and wife in name only. Oh, that is no secret. You will hear it around the camp. You take a great interest in Khardan," she said suddenly, her eyes piercing Mathew's heart with a suddenness for which he was unprepared.

"He saved me from the slavers," Mathew said, his skin on fire. "And he saved me again this night. It is only natural—"

"By Sul!" said Zohra in amazement. "I believe you are in love with him!"

"No, no!" Mathew protested warmly. "I . . . admire him, that is all. And I am grateful. . . ."

"Is this the custom in your land across the sea?" Zohra asked curiously, reclining among the cushions. "Do men love men there? Such a thing is prohibited by our God. Is it not by yours?"

"I—I . . ." Poor Mathew had no idea what to say, where to begin. "You believe me then?" He grasped at this straw, hoping to save himself from drowning. "You believe that I do truly come from a land across the sea?"

"What does that matter!" Zohra brushed away the insignificant with a wave of her hand. "Answer my question."

"As . . . as a matter of fact," Mathew faltered, "such love as you . . . you mention is *not* prohibited by our God. Love . . . between any two people . . . is considered sacred and holy, so long as it is true love and caring and not . . . not simply lust or self-gratification of the body."

"How old are you?"

"I have seen eighteen summers in my land, madam," Mathew replied.

A sudden longing for that land, for those summers spent among the spreading oaks, came to the young wizard. His eyes filling with tears, he hurriedly bent his head so that she would not see. Perhaps she did and sought to turn his thoughts from his homesickness. If that was her intent, she succeeded admirably with her next question.

"And do you lie with men or with women?"

Mathew's eyes flared open; the blood rushed to his face until he felt it was a wonder it didn't drip from his gaping mouth.

"I—I have . . . never . . . lain . . . I mean . . . had that kind of . . . relationship with . . . anyone, m-madam!" he stammered.

"Ah, good," she said gravely, thoughtfully drawing the end of her veil between her jeweled fingers. "Our God, Akhran, forgives much, but I do not think he would be understanding in such a matter. And now," she continued, an amused smile playing about her lips, "you claim to be a sorcerer? How is this possible? The Gods give this gift only to women? Or"—a sudden thought occurred to her—"perhaps you have this because you have never—"

"I assure you, madam," said Mathew, regaining his dignity, "that the men of my land have long practiced this art and that what . . . we spoke of . . . has nothing to do with it."

"But"—Zohra appeared bewildered—"how is this possible? Do you not know of the Too-Learned Wizards and the curse put upon them by Sul? Men are forbidden to practice magic!"

"I do not know of what you speak, madam," said Mathew cautiously. "If, by the story of the Too-Learned Wizards, you mean the story of the Reproach of the Magi—"

"Tell me this tale," said Zohra, settling down more comfortably among the cushions.

Mathew glanced hesitantly toward the outside. "I would be honored to do as you request, madam, but are you certain it is safe? Won't—"

"My husband come seeking me? I think not," Zohra said with a mocking smile that held—for Mathew's eyes—a trace of bitterness. "Besides, I am safe here with you, am I not? Are you not mad? Go on. Tell your tale."

Mathew tried to collect his thoughts—a difficult task. He remembered hearing this story his first day upon entering the Wizards' School as a young child, awed by the black-robed archmagi, the rows of wooden desks, the towering stone buildings. He had never, in his wildest imaginings, pictured himself relating it while sitting in a tent in the middle of the desert, the fiery eyes of a wild and lovely woman fixed upon him.

"It is our belief that our God has gifts and graces that he bestows upon his faithful," said Mathew, looking questioningly at Zohra, who nodded gravely to show she understood. "But Sul—as center of all—alone possesses the magic. He shares this gift with those of learned and serious manner who come to him in humility, pledging to serve him by spending their lives in study and hard work; not only in the pursuit of magic, but in pursuit of knowledge of all things in this world.

"Long ago a group of magi studied so diligently that they became the most learned and the wisest men and women in the world. They knew not only magic, but languages, philosophy, science, and many other arts. Because they had all learned each other's languages and customs, they were able to come together and further increase their knowledge. Instead of looking each to his own God, they began to look increasingly to Sul, the Center. They saw, when they looked into the center, the strife and turmoil in the world, and they knew that it was caused by the rankling and arguing and bickering of the Gods, who could not see the truth but only one part of the truth. Gradually the magi became of one mind, and this mind told them to use their magic to try to reach some resolution among the Gods.

"Unfortunately, feeling threatened, the Gods come to Sul and demanded that magic be withdrawn from the world. This Sul could not do, magic having become too pervasive within the world. Sul himself became enraged at the magi for abusing his gift, and he chastised them severely, accusing them of attempting to aspire to become Gods.

"But the magi reproached him, saying that their concern was only for the suffering of their fellow humans and crying out that the Gods had forgotten this in their selfish arguing. Sul was chagrined and so begged their pardon. But Sul said, something must be done to appease the Gods or they would insist that magic be removed from the world. Therefore the magi agreed on a compromise.

"Magic must be based in material objects—charms and amulets and potions—so that those who practice it are constrained by their own human limitations as well as by the physical properties of the objects in which the magic resides. Thus the Gods would not perceive magic as being a threat to their power, and the magi could still go abroad and work for the benefit of humanity. And that," concluded Mathew in relief, "is my tale."

"Sul did not cut out their tongues?" asked Zohra in disappointment.

"Cut out their— No, certainly not!" Mathew said, shocked. "After all, Sul is a God, not a—" He had been about to say "barbarian," but it suddenly occurred to him that, from what he had witnessed, the Gods of these people *were* barbarians! Stuttering, he fell silent.

Fortunately, lost in her own thoughts, Zohra had not noticed.

"And so you are a sorcerer? You practice the art of Sul? What magic can you do? Show me."

"Madam," said Mathew, somewhat confused, "I can do a great many things, but I need my charms and amulets, which were lost when our ship—our *dhow*—sank in the sea. If I have the proper tools, I can fashion others and then I will be pleased to show you my skills."

"But surely you can do the usual things: healing the sick and injured, calming animals, that sort of magic."

"Madam," said Mathew hesitantly, thinking that perhaps she was testing him, "I could do that when I was a child of eight. My skills are much further advanced, believe me."

Zohra's eyes widened slightly. She ceased toying with her veil, her fingers stopping, frozen in mid-motion. "Explain."

'Well . . .'' Mathew hesitated, wondering what she expected of him. "I can see into the future, for one thing. I can fight evil spirits sent by Sul to test us, as well as those inflicted upon us by the Dark Gods. I can help restless souls of the dead find repose. I can defend those threatened by danger from weapons physical or magical. I can summon certain minor servants of Sul and keep them under my control, although that is very dangerous, and—as an apprentice—I'm not really supposed to do so except in the presence of an archmagus. I am young," he added apologetically, "and still learning."

Sitting up straight from her formerly lounging position on the cushions, Zohra was staring at him in awe, a glittering in her eyes as of the sun on quartz. "Can you truly do this!" she breathed. The glint in her eyes became suddenly dangerous. "Or perhaps you *are* mad, after all . . ."

Mathew was suddenly very, very tired. "In this matter," he said wearily, "I am not. You can test me. If you will give me some days to work and provide me with the material I require. . . ."

"I will," said Zohra fiercely, rising to her feet with a feline twist, her bracelets jangling. She smiled at him. "If you speak truly, you may become the most valued and favored of anyone's wives, Mat-hew!"

Mathew flushed but was too exhausted to reply. When Zohra saw his white, drawn face, her expression softened, but only for an instant and then only when the young man was looking wistfully at his bed and not at her.

Preparing to leave, she paused at the tent entrance. "What God do you worship?"

"He is called Promenthas," Mathew replied, looking back up at her, astonished that she should ask, more astonished that she should care.

"May the peace of . . . Promenthas . . . be with you this night, Mat-hew," Zohra said with unwonted gentleness.

Touched, the young man could not speak but averted his gaze, sudden tears flooding his eyes. Smiling to herself, Zohra bent down, extinguished the light of the oil lamp, and then glided from the tent, her soft slippers making no noise over the sand-swept ground.

And it seemed that the peace of Promenthas was with him, even in this terrifying and alien land, for the young wizard slept soundlessly and dreamlessly for the first night since his ordeal began.

Chapter 14

The next few days passed in gloom for the tribes camped around the Tel. After their initial pleasure in heaving tweaked the Amir's nose subsided, the people began to take stock of their situation and discovered it to be grim.

Once again the tribes found themselves united—if only in their misery. The loot the men had managed to steal would last a while, but not a year. Neither the Akar nor the Hrana were farmers. Both depended on grain and other staples purchased from the city to survive. And if the Amir's wife could conjure up a magical horse, there was little doubt she could produce a magical sheep as well. The prospects of Jaafar and his people selling their animals and their wool in the markets in the fall seemed dim. Not only did their prospects for survival appear to be bordering on desperate, they were trapped out in the middle of the desert, forced to remain camped around an oasis whose water level was dropping, whose grass was gradually being consumed by the horses, while every passing day brought nearer summer and the threat of the violent winds of the *sirocco*.

There was some hope that the Rose of the Prophet might yet bloom and free them. It hadn't died out completely—an astonishing phenomenon, considering that the shriveled cacti appeared prepared to blacken, wither, dry up, and blow away if someone breathed on them crooked. But as for blooming, it seemed likely that flowers would sprout from Jaafar's bald head first—as Majiid observed bitterly to his son.

The tribal leaders, Khardan, Majiid, and Jaafar, spent long

hours in discussion and occasionally heated debate over what to do. At length, all agreed that the Sheykhs' djinn were to be summoned and ordered to go in search of Akhran, apprise him of the situation, and receive the God's permission to leave the Tel until the storm season was over.

Fedj went alone; Sond pleaded some nameless indisposition. After several days Fedj returned downcast, stating that the Wandering God was living up to his name and had disappeared.

The men were cast into gloom. The sun grew hotter and hotter, the grass became more difficult to find, the level of the water in the pool sank a little each day, and the tempers of those in camp became more volatile.

"I say we leave!" Majiid said following Fedj's return. "We move to our summer camp. You move back to the foothills with your sheep . . . and our horses," he added bitterly, beneath his breath.

Jaafar, groaning as usual, did not hear the sarcastic comment. Khardan heard, but preoccupied with some deep thought, he did nothing more than cast his father a warning glance.

"And risk the wrath of Akhran?" Jaafar cried. He shook his head.

"Bah! Akhran may not take it into his head to think about us for another hundred years. What is time to a God? By then we'll all be dead and it won't matter. Or," Majiid continued grimly, "we can stay here three months and we'll all be dead and again it won't matter."

"No, no!" Jaafar flung up his hands in protestation. "I remember the storm, even if you have forgotten—"

"Wait," Khardan interrupted, seeing his father beginning to swell with the prospects of an argument, "I have an idea. Suppose we do as the Amir thinks we're going to do? Suppose we attack Kich?"

Jaafar groaned again. "How does this solve our problems? It only adds to them!"

Majiid, brows bristling, glared at his son. "Go join the madman in the tent of your wife. . . ."

"No, listen to me, Father, Sheykh Jaafar. Perhaps this is what the God has meant for us to do all along. Perhaps this is why he brought us together. I am not opposed to leaving the Tel, but before we part, let us do this one thing!"

"Two tribes, raiding Kich! You did it once, by luck. Such luck won't happen again."

"It doesn't have to be two tribes! It can be three! We bring Zeid in on this with us! Together we'll have enough men to raid the city and this time we'll do it right. We can acquire wealth enough to last us a lifetime, besides teaching the Amir and his Imam to think twice before insulting *Hazrat* Akhran."

As Khardan spoke, his gaze went to Meryem, who was just entering Majiid's tent. Undoubtedly by chance, she always happened to be the one available to bring food and drink to the men.

Seeing the girl, noting her sidelong glances directed at his son, Majiid—who had been about to reject the scheme of raiding Kich—suddenly changed his mind. He had decided that Meryem would make an ideal wife for Khardan. His grandchildren would be descended from the Sultan! They would have royal blood in their veins as well as—what was more important—the blood of the Akar.

Besides, Majiid felt *his* old blood stir at the thought of raiding the city. Not even his grandfather—a legendary *batir*—had done anything so daring.

"I like it!" he said when Meryem had gone. One did not discuss matters of politics before women.

"I, too, find it interesting," said Jaafar unexpectedly. "Of course, we would need more horses—"

"It all depends on Zeid," interposed Khardan hastily, seeing his father swell up again. "Perhaps we can persuade him to give us his swift *meharis*. Will our cousin join us, do you think?"

"No one loves a good raid more than Zeid!"

"Pukah, what is the matter? Where are you going? You have not been dismissed," Khardan said, catching sight of the djinn slinking out of the tent.

"Uh, it occurred to me, master, that you might like your pipe. . . ."

"I will tell you if I do. Now sit down and keep quiet. You should be interested in this. After all, it was you who brought about our alliance."

"I wish that you would forget such a trifling matter, master," said Pukah earnestly. "After all, are you certain that you can trust Sheykh Zeid? I have heard it said that his mind is like the dunes—always shifting its position as the wind blows."

"Trust him?" said Majiid brusquely. "No, you can't trust him. We can't trust each other, why should this be different? We'll send him a message—"

The Sheykhs and the Calif fell to arguing over what they should say and what they should offer and Pukah finally managed to slink, unnoticed, from the tent.

Each day, rising before dawn, the djinn had been traveling to Zeid's camp, where he spent the morning hours watching with increasing gloom the Sheykh's building up of his forces. Not content with drawing on his own men, Zeid had summoned all of the southern tribes. More and more men and their camels were pouring into camp all the time. It was obvious that Zeid's attack on the Tel was going to occur in a matter of weeks, if not days.

Pukah wondered fleetingly if a proposed raid on Kich might not interest Zeid enough to make him forget about attacking his cousins. He immediately rejected this notion, however, knowing that Zeid was certain to think this was just another of Khardan's tricks.

Pukah, sighing, continued working on his plan to be away from camp when the attack occurred, thereby avoiding the wrath of his master when Khardan discovered the truth.

Other people beside the djinn were watching Zeid with considerable interest. Spies of the Amir reported that the Sheykh was calling up those under his *suzerain* or those who owed him favors or money or both and that he was apparently preparing for a major battle. The rumor spread rapidly that the nomads' target was Kich.

The cities in Bas, seeing the huge blade of the Emperor's scimitar hanging over their necks, began sending Zeid gifts. The Sheykh was inundated with concubines, donkeys, and more coffee, tobacco, and spices than he could use in a decade. Zeid wasn't stupid. He knew that the southern cities, aware of the buildup of his forces, were hoping he was coming to their rescue, not to dance on their graves.

Zeid heard the rumor about attacking Kich and laughed at it, wondering how anyone could believe it. The Sheykh knew the Amir by reputation. Qannadi was a cunning, crafty general; one to be respected and feared.

"My feud is not with the Amir or with the God of the Amir," Zeid repeatedly told ambassadors from the cities of Bas. "It is with my ancient enemies, and as long as Qannadi leaves me alone, I, Sheykh Zeid al Saban, will leave Qannadi alone."

Qannadi heard Zeid's words but didn't believe them. He saw the flood of gifts pouring into the desert, he saw the cities of Bas—who had once trembled and hung their heads at the sound of his name—begin to take heart and lift their heads and talk back to him. The Amir was angry. He had counted on the cities to the south falling into his hands like rotten fruit, their governments corrupted from within by his own double-dealing agents. The rumor of strength coming from the desert was making this increasingly more difficult, and it was all the fault of these nomads. The Amir was beginning to think that the Imam had been right to insist that they be harshly dealt with.

But Qannadi was a cautious man. He needed more information. Zeid was undoubtedly planning a move northward, that much Qannadi had from his spies. But the imbeciles also added that they believed he was going to attack Majiid and Jaafar, not ally with them. This made no sense to the military-minded general. It never occurred to him that a blood feud dating back centuries would take priority over the threat that he posed to them here and now. No, Qannadi needed to know what was transpiring among the tribes camped around the Tel.

He had planted his spy there, but he had heard nothing from her. Each day, with growing impatience, he demanded of Yamina if Meryem had made her report.

He waited many days in vain.

Meryem was having problems of her own. She was not, as she claimed to be, a daughter of the Sultan. Rather, she was a daughter of the Empéror—her mother having been one of his many hundred concubines. She had been given to the Amir as a present by the Emperor and thus came into Qannadi's *harem*. Much to Meryem's disappointment, the Amir had not married her but had merely taken her as his concubine. She

was, as Qannadi told Feisal, an ambitious girl. She wanted
the position of wife to the Amir, and it was this that induced
her to take the dangerous role of spy when Yamina offered it
to her.

The danger Meryem had foreseen. But not the discomfort.
Accustomed to a life of luxury in the Emperor's grand palace
in the capital city of Khandar, then to life in the rich palace of
the late Sultan in Kich, Meryem found life in the desert
disgusting, dirty, and appalling.

She was, had she known it, the pampered pet of Sheykh
Majiid's *harem*. Her gentleness and beauty, plus her scandalous
stories of life in the Sultan's court, made her a favorite with
Majiid's wives and daughters. Badia, Majiid's head wife,
spared Meryem from doing truly hard tasks, such as herding
the horses, milking goats, drawing water, hauling firewood.
But Meryem was expected to earn her keep in the *harem*.
After twenty years of doing nothing except gossiping and
lounging around ornamental pools, Meryem found this hateful
in the extreme.

Plus, she was increasingly frustrated in being unable to get
near Khardan and thus find out the information she had been
sent here to gather. She repeated her woes to Yamina.

"You have no idea how wretched my life is here," Meryem
said bitterly.

Alone in her tent, she held in her hands what appeared to
be a mirror in a gilt frame. If anyone came in (which was
unlikely considering the late hour of the night), they would
have seen her admiring her face, nothing more.

In reality the mirror was a device of great magical power
that allowed the sorceress who possessed it to summon the
image of another sorceress onto its surface and thereby
communicate with her.

"I live in a tent so small that I must crouch to enter. The
smell is unbelievable. I was sick with it for three days after I
came here. I am forced to wait on the men hand and foot like
a common house slave. My beautiful clothes are in tatters.
There is nothing to eat except mutton and gazelle, bread and
rice. No fresh fruit, no vegetables. No wine, nothing to drink
but tea and coffee—"

"Surely you have some diversions that make up for these
inconveniences," interrupted Yamina with a distinct lack of

sympathy. "I saw the Calif, you recall. A handsome young man. I was impressed, quite impressed. Such a man must make one's nights exciting. Anticipation of pleasure in the darkness makes the hours of daylight go by swiftly."

"The only thing I anticipate in the night is the pleasure of being bitten to death by bugs," said Meryem bitterly.

"What?" Yamina appeared truly startled. "You have not yet seduced this man?"

"It isn't as if I haven't tried," said Meryem petulantly. She could not bear to see Yamina—who had once been jealous of the younger, prettier girl—gazing at her smugly. "This man has notions of honor. He promised to marry me before taking me, and I fear he truly means it! And only by marrying him can I truly discover what is going on in this camp. I tried spying on the meetings of the Sheykhs, but they stop talking every time I enter. If we were married, however, I know I could persuade him to tell me what they were planning—"

"Then marry him! What is stopping you?"

Briefly, Meryem related her tale, elaborating on Zohra's interference but leaving out the fact that she—Meryem—had been replaced in Khardan's *harem* by a young man. That choice bit of information would become the joke of the *seraglio*! It was a blow from which Meryem's pride would never recover—a blow that she promised herself would someday be avenged.

"There is but one thing to do," Yamina said crisply, having heard the tale. "You know what that is."

"Yes," Meryem replied with seeming reluctance and hesitation, though inwardly rejoicing. "Such a thing goes against the teachings of the Imam, however. If he were to find out . . ."

"And how is he to find out?" Yamina demanded. "If you do it properly, no one will know, not even the woman's kin."

"Still," persisted Meryem stubbornly, "I want your sanction on this."

Yamina was silent, her lips pursed in displeasure.

Meryem, abject and humble, awaited the answer. She knew that Yamina was quite capable of betraying her by turning her over to the Imam. Forcing Yamina to give her sanction to murder would put the blame upon her; she must keep it secret, and Meryem would be safe.

"You know," Meryem added softly, "that the mirror is quite capable of recalling faces and the words they have spoken in the past, as well as transmitting those of the present."

"I am aware of that! Very well, I sanction it," Yamina said in a tight voice. "But only after all other means have failed. Men think with their loins. The Calif's honor will come to mean little enough to him when he holds you in his arms. And the marriage bed is not the only bed where business can be discussed, my dear. Or could it be"—Yamina added sweetly—"that your charms are fading, that you have attempted this and failed? Perhaps this Zohra or the other wife holds greater attraction for him than you do?"

"I have failed in nothing!" Meryem retorted angrily. "It is me whom he loves. He spends his nights alone."

"Then there should be no problem enticing him to spend his nights in your tent, Meryem, my child." Yamina's voice hardened. "The sands in the hourglass dwindle. The Amir grows impatient. Already he has mentioned his disappointment in you. Do not let that disappointment grow to displeasure."

The mirror in Meryem's hands went dark—almost as dark as the girl's scowling face. Beneath her anger and her hurt pride ran an undercurrent of fear. Unlike a wife, a concubine was at the mercy of her master. The Amir would never mistreat her—she was the Emperor's daughter, after all—but he was at liberty to give her away as one might give away a singing bird. And there was a certain one-eyed, fat captain—a friend of the general's—who had been casting that one eye in her direction. . . .

No, Meryem would have Khardan. Never before had she doubted her charms—they had worked on many men, not just the Amir. But this man, this Calif, was different. He could be the rare exception to Yamina's rule. He would not be easy to seduce. Still, as long as she was careful and did not play the harlot but the innocent, loving victim, Meryem thought she might just succeed. . . .

Putting away the magical mirror, the Amir's concubine went to her bed, falling asleep with a sweet and not altogether innocent smile upon her face.

THE WILL OF THE WANDERER

*   *   *

The other newcomer to a *harem* was leading a life almost as easy as Meryem's, though not for the same reasons.

The life of a madman was not an unpleasant one among the nomads. Mathew no longer lived with the fear of imminent and terrible death (except from the bite of the *qarakurt,* for though he never saw one, Pukah's description of the deadly black spider haunted him). He was not shunned, as he had feared, or kept shut up away from other people. In this he had to admit that these barbarians were more humane in their treatment of the insane than those of his own land, who locked the mentally ill away in foul places that were little better (and many times worse) than prisons.

The tribesmen went out of their way to be kind to him—always rather cautiously and warily but kind nonetheless—speaking to him and bowing as they passed, bringing him small gifts of food such as rice balls or *shish kabab.* Some of the women, finding that he had no jewelry of his own, gave him theirs (Zohra would have adorned him head to toe had he allowed it). Mathew would have returned it had not Zohra told him that, in this way, the women were making certain that Mathew would have some money of his own should he ever find himself a "widow."

Children stared at him wide-eyed, and he was often approached by young mothers with requests to hold their newborn infants, if only for a few moments. At first Mathew was touched by all this attention and was beginning to consider that he had misjudged these people whom he had thought uncouth savages. One day, however, Zohra opened his eyes to the truth.

"I am pleased that your people seem to like me," Mathew said to her shyly one morning as they walked to the oasis to draw water for the day's usage.

"They don't like you," she said, glancing at him in amusement, "any more than they like me. They are frightened."

"Of me?" Mathew stared at her in astonishment.

"No, no! Of course not. Who could be frightened of you?" Zohra said, casting a scornful glance at Mathew's frail figure. "They fear the wrath of *Hazrat* Akhran. You see, the souls of babies waiting to be born sleep in the heavens, in a beautiful land where they are tended by the djinniyeh. The

Wandering God visits each babe, bestowing his blessing upon it. Now, most babies sleep through this visit, but sometimes there is one who awakens, opens his eyes, and gazes on the face of God. The radiance dazzles him. He takes leave of his senses and thus is he born here upon the world.''

"That's what Khardan meant when he told them I'd seen the face of the God," Mathew murmured.

"Yes, and that is why they dare not harm you. That is why the gifts and attention. You have seen the God and so will recognize him when you return to him. The rest of us will not know him. The people hope that when they die and reach the heavens, you will introduce them."

"And I'm supposed to get there before them?"

Zohra nodded gravely. "They consider it likely. You are, after all, a sickly looking thing."

"And holding the infants. Is this some kind of blessing? . . ."

"You are warding off the evil eye."

Mathew stared in disbelief. "The what?"

"The evil eye—the eye of envy—which, we believe, can kill a living thing. So that other mothers will not be envious of her newborn infant, the mother puts the babe in your arms, for who could envy a child that has been held by a madman?"

Mathew had no answer to this and began to wish he hadn't asked. The gifts and kindnesses suddenly took on a new and sinister aspect. These people were all eagerly waiting for him to die!

"Oh, not eagerly," Zohra said off-handedly. "They don't particularly care one way or the other. They just want to make certain that you will remember them to the God, and—in this harsh land of ours—it is best not to take chances."

A harsh land, a harsh people. Not cruel and savage, Mathew was beginning to realize, as he struggled to align his nature to their way of thinking. But resigned, accepting of their fate—no, even proud of it. Death was a fact, as much a part of life as birth and attended with rather less ceremony.

In Mathew's homeland death was accompanied by solemn ritual—the gathering of priests and weeping family around the dying person, the gift of prayer to carry the soul heavenward, an elaborate funeral with burial in the sacred cathedral grounds, a strict period of mourning observed by friends and family.

In the desert, among the nomads, the dead were placed in shallow, generally unmarked graves scattered along the roads the nomads wandered. Only the resting places of a particularly heroic *batir* or a Sheykh were commemorated by covering the grave with small stones. These became almost like shrines; each passing tribe paid tribute by adding a stone to the grave.

And that was all. Death in the desert was the same as life in the desert—stark, frightening, and comfortless. Mathew had made his decision. He had chosen to live. Why? Out of cowardice, he presumed. But deep down, he knew that wasn't the reason.

It was Khardan.

Khardan had seen that he was dying inside. Mathew recalled the Calif's words, spoken during that wild, sublime, terrifying moment of rescue. *Come alive, damn you! Come back to life!* Khardan's arms had carried him from the grasp of his captors. Khardan's hand had stayed the hand of his would-be executioner. Khardan's will had drawn him into making the choice. Mathew did not love Khardan, as Zohra had suggested. The young man's heart had been torn open, the wound was fresh, raw and bleeding. Until it healed, he could not feel strongly about anything or anyone.

"But because of Khardan, I am alive," Mathew said to himself in the darkness of his tent. "I do not know yet what that means. I do not know but that death would have been preferable. All I know is that Khardan gave me my life, and in return, I pledge this life of mine—poor and unworthy as it may be—to him."

Chapter 15

Once again an uneasy alliance was created between the tribes of the Tel. The Sheykhs and the Calif called a meeting of the *aksakal*, the tribal elders, of both Hrana and Akar and presented to them the proposal to raid Kich. A torch tossed on an oil-soaked tent would have caused no greater conflagration.

No one trusted anyone. No one could agree on anything, from the merits of the plan itself to the division of spoils that had yet to be taken. No one could make a decision. One side or another stormed out in a rage. Everyone constantly changed views. First the Akar were for it and the Hrana opposed. Then the Hrana came out for it and the Akar decided it was nonsense. The Sheykhs changed their minds according to who presented the best argument at the particular moment, and like a horse that has eaten moonweed, everyone galloped around in a circle and got nowhere very fast.

Life in the camps around the Tel continued much the same. The Rose of the Prophet did not die, but it didn't bloom either. Not that anyone thought about it now or paid much attention to it anymore, their minds being preoccupied with the rumors of war against someone—Zeid, the Amir, each other—that flew around the camp like vultures.

In the realm of the immortals, Sond spent much of his time moping about his lamp in a fit of gloom. Usti, terrified to leave the charcoal brazier lest Zohra catch a glimpse of him, remained hidden from view and lost considerable weight. Pukah made his daily trip south, watching Zeid's numbers increase daily and trying desperately to think of a way to extricate himself from this mess.

In the mortal realm, Meryem watched and waited for a chance to work her charms on Khardan, and Zohra taught Mathew to ride a horse.

At last Zohra had discovered a companion to share her lonely rides. Mathew had not been in camp two days before she made him come with her. Zohra's reasons for this were not entirely selfish; she was truly concerned about the state of the young man's health.

The fact that she should care about him astonished her. At first it displeased her as well. It was a sign of weakness. She had meant merely to use the young man to inflict further wounds on Khardan. Then she admitted that it was pleasing, for a change, to have someone to talk to, someone interesting and different, someone to whom—at the same time—she could still feel herself the superior. It was, she thought, very much like having a second wife in the *harem*. And of course, there was always the possibility he was telling her the truth about at least some of his skills in magic. She might actually learn from him.

What Zohra did not admit to herself was that she saw in Mathew someone as lonely as she was. This and their shared, secret admiration for Khardan formed a bond between them that neither was to know—for a time—existed.

Watching Mathew closely, Zohra became increasingly concerned for his health. The frail body and too-sensitive mind would not last long in this world. Riding would provide exercise, it was a useful skill to acquire, and it would keep the young wizard from his unfortunate tendency to brood too much on things that could not be changed and should—according to those of the desert—therefore be accepted.

Mathew agreed to go riding at first because he was thankful for anything to keep from longing for his home. And he had to admit that it certainly occupied his mind. First he had to overcome his fear of the animal itself—more intelligent than a camel, the horse (so Mathew imagined) took an instant dislike to him, gazing at him with a distinctly unfriendly eye. Then he had to concentrate on staying in the saddle. After a few tumbles onto the hard granite, his mind was occupied with something else—pain.

"This is the end," he told himself, trudging back into camp, so stiff and sore he could barely walk. "This time I was lucky. Next time I will break my neck."

Limping along, he looked up to see Khardan standing before him.

The Calif had been out hunting; he wore the mask of the *haik* to protect him from wind and sand. All Mathew could see of his face were the piercing black eyes, and they were grave and solemn.

Fearful he had done something wrong—he was dressed, after all, in men's clothing, Zohra having insisted on this—Mathew flushed and began to stammer out an apology.

"No, no," Khardan interrupted him. "I am pleased to see that you are learning to ride. It is a man's skill and one that is blessed by Akhran. Perhaps, someday, I will take you out and teach you what I know. Until then"—his gaze went to Zohra, standing slightly apart, her own face concealed by the mask of the head covering—"you are with a teacher almost as skilled."

Pleased at Khardan's words and the unusual fact that the Calif had actually stopped to speak to him, Mathew saw that Zohra was no less astonished at his unexpected praise and that the ordinarily fierce eyes of the woman were introspective and thoughtful as she returned to her tent.

To gain Khardan's respect was a goal worth risking one's life for, Mathew decided, and he vowed to learn to ride if it killed him—which seemed not unlikely. It also gave him the opportunity to discuss magic with Zohra, something that he feared to do when they were in camp. The young man had discovered that his powers and skills in the art—which, in his country, made him an apprentice—were far greater than anything the women of the desert could ever have dreamed.

And it wasn't long before he found out the reason why—an astounding one, as far as he was concerned.

"The magic I have seen you perform is done with charms and amulets—crude ones at best." The two were resting in the shade of the oasis, letting their tired horses drink and nibble at the dwindling grass. "Where are your scrolls kept, Zohra?" Mathew continued. "That is the key to truly powerful magic. Why do you never use them?"

"Scrolls?" Zohra seemed puzzled and not even really interested for the moment.

Her attention was on the hunting being done by Khardan and the men of the Akar, who were using their falcons to bring down gazelle from a herd that had come to the oasis in search of water.

Mathew, too, paused a moment to watch the chase. He had seen falconry practiced in his own land, but never anything remotely similar to the way it was done here. Like everything else, it was brutal, savage, and efficient. Had anyone told him that a bird could bring down an animal as big as a gazelle, he would have scoffed in disbelief. But he was seeing it and he still couldn't believe it.

Khardan, falcon on his wrist, removed the hood from the bird's head. The falcon soared into the air. Flying over the gazelles, it chose its victim and dove for it, aiming for the head of the animal. The gazelle, who could generally outrun packs of hunting dogs, couldn't outrun the swiftly flying bird. Swooping down, the falcon struck the gazelle in the head and began pecking out the animal's eyes. Soon blind, the creature tripped, stumbled, and fell to the ground—easy prey for the hunters. Mathew had seen Khardan training his falcons to perform this feat by placing meat in the eye sockets of a sheep's skull. The young wizard had thought at the time it was some macabre sport, until he saw now that it meant survival.

"Mat-hew! Look at that!"

Zohra pointed excitedly. The falcon of Achmed had made a particularly splendid kill. Mathew, watching, saw Khardan put his hand on Achmed's shoulder, congratulating the young man and praising his work with the bird. Majiid joined them and the three stood laughing together.

Mathew's heart ached, his loneliness came near to overwhelming him.

"Scrolls," he continued grimly, putting it out of his mind, "are pieces of parchment on which you write the spells so that they may be used whenever you need them."

Zohra's response confounded him. "Write?" she said, glancing at him curiously. "What do you mean, 'write'?"

Mathew stared at her. "Write. You know, write down words so that they may be read. As in books."

"Ah, books!" Zohra shrugged. "I have heard of such things used by city dwellers, who also, they say, burn cattle dung to keep warm." This in a tone of deep disgust.

"You cannot read or write!" Mathew gaped.

"No."

"But"—Mathew was bewildered—"how do you read and study the laws of your God? Are they not written down somewhere?"

"The laws were spoken by the mouth of Akhran into the ears of his people and so have been passed from the mouths of his people into the ears of those who came after them. What better way? Why should words go onto paper, then into the eye, and then into the mouth, and then into the ear? It is a waste of time."

Mathew floundered for a moment in this quagmire of irrefutable logic, then tried again. "Books could have kept the knowledge and wisdom of your forefathers. Through books that knowledge would have been preserved."

"It is preserved now. We know how to raise sheep. Khardan's people know the ways of horses. We know how to hunt, where to find the oases, what time of year the storms come. We know how to raise children, how to weave cloth, how to milk a goat. Your books never taught you that!" Mathew flushed. That much was true. His attempts at doing women's work had proved a dismal failure. "What more is there to know?"

"Books taught me to speak your language, they taught me something about your people," he added lamely.

"And was it the truth they taught?" Zohra asked him, turning her eyes on him, their gaze steady and unwavering.

"No, not much," he was forced to admit.

"There, you see? Look into a man's eyes, Mat-hew, and you can tell if he is lying to you. Books tell lies and you will never know it for they have no heart, no soul."

There are men whose eyes can lie, Mathew thought but did not say. Men with no heart, no soul. Women, too, he added mentally, thinking of blue, limpid eyes that had been watching the two of them of late—eyes that seemed to be constantly spying on them, yet could never be discovered looking directly at them. Eyes that always glanced away or were cast down in modesty, yet—when he turned—he could feel them, boring through his flesh.

Thinking of Meryem had distracted his thoughts. Resolutely he forced them back to the moment. Books were not, apparently, the way to introduce Zohra to the study of magic. He came about on a new tack, sailing his ship into what he hoped were calmer waters.

"Scrolls aren't books," he began, fumbling for an explanation that would convince her. "Magical scrolls aren't, at least. Because Sul decreed that magic be based in material objects, writing down the spells on scrolls was the only way the sorcerers could make their spells work. Before that—according to the histories—all they had to do was pronounce the arcane words and the minion of Sul was summoned, or the wood burst into flame, or whatever you wanted happened. Now the sorcerer must write the words upon parchment. When he reads them aloud, he obtains— hopefully—the desired result."

Now Zohra was watching him with eager interest, the hunt forgotten. "You mean, Mat-hew, that all I have to do to summon a servant of Sul to come perform my bidding is to write down these words upon something, read them, and the creature will come?"

"Well, no," Mathew said hastily, having a sudden terrifying vision of demons running loose through the camp. "It takes many years of study to be able to perform magic as powerful as that. Each letter of the words you write must be perfect in shape and form, the exact wording must be used, and then the sorcerer must have rigid control or the servant of Sul will turn the sorcerer into a servant of Sul. But there are other spells I could teach you," he said quickly, seeing Zohra's interest begin to wane.

"Could you?" Her eyes flared, bright and dangerous.

"I—I'd have to think about it. To recall some." Mathew stammered, pleased that he had kindled her interest.

"When can we start?"

"I need parchment, preferably sheepskin. I need to make a stylus, and I need ink."

"I can get you all that today."

"Then I'll need some time to practice, to draw my thoughts together. It has been some time and much has happened since I have used my magic," Mathew said wistfully, feeling the wave of homesickness sweep over him once more. "Perhaps, in a few days. . . ."

"Very well," Zohra said. Her voice was suddenly cold. "Let's go. We should be returning to camp before the heat of afternoon."

Mathew sighed, his feelings of loss and loneliness—almost forgotten for a moment—returning.

Who was he fooling? No one but himself. What could he ever be to Khardan except a coward who had saved his skin by dressing as a woman and pretending to be mad? Certainly he could never be a friend, never a companion—like a younger brother. And Zohra. He thought her beautiful in the wild and savage way this land was sometimes beautiful. He admired her in much the same way he admired Khardan, envying her strength, her pride. He had something he could offer her, and he hoped it would gain her respect and admiration for himself. But it was obvious, she was using him for her own purposes—to ease her own loneliness, to learn more about magic.

No, he was alone in a strange land and he would always be so.

The thought struck him a blow that literally took his breath away.

Always.

He had not looked into his future in this land because—up until now—he did not think he had one. He had looked forward only to death.

Always.

Now he had life, which meant he had an "always"—a future.

And a future, no matter how bleak, meant hope.

And hope meant that perhaps, somehow, he could find a way to get back home.

Chapter 16

As the days passed and Meryem spent more time among the nomads, she began to fear that her attempt to seduce Khardan would fail. Honor was the nomad's single most valued possession—one that belonged to rich and poor, male and female alike. A man's word, a woman's virtue: these were more precious than jewels, for they could not be traded or sold, and once broken were lost forever. Honor was necessary to the nomad's survival—he had to be able to trust his fellow man on whom his life depended, he had to be able to trust in the sanctity of the family on whom his future depended.

This was not something Meryem could easily explain to the Amir, however. Qannadi was not a patient man. He expected results. He did not tolerate excuses. He had sent his concubine to gather information, and he expected her to succeed. Khardan possessed the information Meryem needed. Once in her bed, his head pillowed on her soft breast, lulled by the touch of her skilled hands, he would reveal to her anything she wished.

"He is, after all, only a man," Meryem argued with herself. "Yamina is right. A man's brains are between his legs. He cannot resist me." Impatiently she watched and waited for just the proper moment, and at last she had her chance.

It was twilight. Walking wearily through camp after another day's pointless arguing with his father and the other tribesmen, Khardan glanced up to see Meryem come out from behind a tent and start across the compound, her slender shoulders bent beneath the weight of a yoke from which dangled two full skins of water. This was typically women's work, and Khardan, pausing to watch and admire the grace of the diminutive figure, thought nothing of the burden she bore until he noticed her steps falter. Meryem let the skins down slowly to the ground so as not to lose a drop of the cool water. She lifted a limp hand to her forehead, her eyes rolling upward. Springing forward, Khardan caught her just as she was falling.

His own tent was closest. Carrying the unconscious woman inside, he laid her down upon the cushions and was just about to go and get help when he heard her stir. Returning, he knelt down beside her.

"Are you all right? What is wrong?" He looked at her in concern.

Meryem, half sitting up, gazed around her dazedly. "Nothing is wrong," she murmured. I . . . just felt faint suddenly."

"I'm going to call my mother." Khardan started to rise.

"No!" Meryem said rather more loudly than she had intended. Khardan looked at her, startled, and she flushed. "No, please, don't trouble your mother on my account. I am much better. Truly. It is . . . so hot." Her hand artfully disarrayed the folds of the caftan she wore so that a tempting expanse of throat and the swelling of her smooth, white breasts could be seen. "Let me rest in here, where it is cool, for just a moment, then I will return to my work."

"Those skins are too heavy for you," Khardan said gruffly, averting his gaze. "I will mention this to my mother."

"It isn't her fault." Meryem's blue eyes shimmered with tears. "She . . . she told me not to do it." The soft hand reached out and clasped Khardan's. "But I do so want to prove to you that I am worthy of being your wife!"

Khardan's skin was swept by flame, his blood burned. Before he quite knew what was happening, Meryem was in his arms, his lips were tasting the sweetness of her lips. His kisses were eagerly returned, the girl's body yielding to his with a passion rather unexpected in the Sultan's virgin daughter. Khardan did not notice. His mouth was on the milky white throat, his hands seeking the softness beneath the caftan's silk, when it suddenly occurred to the Calif what he was doing.

Gasping for breath, he pushed Meryem away from him, almost throwing her back into the cushions.

Khardan was not the only one losing control. Consumed by a pleasure she had never before experienced in the arms of a man, Meryem grasped Khardan's arm.

"Ah, my love, my darling!" she breathed, drawing him back down upon the cushions, forgetting herself and acting with the wantonness of the Amir's concubine. "We can be happy now! We don't have to wait!"

Fortunately for Meryem, Khardan was too immersed in his own inner battle to notice. Tearing himself free of her hold, he rose to his feet and staggered to the tent entrance, breathing as though he had fought a deadly foe and just barely escaped alive.

Hiding her face in the cushions, Meryem burst into tears. To Khardan, they seemed the tears of offended innocence, and he felt himself a monster. Actually they were tears of anger and frustration.

Mumbling something incoherent about sending his mother to her, Khardan hastened from the tent. After he'd gone, Meryem managed to compose herself. She dried her eyes, twitched her clothes into place, and was even able to smile. The smoldering coals of Khardan's love had just burst into a raging fire, one that would not be quenched easily. Blinded by his desire, he would be prepared to believe any miracle that would suddenly make it possible for them to marry.

Leaving his tent, Meryem met Badia, who was hurrying to her side. In answer to her future mother's worried questions, Meryem said only that she had fainted and that Khardan had been kind enough to stay with her until she felt better.

"Poor child, this separation is torturing both of you," said Badia, putting her arm comfortingly around Meryem's small waist. "A way out of this dilemma must be found."

"Akhran willing, it shall be," said Meryem with a sweet and pious smile.

"Usti, what are you doing out of your dwelling? I did not send for you!" Zohra poked the fat djinn in his belly as he lay napping upon the cushions. "And what is that thing upon the floor?"

With a startled snort Usti sat bolt upright. His mounds of

flesh rolling and rippling in waves, he blinked at his mistress in the light of her oil lamp. "Ah, Princess," he said, frightened. "Back so soon?"

"It is just past dinnertime."

"I take it you have dined?" he asked hopefully.

"Yes, I dined with the madman. And I ask you again what this is, you lazy excuse for a djinn."

"A charcoal brazier," said Usti, glancing at the object sitting upon the floor.

"I can see it's a charcoal brazier, djinn-with-the-brains-of-a-goat!" Zohra fumed. "But it isn't mine. Where did it come from?"

"Madam should be more specific," he said plaintively. Seeing Zohra's eyes narrow dangerously, Usti added hurriedly, "It is a gift. From Badia."

"Badia?" Zohra stared at her djinn. "Khardan's mother? Are you certain?"

"I am," Usti replied eagerly, pleased to have—for once—impressed his mistress. "One of her own servants brought it over and said distinctly that it was for 'her daughter Zohra.' I have been waiting up to deliver it to you."

" 'Daughter.' . . . She said . . . 'daughter'?" Zohra asked softly.

"And why not? You *are* her daughter, if only in the eyes of the God."

"It's just . . . she never sent me anything before," Zohra murmured.

Kneeling down, she examined the brazier. It was made of brass, of truly fine workmanship and design, like nothing she had ever seen before. Three legs, carved to resemble the feet of a lion, supported the pot. Ornately carved holes around the lid emitted the smoke. Peering inside, Zohra saw six pieces of charcoal nestled in the brazier's brass belly. Since trees were scarce, the charcoal itself was a gift nearly as valuable as the brazier.

Instantly the idea came to her that the brazier came from Khardan. "The man is too proud to give it to me himself," she guessed. "He fears that I would refuse it, and so he uses this ruse to present it to me."

"What did you say, madam?" asked the djinn, nervously stifling a yawn.

"Nothing." Smiling, Zohra ran her finger along the delicate swirls and curlicues of the lid. "Return to your own brazier. I have no need of a fat djinn this night."

"Madam is all kindness!" remarked Usti. With a relieved sigh he transformed himself into smoke and fled gratefully to the peace and tranquility of his own dwelling.

Kicking the djinn's brazier aside with her foot, ignoring the pitiful lament of protest that came from within, Zohra placed the new brazier upon the floor beneath the tent opening. Lighting the charcoal, she was aware of a faint perfumelike fragrance in the smoke, perhaps the wood of a rose or lemon tree. She had never smelled anything like it before.

Undoubtedly Khardan has given it to me, she thought as she made ready for bed. Lying down, she watched the smoke from the brazier drift upward through the tent flap. But why? What can be his motive? He is—to all appearances—furious with me for having supplanted the blond rose he plucked from the Sultan's garden. He has not spoken to me, not one word since the night of his return. Perhaps his anger has cooled and he does not know how to show it except in this way. I will show him that I, too, can be magnanimous. After all, once again I have been the victor. Tomorrow perhaps I will smile upon him. . . .

Perhaps.

Smiling now at the thought, Zohra extinguished the oil lamp and lay down among the cushions, drawing the woolen blankets over her. The charcoal in the new brazier continued to burn, spreading a soothing warmth through the tent, banishing the chill of the desert night.

Hiding in his own brazier, Usti picked up his scattered furniture and comforted himself for his hard life by drinking plum wine and consuming large quantities of sugared almond paste.

The night deepened. Zohra sank into a dreamless sleep. The smoke from the brazier continued to rise through the opening in the tent, but it no longer drifted upward in a thin, wavering line. Slowly, imperceptibly, the smoke came to life, curling and twisting in an evil, sinuous dance. . . .

Chapter 17

The camp slept. Mathew, lying awake on his cushions, thought he had never heard such loud silence. It actually echoed in his head. Sitting up, he strained to hear a noise—any noise that would be a comfort to his loneliness. But not a baby whimpered, not a horse whinnied nervously as it caught the scent of prowling lion or jackal. Nothing stirred in the desert tonight, seemingly.

Mathew sat up, shivering in the cold. Wrapping another cloak around him, he lit his oil lamp and prepared to work.

He drew forth a piece of parchment and spread it out upon the smooth surface of the tent floor. Zohra had brought him the quill from a falcon to use as his writing instrument. He wasn't certain of its effectiveness in copying magical spells—he would have preferred a raven's feather as was used in the schools. But he couldn't recall anything in his texts stating that the quill itself possessed any inherent magical properties. Hopefully it was just tradition that dictated the nature of the quill used. Dipping it into the small bowl of ink that was made from burned sheep's wool with gum water added to the cinders, Mathew slowly and laboriously began to draw the arcane symbols upon the parchment.

This was the third night he had devoted to his work, and he found that he spent most of the day looking forward to this time of peace and quiet when he could lose himself in his art. Everyone rested through the heat of the day in the afternoon, which gave him time to nap and catch up on lost sleep. He already had a small packet of scrolls neatly tucked away in his pillow.

As he worked, he smiled with pleasure over the memory of Zohra's reaction to the performance of his first, simple spell. Taking a bowl, he had filled it with a handful of sand. Then, holding a scroll, he had spoken the arcane words with some trepidation. Would the falcon quill work? What about the ink? Had he spelled every word correctly and was he speaking the words of the cantrip in the proper cadence?

His fears had proved groundless. Moments after he had completed reading the spell, the words on the paper began to writhe and crawl. Zohra—her eyes wide as a terrified child's—shrank back into a corner. She might have run from the tent had not Mathew, dropping the parchment into the bowl, grasped hold of her hand reassuringly. She had clung to him, watching as the words spilled from the parchment into the bowl. When the letters touched the sand, it began to change form, and within seconds the parchment had vanished, the words disappeared, and a bowl of cool, pure water stood on the floor of the tent.

"Here, you may drink it," Mathew had said, holding it out to Zohra.

She would have nothing to do with it, however. He had drunk it himself—an odd experience, with her watching him, waiting half in hope and half in dread for something dire to occur to him. Nothing did, but she still had refused to drink the enchanted water. Mathew, sighing, knew that if Zohra wouldn't touch it then certainly no one else in the camp would even consider such a thing. His dreams for bringing water to the desert in a magical manner ended rather abruptly at this point. It also occurred to him—not without some bitterness—that the nomads probably wouldn't want any more water in the desert anyway. They seemed to gain a grim satisfaction out of battling with their cruel land.

Part of Mathew's brain was thinking idly of this, part of it was concentrating upon the work at hand when both parts came together with a suddenness that sent a physical jolt through his body.

Somewhere in the camp, powerful magic was being worked.

How he knew this, he could not tell. He'd never experienced such a sensation before, except, perhaps, when he'd performed his own spells. Or maybe he'd always experienced it at the school and simply never noticed, so pervasive was the magic there. No matter what the reason, the enchantment prickled his skin, shortened his breath, and he felt the hair on his head rise as it does when one stands too near where lightning strikes.

And it was black magic, evil magic. This Mathew recognized instantly, having been taught to be able to discern the difference, something a wizard must learn to detect in the event that he comes across a strange scroll or spellbook.

Mathew hesitated. Should he get involved? Might not he be putting himself in deadly danger, exposing his own power to whoever was practicing this? He tried to ignore it and turned back to his work. But his hand shook and he made a blot upon the parchment, ruining it. The aura of evil was growing around him.

Mathew rose to his feet. He might be a coward when it came to flashing steel but not to magic. The arcane he knew, he understood, he could fight. Besides, he admitted to himself ruefully as he hurriedly grabbed up the bag of scrolls and slipped out of the tent into the moonlit night, his curiosity was far outweighing his fear.

The source of the enchantment was easy to locate. It beat upon his face like the heat of the afternoon sun. He could literally almost hear its pulsing heartbeat. It was coming from Zohra's tent!

Had the woman duped him? Was she really a powerful sorceress, involved in the black arts? Mathew, creeping nearer, couldn't believe it. Wild, quick-tempered, fierce, but honest—to a fault. No, he thought grimly, if Zohra wanted to kill you she would simply come into your tent and stab you through the heart. None of the subtlety of black magic for her.

Which meant . . .

His own heart in his throat, Mathew quickened his steps. The distance between their tents wasn't great; they were, after all, together in Khardan's *harem*. But to Mathew it seemed an eternity passed before he was able to reach the tent and thrust aside the entry flap.

He stopped, staring, transfixed in horror.

A luminescent cloud of smoke hovered over Zohra's slumbering figure. Just as he sprang into the tent, the cloud dipped down and slowly slipped into the woman's nostrils. She drew it inside her with her own indrawn breath.

She breathed out, but her next breath didn't come. Zohra's eyes opened. She tried to inhale and the cloud flowed into her mouth, strangling her. Her eyes widened in terror. She struggled against it, her hands clawing at the shimmering, deadly cloud. Her frantic fingers closed on nothing but smoke.

What was this apparition? Mathew had no idea; he'd never seen or heard of anything like it. Whatever it was, it was killing Zohra. She would be dead in minutes, already her struggles were weakening, the smoke continuing to seep into the woman's nose. Where was it coming from? What was its source? Perhaps if that were destroyed . . .

Glancing hastily about, searching frantically for a scroll or a charm, Mathew saw the charcoal brazier, he saw the smoke rising from it and drifting—not up and out of the tent—but over to Zohra's bed. The charcoal . . . burning . . .

Lunging outside the tent, Mathew scooped up a handful of sand, hurried back in, and flung it on the glowing hot brazier, thinking it might distract the thing. But it had no effect. Completely ignoring him, concentrating totally on its victim, the deadly smoke continued to enter Zohra's body, suffocating her. Her face was dark, her eyes rolled back in her head, her body convulsed with her futile efforts to draw breath.

Falling to his hands and knees, Mathew scooped up handfuls of sand and flung them one after another over the brazier. At first he thought he had failed, that smothering the fire would not stop the magic. He couldn't fight this thing, he realized in anger and despair. Not with the few scrolls he had. He would have to watch Zohra die. . . .

Desperately Mathew continued to fling sand until the brazier was practically buried. Zohra's body had gone limp, her struggles had ceased, when suddenly the smoke stopped moving. The cloud's awful luminance began to dim and waver. Strengthened by renewed hope, Mathew grabbed up a felt blanket and flung it over the sand-covered brazier. Tamping it down, he began to press it firmly around the object, cutting off any possible source of air.

A wave of anger and hatred hit him a physical blow, flinging him backward. With a howl of rage that he heard in his soul, not with his ears, the cloud surged out of Zohra's

body. Rearing up into the air, it dove down for him with
incredible speed, shimmering hands reaching for this throat.

Mathew could do nothing, there was no time to react to
defend himself. Suddenly a cool breeze, blowing through the
entrance at his back, drifted into the open tent flap. As if
fanned by wings, the cloud separated and broke apart. Soon it
was nothing more than wisps of eerily glowing smoke darting
aimlessly and furiously about the tent. And then they, too,
were gone.

Bowing his head, his body bathed in sweat, Mathew drew
a shuddering breath. Rising on unsteady feet, he hastened to
Zohra's bedside. She lay still and unmoving, her face a
deathly white in the moonlight, her eyes closed. He put his
hands upon her heart and felt it beating, but very, very
faintly. She was no longer under enchantment. The magic
had been smothered with the charcoal. But still, she was
dying.

Not knowing what else to do, realizing only that the thing
had sucked the breath of life from her body and that it must
be put back, Mathew opened her mouth and breathed his own
life into hers.

Time and again he did this, uncertain if it would work, but
feeling that he must do something. And then he felt the chest
beneath his hand move; he felt a stirring of air from her
mouth touch his lips. Elated, he kept forcing breath into
Zohra's body. Her eyes—wide and terrified—fluttered open,
her hands reached out and caught hold of his face.

"Zohra!" he whispered, stroking her hair back from her
forehead soothingly. "Zohra. It is Mathew. You are safe.
The thing is gone!"

She stared at him a moment, frightened, disbelieving. Then
she gave a shuddering sob and buried her face in his breast.
He held her close, smoothing her hair, rocking her like a
child. Shivering with fear and the horrible memory, she clung
to him, weeping hysterically, until gradually the hypnotic
motion of his soothing hand and the soft, reassuring murmurs
of his voice drove away the worst of the terror. Her sobs
quieted.

"What . . . was it?" she managed to ask.

"I don't know." Mathew's eyes went to the brazier, now
covered with the blanket. "It was magic, whatever it was.

Strong magic. Black magic. It came from that charcoal brazier.''

"Khardan tried to kill me!" Zohra gasped out, a last sob wrung from her body. She hid her face in her hands.

"Khardan? No!" Mathew said, holding her tightly and calming her again. "You know how he feels about magic! He wouldn't do anything like this. Come to your senses, Zohra."

Wiping away her tears with the heel of her hand, Zohra seemed to come suddenly to the realization that she was being held in Mathew's arms. Her face flushing, she drew away from him. He, too, was embarrassed and uncomfortable and released her quickly.

Standing up hurriedly, Mathew walked over to the brazier and cautiously removed the blanket.

"Where did you get the thing?"

Zohra, after a few tries, her fingers still numb and trembling, lit the oil lamp and held its wavering flight over the brazier. Mathew brushed away the sand to reveal it, standing in the center of the tent.

"It's cold," he reported, staring at it in awe. He looked back up at Zohra, puzzled. "What do you mean, Khardan tried to kill you?"

"He sent this to me," Zohra said. Her fear dying away, it was being replaced by anger.

"*He* sent it to you?" Mathew repeated, still refusing to believe it.

"Well," Zohra amended, "I assumed . . ." She drew a shivering breath. "This was brought to my tent by a servant who said that she had been sent by Badia, Khardan's mother—"

Mathew glanced up at her swiftly. "Meryem!"

"Meryem?" Zohra appeared scornful. "I'd sooner suspect a kitten!"

"Even kittens have claws," he murmured, reliving with sudden, vivid clarity the night of his near execution. "I saw a look on her face when you thwarted her marriage to Khardan. She could have killed you then, Zohra, if she'd had the means. Lately I've seen her watching us. You stand in her way of marrying the Calif and she means to take care of that small matter."

Zohra's eyes flared with wild anger. She took a step toward the tent flap.

"Wait!" Mathew grabbed her. "Where are you going?"

"I'll confront her with this! I'll drag her before the Sheykhs! I'll accuse her of being the witch she is—"

"Stop, Zohra! Think! This is madness! She will deny everything. She has been in the *seraglio* all night, probably being careful to keep in the sight of the women of Majiid's *harem*. You have no proof! Just my word and I am a madman! Smoke tried to kill you? You will look a fool, Zohra—a jealous fool, in Khardan's eyes."

"*Makhol!* You are right," she murmured. Slowly her anger drained from her, leaving her exhausted. She sank back down on her cushions. "What can I do?" she mumbled, clasping her head in her hands, her long black hair tangling between her fingers.

"I'm not certain," Mathew said grimly. "First we must figure out why she did this."

"You said it yourself. To marry Khardan!" Zohra's eyes burned, a dreadful sight in her livid face. "If I am dead, then he can take another wife. Surely that is obvious."

"But why such haste? Why risk revealing herself by this use of magic that only a truly powerful sorceress would know, especially when she lied to Khardan and to everyone in the tribe about her skills in the art. The odds are, of course, that she would never be discovered. This attempted murder was very clever of her. You would have been found dead in the morning. It would have looked as if you had died in your sleep."

Zohra, shuddering, made a strangled sound, choked, and covered her mouth with a hand.

"I'm sorry," Mathew said softly. Sitting beside her, he put his arm around her again and she wearily laid her head on his chest. "I forgot. . . . I thought I was in the classroom again. Forgive me. . . ."

She nodded, not understanding.

"You had better rest now. We'll talk about this more tomorrow—"

"No, Mat-hew!" Zohra clutched at him fiercely. "Don't leave me!"

"You will be safe," Mathew said soothingly. "She can't

do anything else tonight. She's already taken a great risk. She must wait until morning to see if her magic worked."

"I can't sleep. Go on . . . go on with what you were saying."

She drew away from him. Mathew, swallowing, struggled to recall his chain of thought under the gaze of those black, fiery eyes.

"Haste, Mat-hew. You mentioned haste."

"Yes. She knows that undoubtedly, within a month or so, she will have a chance to marry Khardan. If she were truly the innocent girl she pretends, such a short time would not matter. But she isn't an innocent girl. She is a powerful sorceress who wants, who *needs* to marry Khardan immediately and who will commit murder to do it."

He pondered. "Where would she have come by such magical arts?"

"Yamina, the Amir's wife, is a cunning sorceress," Zohra said slowly, staring at Mathew, both of them thinking the same thing.

"And Meryem comes from the palace. Truly, this begins to make more and more sense! Wasn't it providential of Khardan to come upon Meryem in the garden like that! Some God was surely smiling on her."

"Quar," muttered Zohra. "But, what could be her motive in coming here? Is she an assassin?"

"No," Mathew said after a moment's thought. "If she were sent to kill Khardan, she could have done it a dozen times over before this. She tried to kill you, but only because you stand in the way of her marriage. That's the key. She must marry him and quickly. But why?"

"And we cannot tell anyone!" Zohra said, rising impatiently and pacing the tent. "You are right, Mat-hew. Who would believe us? I am a jealous wife, you—a madman." She twisted the rings on her fingers round and round in her frustration.

"Ah, how stupid we are!" Striking her forehead with hand, Zohra turned to Mathew. "It is very simple. There is no need to worry about any of this. I will kill her!"

Moving to the bed, Zohra slid her hand beneath her pillow, grabbed the dagger, and slipped it inside the folds of her gown. She moved swiftly and calmly, and she was halfway out of the tent before Mathew's dazed brain caught up with her.

"No!" Flinging himself after Zohra, he grabbed hold of her arm. "Y—you can't kill her!" he stammered, shocked.

"Why not?"

Why not? Mathew wondered. Why not kill someone who has just tried to kill you? Why not kill someone you believe is a threat, a danger? I could say that life is a sacred gift of the God and only the God has the right to take it back. I could say that taking the life of another is the most dreadful sin a person can commit. That was true in my world, but is it true in this one? Perhaps that belief is a luxury in our society. If I had John's murderer before me, would I extend my hand to him in forgiveness, as we are taught? Or would I extend it to clutch him by his throat . . .

"Because . . . if you kill her," Mathew said slowly, "no one will know of the foul deed she has committed. She will die with honor."

Zohra stared at Mathew intently. "You are wise for one so young." Sighing in disappointment, the woman lowered the tent flap and stepped back inside. "And you are right. We must catch the snake that hides beneath golden hair and put her on display for all to see."

"That . . . that might take some time." Mathew had no idea what he was saying. I nearly let her go, he thought, trembling. Killing that girl seemed perfectly logical! What is this land doing to me?

"Why?" Zohra's question forced him to concentrate.

"When . . . um . . . Meryem discovers she's failed, she'll be nervous, wary, on her guard. Did her magic go awry? Perhaps you didn't use the brazier at all and will use it tomorrow or the next night. Or did you, somehow, manage to thwart her? If so, do you suspect her? She will be leery of using her magic again too soon, although she may resort to more conventional means of getting rid of you. I do not think I would accept any food or drink from your father-in-law's tent."

"Usti!" said Zohra suddenly.

Mathew stared at her blankly, not understanding.

Kicking aside cushions, Zohra snatched up a charcoal brazier from the tent floor. It appeared to be a very old brazier that had seen a great deal of usage, if one could judge by the scratches and dents on its surface. Tapping it three times with her fingernail, Zohra called out, "Wake up, you drunken sot."

A voice from within was heard to groan. "Madam," it said groggily, "have you any idea what time it is?"

"Had it been left to you, Fat One, I would never have disturbed your rest again! Appear. I command you."

After a night of shocks, it seemed that there was one more waiting for Mathew.

He had not thought any more about the young man who claimed to have been a djinn. Not seeing him around camp, he assumed him to be as mad as, supposedly, he was himself. He'd heard casual talk among the tribesmen concerning djinn doing this and djinn doing that, but he assumed it was much the same as in his country where people spoke of the "faerie" —beings who were supposed to enter houses at night and switch babies or mend shoes or other farfetched legends. Now he could only watch in speechless amazement as another cloud of smoke rose from a charcoal brazier.

This smoke was obviously not threatening, however— coalescing into the form of a rotund man of middle years, with a red, bulbous nose and a bald, round head. Dressed in silken nightclothes, the man had obviously been rousted from a warm and comfortable bed.

"What is it, madam," he began in martyred tones, then he suddenly caught a glimpse of Zohra's pale face, still bearing traces of the horror that she had undergone. "Madam?" he repeated fearfully. "What—what is wrong?"

"Wrong? I was nearly murdered in my bed this night while you slept the sleep of the grape! That is what is wrong!" Zohra waved her hand, expressive of her contempt. "And *you* would have had to answer to Akhran for my death! I dread to think," she said in a hushed voice, "of your fate at the hands of the God!"

"Princess!" the djinn wailed, falling to the floor with a thud that shook the very ground beneath their feet. "Are you serious?" He glanced from Zohra's face to Mathew's. "Yes, you are serious! Ah, I am the most wretched of immortals! Be merciful, madam. Do not tell Holy Akhran! I swear I will make it up to you! I will clean your tent, every day. And never complain once when you rip up the cushions. See"—

grabbing a cushion, Usti tore it apart in a frenzy—"I will even spare you the trouble by ripping them up myself! Only do not tell the Most Holy and Extremely Short-tempered Akhran!"

"I will not tell him," Zohra said slowly, as if considering the matter, "if you will do one thing. We know who it is who tried to murder me. It will be your duty to watch her day and night. And I need not tell you what will happen should you fail—"

"Fail? Me? Like a *saluka*—a hunting hound—I will be on her— Did you say her?" Usti's eyes bulged from their layers of fat.

"The girl, Meryem."

"Meryem? Madam is mistaken. A more sweet and charming little—"

Zohra's eyes flashed.

"—little whore I have never seen," Usti mumbled, crawling backward on his knees, his head bowed. "I shall do as you command, of course, Princess. Henceforth you shall sleep the sleep of ten thousand babes. Worry not. Your life is in my hands!" So saying, the djinn disappeared, melting into the air with unaccustomed alacrity.

Sinking back down onto the cushions, her strength gone, Zohra murmured, "My life . . . in his hands. Akhran help us all."

Mathew, still staring in disbelief at the place where the djinn had been groveling, could only agree.

Chapter 18

"Caring for a madman. That's all you are considered fit for, Pukah, my friend," muttered Pukah disconsolately. Flitting through the air, making his daily trip south, the djinn enlivened his journey by feeling terribly sorry for himself. Pukah'd actually had very little to do with Mathew, although he had convinced himself that he did nothing night and day but watch the young wizard. Generally Pukah lounged around outside Mathew's tent, his brain bubbling with fermenting schemes. When he did happen to peek in, it was more in hope of seeing the beautiful immortal again than keeping a watchful eye on the young man. Pukah noticed Mathew pottering about with sheep's skin and a foul-smelling ink but thought nothing of it. After all, he was mad, wasn't he?

Thus Mathew worked on his magic completely without Pukah's knowledge. The young wizard was able to fashion—as best he could—charms and amulets, as well as scrolls, and he began to instruct Zohra in their use. She, in turn, taught him what she knew of the healing arts of magic. Mathew had little knowledge in that field. In his land the sick and injured were tended by magi specialized in medicine. Pukah knew that Zohra was alone with Mathew for long periods during the day, but he took no particular notice of that either. His master's wife spent her time with a man who thought he was a woman. What of it? She'd done stranger things. Pukah had his own problems, and one of those problems was suddenly about to bloat like the carcass of a dead elephant.

Arriving at his usual observation post, Pukah had just

settled himself comfortably upon a passing cloud when, looking down, he received a most uncomfortable shock.

"Now, may Sul take Zeid!" said the djinn. "May he take the wretch and deliver him into hell and afflict him with ten thousand demons that will do nothing but puncture his fat belly day and night with ten thousand poison spears! Ah, me, friend Pukah, you are in serious trouble now!"

"Well, well. If it isn't little Pukah," exclaimed a booming voice. "*Salaam aleikum.* Pukah. Have you got any more of your master's secrets you are willing to give away today?"

"*Aleikum salaam,* Raja," Pukah said cautiously.

"What think of you my master's army?" Raja asked. He gazed down from the cloud upon a veritable horde of *meharistes,* his glistening black-skinned chest swelling with pride. "We are all assembled, and as you see, preparing this day to ride north."

"I think it is a very nice army, as armies go," Pukah said, attempting to stifle a yawn.

"Nice!" Raja bristled. "You will see what a 'nice' army it is when it kicks your master in the ass!"

"Licks my master where?"

"Kicks, you donkey-headed fool," Raja snarled.

"You had much better say 'licks' because that is what will be happening," Pukah said gravely. "I tell you this only because I like you, Raja, and I am fond of your master, Sheykh Zeid, a very great man, and one whom I would not want to see humiliated before his tribesmen."

"Tell me what?" Raja regarded Pukah suspiciously.

"That you had much better turn around and go back to your business of watching camels hump one another or whatever it is that they do, because if you ride to attack Sheykh Majiid al Fakhar and Skeykh Jaafar al Widjar and Amir Abul Qasim Qannadi, then you will surely—"

"Amir?" Raja interrupted in astonishment.

"What did you say?"

"What did *you* say?"

"I thought you mentioned the Amir."

"Only because *you* mentioned the Amir!"

"Did I?" Pukah inquired uneasily. "If I did, please overlook it. Now, to continue—"

"Yes, you will continue, little Pukah," said Raja threateningly. "Continue talking about the Amir, or by Sul, I will take hold of your tongue, split in two, pull it out of your mouth, wrap it around your head, and tie it in a knot behind your neck."

"You are very boastful now, but my master and his new friend will soon cut you down to size," Pukah remarked scornfully, though he thought it best to put a mile or so of sky between him and the angry Raja.

"What new friend?" Raja thundered, the clouds around him darkening with his rage, lightning crackling around his ankles.

"As I said, I have a truly soft spot in my heart for your master—"

"And another in your head!" Raja growled.

"—and so I think you had better warn Zeid that my master, Khardan, upon hearing of your master's plan to attack him, traveled to the city of Kich, where he was entertained with all honor by the Amir, who was so enamored of my master that he did everything in his power to get him to stay longer. The Imam himself came to join his pleas with those of his Amir. Qannadi sent for his head wife, Yamina, who performed splendid feats of magic all for my master's pleasure. My master refused their invitations, however, saying regretfully that he must fly back to the desert because an old enemy was gathering forces to make war upon him.

"Qannadi was furious. 'Name the wretch!' the Amir cried, drawing his sword, 'that I may personally cut him into four equal parts and feed him to my cat.'

"This, you understand, my master was loathe to do—you know how proud a man he is—saying that it was his fight and his alone. But Qannadi proved insistent, and so my master— most reluctantly, you understand—said that his enemy's name was Sheykh Zeid al Saban. The Amir swore upon the steel of his blade that from that day forward Khardan's foes were his foes, and the two parted with much affection, the Amir giving Khardan one of his daughters in marriage and inviting Khardan and my master's men to enjoy the spoils of the city before they left.

"This my master did, with much delight. The Amir's daughter resides in Sheykh Majiid's tent, and we wait only for the Amir and his forces—who are on their way—to celebrate the joyous occasion of their wedding.''

Pukah ended, having run out of breath, watching Raja warily to see the djinn's reaction. As the astute Pukah had guessed, Sheykh Zeid had received an account of Khardan's visit to Kich from his spies, but the details had been imperfect. Pukah had mingled just enough truth with his lies to make this wild story sound plausible.

The djinn knew it sounded plausible because Raja suddenly disappeared with a thunderclap, the clouds swirling around him in a black vortex. Pukah heaved a sigh of relief.

''Now, Pukah, you are certainly very clever,'' said Pukah, lounging back upon the cloud.

''Thank you, my friend,'' Pukah replied. ''I think I must agree with you. For surely, upon hearing this news that the great amy of the Amir is allied against him, Zeid will take fright. He will disband his men and return to his homeland. You have spared your master the annoyance of being attacked by these sons of she-camels. By the time Zeid (may his beard grow up his nose) learns the truth—that the Amir has no interest at all in your master—it will be well into summer and too late for the Sheykh to launch an attack. Now that you have—once again—saved your master, you have time to help poor Sond out of his difficulty, for which he will—no doubt—be eternally grateful.''

''A beautiful plan,'' Pukah informed his better half. ''It won't be long, I foresee, before he and Fedj are working for me—''

''Ah, Pukah,'' the alter ego interrupted, tears in his eyes, ''if you keep on as you are going, the Holy Akhran will fall on his knees and being to worship *you*!''

''What? This is impossible!'' Zeid roared, reining in his camel with a suddenness that nearly sent the beast foundering in the sand.

''So I thought, *sidi*,'' said Raja, breathing heavily from exertion. ''Knowing what a liar this Pukah is, I flew to Kich to see for myself.''

''And?''

''And I discovered that the Amir has recalled some of his troops from the south. As we speak, they are gathering in the city; the soldiers talk of a rumored journey eastward, into the desert.''

"But he has not moved out yet?"

"No, *sidi*. Perhaps the marriage is still being negotiated. . . ."

"Bah! I cannot believe this is possible! An alliance between city and desert? *Hazrat* Akhran would never permit it. Yet," muttered the Sheykh into his beard, "it is certainly true that Khardan left the city in a shambles and was not chastised for his daring; the Amir allowed him to ride away free as the wind. And he was seen bearing upon his horse a woman of the palace, reputedly as lovely as the bending willow. . . ."

"What is your command, *sidi*?" Raja asked. "Do we return to our homeland?"

The Sheykh, looking back behind him, saw his vast army of *meharistes,* saw the sun flash upon sword and dagger, upon lance and arrow tip. He saw, behind them, another army, this one made up of women and their children, following their men to set up camp for them and to tend to their wounds after the battle. Here were gathered together all the tribes who owed him allegiance. It had taken many long hours of negotiating and compromising and the salving of old wounds to bring them together. Now all were eager for war. And was he going to tell them to turn back? Tell them Sheykh Zeid ran from the field, his tail between his legs, because another, larger dog had entered the fray?

"Never!" Zeid cried with such fierceness that his voice carried up and down the ranks, causing the men to join in the yell with wild enthusiasm, although they had no idea what they were cheering.

Grabbing his banner from his staff-bearer, Zeid waved it in the air. "Ride, my men! Ride! We will descend upon our foe like the wind!"

Banners waving, the *meharistes* galloped north, toward the Tel.

"I tell you, Sond, *Hazrat* Akhran was most emphatic in insisting that we undertake this journey." Pukah spoke to his fellow djinn in a soft undertone. The two were waiting in attendance upon their masters, who were—once again—meeting in Majiid's tent to argue about the best way to approach Sheykh Zeid. "Of course," Pukah added deprecatingly, "I realize that this proposed rescue attempt is going to be perilous in the extreme, and if you would prefer not to go . . ."

"I will go"—Sond swore an oath—"were it into the abyss of Sul itself! You know that, Pukah, so don't be a fool."

"Then ask your master's permission," Pukah urged. "Or would you rather wait here, serving coffee while your heart bleeds with grief, not knowing what terrible torment Nedjma may be enduring? Our masters can spare us for the short space of time it will take us to locate the Lost Immortals, rescue them, and return covered in glory. The Tel is as dull as the Realm of the Dead. What could possibly happen while we are gone?"

"You are right," Sond said after a moment's thought. "You have received your master's permission?"

"Khardan was most proud to send me upon work of the God," boasted Pukah.

Now, Pukah had not actually spoken to the God at all, but he felt safe in assuming that *Hazrat* Akhran would want them to do this, and so he took the liberty of sparing the God worry by issuing Akhran's orders for him and relaying those orders to Khardan.

"Undoubtedly my master has spoken to yours about the matter already," Pukah continued. "Majiid will be expecting you to go."

Sond saw himself freeing Nedjma from her cruel bondage. She would fall into his arms, fainting, weeping, blessing him as her savior and vowing to be his forever. . . . And Akhran—the God would surely reward him handsomely, perhaps a palace of his own where he and Nedjma could dwell. . . . "I will ask my master this evening," the djinn said decisively.

The two were serving *berkouks*—pellets of sweet rice—to the Sheykhs and the Calif when their fellow djinn, Fedj, swirled down through the tent flap opening with the fury of a windstorm.

"What is the meaning of this?" Majiid demanded. Rice flew about the tent, his robes billowed in the wind, sand and dust rose from the tent floor in a stinging cloud.

"I beg pardon, *sidi*."

Gasping for breath, the djinn whirled around until his form began taking shape out of the cyclone. Falling on his knees before Jaafar, who was regarding him with his perennially worried expression, Fedj burst out, "I have seen a huge army coming toward us. It is located three days' ride south from our camp!"

"Zeid?" flashed Khardan, rising to his feet.

"Yes, *sidi*," Fedj replied, talking to Jaafar as if it were his master who had asked the question. "He has many hundred *meharis* with him, and their families follow behind."

"*Ykkks!*" Pukah dropped a tray of candied locusts.

"Ah, you see, Father?" the Calif said in excitement. "Our arguments were all in vain. We need make Zeid no offer! He comes to join us in friendship."

"Mmmm," growled Majiid. "This is also how the *meharistes* ride to battle."

"It makes little difference," Khardan said, shrugging. "Zeid knows our credo: 'The sword always drawn and the same word for friend or foe.' Nonetheless, I think they will prove friendly. Pukah, here, assures me of it."

He glanced at Pukah with a smile. The djinn's return grin was that of a fox who has just drunk poisoned water, but Khardan was too preoccupied to notice. "Now we can discuss with them our plan to band together and raid Kich! There can be no more arguments among our people when they see the camel riders coming to us in the name of peace! Truly *Hazrat* Akhran has sent Zeid at precisely the right time!"

Pukah uttered an alarming groan. "Too many sweets," he said miserably, laying his hands on his belly. "If I may be excused, master—"

"Go! go." Khardan waved his hand, impatient with the continued interruptions. Resuming his seat, he leaned forward, the Sheykhs drawing close to him. "Now, here is my suggestion. Three days from hence, we will ride out to meet Zeid and—"

The Sheykhs and the Calif bent their heads together and were soon absorbed in deep discussion. Sond took advantage of the opportunity to leave the tent and follow Pukah. The djinn, looking truly ill, was slumped against a tent pole.

"Well, what are you doing out here?" Pukah snapped, seeing Sond's downcast expression. "If we are to leave this night, you had much better be back in there, asking permission of your master."

"You still intend to go?" Sond stared at him in astonishment.

"Now more than ever!" Pukah averred solemnly.

"I don't know." Sond appeared dubious. "If our masters are going to raid Kich with Zeid, then we will be needed. . . ."

"Oh, we will be back before *that* event takes place, you may be certain," said Pukah. "Probably about a thousand years before," he muttered.

"What did you say? Are you feeling all right?"

"I need to get away," Pukah stated with firm conviction. "The strain I've been under, arranging this . . . uh . . . alliance, has taken its toll on me. Yes, I definitely need to get away! The sooner the better."

"Then I will go speak to my master right now," Sond said, disappearing.

Pukah stared after him, his gloomy gaze following the djinn back to the tent where the Sheykhs sat discussing their plans to enlist Zeid's aid to raid Kich. If they only knew that instead of riding out to be met with kisses on the cheeks they were going to be met with daggers in the guts! . . . Pukah groaned.

He noticed, as he gazed despairingly at the tent, a small figure slipping away from it. But so lost was the djinn in his own fear and misery that he lacked the curiosity to wonder why a woman would have been so interested in what was going on inside that she had paused to listen. Or yet why she was now in such a hurry to leave.

The Amir was in his bathing room. Lying naked on a table, he was suffering untold tortures under the massaging hands of his manservant when a slave arrived to announce that Qannadi's head wife and the Imam needed to see him on a matter of extreme urgency.

"Ah!" grunted the Amir, propping himself up on his elbows. "They've heard from the girl. Toss that towel over me," he instructed his servant, who was already covering his master's body. "No, don't stop. Unless I have misjudged my barbaric desert friend, I will be riding soon and I need the kinks worked out of these old muscles."

Nodding silently, the manservant began his work again, his huge hands mercilessly pummeling and kneading the muscles in Qannadi's legs. A stifled cry came from the Amir's throat.

"The blessings of Quar be upon you," said the Imam, entering the steamy bathing room. "From the sound, I thought you were being murdered, at the very least."

"So I am!" Qannadi said, gritting his teeth, sweat pouring down his face. "The man delights in his work. I'm going to make him Lord High Executioner one day. *Ahhh!*" The Amir sucked in a breath, his hands clenched over the end of the marble table on which he lay. The manservant, grinning, started on the general's other leg. "Where is Yamina?"

"She comes," said Feisal imperturbably. "She has had news."

"I expected as much. Ah, here is my lovely wife."

Yamina entered the room, her face modestly veiled with only the one eye visible. Walking delicately to avoid stepping in puddles, she circled the sunken marble bathing pool. Lilies floated upon the perfumed water. Sunlight poured down through a skylight in the ceiling above, comfortably warming the enclosed room, its rays dancing upon the water's surface.

"You have heard from the girl?"

"Yes, husband," Yamina replied, bowing to him and bowing yet again to the Imam—the woman's single visible eye casting the priest a sultry glance that he caught but chose to ignore.

"So she finally seduced the desert prince?"

"We did not discuss the matter," Yamina said reproachfully, with an apologetic glance for the Imam for speaking of such sordid matters. "Meryem's time was short. She is constantly watched, she says, by Khardan's head wife, whose jealousy of her knows no bounds. Meryem has discovered that what we heard rumored is true. Sheykh Zeid al Saban and his *meharis* are within three days ride of the Tel. The nomads are meeting now to make plans to"—Yamina paused for effect—"join forces and raid Kich!"

"Ouch! Damn you for a blackhearted bastard! I'll rip your throat out someday!" Half sitting up, the Amir glared behind him at his manservant.

Accustomed to being sworn at and threatened by Qannadi, who could not get along without him, the manservant merely grinned and nodded, his hands continuing to twist and pound Qannadi's battle-scarred flesh.

The Amir transferred his glare to the Imam. "It seems you were right, Priest," he said grudgingly.

Feisal bowed. "Not I, but our God. You do not intend to let them near the city?"

"Of course not! Kich would be in an uproar. I had enough trouble settling the populace down after Khardan's last little visit. No, we'll ride out and make short work of this puppy."

"There is to be as little bloodshed as possible, I hope," the Imam said earnestly. "Quar would be displeased."

"Humpf. Quar wasn't displeased at the blood that was shed taking this city, nor does he seem displeased by the thought of the blood we're shortly going to be shedding in the south. He'd rather have dead souls, I presume, than no souls at all?"

Yamina's eye widened at such sacrilegious talk. Glancing at the Imam, she was not surprised to see his face flush, the thin body quiver with suppressed rage. Drawing near the Imam, her hand hidden in the folds of her silken robes, Yamina closed her fingers around the priest's wrist, cautioning him to control himself.

Feisal needed no such warning, however. His skin crawled at the touch of the woman's cool hand pressed against his hot flesh, and he removed his wrist from her grasp as diplomatically and unobtrusively as possible, meantime issuing a rebuke to the Amir.

"Naturally Quar seeks the souls of the living, so that he may pour his blessings down upon them and so enrich their lives. He knows to his great grief, however, that there are those who persist in walking in darkness. For the sake of their souls and to free them from a life of wretched misery, he condones the killing of these *kafir* but only so that they may come to see in death what they were blind to in life."

"Hunh!" grunted Qannadi, growing uncomfortable as always in the presence of the burning-eyed priest. "Are you saying then that Quar will have no objection if we put these nomads to the sword?"

"Far be it for me to interfere with military affairs," said the Imam, noting the Amir's darkening face and proceeding with caution, "but—if I may make a suggestion?"

Feisal spoke humbly, and Qannadi nodded.

"I think I know how we can pull the teeth of this lion instead of cutting off its head. Here is my plan. . . ."

Feisal presented his proposal clearly, succinctly, precisely; his orderly mind had taken care of every detail. Qannadi listened in some astonishment, although he should have known, from past dealings with the priest, that this man was as ingenious as he was devout. When the Imam had finished, Qannadi nodded again grudgingly, and Yamina, seeing her husband bested, cast the Imam a proud glance.

"And if this fails?" the Amir asked gruffly, waving his manservant away. Wrapping himself in the towel, he heaved his aching body off the marble table. "If they refuse to convert?"

"Then," said the Imam devoutly, "it will be *jihad*! May Quar have mercy upon their unworthy souls."

Chapter 19

Huddled in the cool shadows of Mathew's tent, her feathery white wings drooping, Asrial hid her face in her hands and wept.

It was not often the guardian angel gave way to her despair. Such a lapse in discipline would have brought raised eyebrows and stern, cold stares of reproach from the seraphim and undoubtedly a lecture from some cherubim upon putting one's trust wholeheartedly in Promenthas, believing that all was the will of the God, and all were working toward the Greater Good.

Thinking of such a lecture, hearing in her mind the sonorous voice, only made Asrial's tears flow faster. It wasn't that she had lost her faith. She hadn't. She believed in Promenthas with all her heart and soul; to work his will upon this material plane was the greatest joy she could know. So it had been for eighteen years, the years she'd been given Mathew to guide and protect.

But now?

Asrial shook her head bleakly. The young man she guarded was not alone in his anguish and misery. Asrial had watched, horrified, as the *goums* cut down the charges of her fellow angels. She had seen the other angels, helpless to intervene, fall to their knees in prayers to Promenthas and then rise again to comfort the souls of the newly departed and lead them to their safe rest.

Asrial alone had not been content to pray. She loved Mathew dearly. She remembered spending night after night, hovering over his crib when he was a baby, taking simple delight in just watching him breathe. To see him foully murdered, dying upon this alien shore. To have to face his bewildered soul and try to wean it away from the life he loved so dearly and had just begun to experience. . . .

It was the angel's unheard prompting that had caused the young wizard to run for his life. It was Asrial's invisible hand that had snatched the black hood from the wizard's head, revealing his delicate face and the long coppery-red hair. Why had she done it? She had a wild hope that his youth and beauty might touch the hearts of the savages and that they would leave him in peace. She'd had no idea that the man with whom she was dealing had no heart; that the only emotion the sight of Mathew's beauty touched was greed.

When Asrial saw the young man taken into the caravan, to be sold as a slave, she knew she'd made a mistake. She'd allowed herself to become personally attached to a human. Inadvertently she'd tampered with the plan of Promenthas, and now her charge was suffering for it. That first night when Mathew had wept himself to sleep in the trader's caravan, Asrial had flown home to Promenthas. Falling upon her knees before the God, she had kissed the hem of his white robes and prayed for forgiveness and a swift death for the suffering human.

Promenthas had been on the verge of promising her just what she'd asked, but then they had been interrupted by Akhran, the Wandering God—a frightful being to Asrial. Trembling, she had crept into the nave to wait impatiently until the Gods had finished their conversation. Already she was imagining Mathew's release from his dreadful life, the look of peace that would come upon his face, the joy when he knew that his soul was, at last, to return home.

And then, after talking with the barbaric Wandering God, Promenthas had changed his mind! Mathew was to live, it seemed. Why? Of course Asrial had not been given a reason. Faith. Trust in the Lord. She must do what she could to keep the young man alive, and not only that, but somehow she must place him in the hands of those who worshiped Akhran.

Bitterly disappointed, feeling Mathew's terror and misery wrench her heart, Asrial had nevertheless obeyed the commands of her God. It was she who alerted the guard to the fact that

Mathew was slowly starving himself to death; she who touched Khardan with her feathery wings so that he would turn his head and see the young man about to be sold into slavery.

And all for what? So that Mathew could now, under the guise of a woman, live among people who considered him mad! What was Promenthas thinking? What could this one human, this eighteen-year-old boy, do to end the war raging in the heavens. . . .

"Child!"

Asrial started and looked up in fear, thinking perhaps that the barbaric, savage djinn who had been pursuing her had discovered her at last. Instantly she began to fade away.

"Child, do not go!" came the voice again, and it was soft and gentle and pleading. Asrial stopped, her wings shivering in terror.

"What do you want of me? Who are you?"

"Look to your feet."

Asrial glanced down and saw the small crystal globe containing the two fish lying upon the floor of the tent. She stared at it, alarmed. It should not be sitting about in the open like this. Mathew was always so careful. She was certain he had concealed it safely in the pillow before going out to ride with Zohra this morning. Hastily she started to pick it up and return it to its hiding place, but the voice stopped her.

"Do not touch the globe. It might waken him."

Asrial, kneeling down beside it, could see that one of the fish—the black one—was asleep, floating inertly, eyes closed, near the bottom of the globe. The other fish, the golden one, swam in circles near the top, keeping the water moving in lulling, hypnotic ripples.

"Who are you?" asked Asrial in awe.

"I cannot tell you. To speak my name would break the spell. He would awake and know what I have done. Now listen and obey me, child. We haven't much time. My power wanes. There are two within this camp who prepare to go seek the Lost Ones. You must go with them."

Asrial gasped, her wings fluttered. "No! I cannot! I dare not leave my charge!"

"You must, child. It is for him you do this. If not, he faces a cruel fate. He will die slowly by the most foul means man can devise—a sacrifice to a Dark God who thrives on pain and suffering. Your human will linger for days in hideous agony, and at the end his soul will be lost, for in his final moments, in the madness of his pain, he will renounce Promenthas. . . ."

"But I cannot leave him." The angel wept and covered her ears with her hands. But this did not blot out the voice that continued to whisper within her heart.

"You can. He will be safe as long as he carries us. He is the Bearer and as such cannot be harmed. He will be safe—until the one who seeks him finds him again!"

"The man in the palanquin!" Asrial cried, a prey to terror.

"Yes. Already he comes searching for him. Every moment that passes, the danger draws nearer."

"I must talk to Promenthas!"

"No!" Though the fish continued to swim in seemingly unconcerned, lazy circles around the globe, the voice was insistent, stern, commanding. "No one—least of all a God—must know, or all will be ruined. Go with them, child. It is your protege's—and perhaps the world's—only chance."

"Chance! Chance for what?" Asrial cried desperately.

But the fish spoke no more. Around and around it swam, its gills moving in and out, its graceful tail and fins sending the water washing in gentle waves against the sides of the crystal, rippling around its slumbering companion.

Afraid to touch the globe, Asrial dropped a silken scarf over it, then sank back upon the cushions of Mathew's bed.

"What should I do?" she murmured, distractedly plucking out small pinfeathers in her wings. "What should I do?"

Chapter 20

"No, you read it," Mathew insisted, putting the scroll back into Zohra's reluctant hands. "Go ahead. Read the words."

"Isn't it enough that I wrote them?"

Zohra smoothed the parchment out upon the floor of the tent, her eyes fixed upon it with a gaze of mingled pride and awe and dread. Drawing a deep breath, she lifted the scroll and held it over the bowl of sand. Then, at the last moment, she shoved it toward Mathew.

"You!"

"No, Zohra!" Mathew pushed the scroll away. "I've told you. It is *your* spell. *You* wrote it. *You* are the one who must cast it!"

"I can't, Mat-hew. I don't want it!"

"You don't want what?" Mathew said softly. "The power? The power that will make you a great sorceress among your people? The power to help them. . . ."

Zohra's eyes flashed. Her lips compressed, the hand holding the parchment let it fall to the floor, and her fingers clenched into a fist. "The power to rule them!" she said fiercely.

Mathew sighed, his shoulders slumping. "Yes, well"—he gestured at the bowl of sand—"you won't be able to do anything until you overcome this fear—"

"I'm not afraid!" Zohra said angrily.

Snatching up the scroll, she carefully smoothed it out as Mathew had taught her. Holding it above the bowl of sand, she slowly and deliberately repeated the arcane words.

Mathew held his breath, averting his eyes, unable to watch.

What if the cantrip failed? What if he had misjudged her? What if she didn't possess the magic? Picturing her disappointment, he shuddered. Zohra did not handle disappointment at all well. . . .

A quick intake of breath from Zohra caused Mathew to look back at the scroll. Relief and pride flooded through him. The words were beginning to writhe upon the parchment. One by one they slid off, tumbling into the bowl. Within seconds the sand had been transformed to cool, clear water.

"I did it!" Zohra cried. Transported with delight, she threw her arms around Mathew and hugged him. "Mat-hew! I did it!"

No less elated than his pupil, feeling for the first time since he'd come to this terrible land a tiny surge of joy bubble up through the barren desert of his soul, Mathew clasped Zohra close. The human contact was intensely satisfying. For an instant the bleak wind did not blow quite so coldly. Their lips met in a kiss that, for Zohra, was laced with fire but was—for Mathew—a kiss of heartbroken loneliness.

Zohra sensed this. Mathew felt her stiffen, and she thrust him away from her. The young man lowered his head, swallowing the shame, the guilt, the sense of loss whose bitter bile was choking him. Glancing at the woman, he saw her face—cold, stern, proud, and contemptuous. . . . The open wound inside him bled freely, its pain overcoming him.

"Can't you understand!" he shouted at her, suddenly angry. "I don't want to be here! I don't want to be with you! I want to go home! I want to be with my own people in my own land! To see . . . trees again! To walk on green grass and drink water—all the water I want—and then to lie in the middle of an icy-cold stream and let it wash over me. I want to hear birds, leaves rustling, anything, except the wind!" He tore at his hair, gazing around the tent in his frenzy. "My god! Doesn't it ever quit blowing?"

He gasped for breath, the pain in his chest suffocating him. "I want to sit in the blessed silence of the cathedral and repeat my prayers and . . . and know that they are going to the ears of Promenthas and not being scattered like so much sand by this damnable wind! I want to continue my studies! I want to be with people who don't look away when I approach, then stare at me when I am past. I want to talk to people who

know my name! It's Mathew, *Mathew*! Not Mat-hew! I want
. . . my father, my mother . . . my home! Is that so wrong?''

He looked into her eyes. She lowered her long lashes
almost immediately, but he saw there what he had expected—
scorn, pity for his weakness. . . .

"I wish Khardan had killed me that night!" Mathew burst
out in bitter agony.

Zohra's response startled him. She reached out hastily and
placed her hand upon his lips. "No, Mat—Matchew!" Her
struggle to pronounce his name correctly touched him, even
through his despair. "You must not say such a thing. It will
anger our God, who blessed you with life!" Fearfully she
glanced about. "Promise me you will never say such a thing
or think it," she whispered insistently, not moving her hand
from his mouth.

"Very well," Mathew mumbled as best he could through
her fingers.

She patted him, as one does an obedient animal, and
withdrew her hand. But she continued to watch him anxiously,
her gaze straying from him more than once to the tent entrance.
It suddenly occurred to Mathew that she was truly frightened,
truly expecting this God of hers to hurl aside the tent flap,
draw his flaming sword, and carry out Mathew's wish on the
spot.

How personally these people take things, Mathew thought,
feeling even more alien and alone. How close they are to
their God, involving him in every part of their lives. They
argue with this Akhran, they curse him, they bless him, they
obey him, they ignore him. A goat fails to give milk, a
woman breaks a pitcher, a man stubs his toe. . . . They cry
out to their God with their petty woes. They blame him for
them, although—Mathew had to admit—they were equally
generous in their praise of him when things went right. This
Akhran is more like a father than a God—a father who was
as human as themselves, with all a human's failings. Where
is the awe, the reverence, the worship of One who is without
fault?

One who is without fault. . . .

"Promenthas! Heavenly Creator," Mathew sighed, "forgive
me! I have sinned!"

"What . . . what do you say?" Zohra regarded him

suspiciously. He had unconsciously spoken the prayer in his own language.

"It is by your holy will I am here. Promenthas! It is by your will that I am alive!" Mathew gazed up into the heavens. "And I have not seen that! I have been lost in pitying myself! I did not realize that, in so doing, I was questioning you! You brought me here for a reason—but what reason? To bring knowledge of you to these people? That can't be! I am not a priest! Your priests died, and I was spared. For what purpose? I don't understand. But I am not meant to understand," Mathew counseled himself, remembering his teachings. "Mortal mind cannot comprehend the mind of God." Yet these people seem to, easily enough.

"Matchew!" Zohra cried fearfully, tugging on his sleeve. "Matchew!"

Blinking, he stared at her. "What?"

"Don't talk in those strange words. I don't like it. I am certain it will offend Akhran."

"I—I'm sorry," he said flushing. "I was, I was praying . . . to my God."

"You can do that at night. I want to learn another spell. And, Matchew"—she cast him a stern glance—"do not try to kiss me again!"

He smiled wanly. "I'm sorry." He drew a deep breath. "And Zohra, you have been speaking my name . . . just fine."

"Of course," she said, shrugging. "I knew I was saying it right, Mat-hew. It was you who were not hearing it right. Sometimes"—she regarded him gravely—"I think you *are* mad. But only a little," she added, stroking his arm soothingly.

"Now," she continued, scooting the bowl toward him. "You say that we can see pictures in the water. Show me how to work this spell. I want to see pictures of this home of which you speak."

"No! I can't!" Mathew drew back, truly alarmed. "I don't want to be reminded!" If he saw his homeland, his parents' dwelling, standing among the pines upon the high cliffs, the rose-red clouds of sunset, his heart would break. He might go truly mad, more than just a little.

"I was wrong in what I said before," he continued steadfastly. "My God told me that I am here to do His bidding, whatever that may be. Longing for something that I am obviously not meant to have is . . . is sacrilege.''

Zohra nodded, her dark eyes grave. "I have long seen this sickness in you,'' she said. "Now perhaps you will heal. But what can we see in the bowl?''

"We will look into the future,'' Mathew said. He thought this would please her and he was right. Rewarded by a warm, eager smile, he pushed the bowl of water over toward her. "You will perform the spell. We will look into your future and that of your people.'' Truth to tell, he didn't much want to see into his own.

Zohra's eyes glistened. "Is this the way?'' she asked, kneeling before the bowl.

"You are too rigid. Relax. There. Now listen to me carefully. What you will see are not 'pictures' of what will happen. You will see symbols that represent events looming in your future. It will be up to us to interpret these symbols, in order to understand their meaning.''

Zohra frowned. "That seems silly.''

Mathew hid his smile. "It is Sul's way of forcing you to think about what you see and study it, not just accept it and go on. Remember, too, that what you see may never come to pass, for the future is shaped by the present.''

"I am beginning to wonder why we bother!''

"I did not promise this would be easy! Nor is it a toy to play with,'' Mathew responded sternly. "There is a danger involved in scrying, for—if we see something bad happening —we have no way of knowing if we should alter the present so as to change the future or to continue as we are.''

"If we see something bad, we should try to stop it!''

"Perhaps not. Look,'' Mathew said patiently, seeing her mounting frustration, "suppose you look into the water and you see yourself riding your horse. Suddenly your horse stumbles and falls. You are thrown from the animal and break your arm. This is a bad thing, right? And you would do what you could to prevent it from happening?''

"Of course!''

"Well, let us say that if the horse doesn't fall, he carries you into quicksand and you both die.''

Zohra's eyes opened wide. "Ah, I understand,'' she

murmured, looking at the water with more respect. "I'm not certain I want to do this, Mat-hew."

He smiled at her reassuringly. "It will be all right." He felt safe, knowing that the symbols were generally obscure and complex to decipher. She probably wouldn't understand them at all, and it might take Mathew days to figure out what Sul meant. Meanwhile the scrying would entertain her and turn her thoughts from . . . other matters.

"Relax, Zohra," he said softly. "You must clear your mind of everything. Empty it so that Sul may draw his images upon it as a child draws in the sand. Close your eyes. Begin to repeat this phrase." Slowly he spoke the arcane words of the spell. "You say it."

Zohra stumbled over the words, speaking it clumsily.

"Again."

She said it again, this time more easily.

"Continue."

She did so, the words coming to her lips easier each time.

"When you believe you are ready"—Mathew lowered his voice almost to a whisper so as not to disturb her concentration—"open your eyes and look into the water."

At first, despite his instructions, Zohra's body was stiff and tense from nervousness and excitement. It was a natural reaction and one reason that the chant was repeated—to force the mind into calm waters where it could drift until Sul claimed it. Mathew saw Zohra's shoulders gradually slump, her hands cease trembling, her face grow peaceful, and he felt a true sense of pride and accomplishment, knowing that his pupil had succeeded. She had entered the trance. Mathew had often wondered why powerful archmagi should spend their time in teaching young people when they could, for example, be managing royal kingdoms. Now he was beginning to understand.

With a deep sigh Zohra opened her eyes and stared into the water. A tiny line of irritation creased her brow.

"At first you will see nothing," Mathew said gently. "Be patient. Keep looking."

Zohra's eyes blinked, she caught her breath.

"Tell me what you see."

"I see"—her voice was hesitant—"birds of prey."

"What kind of birds?"

"Hawks. No, wait, there is one falcon among them."

That symbol was easy enough to interpret, Mathew thought. "What are they doing?"

"They are hunting. It is *aseur,* after sunset, night is falling."

"What do they catch?"

"Nothing. They fight among themselves and so their prey escapes."

That certainly wasn't unexpected. There wasn't a day went by that some minor squabble didn't break out between the two tribes camped around the Tel. Mathew nodded, "Go on," he said wryly.

"Other birds are coming. Eagles! A great many. . . ." Zohra suddenly gasped. "They are attacking!"

"What are?" Mathew asked, alarmed.

"The eagles! They are attacking the hawks! Scattering them across the sky! The falcon. . . . Ah!" Zohra put her hands over her mouth, her eyes staring into the water in horror and shock.

"What?" Mathew almost shrieked. It took all his willpower not to grab the bowl of water and stare into it himself, despite the fact that he knew he wouldn't be able to share her vision. "What happens, Zohra? Tell me!"

"The falcon falls to the sand . . . his body pierced by sharp claws. . . . The hawks are destroyed, killed or carried away by the eagles to their nests . . . to feed . . . their young. . . ."

"Anything else?" Mathew demanded impatiently.

Zohra shook her head. "The sky is dark now. It is night. I can see nothing more. Wait. . . ." She stared into the bowl in perplexity. "I'm seeing this all again!"

Mathew, confused and fearful, trying to make some sense of this terrifying vision, looked up at her quickly. "Exactly the same as before?"

"Yes."

"Exactly!" he said insistently. "Any change? No matter how slight. . . ."

"None . . . except that it is *fedjeur,* before morning. The hawks and the falcon are hunting at sunrise."

Mathew breathed a shivering sigh of relief. "Go on," he said almost inaudibly.

"I don't understand."

"I'll explain later."

"The hawks are again fighting among themselves. The prey escapes. The eagles are coming. They are attacking. I can't watch!"

"Yes, you can!" Mathew came near shaking her and dug his nails into his palms to control himself. "What now?"

"The eagles strike the falcon. He falls . . . but not into the sand! He falls . . . into a pit of . . . mud and dung. . . . He lives and struggles to rise up out of the pit. He yearns to fight. But the eagles fly away, pursuing the hawks."

"The falcon?"

"He is hurt . . . and his wings are caked with . . . filth. . . . But he is alive."

"And?"

"And the sun is shining."

She fell silent, peering intently into the water.

"Nothing else?"

Zohra shook her head. Slowly, blinking her eyes, coming back to herself, she turned to look at Mathew. "That was very bad, wasn't it?"

"Yes," he answered, averting his face.

"What does it mean?"

"I . . . I must study it," he answered evasively.

"No," she said. "There is no need to study it, Mat-hew. I know what it meant. I know in my heart. A great battle is coming! My people will fight and they will die! Isn't that what it means?"

"Yes, partly," Mathew said. "But it is not that simple, Zohra! I warned you it wouldn't be. For one thing, Sul is offering you hope! That is why there were two visions."

"I see no hope!" she said bitterly. "The hawks are attacked and they are killed!"

"But in the first, it is sunset, then night. In the second, it is sunrise, then the sun is shining. In the first, the falcon dies. In the second, Khardan lives."

"Khardan!" Zohra stared at him.

Mathew flushed. He hadn't intended to stay that.

Zohra's lips pressed firmly together. She stood up and stared for the tent entrance. Twisting to his feet, guessing her intention, Mathew caught hold of her arm.

"Let go of me!" Her eyes flared dangerously.

"Where are you going?"

"To tell my father, to warn them."

"You can't!"

"Why not?" Angrily she shook free of him and started to shove past.

"How will you explain it?" Mathew cried. Catching hold of her again, he gripped her arms, forcing her to look at him. "How will you explain the magic, Zohra? They won't understand! You'll put us both in danger! And we don't know what Sul is trying to tell us yet!"

Promenthas forgive me my lie, he prayed silently.

"But we are going to be attacked!"

"Yes, but when? It could be tonight. It could be thirty years from tonight! How can you tell?"

He felt the bunched muscles in her arms start to ease, and he breathed a sigh of relief. He released his hold on her. Turning her back to him, Zohra brushed her hand across her eyes, wiping away tears he was not intended to see.

"I wish I'd never done this thing!" Frustrated, she stamped on the water bowl, shattering the crockery and deluging cushions, robes, and the tent floor.

Mathew was about to say something comforting—meaningless, perhaps, but comforting—when a cloud of smoke appeared in the tent, coalescing into the large, flabby body of the djinn. Usti glanced around at the destruction gloomily. "Princess," he said in a quavering voice, "it is customary to take laundry to the water, not bring the water to the laundry. I suppose I will be asked to clean up this mess?"

"What do you want?" Zohra snapped.

"A little rest, if you do not mind, madam," Usti said plaintively. "I have been watching the woman, Meryem, for days now, and the most exciting thing she has done is learn how to milk a goat. And while spending twenty-four hours a day with the constant sight of a nubile white body and golden hair before my eyes would have been the dream of my youth, I find that at this age my mind turns to thoughts of broiled mutton, a nice bit of crispy lamb, sugared almonds. All to be digested pleasantly while lying stretched out upon my couch. . . ."

"What is she doing now?" Mathew interrupted the djinn's blissful ramblings.

"Sleeping through the heat of the afternoon, *sidi*," said Usti morosely, "as should all sane people. I make no disparaging remark on your affliction," the djinn added, bowing.

Mathew sighed and glanced at Zohra. "I suppose it won't do any harm to ease up on watching her," he said. "As Usti says, days have passed and she hasn't tried anything. I wonder why." Here was yet another problem to ponder. "What do you think?"

"Mmm?" Zohra looked around at him. Obviously she hadn't heard a word. "Oh." She shrugged. "I don't care. I grow bored with this chasing after nothing anyway. Leave the girl alone."

"At least for the afternoon. I'll clean this up," Mathew offered, still feeling the sense of unreality and uneasiness he always experienced talking to a being he wasn't fully convinced he believed in. "You may go."

Usti granted him a grateful look. "Akhran's blessings on you, madman," he said fervently, and quickly disappeared before anyone could change his or her mind.

"My head throbs," Zohra said heavily, putting her hands to her temples. "I am going to my tent to think what must be done."

"Hope, Zohra," Mathew said to her softly as she walked past him. "There is hope. . . ."

The dark eyes stared into his searchingly, their gaze warm and intense. Then, without a word, she stepped around him and left his tent, gliding across the empty compound that was baking in the hot sun.

Turning back, Mathew began listlessly picking up fragments of the water bowl. Holding the broken pieces in his hands, he came to a stop, staring at them unseeing. Hope? he said bleakly. Yes. Hope to save Zohra and her people from the night, hope to save them from annihilation.

But only if Khardan plummets from the sky. Not to die in glory, but to live. . . .

To live in shame and degradation.

Chapter 21

Usti was correct in reporting that Meryem hadn't done anything remarkable in the past few days—or at least anything that had been discovered by the djinn. This was due to several factors, not the least of which was Meryem's discovery of Usti. The bumbling djinn was no clever spy, and it had been easy for the sorceress to discern she was being watched and by whom. Of course this told her all she needed to know: somehow Zohra had survived the murder attempt, her suspicions were aroused, and she now believed Meryem to be a sorceress of considerable power. Meryem guessed, although she did not know for certain, that she had the madman to thank for all this. She intended to see that he received her compliments.

Meanwhile, knowing she was being watched forced her to take extra precautions. She was still no nearer marrying Khardan, and it began to look as if she must fail in her assignment when—by Quar's blessing—she happened to pass Majiid's tent just as the men were informed of the approach of Sheykh Zeid and his *meharistes* from the south. A few minutes spent listening told her all she needed to know.

A swift call summoned Yamina to the mirror, and it had been a simple matter to impart the vital information Meryem had learned to the Amir's wife while sharing the news with Majiid's wives at the same time. Since spying on their menfolk was accepted practice, none of the wives questioned Meryem's having overheard such important news or her right to spread it. They found it most welcome and discussed it and its implications far into the night.

Yamina sent Meryem a message in return, stating that the Amir had received the news and was making his plans accordingly. The message also added that he looked forward to welcoming Meryem into the *seraglio*. Meryem, who should have been gloating like a miser over newfound wealth, suddenly discovered that the gold had turned to lead. In particular, the thought of sharing the Amir's bed—which had before been her highest goal—was distinctly unappealing. It was Khardan she wanted.

Never before had a man taken such possession of her mind and soul. She didn't like the feeling. She fought against it. And not a day went by but that she didn't find some opportunity to see him, to be near him, to make him aware of her, to watch him in secret. She did not love him. Hers was not the nature to love. She was consumed by desire for him; a physical yearning that she'd felt for no other man in her life.

Had she been able to satisfy that desire, a few nights of passion might have quenched it. Knowing she could not have what she wanted increased its value tenfold. He tantalized her. Her nights were spent in sweet, tormenting fantasies of his love; her daily menial tasks were made bearable by dreams of introducing him to the pleasures taught in a royal *seraglio*.

And the Amir was going to make war on him.

Khardan might well be killed! Might? Hah! Meryem knew enough of the man to realize that for him there would be no surrender. Were the foe to outnumber him a thousand to one, he would die fighting. What could she do?

She had only one idea. She would try to persuade him to flee with her to Kich. The Amir could use a man such as Khardan in his armies. He would be near her, in the palace, and once the nomad had tasted the pleasures of city life, Meryem was postive he would not want to return to this one.

Knowing the loyalty Khardan felt for his people, Meryem was somewhat dubious about the success of her plan, but there was no harm in trying. At least it would give her an excuse to talk to him, to be alone together in the privacy of his tent.

Consequently, on the afternoon when Zohra and Mathew were absorbed in their contemplation of terrifying visions and Usti was absorbed in the contemplation of a bottle of fine wine, Meryem rose from her supposed nap and crept out into the camp that slumbered beneath the sweltering sun.

Silently, unobserved by anyone, Meryem slipped into Khardan's tent. He was asleep, his strong body stretched out full length upon the cushions. For long moments she stood watching him, delighting to torment herself with the ache of her longing. One arm was thrown across his eyes to protect them from a beam of sunlight that had slanted over the bed and was now gone with the approach of evening. His breathing was even and deep. The front of his tunic was open, revealing the strong, muscular chest. Meryem envisioned sliding her hand inside, caressing the smooth skin. She envisioned her lips touching the hollow of his throat and was forced to shut her eyes and regain control of herself before she dared approach him.

Feeling her glowing cheeks cool, she knelt down on shaking knees by his bed and laid a gentle hand upon his arm.

"Khardan!" she whispered.

Startled, he blinked and half sat up, his hand reaching instinctively for his sword.

"What? Who—"

Meryem shrank back in terror. "It is only me, Khardan!"

His expression softened at the sight of her, then he frowned. "You should not be here!" His voice grated harshly, but she knew—with a thrill—that it was not the harshness of anger but of passion.

"Don't send me away!" she pleaded, pressing the palms of her hands together. "Oh, Khardan, I am so frightened."

She was pale and trembled from head to toe, but it wasn't from fear.

"What is it?" Khardan said, instantly concerned. "Who in this camp has given you reason to be afraid?"

"No one," Meryem faltered. "Well"—she amended, lowering her eyes and looking at him through the long lashes— "there is someone who scares me."

"Who?" Khardan demanded in a deep voice. "Tell me the name!"

"No, please. . . ." Meryem begged, affecting to try to draw away from him. Though this had not been her intent in coming here, the opportunity to strike out at her enemy was too good to pass up.

Khardan continued to argue, and as he was much too strong for her, she yielded to his pressing demands.

"Zohra!" she murmured reluctantly.

"I thought as much," Khardan said grimly. "What has she done? By Akhran, she will pay!"

"Nothing! Truly. It is just that sometimes, the way she looks at me. Those black eyes. And then she is such a powerful sorceress. . . ."

Khardan regarded Meryem fondly. "Such a loving little bird as you, my dear, would not speak ill of anyone, even the cat. Do not be afraid. I will have a word with her."

"Ah, but Khardan!" She wrung her pretty hands. "This is not why I came! It is not for myself that I am frightened."

"For whom then?"

"For you!" she breathed. Hiding her face in her hands, she began to weep, being careful as she did so to cry only enough tears to give a shimmer to her eyes, not to make her nose red and swollen.

"My treasure!"

Putting his arms around her, Khardan held her close, stroking the blond hair that had slipped out from beneath her veil. She could feel his body tense, straining against the bonds he had bound around himself. Her own passion rose. She let slip the veil from her face, revealing her full, red lips.

"What have you to fear for me?" he asked, his voice husky, holding her away from him slightly to look into her eyes.

"I have heard . . . about this terrible Sheykh Zeid!" she said in a tear-choked voice. "I know that there may be a battle! You might die!"

"Nonsense." Khardan laughed. "A battle? Zeid is coming in answer to our prayers, gazelle-eyes. He will ride with us to raid Kich. Who knows," he added teasingly, brushing back a handful of golden curls, "by next week I might be the Amir."

Meryem blinked. "What?"

"Amir!" he continued, just for something to say. His towering fortress of strength was rapidly crumbling. "I will be the Amir and you will show me the wonders of the palace. Particularly the secret hole in the wall that looks into the bathing room and the hidden chamber where the blind musicians play.''

Meryem wasn't listening. Was it possible? Why had she never considered this before? But could it be worked? There was still this terrible battle. . . . She had to think. To plan. Meanwhile, here was Khardan, his lips brushing against her cheek, burning her skin. . . .

''I must go!'' she gasped, tearing herself from his embrace. ''Forgive the foolish fears of a weak and silly woman.'' She backed out of the tent, her heart pounding so that she couldn't hear her own words. ''Only know that she loves you!''

Though his arms and hands released her and he let her go without trying to stop her, his eyes held her still, and it was all she could do to flee their warm embrace. Literally running, she escaped back to the cool solitude of her tent.

Yes, she would sleep in the Amir's bed.

But it would be Khardan, not Qannadi, who lay beside her!

Chapter 22

Sheykh Zeid was now within two days ride of the camp around the Tel. Everyone waited eagerly to see what tomorrow morning would bring, for if Zeid were coming as a friend, he would send vaunt-couriers ahead of him by one day to announce his coming. If he were a foe, he would send no one. Since the *spahis* lived for fighting, they were as prepared for one eventuality as the other. Most—like Khardan—considered it unlikely that Zeid would opt for war. After all, what possible reason could he have for attacking them?

Pukah could have given one. Pukah could have given them several. The djinn was the only person in camp *not* looking forward to tomorrow morning. He knew that no vaunt-courier would appear bearing guest-gifts and salutations from his master. He knew that instead there would be masses of fierce *meharistes* galloping down on them. Zeid's men were true children of battle—the highest compliment one nomad can pay another. Strong and courageous to the point of folly, the Aran fought as well on foot as on the backs of their *meharis*, each man trained to run alongside his camel, using one hand to pull himself up onto the animal's back by the saddle while slashing out with his sword in the other. Pukah chafed to be gone. He *had* to be gone by morning and intended to leave this night—Sond or no Sond.

Majiid had been most reluctant to part with his djinn, and the fact that Sond was running off on another wild errand for Akhran didn't help matters. The Sheykh was beginning to have his doubts concerning his wisdom of the Wandering

God these days. The Rose of The Prophet looked to be on verge of death. He'd lost horses to the Hrana. (Majiid's worst nightmares consisted of seeing his precious animals plodding along ignominiously behind a flock of bleating sheep.) Then there'd been the Amir's refusal to buy the horses, the Calif's near arrest, and finally the arrival of a madman in their midst.

"What more could Akhran do to me?" Majiid demanded of his djinn. "Beyond setting fire to my beard, of course. Now he wants to take you away from me!"

"It is a most urgent matter," Sond pleaded, driven by his love for Nedjma to pursue the argument in the glare of Majiid's anger. "You, my master, are seeing things by night instead of by day. You may have lost horses, but you have gained mutton. You and Jaafar have managed to intimidate that old bandit Zeid, who is eager to be your friend. Khardan escaped the Amir's wrath and tweaked the man's nose into the bargain by carrying away the Sultan's daughter, and now you will have vengeance upon the city and become wealthy in the process!

"I will be gone only a few days at the most, *sidi*," Sond said in conclusion. "You will never miss me. Usti, the djinn of your daughter-in-law, has agreed to supply your needs until I return." (This Usti had done, but only after great quantities of *qumiz*, and then he had been unable to recall his agreement in the morning. This didn't matter to Sond, however, who truly expected to be back before Majiid could think of wanting him.) "And if I may remind my Sheykh," Sond continued smoothly, "now is hardly the time to offend *Hazrat* Akhran."

That much Majiid had to admit, albeit reluctantly. Such a daring undertaking as a raid on a walled city would require all the blessings the Wandering God had to bestow and then some. "Very well," he said finally, giving grudging assent. "You may go. But I command you by the power of the lamp to be back before we launch our attack on Kich."

"To hear is to obey, *sidi*," the overjoyed Sond cried, throwing his strong arms around his master and kissing him soundly on both cheeks—a proceeding that highly scandalized Majiid, who felled the djinn with one blow of his powerful fist. The swelling of Sond's jaw was nothing compared to the swelling of his heart with love, however. He hastened into his lamp to prepare for his journey.

Pukah, meanwhile, restlessly prowled the camp, trembling in dread whenever anyone rode up, fearful news would come that Zeid was attacking sooner than the djinn anticipated. It was evening, the time when the barren sands came alive with sparkling purples and golds. Oblivious to the beauty, Pukah sat some distance from camp in the shadow of the Tel, watching with increasing gloom the people coming out of their tents to take advantage of the cool night breeze.

"I will give Sond one hour," Pukah stated, his eye on the rim of the sun that was slowly disappearing into the far distant hills. "When it is dark, we are leaving."

He was speaking to himself, as usual, and so was considerably surprised and more than a little alarmed to find this pronouncement met with a small, soft sigh.

"Who's there?" he cried, leaping to his feet. "Who spoke?" He drew his sword.

"Oh, please! Put your weapon away!" said a sweet voice, the sweetest voice Pukah had ever heard in all his centuries. Dropping the sword, he fell to his knees.

"It is you, my enchanter!" he cried, spreading his arms and looking around wildly. "Please, show yourself. I will not harm you, I swear it! I would sooner let myself be pierced by red-hot needles run into the soles of my feet—"

"Don't say such dreadful things, I beg of you!" the voice pleaded.

"No, no! I won't. I'm sorry. Please, only let me see you that I may know you are real and not a dream!"

A cloud of golden rain began to shimmer before the djinn's dazzled vision. Out of the rain stepped the form of a woman. She was dressed in voluminous white robes with long white sleeves. Wings surpassing the whiteness and delicacy of a swan's sprang from her shoulders, their feathery tips brushing the ground. Silver hair curled about a face so ethereal in its wistful loveliness that Pukah didn't feel a thing when his heart leaped from his chest and fell with a thud at the woman's bare, white feet.

"Please, tell me your name, that I may whisper it to myself every second from now throughout eternity!"

"My . . . my name is Asrial," said the immortal vision of loveliness.

"Asrial! Asrial!" Pukah repeated in rapture. "When I die, that name will be the last word upon my lips."

"You can't die; you're immortal," Asrial pointed out unromantically. Her voice shook as she spoke, however, and a tear sparkled like a star upon her cheek.

"You are in trouble, in danger!" Pukah guessed instantly. He threw himself upon his belly in the sand, arms outstretched. "I beg you! Let me help you! Let me sacrifice my unworthy life for just the reward of removing that tear from your cheek. I will do anything, anything!"

"Take me with you," said Asrial.

"Anything but that," Pukah said heavily.

Sitting up, leaning back on his heels, he regarded the angel with a mournful expression. "Ask me for something simple. Perhaps you'd like the ocean to cool your feet. I could it put it over there, to your left. And to the right, a mountain, to complete the view. The moon, to hold in your hand, and the stars to adorn your hair. . . ."

"Can you truly do such things?" Asrial's eyes widened.

"Well, no," Pukah admitted, realizing that he might suddenly be called upon to supply one or more of the above. "But I am very young. Someday, when I am older, I expect to be able to perform these and other such miracles like that!" He snapped his fingers. "You see," he added confidentially, "I am the favorite of my God."

"Ah!" The angel's pale, wan face brightened until it seemed to Pukah he was blinded by her radiance. "Then surely you have nothing to fear and my coming with you will be only a minor inconvenience. I will keep out of your way," she promised. "I won't be any trouble, and I might be of some small help. I am not a favorite of my God as are you," she added shyly, "but Promenthas is very powerful and a loving father to his children."

"Are you his daughter?" Pukah was beginning to fear that he'd chosen the wrong immortal to try to impress.

"No, not literally," Asrial said, blushing. "I meant only that all those who worship Promenthas are viewed by him as his children."

"So, you worship Promenthas," Pukah said, stalling for time, wondering how he could get out of this.

"Yes," she answered. "Do you mind if I sit down? It's been a . . . a trying day. . . ."

"Oh, please!" Pukah sprang to his feet. "What would you prefer? A cloud? A cushion of swan's down? A blanket of lamb's wool?" He produced all three, this being a relatively simple trick.

"Thank you," she said, selecting the blanket. With her own hands—such lovely hands, Pukah saw with a sigh—she spread it upon the desert floor and sank down onto her knees.

"Excuse me," she said. "What are you looking at?"

"Your wings. Forgive me, but I was just wondering how you manage to sit like that without crushing them."

"They fold back, out of my way. Like this." She turned slightly to give him a view of the graceful sweep of her feathers trailing on the ground behind her.

"Ah!" said Pukah, overwhelmed by the beauty of the sight. He caught hold of his hand, just as it was straying out to touch one of the feathers. Clasping it firmly, he held it behind his back, out of temptation.

"It is unusual to see a female immortal on this plane." A sudden jealous thought struck Pukah. "The madman is your master. In what capacity do you serve him?" he demanded savagely.

"The madman—I mean Mathew—is *not* my master. We do not serve humans as do you," she added, regarding Pukah with lofty reproof. "I serve only Promenthas, my God."

"You do?" Pukah cried, ecstatic. "Then why are you with the madman?"

"Mathew is not mad!" Asrial returned angrily. "I am his guardian."

"You?" Pukah seemed to find this amusing. "From what do you protect him? Vicious attacks by butterflies? A sparrow coming too near?"

"I saved his life when all the rest of his companions were slaughtered by the foul followers of Quar!" Asrial cried, stung. "I kept him alive when he was in the fiendish clutches of the evil slave trader. I kept him alive when your master would have had his head on his sword!"

"That is true," Pukah said thoughtfully. "I saw that myself

and I found it hard to believe. Khardan is not generally one to show mercy.'' He regarded her with new respect. ''I think, then, that your mad— Forgive me . . . your Mathew . . . is a human fortunate in his God's choice of a guardian. I also think that your Mathew is still in much need of guarding, if you will forgive my mentioning such a distressing fact,'' he added gently.

''Oh, Pukah!'' Asrial's eyes filled with tears. ''I do not want to leave him! But I have no choice, it seems. If I do not go on this journey with you, I have been told that a terrible fate will most certainly befall him!''

''Do you know where we are going?'' Pukah hedged.

''I was told you seek the Lost Immortals.''

''Who told you?'' Pukah demanded, startled and displeased. ''Sond! That's it! You know Sond! He knows you! Ah, I should have guessed as much! Breaking his heart over Nedjma, is he? Meanwhile dallying with another immortal—''

''I don't know what you are talking about!'' Asrial said coldly, drawing her robes closely about her. ''I never heard of this Sond. As for who told me, I can't tell you. It is a secret, one on which—perhaps—my Mathew's very life depends.''

''I'm sorry. Don't cry. I'm a jealous fool!'' Pukah said remorsefully. ''It's only that I love you to distraction!''

''Love?'' She looked at him in perplexity. ''What is this talk of love and jealousy and dalliance among our kind?''

''Are there male angels among you?''

''Yes, most assuredly.''

''Don't you fall in love?''

''Certainly not. Our thoughts are on paradise and the good work that we strive to do among men. We are wholly occupied in our worship of Promenthas. It is he who has our love, and it is a pure love, unstained by the corruption of bodily lust that so afflicts humans. And is this not true with you?''

''Er, no,'' said Pukah, feeling somewhat uncomfortable beneath the gaze of those cool, innocent eyes. ''We have our share of bodily lust, I'm afraid. I can't quite picture paradise without it, if you'll forgive my saying so.''

''That's what comes of being around humans so much,'' Asrial stated.

''Well, for that matter,'' Pukah added, nettled by her

superior tone, "I notice that your talk about 'your Mathew' goes a bit beyond that of your everyday bodyguard."

"What do you mean by that?"

"I mean that perhaps you're eager to do more than just *guard* his body. . . ."

"How dare you!" She flounced to her feet, her wings spreading in her indignation. Her face had flushed a deep rose, her eyes sparkled with her anger, the outspread wings fanned the evening air, filling Pukah's nostrils with the pure, sweet smell of holy incense. He fell to the ground again.

"I dare because I'm a wretch, a miserable excuse for a djinn, not worthy of you to spit upon!" he cried woefully. "Forgive me?"

"Will you take me with you?"

"Please don't ask that of me, Asrial!" Pukah begged, looking up at her earnestly. "It is dangerous. More dangerous than you can possibly imagine. More dangerous than I've let on to Sond," he admitted shamefacedly. "If you must know the truth, *I'm* going only because I've messed things up around here so badly that I'm afraid my master will turn me over to Akhran for punishment. And all know that while the Wandering God has many faults, showing mercy is not one of them. I hope, by searching for the Lost Ones, I can somehow make reparation for the serious trouble I'm about to bring down upon my master's unsuspecting head."

"You did not do this purposefully to cause him harm?"

"No, oh, no!" Pukah cried. "I can say that truthfully, if I can say nothing else to my credit. I meant, all along, only to help him." Choking, he wiped his eyes, muttering something about sand flying down his throat.

"Then," said Asrial shyly, reaching out her hand to him, "together we will work to help your master and my Mathew and save them from the trouble that we *both* have inadvertently brought to them. Can you put up with me?"

"If you can put up with me," Pukah said humbly.

"Then I may come?"

"Yes." Pukah sighed. "Though it goes against my heart. Ah, look. Here is Sond, and with good news by that stupid grin on his face. I better tell you the rest of the story. And—er —don't mention anything to Sond about . . . about what I just said? He wouldn't understand! The reason we are going is that

Sond's beloved, a djinniyeh named Nedjma, was kidnapped by an evil being known as an 'efreet. This 'efreet—going by the name of Kaug—dwells in a most fearsome place beneath the Kurdin Sea, and it is there that we must begin our search for the Lost Immortals.

"Ah Sond! About time. We were just speaking of you. This is Asrial. She's coming with us. . . . Yes, she has wings. She's an angel. . . . Don't ask questions. We don't have time. I'll explain everything to you on the way!"

Chapter 23

Zeid was within one day's ride of the Tel. Khardan, his father, and Jaafar were up early that morning, eyes turning toward the south. The sun rose over the Sun's Anvil, burning fiercely in the sky. Everyone waited expectantly.

At length three *meharis* appeared. But they were not vaunt-couriers. They did not ride into camp, which would have been a show of friendly intent. They stood upon a tall sand dune, the sun glinting off the banner of Sheykh Zeid al Saban and off the swords the men held—blades bare—in their hands.

It was a challenge to do battle.

Mounting their horses, Khardan and Majiid galloped out to meet them; Jaafar following on an ancient she-camel, who plodded through the sand with extreme reluctance and who managed to carry the Sheykh to the brief parley in time to see it end.

"What does our cousin mean that he brings war upon us?" Majiid demanded, urging his horse forward until it stood nose-to-nose with the lead camel rider—Sheykh al Saban's standard bearer.

"We do not come in war, but in peace," said the *mehari* formally. "Acknowledge that you are under the *suzerain* of Sheykh Zeid al Saban and pay him tribute of the following"— the *mehari* recited a list of demands that included, among other things, thirty fine horses and one hundred sheep—"and we will leave in peace," the *mehari* concluded.

Majiid's brows bristled in anger. "Tell Sheykh Zeid al Saban that I would sooner place myself under the *suzerain* of Sul and that the only tribute I will pay him will be in blood!''

''So be it!'' the *mehari* said grimly. He pointed to the south where the Sheykhs and the Calif could see the vast army of *meharistes* assembled. ''We will be waiting to collect.''

Raising their sabers, the camel riders saluted their foe, then turned and dashed off, the tassels that hung from the camels' saddles bouncing wildly about the animals' long, thin legs.

Hastily Khardan and the Sheykhs returned to camp—Majiid grinning broadly at the prospect of a battle, Jaafar groaning and moaning that he was cursed. Khardan, his face dark with fury, stalked into his tent and kicked the basket where Pukah lived.

''Come out, you miserable wretch, that I may yank off your ears!''

''Have you forgotten, Brother?'' Achmed peered in the tent flap. ''You gave him permission to leave.''

''Yes, and now I understand the reason why he was so eager to be gone before this day dawned!'' Khardan muttered with an oath. ''I wonder how how long he's known Zeid meant to attack us.''

''Still, Khardan, it *is* a fight!'' Achmed could not understand his brother's anger.

''Yes, but it's not the fight I wanted!'' Khardan's fist clenched.

''Ah, well,'' said Achmed with the philosophy of one who is seventeen, possessor of a new sword, and about to ride into his first major battle, ''we attack the camel riders today, Kich tomorrow.''

Khardan's stern face relaxed into a smile. Putting his arm around his brother, he hugged him. ''Remember what I've taught you! Make me proud!''

''I will, Khardan!'' Achmed's voice broke, excitement and emotion overcoming him.

Seeing his embarrassment, Khardan cuffed the boy affectionately across the face. ''And don't fall off your horse!''

''I was a child then! I haven't done that in years! I wish you'd just shut up about that!''

Achmed shoved his brother. Khardan shoved him back, harder. Their friendly tussle was broken up only by the sound of a ram's horn.

"There's the call!" Achmed's eyes shone.

"Go along. Get ready," Khardan ordered. "And don't forget to visit your mother."

"Will she cry?"

Khardan shrugged. "She's a woman."

"I don't think I can take that," Achmed muttered, his eyes cast down, face flushing.

Khardan permitted himself a smile, knowing his brother would not see it. He remembered himself at seventeen, bidding his mother good-bye. There had been tears then, too, and it had not been his mother alone who cried. The memory had shamed him for days. Now he was older and could understand. He had a difficult visit of his own to pay.

"You are a man now," he told his brother severely. "It is for you to play a man's part. Would you go into battle without your mother's prayers?"

"N-no, Khardan."

"Then leave!" Khardan shoved him again, this time in the direction of Majiid's harem. "I will see you when we ride. You are to be on my right."

It was the place of honor. His face glowing with pleasure and pride, Achmed turned and raced across the compound to Majiid's tents.

Khardan stared in that direction longingly, his thoughts *not* on his mother. Although it would not be considered proper, since they were not married, he still meant to bid Meryem good-bye. But there were other farewells he had to make first, much as he disliked it.

Turning, he left his tent. Walking the short distance across the compound to the dwellings of his wives, he glanced about, instinctively studying the weather, and noticed a darkening in the western sky. Odd time of year for a storm. It looked to be far off, however; probably over the foothills. He thought little of it. Often the clouds never left the hills. Their moisture sucked out of them by the desert heat, they generally dwindled away. His attention was drawn away by a shouted question from one of his *spahis*. Answering that, Khardan did not give the storm another thought.

The camp was in an uproar—men sharpening their blades on the whirring grindstones, gathering up saddles and bridles, bidding their families good-bye, receiving crude charms and protective amulets from their wives. Khardan, pausing, watched a father gather his small children in his arms and hold them close.

The Calif felt a swift spasm of pain contract his heart. He wanted children of his own. As he was the eldest of Majiid's many offspring, one of the greatest pleasures in Khardan's life had been helping to raise his younger brothers, teaching them horsemanship and warfare. To pass these skills on to sons of his own would be his proudest moment. And then to have a little girl (he pictured her with blue eyes and blond hair) clinging to him. To keep her safe from the harshness of the world, protected in the shelter of his strong arms. And when she was older, he could envision her coaxing a new bauble or a pair of earrings from him. Her teasing voice, her gentle hands . . . so like her mother's. . . .

Khardan shook his head, his gaze going to his destination—Zohra's tent. His face dark and grim, he thrust aside the tent flap and entered.

She had been expecting him. This was a visit he was required to pay before leaving to fight. Tradition demanded it, despite the fact that they had not spoken and only rarely even looked in each other's direction since the night he had brought Meryem into camp and into his father's tent.

Zohra, her face cold and impassive, rose to her feet to greet him. She did not bow, as was customary between husband and wife. Someone else in the tent rose, too. Khardan was surprised to see Mathew present, as well, and he looked at Zohra in some astonishment, amazed at her thoughtfulness and foresight in sparing him the humiliation of entering the tent of the madman and bidding him good-bye like a true wife.

This unexpected solicitude on her part did not deter him from his true purpose in coming here, however. Seeing them together increased his anger. He was beginning to think that *Hazrat* Akhran was playing some sort of cruel joke upon him—giving him one wife who was still a virgin and another wife who was a man. The crimson stain on the bridal sheet had saved him from shame in regard to Zohra. Everyone in both tribes knew that he did not visit her tent at night, and there was not a person in either tribe—including Zohra's own—who blamed him, considering how unwomanly she acted. He was spared shame, too, in the case of the madman. But this did not ease the bitter knowledge deep within him that—to all effect—his two wives were more barren than the desert, for the sands at least bloomed in the spring. His wives were like that accursed, dried-up, withering Rose that had brought them here in the first place.

This will end, he said to himself. This will end when Meryem comes into my tent. And then it suddenly occurred to the Calif that maybe this was what Akhran intended all along. Khardan was meant to conceive children with a Sultan's daughter! The blood of sheep would not run in the veins of his sons!

Zohra had dressed herself in a *chador* of deep-blue silk edged with gold. Her face was not veiled, her jewelry sparkled in the light of day that sifted through the tent. Fire smoldered in her dark eyes, as it always did when she confronted her husband. But it was not the fire of desire. Whatever attraction these two had felt had seemingly died—a casualty of the Calif's journey to Kich. Resentment, hatred, jealousy, shame—this was the dagger that separated them now, a dagger whose edge was sharper and cut deeper than any blade forged by the hands of man.

"So, it is to be war," Zohra said coldly. "I trust, husband, that you are not here to receive either my tears or my blessing."

"At least, wife, we understand each other."

"I do not know why you bothered to come at all then."

"Because it is expected and would not look right," Khardan returned. "And it gives me the opportunity to discuss a matter of serious import with you. I do not know the details because Meryem, gentle and loving soul that she is, refused to tell me. But I know that you have done or said something to frighten her. By Sul!" His voice grated. Taking a step nearer Zohra, his fist clenched, he stared at her intently, eyes flaring in anger. "You *do* anything to her, you *say* anything to her, you harm a single strand of golden hair on her head, and I swear by *Hazrat* Akhran I'll—"

Swiftly, silently, without a scream, without breathing a word, Zohra hurled herself at her husband, her sharp nails flashing like the claws of a panther. Her reaction took Khardan by surprise, caught him completely off guard. He had expected an angry denial or perhaps the haughty silence of one who is guilty but considers herself justified. He had not expected to be fighting for his life.

Catching hold of her wrists, he wrested her hands from his face, but not before four long, bloody scratches glistened on his left cheek. She lunged at him again, her hands clutching at his throat. Zohra's strength was above that of the average woman. Add to this the fury, the surprise, and the swiftness of her attack, and Khardan might have been in serious trouble had not Mathew joined in the fray. Grabbing hold of Zohra, the young wizard dragged her off Khardan.

The woman fought and struggled to free herself, kicking and spitting like an enraged cat.

Clasping his arms around her upper body, pinning her flailing hands to her side, Mathew glared at Khardan.

"Get out!" he cried.

"She is a witch!" Khardan said, breathing heavily, his fingers upon his face. Drawing them back, he saw the blood and cursed.

Zohra tried to fling herself at him again, but Mathew held on to her firmly.

"You cannot understand!" Mathew shouted at Khardan angrily. "Just get out!"

The Calif stared at him in some astonishment, amazed to see the young man's face so pale and threatening. Dabbing at the bloody marks with the hem of his sleeve, Khardan cast a final, piercing glance at his wife, then turned upon his heel and left her tent.

"Let me go! Let me go!" Zohra shrieked, foam flecking her lips. "I'll kill him! He will die for this insult!"

Mathew continued holding Zohra, now more out of concern for her than from fear she might harm Khardan. He was right to be alarmed. Her body went suddenly stiff, rigid as a corpse. She stopped breathing.

She was having some sort of fit. Mathew glanced about in desperation, looking for something . . . anything. . . . Catching sight of a waterskin hanging on the tent pole, he snagged it with a free hand and dashed the liquid into the woman's face.

Zohra caught her breath in shock, sputtering and gasping as the water ran down into her mouth. Half-collapsing, she staggered against the sides of the tent. Mathew went to help her, but—with unexpected strength—she shoved him away.

"Wait! Zohra!" Cursing the confining folds of the caftan that wrapped around his legs, nearly tripping him, Mathew managed to catch hold of the woman's wrist just as she was about to storm out of the tent. "You can't blame Khardan! He didn't know she tried to kill you! You can't expect him to understand. And we can't tell him!"

Zohra came to a stop. She did not turn to look at Mathew, but he knew she was listening to him at least, though her body shook with fury.

"We'll find a way to prove it!" Mathew gasped. "After the battle."

Now she looked at him, her eyes cold.

"How?"

"I—I don't know yet. We'll . . . think of something," Mathew muttered. He had never in his life seen any person— man or woman—so enraged. And now she was suddenly cool and calm. A moment before she had been fire, now she was ice. He would never understand these people! Never!

"Yes," Zohra said, lifting her chin, "that is what we will do. We will prove to him that she is a witch. The Sheykh will order death. His men will hold her down upon the sand and I will bash her head in with a rock!"

She'd do it, too, Mathew thought with a shudder. Mopping chill sweat from his face, he felt his legs give way and sank back down weakly onto the cushions.

"What was it you came to tell me?" Zohra asked. Seating herself before a mirror, she picked up a bracelet and slid it over her wrist.

Mathew had to get hold of his scattered thoughts before he could relate in any sort of coherent fashion the reason for his visit to her tent this morning.

"I've been working out the symbols in the dream. And I need to discuss them with you, especially now that it seems there could be a war."

At the mention of the vision Zohra's hand began to shake. Hurriedly she lowered the mirror she had been holding. Glancing back at him with a troubled look, she put her hand to her head, her brow creased in pain.

"No," she said, her voice suddenly hollow and fear-laden.

"This is not it. I would know. I would feel it inside me—a cold emptiness." She pressed a clenched fist over her heart. "Like I felt when I looked into that cursed water. I don't want to talk about it, Mat-hew. Besides"—she tossed her head, banishing the darkness—"this is not war, not really, though they call it that. It is"—she shrugged—"a game, nothing more."

"A game?" Mathew gaped. "But . . . then . . . no one will get hurt? No one will die?"

"Oh, yes, of course," Zohra said, slipping a sparkling ring onto her finger, admiring the flash of the jewel in the light. "They will slash each other with their swords and knock each other from their mounts and some will undoubtedly die, more by accident than anything else. Perhaps Zeid will prove the stronger. He and his *meharis* will drive our men back to camp. He will gloat over his victory, then return to his homeland. Or perhaps our men will drive him back to his homeland, then they will sit and gloat over their victory. The dead will be proclaimed heroes and songs sung over them. Their brothers will take their wives and children into their households and that will be that."

Mathew only partially heard. He was staring into nothing, seeing again—in his mind—Zohra's description of the vision.

"That's it!" he breathed.

"What?" Startled by the timbre of his voice, she looked up from her jewels.

"The hawks were fighting among themselves! The eagles came at them, diving out of the sky!"

"There, you see?" Zohra cast him a triumphant glance. "When armies fall from the skies, then we can worry. Until that moment"—she turned back to adorning herself with her jewelry—"all this stupid battle means is that we will miss our ride this morning."

The storm drifted resolutely down out of the foothills. Only one person in camp paid any attention to the approaching clouds. Meryem, her hand parting the tent flap, stared at it intently, watching it come nearer and nearer. So preoccupied was she that she did not notice Khardan approach until his hand brushed hers.

Startled, she gave a little scream. Swiftly Khardan slipped inside the tent, and Meryem was in his arms.

"Oh, my beloved!" she whispered, shimmering blue eyes searching his face. "I don't want to you to go!"

What could he do but kiss the trembling lips and brush away the tear that crept down her soft cheek?

"Do not grieve," he said lightly. "This is what we have prayed to Akhran for!"

She stared at him in perplexity.

"But you wanted peace with Sheykh Zeid. . . ."

"And we shall have it—after his fat stomach has been relieved of a few pounds." Khardan patted the hilt of his sword. "When he acknowledges us the victor, I intend to offer him the chance to fight together. The chance to raid Kich! What's the matter? I thought you would be pleased."

Meryem's glance had strayed to the storm cloud. Swiftly she looked back at Khardan.

"I—I am afraid," she faltered. "Afraid of losing you!"

She buried her face in his chest. Khardan stroked the golden hair, but there was a note of irritation in his voice when he answered.

"Have you so little faith in my skill as a warrior?"

"Oh, no!" Meryem hastily dried her tears. "I am being a foolish female. Forgive me!"

"Forgive you for being female? Never!" Khardan said teasingly, kissing the supplicating hands she held up so prettily before her. "I will punish you for it the rest of your life."

The thought of such punishment made Meryem's heart beat so rapidly she feared he might notice and consider it unmaidenly. Hoping the flush staining her cheeks would be taken for confusion and not the immodest desire that swept her body, Meryem hurriedly lowered her head before his intense gaze. Removing a necklace she wore around her throat, she offered it to him timidly.

"What is this?" he asked, taking the object in his hand.

"A silver shield," she said. "I want you to wear it. It was . . . my father's, the Sultan's. My mother made it for him, to protect him in battle. Its protection isn't very powerful. But it carries with it my love."

"That is all the power I need!" Khardan whispered, clasping

the shield tightly in his hand. He kissed her again, nearly crushing her in his embrace.

With difficulty Meryem caught her breath. "Promise me you will wear it?" she said insistently

"You shall put it on me with your own hands!"

Almost reverently he removed the head-cloth.

Meryem saw the four long scratch marks upon his face and gave a small scream. "What is this?" she asked, reaching out hesitantly to touch them. "You are hurt!"

"Nothing!" Khardan said harshly, averting his face, bowing his head so that she could slip the silken ribbon over his curling black hair. "A tangle with a wildcat, that is all."

Thinking she knew the particular breed of cat, Meryem smiled to herself with pleasure. Wisely saying nothing more, she slid the ribbon over his head, her fingers brushing through his hair. She felt his body tremble at her touch, and she stepped back quickly, her worried glance straying, once again, to the approaching storm.

The ram's horn, bleating loudly, recalled Khardan's attention.

"Good-bye, gazelle-eyes!" he said, his face flushed with passion and excitement. "Do not weep! I will be safe!" His hand closed over the silver shield.

"I know you will!" Meryem said with a brave, tearful, secret smile.

Chapter 24

Seated astride the magical ebony horse, the Amir looked down from his vantage point on the back of the cloud-shaped 'efreet, watching as the *meharistes* of Sheykh Zeid dashed across the dunes, their swift camels seemingly outpacing the wind. Below him he could see the activity in the camp around the Tel: the men racing for their horses, the women with their children gathered outside their tents, waving their outstretched hands in the air, their shrill voices raised in an eerie war chant to hearten their men.

Gathered around the Amir was a vast army, each soldier mounted upon a steed as magical as his own. Unaccustomed to the height and the strangeness of being carried through the skies on the back of an 'efreet, many of Qannadi's men cast nervous glances beneath them. More than a few faces were pale and sweating, and several—to their eternal shame—leaned over their saddles and were quietly sick. But these were well-disciplined, seasoned troops. They spoke no word. Their eyes upon their captains, who were meeting with the Amir, they waited for the signal that would send them from this black, lightning-fringed cloud to the ground below where they would do what they did best—fight and conquer.

"You have your orders. You know what to do," the Amir said crisply. "The Imam asks me to remind you that you fight to bring the light of Quar to the darkness of the souls of these *kafir*. We fight these men only long enough to show the strength and might of our army. I want to divide them, demoralize them. I don't want them killed!"

The captains answered in the affirmative, but with a distinct lack of enthusiasm.

"Wreck their camp as we did that of the sheepherders earlier this day. Leave the elderly and the infirm behind, unharmed. We don't want them. They are of no use to us. Women of childbearing age and children are to be captured and taken back to the city. They are not to be molested. Any man caught violating a woman will swiftly find himself a place among the palace eunuchs."

The captains nodded. The Amir was always strict in regard to this, as several eunuchs had reason to know to their bitter sorrow. The Amir had performed the operation himself, on the spot, with his own sword. It was not that he was a kindly man. He was simply a good general, having seen in wars in his youth how quickly a well-disciplined army can degenerate into an uncontrollable mob if allowed to slip the leash.

The Amir glared around his troops, letting his threat sink in. Fixing his eyes upon two of his captains, Qannadi continued, speaking to them specifically. "Those of you riding south to attack the Aran, the same orders apply. All captives are to be brought to Kich. Any questions?"

"We don't like this about the men, sir; just leaving them out here. We've heard about these nomads. They fight like ten thousand devils, and they would cut out their own hearts before they'd surrender. Begging the Amir's pardon, but they'll never convert to Quar. Let us kill them and send Him their souls now instead of later."

There were mutterings of agreement. Privately Qannadi sided with his captains. He knew that the nomads would eventually have to be wiped out. Unfortunately the Imam would have to come to see this, too. And right now the only thing those almond eyes—blind with holy zeal—saw was the glory of converting an entire people to the knowledge of the One, True God.

"You have your orders," Qannadi said harshly. "See that they are obeyed. When the men have been beaten on the field and left to starve, they will receive word that their families are being well-treated in Kich and have found true spiritual solace in Quar." Qannadi was repeating the Imam's words. But those who knew him well saw the slight twist of the man's lip.

"However, if you are attacked," the Amir said slowly and precisely, "there is nothing you can do but kill to defend yourselves."

Nodding, relaxing, the men grinned.

"But when I give the order to withdraw, all fighting is to cease. Take a few prisoners among the men—in particular strong, young ones. Is this understood? Any further questions . . . Fine. The blessing of Quar be with you."

At this point the captains would have responded with a mighty shout, but they had been counseled to keep strict silence and so they disbanded in quiet, each man returning to his command.

"Gasim, a word with you." The Amir gestured to his favorite, the one-eyed captain who had been casting that eye upon the lovely Meryem. Gasim rode up in response to the Amir's command, bringing his horse close alongside that of his commander. "Captain"—the Amir's voice was low—"you know that I put up with this nonsense of taking prisoners to keep the Imam happy. There is one man, however, whose soul must be in Quar's hands this night."

Gasim raised his single eyebrow, the other being concealed behind the patch that covered the empty socket where his eye had been prior to a vicious sword slash. "Name him, my General."

"Their Calif—Khardan. You know him by sight. You saw him at the palace."

"Yes, Amir." Gasim nodded, but Qannadi saw the man appeared uneasy.

"What's the matter?" The Amir's voice grated.

"It is just . . . the Imam said that the Sheykhs and the Calif were to be left alive, to lead their people to the knowledge of the truth of the God . . ." Gasim hesitated.

The Amir shifted in his saddle and leaned forward, thrusting his chin into Gasim's face. "Whose wrath do you fear most? Mine upon this world or Quar's in the next?"

There could be only one answer to that. Gasim was well-acquainted with the Amir's legendary torture chambers. "Khardan will die!" he said softly, bowing.

"I thought he might," Qannadi returned wryly, sitting back in his saddle. "Bring me his head so that I may know my orders have been carried out. You are dismissed."

The captain saluted and galloped off, the hooves of his horse eerily silent as they beat upon the cloudy chest of the 'efreet.

"You know what you are to do, Kaug?" the Amir asked, looking into the two huge staring eyes among the mist.

"Yes, *Effendi*."

The Amir's gaze returned to the desert beneath him. The *spahis*, mounted upon their horses, were galloping out to meet the camel riders—swords flashing in the air, their voices raised in wild shouts.

An odd way to welcome friendly allies, Qannadi thought idly. But what could you expect of these savages?

Lifting his hand, he gave the signal.

Chapter 25

Leaving Zohra's tent, Mathew looked up at a swiftly moving, dark-black cloud and saw an army descending from the sky.

At first he could neither speak nor react. Paralyzed with astonishment, he stared, openmouthed. Soldiers—hundreds of them—mounted on winged horses, soared out of the towering thunderhead. They rode in tight formation, spiraling downward like a human cyclone, heading for the ground, heading for the camp around the Tel. The golden ram's head, stitched upon their uniforms, now bore the wings of eagles sprouting from its skull.

Mathew gave a strangled cry. Hearing him shout, Zohra ran from her tent. Several women, standing near him, their eyes on the husbands who were just galloping out of sight, turned to stare at him in alarm. Wordlessly, unable to talk, Mathew pointed. The first riders were just touching the ground, their magical steeds hitting the desert floor at a gallop.

Zohra clutched at her chest, her heart frozen by cold, numbing fear. "The vision!" she gasped. "Soldiers of Quar!"

A fierce wind swept down out of the cloud, raising a stinging, blinding storm of sand that swirled around the camp. Catching hold of tent poles, the wind—like a huge hand—yanked them from the ground and sent them flying, bringing the fabric crashing down upon those inside. Shrieks and wails of terror rose into the air. The winds increased to gale force and the darkness deepened, split occasionally by jagged lightning and deafening cracks of thunder.

Some of the women tried to flee, to escape, running after the *spahis,* who had already disappeared. Blankets, swept along the desert floor by the wind, encircled the legs of their victims, tripping them, bringing them down. It seemed as though all inanimate objects had suddenly come to malevolent life. Brass ware, iron pans, and crockery slammed into their former mistresses, knocking them senseless to the ground. Rugs wrapped around their weavers, smothering them.

Then, out of the storm came the soldiers of Quar. They rode through the camp, the storm winds dying swiftly to allow them to do their work. Leaning down, the soldiers grabbed wailing children up in their arms and carried them off. Others dragged the comatose bodies of the women across the saddles and ordered their steeds back to the air.

Not all their prey was easily captured. Although supposedly sheltered and protected in the *harems,* the women of the desert were in reality the same valiant warriors as their husbands and fathers and brothers. The women did not fight for glory but they fought nonetheless—a daily battle, a battle against the elements, a battle to survive.

Badia caught up a broken tent pole and swung it. Smashing against the shoulders of a soldier, it knocked him from his mount. A brass pot, hurled with deadly efficiency by a grandmother with long years of matrimonial bickering behind her, struck a soldier on the back of his head, felling him instantly. A twelve-year-old girl leaped for the bridle of a galloping horse. Catching hold of it, she used her weight to drag the animal off balance as she had seen her father do many times during the *baigha* games. The horse fell, its rider tumbled to the ground. The girl's younger brother and sisters fell upon the soldier, beating him with sticks and pummeling him with their small fists.

But the battle, against overwhelming odds, was a losing one.

The wind blew Mathew off his feet, driving him to his hands and knees. He caught a glimpse of Zohra running back into her tent, then—blinded by the stinging sand—he could see nothing. Fighting the whipping gale, he struggled to stand and saw Zohra emerge, dagger in hand, just as the tent blew down

The tent! Mathew thought instantly of two things: the fish and his magic. Panicked, he turned to see his own tent take wing and flap off like a huge bird, his scrolls and parchments sailing after it. This time the wind inadvertently aided him, for it was at his back as he ran to save his possessions. Lunging after them, he caught what scrolls and parchments he could, searching frantically as he scrambled here and there among the debris for the glass globe, containing the two fish.

A glint of light caught his eye. There was the globe—right beneath the pounding hooves of a galloping horse!

Mathew heard echoing in his ears the cold voice promising what would happen to him if he lost the fish. His heart in his throat, he watched, cringing, as the iron shoes smashed the globe into the ground. The horse's rider, clutching two squirming, screaming children in his arms, thundered past Mathew without a glance. Dazed by the confusion about him, the young wizard was turning away in despair to look for Zohra when the same flash of light caught his attention. Looking down, he saw the glass globe, blown by the wind, rolling toward him.

Numb with shock, Mathew stared at it in disbelief. It was completely unharmed, not even scratched.

"Mat-hew!" He heard a shout behind him. Hastily he picked up the glass globe and, after a quick glimpse to ascertain that the fish were safe and unharmed, thrust it into the bodice of his women's robes.

"Mat-hew!" The shout was a warning.

Whirling, Mathew saw a soldier on horseback reaching out to grab the "woman" and haul her up into the saddle. Reacting with a coolness that astonished him, Mathew caught hold of the soldier's outstretched arm. Bracing himself, he pulled with all his strength, jerking the man from the saddle.

The soldier fell on top of Mathew, carrying them both to the ground. Grappling with the man, Mathew fought to free himself, then he heard a horrifying scream and felt the heavy body on top of his go rigid, then limp, sagging over him. The silken scarves of a *chador* swirled about Mathew's head like a blue and golden cloud. The weight was yanked off him, a hand helped him to his feet. Standing up, Mathew saw Zohra remove her bloodstained dagger from the soldier back.

Her long black hair streaming in the wind, she turned, dagger in hand, ready to face her next foe.

"Zohra!" Mathew shouted desperately above the shrieks and screams, the neighing of horses, the yells and commands, "Zohra, we must find Khardan!"

If she heard him, she paid no attention to him.

Frantically Mathew spun her around to face him. "Khardan!" he screamed.

Seeing a soldier intent on riding them down, Mathew dove for cover beneath a partially collapsed tent, dragging a struggling Zohra with him.

Though Mathew knew they wouldn't be safe here long, the tent offered some protection and there might be—there *had* to be—time enough to make Zohra understand the danger.

"Listen to me!" Mathew gasped. Crouched in the darkness, he caught hold of the woman by the shoulders. "Think of the vision! We have to find Khardan and convince him to flee!"

"Flee! hah!" Zohra's eyes flamed. She stared at him contemptuously. "Remain here if you want, coward! You will be safe in your women's clothing. Khardan will die fighting, as will I!"

"Then night will come to you and your people!" Mathew cried.

Starting to crawl out the tent, Zohra paused. Outside, hooves thundered about them, the cries of women and children echoed shrilly in their ears.

"Think of the vision, Zohra!" Mathew said urgently. "The falcon pierced by many wounds. Night falling. Or the falcon, wings mired in the mud, struggling to fight with the coming of day!"

Zohra stared at Mathew, but he knew, from the expression on her livid face that her eyes did not see him. They were seeing, once again, the vision. The dagger fell from nerveless fingers. Her hand—covered with the soldier's blood—pressed against her heart.

"I can't ask him to do such a thing! He would despise me forever!"

"We won't ask," Mathew said grimly, searching about for some type of weapon and settling for an iron pot

Absorbed in his fear, he did not notice the ominous silence that had now settled over the camp, making it possible for them to talk without yelling.

"But how will we find him?"

"Surely your men will turn back, once they know what is happening?"

"Yes!" said Zohra excitedly. "They will come to us and

so will Zeid! They will fight together to defeat these foul sons of Quar!''

''Not if the vision is true. Something will happen to separate them. But you're right. Khardan will return to the camp—if he can. Come on!''

Cautiously he emerged from the tent. Zohra crept out after him. They both halted, staring in shock. The battle was over. The camp was completely destroyed. Tents lay on the ground like dead birds, their fabric rent and shredded by wind, sword, and horses' hooves. Livestock had been ruthlessly butchered. Waterskins lay split open, their precious liquid soaking into the desert sand. There wasn't a thing left, it seemed, that hadn't been broken, smashed, or ripped to shreds.

Those few who had put up a fight had been subdued at last, the soldiers carrying them up into the welcoming arms of the 'efreet, whose huge body shrouded the sky in darkness. Now that the captives were safe, the storm wind began to rise again.

At the edge of the camp, barely visible through the swirling sand, Mathew caught a glimpse of color—rose-pink silk. Staring, he saw a strange sight. A woman with golden hair, her veil having blown from her head, was talking with a soldier on horseback. She was speaking earnestly, angrily it seemed, for she stamped her foot upon the ground and pointed insistently toward the south.

Meryem! How strange, Mathew thought. What is she doing? Why hasn't she tried to escape? Turning to glance in the direction he indicated, Mathew drew a breath.

''Look!'' he shouted, peering through the gathering gloom, his eyes gummed with sand. ''There they are! There is Khardan! I can see his black horse! Hurry!'' He started running. ''Or we'll be too late.''

A hand caught hold of his arm; nails dug painfully into his flesh. Turning, he saw Zohra gazing bleakly above them. From out of the clouds came another spiral of horses—fresh soldiers riding down to meet the returning nomads.

''I think, Mat-hew, that we are already too late!'' she said softly.

Chapter 26

Unaware of what was happening in their camp, Sheykhs Majiid and Jaafar led the charge across the desert to meet Zeid. Unaccustomed to riding, Jaafar jounced up and down in the saddle, stirrups flying and there appeared every likelihood that the Sheykh would fall from his mount and break his neck before ever reaching the field of battle. Majiid had tried to persuade the Sheykh to stay behind, but Jaafar—more than half-convinced that this was all some devious plot of Majiid's—had insisted on riding with the leaders, refusing to let his "ally" out of sight. Thus did all the Hrana and the Akar ride into combat—keeping one eye on the enemy in front and the other eye on those who rode at their side.

So occupied were they in warily watching each other that they never thought to look up into the sky that was growing darker and darker by the moment. They might never have noticed it at all had not Jaafar—to the surprise of no one—toppled off his horse to land heavily upon his back in the sand.

The Hrana gathered around him, prepared to stop and assist their fallen leader. Jaafar couldn't talk—the breath had been knocked from his body—but he managed to wave his men on, pointing furiously at Majiid, warning them not to let the *spahis* get ahead of them.

Lying in the sand, gasping for breath, Jaafar had time to contemplate the heavens while Fedj, his djinn, chased after the horse.

"I hope that damn storm breaks before the fighting starts!"

the Sheykh growled when Fedj returned, leading the horse and coming to assist his master.

Fedj took hold of his master's hand, glancing up as he was about to haul Jaafar to his feet. The djinn's eyes widened. With a startled cry, he let loose of the Sheykh, who tumbled back down into the sand again.

"Storm!" the djinn shouted. "That is no storm, *sidi!* That is Kaug, Quar's 'efreet!"

"Bah! What would an 'efreet be doing here?" Jaafar peered up into the sky in disbelief.

Suddenly Fedj gasped in horror. "Armies!" he shrieked, pointing behind them. "Armies of men on horseback, attacking our camp!"

Twisting around, Jaafar saw the soldiers, mounted on their magical steeds, flying out of the storm cloud, aiming for the tents below.

"Go to Majiid!" Jaafar ordered the djinn. "Go warn him!"

Within an eyeblink Fedj was gone, and within another he materialized directly in front of Majiid's horse, causing the startled Sheykh to rein in so quickly he nearly upset the animal.

"What do you want?" Majiid roared in anger. "Get out of my way! Return to that clumsy oaf you call a master and tell him to ride a donkey into battle next time!"

"Effendi!" cried Fedj. "Our camp is under attack!"

"What fools does Jaafar take us for that we should fall for such a trick?" Khardan demanded furiously, galloping up beside his father. "The enemy is before us, not behind!" He indicated a large cloud of sand through which could now be see the armies of the *meharistes.*

In answer Fedj—his expression grim—simply pointed back at the Tel. Khardan and Majiid reluctantly turned in their saddles.

"Hazrat Akhran be with us!" Khardan breathed.

Majiid, his eyes bulging in disbelief, could only sputter, "Who— What?"

"The Amir's soldiers!" Khardan cried. Grasping the reins, he dragged his horse's head around. The black war charger, foundering in the sand, nearly lost its balance. But Khardan's skill kept it upright until it could get its hind legs beneath its body. Leaping forward, it carried its master ahead at a furious gallop.

The other *spahis* milled about in confusion, shouting and pointing and passing the news along to those who were just riding up. One by one they all turned to dash back to camp, several of the unskilled Hrana riders falling from their mounts or upsetting their horses in their excitement.

"Fly to Zeid!" Majiid ordered Fedj. "Tell him the Amir is attacking and that we call upon him in the name of Akhran to help us defend ourselves against the unbeliever!"

"Done!" cried Fedj, disappearing so swiftly that the air spoke the word for him.

But when the djinn reached Zeid, he found the Sheykh already apprised of the situation, having seen for himself the armies descending from the sky.

"So!" snarled Zeid before the djinn could say a word. "What's the matter? Was Khardan afraid that he could not take us on alone? Well, he was right! We will fight both you and your friend the Amir!"

"What do you mean?" Fedj cried. "The Amir is not our friend! Can't you see he is attacking us?"

Consumed with battle rage, Zeid did not hear. The Sheykh was about to urge his camel forward when one of his men shouted and pointed toward the sky. A contingent of soldiers on their winged horses could be seen dropping down out of the thundercloud, flying southward.

"So that's your master's plan, is it?" Zeid cried grimly.

"What plan? You don't understand! Listen to me!" Fedj pleaded in desperation.

"Oh, I understand! You lure us up here and then the Amir attacks our defenseless camp while we are gone! Qannadi won't get far! Not even magical winged steeds can outrun the *meharis*!"

Shouting commands, dividing his forces, leaving some to guard his rear, ordering others to lead the charge, Zeid wheeled his camel and prepared to race after the soldiers.

"You brainless goat!" Fedj flew after Zeid. "The Amir isn't our ally! How could you think such a thing? And now you're playing into his hands, letting him divide us up." But Zeid, his face red with fury, refused to listen. Soaring to twenty feet in height, Fedj was prepared to grab hold of the camel with his bare hands and shake some sense into the fat little Sheykh. But he was stopped by Raja, Zeid's djinn, who leaped out of his master's saddlebags.

Soaring to thirty feet in height, his black skin glistening in the sun, his muscles bulging, his eyes blazing in fury, Raja leaped at Fedj. The two djinn fell to the ground, landing with a thud that caused the granite floor to crack beneath them. Howling in rage, Raja and Fedj rolled over and over, hands grappling for each other's throat.

Sheykh Zeid, in the meantime, raced over the dunes, chasing after the winged horsemen, his *meharistes* shouting for the soldiers to come down and fight them like men.

Glancing over his shoulder as he thundered northward toward the Tel, Majiid saw the camel riders turn tail—or so it seemed—and dash off back in the direction of home.

"Ah! Coward!" Pulling back on the reins, Majiid caused his horse to rear on its hind legs, the animal's front hooves slicing the air.

"May your wives mate with camels!" he called after the departing Zeid. "May your sons have four legs and your daughters humps! May you— May you . . ."

Majiid could think of nothing else. Fear for his people choked him. Half blind with tears of anger, he galloped on.

Chapter 27

The voice of the 'efreet howled in Khardan's ears, Kaug's breath blew sand into his face. Lightning flared, trying to blind him. Thunder rumbled, shaking the ground beneath his feet. A darkness as of night covered the sun.

Deadly as the diving falcon, Khardan fell upon his prey.

Unfortunately, the Calif had, in his rage, far outridden his men. Alone he smashed into the vanguard of the Amir's troops, attacking them with a fury and a recklessness that caught them completely by surprise. They might well have been facing ten thousand devils, instead of just one man.

The steel talon of his saber ripped into his enemy's flesh. The Rose of the Prophet growing on the Tel was watered with his enemy's blood. On Khardan fought, by himself. His enemies fell before his wrath like wheat to the scythe.

His arms were crimson to the elbow, the hilt of his saber and his hand were gummed with blood and gore so that he could not move his fingers. His horse battled as savagely as its master, lashing out with its sharp hooves, working skillfully to keep its footing on the blood-slick ground.

So fierce was Khardan's attack that his enemies could not get within his guard, though they outnumbered him twenty to one. Time and again they hurled themselves at him, striking with sword and dagger, only to be thrown back. They waited, biding their time, knowing that soon Khardan must grow tired, he must begin to weaken. When the rise and fall of his blade slowed, when they heard his breath begin to whistle in his lungs, his enemies took heart. Surrounding him, they pressed in closely and this time won through.

A sword thrust sliced the Calif's arm, another ripped a bloody gash across his chest. Khardan knew he was hit, but he felt no pain. Grimly he fought on, his horse staggering and plunging in the churned-up sand, its hooves slipping in the brains and mangled flesh beneath its feet.

Then Khardan, battling one foe in front of him, saw— behind him—the flash of a saber. He could not defend himself and knew that this was the end. He would take this last enemy with him, however, and—even as he braced himself for the blow from behind—he cut down the man in front. The blow never came. A cry caused him to glance around. He saw his younger brother Achmed, his sword wet with blood, staring down white-faced at the corpse of the man who had been about to kill Khardan.

"Your left!" Khardan cried out harshly, knowing he must rouse his brother from the shocked daze of his first kill. "Fight, boy, fight!"

Instinctively obeying his brother's voice, Achmed turned, clumsily blocking the soldier's blow. Khardan tried to keep by his brother's side, but a strange feeling was coming over the Calif—a feeling of weariness and exhaustion such as he had never before experienced during the wild madness of battle. He knew he had not taken a serious wound, yet he felt life draining from his body. Darkness covered his eyes, taking on an eerie, bloodred tinge. Time itself slowed. Men and horses came into sight, loomed large in his vision. He tried to fight them, but his sword arm suddenly felt as though it were made of lead, holding a weapon of stone.

And then one single figure appeared before him, riding out of the red-tinged mist. It was a captain of the Amir's soldiers, a man with only one eye. Khardan saw death glittering in that eye, but he could do nothing to defend himself; raising his arm took more strength then he possessed. He saw the stroke of the captain's blade, slicing toward his neck, and it seemed to take forever, the flare of the metal cutting a burning swath through the enveloping mist.

Khardan felt no fear, only a fierce anger. He was going to die, helpless as a babe.

The blade hit his throat and stopped, the sword rebounding

from his neck as though it had struck a steel collar. He saw the one eye of the captain open wide in astonishment, then the man himself disappeared, falling backward off his horse, sinking into the red-tinged mist with a terrible yell.

Khardan blinked, trying to clear his vision, trying to shake off this awful lethargy. He was like a small child lost and wandering aimlessly in a horror-filled night.

He felt himself slide from the saddle, his body nerveless, unable to support him. He slumped down into the warm sand, closing his eyes, longing for sleep.

"Khardan!" came a voice.

Forcing open heavy eyelids, he looked up and saw a face covered by a rose-pink veil hovering above him in the mists.

"Meryem!" he murmured. He could not think how she came to be here. She was in danger! Frantically, he struggled to rise, to save her!

But he was tired.

So very tired. . . .

Chapter 28

Huddled in the meager shelter offered by the trunk of a palm tree, Mathew watched the battle raging around the Tel with the curiously detached interest of a spectator witnessing a drama. He couldn't understand his lack of feeling and began to fear that the harshness and cruelty of this land was robbing him of his humanity.

Mathew had one thought, one purpose—to find Khardan. Nothing else mattered. Silently cursing the darkness, the storm-driven wind, and the swirling sand, the young wizard stared into the surging, heaving, struggling mass of men and horses. The sand blowing into his face made his eyes burn painfully. Tears streamed down his cheeks, soaking the veil he had drawn over his mouth to protect himself from inhaling the dust. Angrily, impatiently, he wiped the tears and grit from his eyes and continued to stare into the mob.

Once he thought he saw Khardan and pointed him out to Zohra, who was crouched next to him. But she shook her head emphatically. The man turned his head, and Mathew, sighing, was forced to admit that she was right. The *spahis* in their swirling robes all looked alike to him. He was trying to recall if Khardan had been wearing anything distinctive that morning, such as a red head-rope or perhaps the red leather boots that he sometimes preferred to his black ones. But the morning seemed very far away, lost in a haze of blood and terror. He couldn't remember anything.

The pounding of horse's hooves behind him and a sharp intake of breath from Zohra caused Mathew to whirl about fearfully. One of the soldiers was riding down on them, sword raised. Mathew saw Zohra's hand dart inside the folds of her *chador,* he saw the flash of her dagger. Instinctively Mathew's hand closed around one of his magical scrolls. Scoffing at himself, he let it go. What would he do? Throw a bowl of water in the enemy's face? He needed a wand—something powerful—to work warrior's magic.

The soldier closed on them. Mathew felt Zohra tense, ready to spring, but the man, seeing now that they were females, arrested the downward stroke of his blade.

"Ah, did we forget you, my beauties?" he asked, laughing harshly. His uniform was streaked with blood. "An oversight. Wait here. I will return for you when I have sent a few more souls of your menfolk to Quar."

He rode off. Mathew caught hold of Zohra as she lunged after him. "Stop it! Are you mad?"

"That son of ten thousand swine! Let me go!" Zohra's face was pale and resolute. "This is hopeless, Mat-hew! We will never find Khardan! I am going to go fight with my people!"

"You'll be captured! They won't fight a woman!"

"I won't *be* a woman!" Zohra cried fiercely.

Not twenty feet from them lay the body of one of the *spahis,* the wind whipping his robes around him. Zohra's gaze fixed upon the body, and it was easy for Mathew to guess her intent. Stripping the veil from her head, Zohra tossed it to the ground and started forward.

"You'll be killed! And Khardan will be lost and so will your people!" cried Mathew. Pressed against the palm tree's trunk, he was suddenly too afraid to move. He saw the soldier's leering face. . . .

"Then at least the souls of my people will come before Akhran with pride, knowing we have avenged our wrongs," Zohra retorted, clambering over the scrub. Sharp needles stabbed into her gown, rending and tearing it.

Mathew glanced wildly at the battle and then at Zohra, moving farther from him every instant. The horror of the slaughter, the carnage he had witnessed struck him with a bloody fist.

"Zohra!" he shouted desperately. "Don't leave me! Don't leave me alone!"

She stopped then and turned to face him. Her long black hair streamed behind her in the wind, her tattered clothes fluttered around her like the feathers of a bird's wings. Her face was sharp as the hawk's beak, her eyes as dark and deadly as those of any bird of prey.

The contempt in those eyes, staring coldly at Mathew, pierced him to the heart. Without a word Zohra turned. Fighting the buffeting winds, she headed once more for the body.

Howling darkness overwhelmed Mathew. Falling back against the tree trunk, he stared into the storm, seeing the nightmare begin all over again. The soldier coming for him, dragging him back to Kich. And once in Kich, the man in the white palanquin would find him. . . . He began to shake.

"Promenthas!" he gasped. "You spared my life! You brought me to this accursed land for some reason! What for? What for?"

Mathew stared beseechingly into the heavens, but there was no answer. His head lowered in despair. How could he expect it? Promenthas was far away. Mathew was in the land of this savage God, this Wandering God, who cared nothing for anyone, not even for his own people. Mathew twisted around to watch Zohra. The desperate notion of following after her entered his mind—at least he wouldn't die alone— when suddenly Mathew caught a glimpse of rose-pink silk, an astonishing sight amidst the blood and the darkness.

Suddenly everything was clear to him. They weren't the only ones interested in rescuing Khardan!

"Zohra!" Mathew screamed to make himself heard above the noise of the battle. "Zohra!"

She turned her head, clutching back the hair that flew into her eyes. Mathew pointed, yelling wildly.

It was Meryem. Mounted on one of the magical horses, she was heading away from the battlefield, riding back toward the ruined camp. Slung across the front of the saddle was the body of a man, a *spahi* to judge by his robes. The man hung head down, his arms dangling limp. Mathew had no doubt that it was Khardan, and he saw, from Zohra's suddenly rigid stance and intense gaze, that she recognized him as well.

Not knowing what else to do, Mathew began to run after Meryem on foot, more out of desperation than with the hope

of catching up with her. His lithe body, toughened by hardship
and exercise, gave him more than he had expected, however.
A heady excitement, doubly welcome after the debilitating
fear, exhilarated him, and it seemed he flew over the hard
ground, his feet barely touching it.

Gradually, with a feeling of grim exultation, he realized he
was gaining on them.

The battle safely behind her, Meryem slowed when she
reached the camp. Checking her horse, she gazed up into the
cloud, and raising a wand she held in her hand, she spoke
arcane words, causing the wand to flare brightly, illuminating
her in a circle of radiant white light.

"Kaug!" she called out. "Extend your hand! Lift us up
into the clouds!"

The man she carried across her saddle stirred and moaned.

"The terrible dream will soon be ended, my darling," she
murmured, running her hand over Khardan's body, delighting
in the feel of the strong, muscular back beneath her fingers.
"A few more moments and we will be far away from this vile
place! I will take you to the Imam, beloved. And I will also
take with me a most interesting story of how the Amir
ordered Gasim to murder you, contrary to the Imam's express
command.

"The Amir will deny it, of course." Her fingers lightly
touched a pouch she wore around her waist, concealed beneath
the flowing, rose-pink silk. "But I have Gasim's dying image,
captured within my mirror. I have his final words revealing
Qannadi's treachery."

The horse shifted about nervously; a lightning bolt crackled
too near.

"Come, Kaug! Get me out of here!" Meryem cried, staring
upward impatiently into the cloud and shaking the wand at it.

She saw nothing, however, the 'efreet being occupied with
the battle. Irritably biting her nether lip, Meryem sighed. Her
eyes turned once more to Khardan.

"It will take more than this, of course, to bring down the
Amir," she told him. "But it will be a start. In the meanwhile,
beloved"—her hand massaged Khardan's shoulders—"when
you awaken, I will tell you how you saved me from the
clutches of the murderous Gasim. I will tell you how I

pleaded with the soldiers to spare your life and bring us safely to Kich. You will be a prisoner, that is true, but a prisoner whose captivity will be the most pleasant in history! For I will come to you every night, beloved. I will bring you to a knowledge of Quar, and''—she drew a deep breath, her fingers tightening convulsively—''I will bring you to a knowledge of more worldly pleasures! Your body will be mine, Khardan! You will give your soul to Quar, and together we will rule—''

Too late, Meryem heard the panting breath and light footsteps. Turning, she caught a glimpse of the white face and red hair of the madman right behind her. She raised the wand, but the madman's hands dragged her from the saddle and hurled her to the ground before there was time for her to recite the spell.

She fell heavily.

Pain shot through her head. . . .

"Zohra! There's no time for that now!" Mathew hissed angrily. Catching hold of Zohra's dagger-wielding hand, he stopped it just above Meryem's breast. "Look at her! She's unconscious! Would you murder her thus?''

"No," said Zohra after a moment's pause. "You are right, Mat-hew. Her death would be quick and easy. I would derive no satisfaction from it.''

Sickened, Mathew turned back to Khardan. "Help me get him down on the ground," he ordered Zohra coldly.

The wind tearing at them, they struggled together to grasp Khardan in their arms and slowly lower him from the back of the horse. Nervously Mathew glanced back at the battle to see if anyone was taking an undue interest in them. But the soldiers were intent upon their fighting, the *spahis* were battling for their lives. Nevertheless, Mathew thought it best that they not call attention to themselves. Reaching out his hand, he touched the horse's bridle, and as he had anticipated, the magical beast instantly disappeared.

"Keep low!' he ordered Zohra, pulling her down next to him.

"What is the matter with Khardan?" Zohra asked, examining him by the fading light of the wand Meryem had dropped upon the ground. Zohra's skilled hands pulled back the blood-soaked robes from the man's chest with unwonted gentleness. "He is wounded, but not seriously. I have seen him take worse hurts in the *baigha*! Yet he seems on the verge of death!"

"He is under an enchantment. But what's causing it? . . . Ah! Here's the answer." Drawing aside the folds of Khardan's *haik*, Mathew gingerly slipped his hand beneath a small piece of jewelry the Calif wore around his neck. "Look, Zohra!"

A silver shield beamed with a bright, magical radiance like a small moon.

Sucking in her breath, Zohra stared at it in awe.

"A parting gift from our sorceress," Mathew said coolly with a glance at Meryem. "Quite clever. She can activate the shield with a word. He probably collapsed as though dead. It not only enchanted him, it protected him from harm until she could reach him."

"How do we break the spell?"

Mathew was silent a moment, then he looked up into Zohra's face.

"I'm not certain we want to, Zohra. If Khardan regains consciousness, he will go back and fight and he will die, as the vision foretold. This is our chance to save him."

Zohra stared at Mathew, then turned her gaze to Khardan, lying amid the wreckage of the camp of his people. Blood covered his robes—his own blood and that of his enemies. Lifting her head, Zohra looked back at the Tel.

The storm wind was dying. The battle, too, was ending. The outcome had been obvious from the start. Taken by surprise and completely outnumbered, the *spahis* had fought valiantly, inflamed by the sight of their wrecked homes, their fear for their captive families. Many of Qannadi's soldiers would find a lasting resting place at the foot of the Tel, their bones picked clean by the slavering jaws of the jackals and hyenas who were already prowling the fringes of the battleground.

But the sheer force of the number of the Amir's troops proved impossible for the nomads to overcome. The bodies of many *spahis* lay scattered about the oasis. Some of them were dead. Most were only wounded and unconscious. Qannadi's soldiers had acted on their orders, fighting their foe with the flats of their swords, clubbing them to the ground. Those who had risen up to keep on fighting had been struck down again and again, until they rose no more.

Mathew watched Zohra, his heart aching. He knew what she must be thinking. Khardan would return and he would fight. He would force the Amir's soldiers to fight until he fell, pierced by many swords. . . .

Her face deathly white, Zohra faced Mathew. "Where shall we go?"

Why go anywhere? Why not just stay here? The words were on Mathew's lips, then he saw a group of soldiers break off from the main body and begin riding back toward the wrecked camp. They carried flaming torches in their hands. Leaning down, they touched the brands to the tents, setting them on fire. They were, apparently, leaving nothing behind for the survivors. Others began moving among the wounded, occasionally lifting the unconscious body of a *spahi* onto the backs of their horses, taking them prisoner. Mathew thought he recognized Achmed, Khardan's brother, being dragged into a saddle. The young man's face was covered with blood.

His gaze going hopelessly from one danger to another, Mathew saw—standing on the rim of a dune, silhouetted against the setting sun—a white palanquin!

He is here! He has come for me! Terror clasped Mathew by the throat, suffocating him. The globe of glass pressed against his skin, its icy cold making him shudder.

"Mat-hew! Do you see? The soldiers are burning the camp! What should we do?"

"Why do you look at me?" Mathew gasped, struggling to breathe. He glared at her accusingly. "I don't know anything about this land! All I know is that we must flee! We must escape!"

His eyes were drawn involuntarily to the dune. He blinked, staring. The palanquin was gone! Had it ever been there? Was it his imagination? Or was he crazed with the horror of everything that had happened? Shaking his head, he glanced hurriedly around.

What was left of the tents, the smashed poles, the blankets and cushions, and all the other possessions of the tribes were ablaze. A few old women, left wailing over their losses, raised their fists, shrieking curses. The soldiers ignored them and went about their work.

Mathew began to strip off Khardan's headcloth.

"What are you doing?" Zohra demanded in amazement.

"Hand me her clothes and her veil!" he ordered, tugging at Khardan's black robes with shaking hands. Not stopping his work, keeping one eye on the soldiers, Mathew nodded his head toward the unconscious Meryem.

To his surprise, he heard Zohra chuckle—a deep throaty sound more like the purring of a giant cat than a laugh. Apparently she approved his plan.

Working swiftly, hidden from sight by the billowing clouds of smoke rolling through the camp, Mathew and Zohra covered Khardan's bloodstained tunic and trousers in folds of rose-pink silk. Avoiding touching the brightly glowing silver shield that hung around the man's neck, Zohra wrapped Meryem's veil about Khardan's head, drawing it up over his mouth and nose, arranging it to hide his beard. While Zohra did this, Mathew hurriedly searched Meryem's unconscious, half-naked body, taking anything he could find that might be magical and hastily stashing it in the folds of his robes. Last, he lifted the now-dark wand from her hand, treating it with the utmost respect, carefully wrapping it in a piece of torn cloth before thrusting it into one of the pouches and hanging it around his waist.

Khardan's body was dead weight when they lifted him, one arm draped over the shoulder of each, his feet dragging on the ground. Mathew staggered beneath the burden. "We can't carry him far!" he grunted.

"We won't have to!" Zohra returned, coughing in the thick smoke. "We will hide in the oasis until the soldiers are gone. Then we can come back to camp."

Mathew wasn't certain he wanted to come back, not until he knew whether the white palanquin had been real or a vision. But he lacked breath to argue. Keeping to the shadows, he and Zohra hurried through the camp, avoiding the light of the burning torches, their own veils wrapped tightly about their heads.

Rounding a blazing tent, they were suddenly confronted by a soldier, who stared at them in the dim light.

"Hey, you women! Stop!"

"Pretend you don't hear!" Zohra muttered. Heads bowed,

dragging Khardan between them, they kept walking. The soldier started after them.

"Dog! Where do you think you are going?" came a harsh voice. "Trying to get out of the work?"

"Captain! Look, some women are getting away!"

This is it! Mathew thought. Stabbing pain tore through his shoulders, bowed beneath Khardan's weight. The smoke and the veil were both slowly stifling him. He was on the verge of exhaustion; it took a conscious effort to force his feet to stumble along the ground. No, this would be the end of them. Grimly he waited for the command. . . .

But the captain, absorbed in setting fire to a pile of silken cushions, glanced in the direction of the fleeing women and gave the soldier a look of disgust.

"Look at them! Bent, sickly old hags. If you must risk having yourself turned into a eunuch, do so with one of the young, pretty girls we stole! Now, get back to your post!"

Mathew exchanged relieved glances with Zohra and saw the black eyes—reflecting the flames of the burning village— smile at him in weary triumph.

"We did it, Mat-hew!" she whispered.

The young wizard could not reply; he didn't have the strength.

They were near the edge of camp. A few feet more and they were in the tall, tassel-headed grass that grew thick about the water. Easing Khardan's unconscious body to the wet ground, Mathew and Zohra collapsed beside him, too tired to go farther.

Huddled in the grass, hidden from view of the campsite, they were afraid to move, afraid to speak, almost afraid to breathe. The soldiers milled about the area for hours, it seemed. Smoke from the burning camp drifted over them, and they could hear the groans and cries of the injured echoing in the darkness.

Time passed, and no one discovered them. No one even came in their direction. The dark cloud disappeared, revealing behind it a full moon, hanging like a grinning skull in the dark sky. Khardan remained unconscious, still under the enchantment. Zohra, by the sound of her regular breathing, had fallen asleep.

The veil had been torn from her head, the moonlight shone

full upon her. To keep himself from giving way to exhaustion, Mathew concentrated on studying Zohra's face. Beautiful, proud, willful, unyielding, even—it seemed—to sleep itself. Smiling sadly, Mathew sighed. How angry she made him, angry and frustrated. And ashamed. He brushed back a lock of black hair from her eyes and felt her shivering in the chill air. Moving as softly and gently as he could, Mathew put his arm around her and drew her near him. She was too tired to wake. Reacting instinctively to the warmth of his body, she snuggled next to him. The scent of jasmine, faint and sweet, drifted to him over the acrid smell of smoke.

Turning his head, Mathew looked at Zohra's husband. The woman's clothes Khardan wore were caked with mud and filth. Recalling the vision, Mathew's soul shrank in fear. Resolutely he shoved the memory aside.

Khardan was alive. That was all that mattered.

Mathew withdrew the rose-pink veil from Khardan's face. The enchantment the man was under must be a terrible one. The strong features twisted. Sometimes a stifled groan escaped his lips, the hands twitched and clenched. But Mathew dared not lift the spell, not yet. He thought he could still hear gruff, sharp voices coming from the direction of the camp.

He could do nothing for the Calif but offer silent sympathy and guard his rest—poor guard though he might be. Reaching out slowly, Mathew took hold of Khardan's hand and held it fast.

Mathew closed his eyes, promising to keep them shut just a moment to ease the burning irritation caused by the sand. The irritation was soon gone. His eyes stayed closed. He slept.

Chapter 29

Exhausted from his fight with Raja that had—as was usual with fights among the immortals—ended in a draw, Fedj hastened back to the camp, only to find the battle over. Searching the battlefield for his master, the djinn discovered Jaafar lying unconscious on the ground. The unfortunate Sheykh had been the first casualty. Arriving at the field of battle on foot, Jaafar was kicked in the head by a horse and fell over senseless, never drawing his sword.

Making certain his master was still alive, Fedj carried him back to what was left of the camp, then went off in search of other survivors. Hearing a soldier shout about someone's trying to escape, the djinn instantly went to investigate. Three women were taking advantage of the smoke to try to sneak away. It appeared that one of the women was sick or injured, for the other two were carrying her. As he flew forward to help them, the djinn saw the rose-colored veil slip down from the face of the injured woman.

Fedj stared in shock, too stunned to even make his presence known.

Though partially hidden by the rose-colored veil, the strong, handsome features, the black beard, were easily recognized.

"Khardan!" the djinn muttered in swift anger. "Fleeing the battle disguised as a woman! Wait until my master hears this!"

So saying, he sped back through the air to Jaafar, who was just sitting up, clutching his head, and moaning that he was cursed by the God.

*   *   *

"Effendi," whispered a voice. "I have located her."

A slender hand parted the curtains of the white palanquin "Yes?"

"She is hiding in the tall grass of the oasis. There are two others with her."

"Excellent, Kiber. I will come."

The curtains of the palanquin were drawn back. A man stepped from them. The litter stood concealed behind a huge dune some distance to the east of the Tel. Making less noise than the wind brushing the desert floor, the *goum* and his master walked along the outskirts of the wrecked camp. Neither gave it a glance; both looked to their destination and soon reached the oasis.

Walking swiftly through the grass, Kiber led his master to where three figures slept, huddled together in the mud.

Leaning over them, the slave trader examined them carefully by the bright light of the full moon.

"A black-haired beauty, young and strong. And what is this? The bearded devil who stole the blossom and put me to all this trouble! Truly the God looks down upon us with favor this night, Kiber!"

"Yes, *Effendi!*"

"And here is my blossom with the flame-colored hair. See, Kiber, she wakes at the sound of my voice. Don't be frightened, Blossom. Don't scream. Gag her, Kiber. Cover her mouth. That's right."

The trader drew forth a black jewel and held it over the three figures on the ground.

"In the name of Zhakrin, God of Darkness and All That Is Evil, I command you all—sleep. . . ."

The trader waited a moment to make certain the spell had taken.

"Very well, Kiber, you may proceed."

Turning, the trader walked away.

Their task completed at last, the soldiers threw their burning brands into the numerous bonfires blazing around the camp. Springing onto the backs of their magical horses, they soared into the air, flying back to the west toward Kich. Kaug had long ago departed, bearing in his mighty hands the main body of the Amir's troops, the Amir, and all those who had been taken captive.

The desert night was alive with the sounds of death: the crackling of the flames; the wailing of an old woman; the groaning of the wounded; the snarls and vicious snaps of carrion eaters, fighting over the bodies.

The survivors who could stand did what they could for those who could not, dragging the wounded back to the fires that would—at least—keep them warm during the chill night. Tribesman helped rival tribesman—shepherd carrying horseman in his arms, horseman dabbing cool water onto the parched lips of a shepherd. No one had strength enough to bury the dead. The bodies of the nomads were hauled near the fires, thwarting the jackals and hyenas, who howled their frustration and made do by feasting on the corpses of the Amir's soldiers.

Majiid, weary and wounded, looked at the bodies as each was brought in. He recognized here a friend, there a cousin, but never the one for whom he searched in vain. He questioned the men. Were there more dead out there? Had they found everyone? Were they certain?

His men only shook their heads. They knew whom the Sheykh both longed and dreaded to find. They had not seen him. No, as far as they could tell, these were the only ones who had met their deaths.

"But I have his sword!" Majiid cried, holding out Khardan's notched and bloodstained weapon. "I found it on the ground beneath his fallen horse!"

Averting their faces, the men looked away.

"He would not let himself be captured!" Majiid thundered. "He would not have surrendered his sword! You are blind fools! I will go look for myself!"

Torch in hand, ignoring the pain of his wounds—and he had taken several—the Sheykh went to conduct his own search of the area around the Tel.

The carrion eaters snarled at him for disrupting their feasting and slunk away, skulking about in the shadows until he and his fearsome fire had gone. Majiid grimly climbed among the rocks of the Tel, turning over the bodies of the soldiers and the dead horses, peering beneath them, dragging them to one side. Only when he grew too weak and dizzy from loss of blood to stand did he finally admit to himself that he would have to give up, at least for the night.

Sinking to the sand, he looked back on the ruins of the camp, on the smoldering fires, the smoke curling into the starlit sky, the figures of his people—what remained of them— silhouetted against the flames, walking slowly with bowed heads.

Tears came to Majiid's fierce old eyes. Snorting, he fought them back, but the fires blurred in his vision, the bleak hopelessness of despair overcame him. Refusing to give way to such womanly weakness, the old man struggled to rise to his feet. His hand brushed across a cactus, growing in the blood-covered ground.

"Curse you, Akhran!" the old man swore viciously. "You have brought us to ruin!"

Grasping the cactus, oblivious to the thorns that gouged his flesh, Majiid took hold of the Rose of the Prophet and tried to drag it out of the sandy soil.

The cactus didn't budge.

Time and again Majiid tugged at it, drove his foot into it, hacked at it with his sword.

Stubbornly the cactus refused to yield.

Majiid sank, exhausted, to the ground and stared at the Rose in wonder until the coming of the dawn.

Never Before Published
Special 16-page Preview of

The Paladin of the Night

Volume 2 in

THE ROSE OF THE PROPHET

by Margaret Weis and Tracy Hickman

While the mortal desert dwellers struggle against the bonds of their captors. Sond, Pukah and Ariel set off to rescue Sond's beloved Nedjma, believed to be held captive in the enchanted cave of Kaug the 'efreet. Their noble plan fails miserably, but Ariel manages to hide as Sond and Pukah are captured. Kaug binds Pukah to life-long servitude—to begin with transporting Sond to spend eternity in the dead city of Serinda. Upon their arrival, however, the three immortals are shocked to find this long-forgotten city has become much livelier of late . . .

Pukah looked around himself with wonder. "This is Serinda? This is where the immortals are being held *prisoner*? Impossible. Market day in Khandar is nothing to this!"

Serinda was indeed lively—for a dead city.

Long ago, so many centuries past that it was not worth remembering, when the great and glorious city of Khandar was nothing but a camel watering hole, a beautiful city named Serinda flourished. Few people living now remember that city.

But today, the streets were so crowded it was difficult to walk through them. They reverberated with noise—merchants extolling, customers bargaining, animals bleating. *Arwats* and coffee houses were doing a thriving business; so packed that their patrons were literally tumbling out the doors and windows. No one seemed to be making any attempt to keep order. Everyone was intent on doing whatever he or she pleased, and pleasure seemed to be Serinda's other name.

Raucous laughter echoed through the streets. Women hanging out of silk curtained windows called out sweet enticements to those below. Gold and silver flowed like water, but not so freely as the wine. Every mark and feature of every race in the world of Sularin was visible—straight black hair, curly golden hair, slanted dark eyes, round blue eyes, skin that was white as milk, skin tanned brown by wind and sun, skin black and glistening as onyx. All jostled together; greeted each other as friend, fell upon each other as enemy; exchanged wine, laughter, goods, gold, or insults.

And every one of them was an immortal.

"Poor Sond!" snarled Pukah, giving the lamp a vicious kick. "Poor Sond! Sentenced to a life of constant merry-making, love-making, drinking and dicing! While I'm chained, day and night, to a beast of an 'efreet who will no doubt beat me regularly—"

"If he does, it will be no more than you deserve," cried an indignant, feminine voice.

Smoke poured forth from the lamp's spout, coalescing into the handsome, muscular Sond. Bowing gallantly, the djinn extended his hand and assisted another figure to step from the lamp—this one slender and lovely with flowing silver hair and feathery white wings, who glared at Pukah with flashing blue eyes.

"What do you mean—I fanned you with my wings?" Asrial demanded angrily.

"What were you two doing in there?" Pukah shouted.

"Precisely what we did in your basket!" retorted Asrial.

"Ah, ha!" Pukah cried, raising clenched fists to Sond.

"Nothing!" Asrial shrieked, stamping her bare foot.

"Pukah, stop it," Sond ordered out of the corner of his mouth. "We have to find Nedjma and get out of here."

Emerging out of the shadows of an alley, the three blinked in the bright sunlight.

"I don't think we'll be having trouble with any guards," said Sond quietly, after a moment's study of their surroundings.

The only ruler in the city of Serinda appeared to be

Chaos, with Disorder as his captain. Every conceivable vice known to mortal flesh was being plied in the streets and houses, the alleys and byways of Serinda.

"You're right," Pukah admitted glumly. "Why don't they all leave, then?'

"Would you?" Sond asked, pausing to watch a dice game.

"Certainly," said Pukah in lofty tones. "*I* know my duty—"

Sond made an obscene noise.

"Pukah!" gasped Asrial, grabbing the djinn. "Pukah, look!" She pointed, "An . . . an archangel!"

Turning, the djinn saw a man dressed in white robes similar to Asrial's, standing in a doorway. His white wings quivering, he was enjoying the favors of a giggling, minor deity of the goddess Mimrim.

Forgetting himself, Pukah sniggered. Asrial flashed him a furious glance.

"You told me angels didn't indulge in that sort of thing," Pukah teased, sweeping Asrial into the shelter of an iron monger's stand.

"We don't!" Asrial blinked her eyes rapidly, and Pukah saw tears glimmering on her long lashes.

"Don't cry!" Pukah's heart melted. Wiping her tears with one hand, he took advantage of the situation to slide the other around the angel's slim waist. "You're too innocent, my sweet child. Knowing their God disapproves, I imagine your higher-ranking angels have learned to keep their affairs private—"

"Affairs? There are no affairs! None of us would ever even think of doing . . . such . . . such . . ." Glancing back at the couple in the doorway, her eyes widened. She flushed a deep red, and hastily turned away. "Something's wrong here, Pukah!" she said earnestly. "Terribly wrong. I must leave and tell Promenthas—"

Pukah's heart suddenly chilled into a lump. "No, don't leave me!" he pleaded. "I mean, don't leave . . . us," he stuttered. "What will you tell your God, after all? I agree with you. Something is wrong, but what? There are no guards. It doesn't look like anyone's being held here against his will. Help us find Nedjma," continued Pukah, inspired. "She'll tell us everything and then you can take that information to Promenthas, just as I'll take it to Akhran."

Asrial appeared dubious. "I'll come with you to find Sond's friend and hear what she has to say. Then I must return to Promenthas. Although I don't quite understand," she added with a tremor in her voice, "how this is going to help Mathew."

"Your protege is with my master," Pukah said, hugging her comfortingly. "Khardan will protect him. When you have reported to your God and I to mine, then you and I will go find both of them!"

"Oh, Pukah!" Asrial's eyes gleamed through her tears. "That would be wonderful! But . . ." The light dimmed. "What about Kaug?"

"Oh damn and blast Kaug!" Pukah snapped impatiently. He was not, in fact, quite as confident as he sounded about the 'efreet's thickness of skull and dullness of wit and did not want to be reminded of him at every turning. "Come on, Sond! Are you going to stand here for the next millennium?"

"I was just considering the best way to search for her." Sond looked bleakly at the hundreds of people milling about in the street. "Perhaps we should split up?"

"Since neither Asrial nor I knew what she looks like that is hardly a good idea," remarked Pukah asperically. "From what you've told me about her, I suggest we just listen for the sound of *tambour* and *quaita* and look for the dancing girls."

Sond's face darkened with anger and he began to swell alarmingly.

"I'm only trying to be helpful," said Pukah in soothing tones.

Muttering in response, Sond began to shove his way through the crowd.

Pukah, with a wink at the angel, followed along behind.

As it turned out, Pukah's suggestion led them straight to Nedjma. Unfortunately, the djinn never had a chance to gloat over it.

It was with some difficulty that they made their way through the "dead" city of Serinda. The two djinn and the angel were continually accosted by merry-makers, seeking to draw them into their revels.

"Shhh!" Pukah suddenly held up his hand for silence.

"What?"

"Listen!"

Rising above the laughter and the giggles and the shouts and the singing, they could hear—very faintly—the shrill, off-key sinuous notes of the *quaita*, accompanied by the clashing jingle of the *tambour*.

Sond glared at Pukah.

"Very well!" The young djinn shrugged. "Ignore it."

Without saying a word, Sond turned and crossed the street, heading for a building whose shadowy arched doorways offered cool respite from the sun. Roses twined up ornate latticework decorating the front. Two djinn in silken caftans lounged around outside the doorways, smoking long, thin pipes. Sond looked neither to the right nor the left, up nor down, but pushed his way past the djinn, who gazed after him in some astonishment.

"Eager, isn't he?" said one.

"Must be a newcomer," said the other, and both laughed.

Raising his gaze to the upper levels of the building, Pukah saw several lovely djinniyeh leaning seductively over the balconies, dropping flowers or calling out to the men passing by in the street below.

Pukah shook his head and glanced at a stern and solemn Asrial. "Are you sure you want to come in here?" he whispered.

"No. But I don't want to stay out here either."

"I guess you're right," Pukah admitted, scowling at the red-bearded barbarian who appeared to be following them. "Well"—he grasped her hand again, smiling as her fingers closed firmly over his—"just stay close to me."

Muttering an apology, tugging Asrial after him, Pukah stepped between the two djinn lounging in the doorway.

"Say, friend, bring your own?" commented one.

"I know that voice!" Pukah said, raising his head and studying the djinn intently. "Baji? Yes, it is!" Pukah clapped the djinn on his muscular forearm. "Baji! I might have known I'd find you here! Didn't you recognize Sond, who just walked past you?"

"Friend, I don't even recognize you," said the djinn, eyeing Pukah calmly.

"Of course, you do! It's me, Pukah!" said Pukah. Then, frowning, "You aren't trying to get out of paying me those five silver *tumans* you owe me, are you, Baji?"

"I said you're mistaken," returned the djinn, a sharp edge to his voice. "Now go on in and have your fun before things turn ugly—"

"Like your face?" said Pukah, fists clenching.

The shrill, anguished bleep of a *quaita* being cut off in mid-note and the clattering of a *tambour* hitting the floor mingled with a female scream and angry, masculine voices raised in argument.

"Pukah!" Asrial gasped. Peering into the shadows of the entryway, she tugged on the djinn's hand. "Sonds' in trouble!"

"He's not the only one!" said Pukah threateningly, glaring at his fellow djinn.

"Pukah!" Asrial pleaded. The voices inside were growing louder.

"Don't leave!" Pukah growled. "This will only take a moment."

"Oh, I'll be right here," said the djinn, leaning back against the archway, arms folded across his chest.

"Pukah!" Asrial pulled him along.

Crystal beads clicked together, brushing against his skin as he passed through them into the cool shadows of the *arwat*. A wave of perfume broke over him, drenching him in sweetness. Blinking his eyes, he tried to accustom himself to the darkness lighted only by the warm glow of thick, jojoba candles. There were no windows. Silken tapestries covered the walls. His foot sank into soft carpeting. Luxurious cushions invited him to recline and stretch out. Flasks of wine offered to make him forget his troubles. Dishes heaped high with grapes and dates and oranges and nuts promised to ease his stomach's hunger while the most enticing, beautiful djinniyeh he'd ever seen in his life promised to ease any other hungers he might have.

An oily, rotund little djinn slithered his way through the myriad cushions that covered every inch of the floor and, glancing askance at the angel, offered Pukah a private room to themselves.

"A charming little room, Effendi, and only ten silver *tumans* for the night! You won't find a better place in all of Serinda!" Catching hold of Pukah's arm, the chubby djinn started to draw him across the room to a bead curtained alcove.

Pukah jerked his arm free. "What's going on here?" He glanced toward the center of the room, where the shouting was the loudest.

"Nothing, *Effendi*, nothing!" assured the rotund djinn, making another attempt to capture Pukah's arm, urging him onward. "A small altercation over one of my girls. Do not trouble yourself. The *mamalukes* will soon restore peace. You and your lady friend will not be disturbed, I assure you—"

"Pukah! Do something!" Asrial breathed, her nails digging into his flesh.

Pukah quickly assessed the situation. A flute player sat gagging and coughing on the carpeted floor; it appeared he'd had his *quaita* shoved down his throat. The *tambour* player lay sprawled amid the cushions, unconscious; one of the drummers was attempting to bring him around. Several patrons were gathered together in a circle, shouting and gesticulating angrily. Pukah couldn't see through their broad backs, but he could hear Sond's voice, bellowing from their midst.

"Nedjma! You're coming with me!"

A shrill scream and the sound of slap was his answer, followed by laughter from the patrons. Irritably shoving away the grasping hands of the proprietor, Pukah ordered, "Stay here!" to Asrial and shoved his way through the circle.

As he had expected, Sond stood in the center. The djinn's handsome face was twisted with anger, dark with jealousy. He had hold of the wrist of a struggling djinniyeh with the apparent intent on dragging her out of the building.

Pukah caught his breath, forgetting Asrial, forgetting Sond, forgetting why they were here, forgetting his own name for the moment. The djinniyeh was the most gorgeous creature he'd ever laid eyes on and there were parts of her on which he longed to lay more than his eyes. From her midriff up, only the sheerest of silken veils covered her body, sliding over her firm, high breasts, slipping from around her white shoulders. Honey gold hair had come loose in her struggle and tumbled about a face of exquisite charm that, even in her indignation, seemed made to be kissed. Numerous long, opaque veils hanging from a jeweled belt at her waist formed a skirt that modestly covered her legs. Noticing several of these veils wound around the heads of the onlookers, Pukah guessed that the djinniyeh's shapely legs, already partially visible, wouldn't be covered long.

"Nedjma!" said Sond threateningly.

"I don't know any Nedjma!" the djinniyeh cried.

"Let her go! On with the dance! Pay your way like everyone else!"

Pukah glanced behind him and saw the proprietor make a peremptory gesture. Three huge *mamalukes* began to edge their way forward.

"Uh, Sond!" Shoving the unsteady footed patrons out of his way, Pukah tripped over a cushion and tumbled onto the cleared area of the dance floor. "I think you've made a mistake!" he said urgently. "Apologize to the lady and let's go!"

"A mistake? You bet he's made a mistake." A huge djinn that Pukah didn't recognize and thought must be one of Quar's immortals thrust his body between Sond and the djinniyeh.

"The girl doesn't know you and doesn't want to," the djinn continued, his voice grating. "Now leave!" Pukah saw the djinn's hand go to the sash he wore round his waist.

His gaze fixed on the djinniyeh, Sond saw nothing. "Nedjma," he said in a pleading, agonized voice, "it's me, Sond! You told me you loved—"

His words ended in a choke.

"I said, leave her alone!" The large djinn lunged at him.

"Sond!" Pukah leaped forward, but a quick hand movement, the flash of steel, and Sond was staring down at the hilt of dagger protruding from his stomach. The huge djinn who had stabbed him stepped back, a look of satisfaction on his face. Slowly, disbelievingly, his face twisted in pain and astonishment, Sond placed his hand over the wound. Red blood welled up between his fingers.

"Nedjma!" Staggering, doubled over with pain, he extended the crimson stained hand to the djinniyeh.

Crying out in horror, she covered her eyes with her jeweled hands. Sond crashed to the floor at her feet and lay there, still and unmoving.

Pukah sighed. "All right, Sond," he said after a moment. "That was very dramatic. Now get up, admit you were wrong, and let's get out of here."

The djinn did not move.

The patrons were gathering around the djinniyeh, offering comfort and taking advantage of the opportunity to snatch away more of the veils. The huge djinn put his arm around the weeping Nedjma and drew her away to one of the shadowy alcoves, the other patrons wailing in protest and demanding that the dance continue. Other djinniyeh soon appeared to soothe away their disappointment.

Clucking to himself about blood ruining his best carpets, the proprietor was pointing at Pukah and demanding payment for damages! The tall *mamalukes*, faces grim, turned their attention to the young djinn.

"Uh, Sond!" Pukah knelt down beside him. Placing his hand on the djinn's shoulder, he shook him. "You can quit making a fool of yourself any time now! If that was Nedjma, she's obviously enjoying herself and doesn't want to be bothered. . . . . Sond." Pukah shook the unresponsive body harder. "Sond!"

There was a flutter of white wing and white robes and Asrial was beside him. "Pukah, I'm frightened! Those men are staring at me! What's Sond doing? Make him get up and let's leave— Pukah!" She caught sight of his face. "Pukah, what's wrong!"

"Sond's dead," said Pukah in whisper.

Asrial stared at him. "That's impossible," she said crisply. "Is this more of your antics, because—" The angel's voice faltered. "Promenthas have mercy! You're serious!"

"He's dead!" Pukah cried. Almost angrily, he grabbed Sond's shoulder and rolled the body of the djinn over on its back. An arm flopped limply against the floor. The eyes stared at the nothing. Pulling the dagger from the wound, the djinn stared at it. The blade was smeared with blood. "I don't understand!" He glared around the room. "I want answers!"

"Pukah!" Asrial cried, trying to comfort him, but the *mamalukes* shoved the angel aside. Grasping the young djinn by the shoulders, they dragged him to his feet.

Pukah lashed out furiously. "I don't understand! How can he be dead?"

"Perhaps I can explain," came a voice from the beaded curtained entryway. "Let him go."

At the sound, the *mamalukes* instantly dropped their hold on the djinn and stepped back from him. The proprietor ceased his lamentations, the patrons swallowed words and wine, several nearly choking themselves, and even this sound they did their best to stifle. No one spoke. No one stirred. The light of the candles flickered and dimmed. The fragrant air was tinged with a sweet, cloying smell.

A cold whisper of air on the back of his neck made Pukah's skin shiver. Reluctantly, unwillingly, but completely unable to help himself, the djinn turned to face the doorway.

Standing in the entrance was a woman of surpassing beauty. Her face might have been carved of marble by some master craftsman of the Gods, so pure and perfect was every feature. Her skin was pale, almost translucent. Hair, thin and fine as a child's, fell to her feet, enveloping her slender, white-robed body like a smooth satin cape of purest white.

Pukah heard Asrial, somewhere near him, moan. He couldn't help her, he couldn't even see her. His gaze was fixed upon the woman's face, he felt himself slowly strangling.

The woman had no eyes. Where there should have been two orbs of life and light in that classic face were two hollows of empty blackness.

"Let me explain, Pukah," said the woman, entering the room amid a silence so deep and profound that everyone else in the room seemed to have suffocated in it. "In the city of Serinda, through the power of Quar, it is at last possible to give every immortal what he or she truly desires."

The woman looked expectantly at Pukah, obviously expecting him to question her. "And that is?" he was supposed to say. But he couldn't talk. He had no breath.

Yet his words echoed, unspoken, through the room.

"Mortality," the woman replied.

Pukah shut his eyes to blot out the sight of the empty eye sockets, of the darkness that bored through him.

"And you are—" he blurted out.

"Death. The ruler of Serinda."

The Paladin of the Night is the magnificent second volume in the **Rose of the Prophet** trilogy. Though the desert dwellers have been scattered like so many grains of sand, they begin to come together to fight both the men and gods who would expect them to be other than what they choose to be.

Read **The Paladin of the Night,** on sale April 1989, wherever Bantam Spectra Books are sold.